The
Lenz

Damien Lutz

"Grief is just love with no place to go."
- *Jamie Anderson*

"Imagination is everything. It is the preview for life's coming attractions."
- *Albert Einstein*

"Passive hope is about waiting for external agencies to bring about what we desire. Active Hope is about becoming active participants in bringing about what we hope for."
- *Joanna Macy, Active Hope: How to Face the Mess We're in without Going Crazy*

ACKNOWLEDGMENTS

Thank you to Shida-san for showing me Ofunato and sharing with me the area's experience of the 2011 tsunami, and to Masato-san, who taught me about the relationship between the forest, the ocean and people.

And a big thank you to my fellow writers for helping me shape up this hot mess—
Jeanne, Joseph, Shelia, Heather,
Paul, RL, Rayleen, Rolando and Ian.

CONTENTS

AUTHOR'S NOTE

The Lenz is set in 2039 Japan. The coastal city of Shibido and the Agu-shi archipelago do not exist today.

Although the Japanese use the surname first when referring to individuals by name, I have intentionally used the westernized format of given name first (and without Japanese honorific titles such as *san*) for better readability for the western audience, for whom this edition is intended.

The Japanese word *yujin* means friend.

PART ONE

The Wall

Job

Fucking Santa.

Hurrying along the crumbling footpath, Yoshi Goto struggled to twist his disappointment into excitement, like a fisherman might wrestle a tangled, empty net. His footsteps splashed puddles of reflected neon signs into angry sparks, and a growing headache ambushed his skull. He cursed the hangovers of unemployment freedom—he wouldn't have had the extra glasses of whisky before bed if he'd known he'd be starting a new job that morning.

But as a shopping mall Santa?

He acknowledged he should be grateful that his agent, Haru Hamada, even still considered him for roles. Haru had barely called since the 'mishap' on the set of *One Man Dreaming* two years prior, and Yoshi had begun to fear any career re-invention was as dead as the polar bears. His financial situation was certainly on the endangered list, barely staying above poverty line with cleaning jobs and the meagre residuals from his previous acting, even if the last two royalty payments had increased. With so many jobs automated in Shibido, employment was a prize, a treasured state of being, especially for an actor competing with entirely computer-generated films produced within a few weeks. Especially for an actor considered one of the most unreliable in the business.

"Now, don't get too excited," Haru had said after waking him with the call. "The job is nothing ground-breaking, but it does require strong character skills. The Santa *yujin* at Glasshouse Shopping Plaza is glitching, surprise-surprise. And it's the first day of Christmas. They need a replacement, this morning."

"But I'm only twenty-one," Yoshi protested, unable to complain directly about the lack-luster of the first role he'd been offered in months.

"They have a great suit that will take care of that. And the plaza is fully augmented. The shoppers' Lenz's will adapt your face to the Santa of their dreams. And the ones without won't know any different. This is a great opportunity for you to skill-up on tech-integrated performance. This role might be your chimney back into the business."

Leaving behind the industrial district's decaying concrete roads, Yoshi checked his watch—7:32 a.m.— and then swiped to load the city maps.

Glasshouse Shopping Plaza sat on the other side of Shibido, up on High Scape's western edge. He could avoid the expense of a direct bus ride by using the free moving walkways around the city—east to the sea-wall, north along the abandoned esplanade, and up the western elevators—to reach the mall with plenty of time to get into character.

Ho-Ho-Ho.

As he left behind the industrial district's decaying concrete roads, it occurred to him that the lack of positivity in his Outlook might have delivered the disappointing Santa job rather than a new lead role. After all, each and every Shibidoan had a duty to contribute to the collective optimism, and to practice it with military diligence. Scientists couldn't say for sure if another Earth Shift could happen, or if its earthquakes and tsunamis would be as severe. The oceans were still rising; no one needed a scientist to see that. One should be grateful for each new day no matter its disappointments. Gratitude for the day, good cheer for your fellow citizen, and maintaining an optimistic spirit—these were Shibido's values, the buoys keeping the city's Outlook afloat in a rising sea of uncertainty.

But as Yoshi headed through a quiet maze of closed electronics and convenience stores, a persistent cloud cover compressed a humidity unusual for winter, which in turn squeezed the truth out of him—it wasn't just role-disappointment bothering him, it was his jangled nerves sabotaging his confidence. He hadn't performed in a year. And when he wasn't covering for malfunctioning delivery bots, he spent most of his days avoiding life by hiding at home.

A notification pinged from his watch:

Reminder:
Your rental payment of ¥82,500
is one week overdue.

Motivated out of his funk by necessity, he passed the Good Time Adult Store where he bid the companion *yujins* in the window a Wonderful Day. Wearing little more than Christmas scarves, the androids were new models.

Business must be banging.

The dating culture of a looming Japanese Christmas Eve could be lonely for the single.

He turned the corner, just past The Undertow's low-hanging lantern sign, and stopped. A crane-bot reached over the walkway to attach a briefcase-sized black box to a light pole. He crossed the road to avoid walking under the crane, not because he considered himself superstitious, but, well, the last thing he needed was bad luck.

As he reached the other side, his watch vibrated, and for a second, he expected to see Haru again. *Perhaps with a better role!* But Tora's digitized face appeared on the small screen instead. Colorful liquor bottles twinkled on glass shelves behind the barman, like he was a genie trapped in a tiny bar. A familiar song played its nostalgia in the background through

Yoshi's earpiece, and he could hear the *squeak, squeak* of Tora twisting a cloth inside a tumbler.

"Morning, Chief. Just checking to see how the job search is going?"

"Hey, Tora," Yoshi replied, summoning a believable cheer. "You're looking at an employed man."

"Congratulations! What's the job?" *Squeak, squeak.*

"I'm Santa at the Glasshouse Plaza. It's no giant leap for an experienced actor, but it's a small step for a struggling one."

"Exactly, exactly, my friend. And a job's a job. You know that, right?"

"I do, of course. I just… it's been a while since I performed."

"You hush that bird noise right now. Keep your spirit high, okay? Tomorrow starts today."

Yoshi cringed—proverbial wisdom just didn't sound genuine coming from an artificial intelligence. He'd grown so comfortable with the avatar's realism he often forgot Tora was nothing more than a digital character simulating friendship, his calls generated by anomalies in Yoshi's biorhythms. But Tora's merry-barman avatar was just what Yoshi's slipping Outlook needed, and that's why he'd chosen him.

"Still with me, Chief?" *Squeak, squeak.*

"Yeah, sorry. I'm just thinking about the role."

"You got some good shine goin' on there. You'll make your Grandpapa proud; don't you be worryin', okay?"

"Thanks, Tora."

"Don't forget it. I'll check in with you after. Wonderful Day."

Tora's face pinched to a dot.

Determined to keep his Outlook on the upward, Yoshi conjured something of a film score in his mind, a gently taut orchestral piece that he synched with his steps. A light drizzle joined in and pitter-pattered his jacket with the steadiness of drummers. He pulled his head deeper into his hood, picked up his pace, and turned right into the main intersection where a clear view of the city emerged.

Fog wrapped the tips of the city center in a cloak of semi-invisibility. Like a giant, odd-shaped piece of paper pressed half-way down upon the uneven grid of buildings, High Scape's patchwork of elevated public spaces appeared to float above the shorter buildings. A living memorial to those lost in the 2022 wave that swept through the city, the elevated district created an urban platform to overlook the sea-wall. Glass and steel pod elevators dripped from its circumference to Low Ground. The auto-pods sliding up and down inside the transparent wells made Yoshi think of water cascading from the sides of a re-emerging Atlantis. He filled with the kind of spontaneous hope that arises when one believes something appearing in the real-world heralds some personal significance.

Increasing the pace of his imagined soundtrack, he turned right again. The footpath became sturdier as he joined other pedestrians on a moving walkway. Low-rise buildings lined both sides of the street, topped by digital billboards competing for attention. But one stood out from them all:

The Maya Lenz
See more of what you want to see

The words morphed into a video of a fresh-faced teen tilting her head back and raising a silver vial to drop liquid into her eye. The video zoomed in to the molecular level to reveal nano-bots colonizing the Lenz across her eye's surface, before completing itself with a rainbow-colored sliver around the iris' edge. The video switched to the girl's view of the world. As she blinked through a menu of icons in the top left of her vision, images and information overlaid her view—a grey sky brightened with an opalized sheen, 3D animations extruded from roads and buildings, and characterization enhanced the people around her.

An idea pinged in Yoshi's head—perhaps the four weeks of Santa work could afford him a Lenz. He could set up a Livey profile on the channels, build up a following, and reboot his career, his life, his whole world.

Inspired, he imagined his account balance increasing with every pay. He saw a Lenzist handing him the silver vial, and after blinking in the nano-bot infused liquid, he opened his eyes again to see—

The travelator ended abruptly, forcing him to stagger forward to awkwardly regain his balance.

With his heartbeat pulsing from the sharp fright—and excitement lingering from his daydream—he strode toward the esplanade district where the north-south travelators awaited to glide him to his reinvention.

But as he turned left onto the road running parallel to the sea-wall, he found himself blocked by a detour truck parked across the road. Black and yellow striped barriers stood guard around it with hornet menace. A message flashed on the truck's side:

Esplanade closed.
Please use alternate routes.

Behind the truck, temporary fencing enclosed the entire district all the way back to the sea-wall, including the travelators.

Yoshi swore. He hadn't visited the city in months and had forgotten all about Maya's mixed-reality project taking over the esplanade—one of five, apparently, being built around the world. Sight drones hovered above, feeding video of the development into the Lenz channels.

Rebuilt after the Shift tsunami, the esplanade district had degenerated into a seedy area of dilapidated housing, failing nightclubs and nasty brothels, before it was eventually abandoned. Maya had purchased the land, stripped the area bare, and erected an immaculate grid of empty buildings as the bones of a totally augmented district.

Looking down the street, Yoshi swore again. A long line stretched back from a temporary auto-bus stop. Newcomers tapped their watches or blinked at their Lenz to book a seat on the next available bus—all smiling, no matter the inconvenience. *A detour is a new adventure*, he assumed they were thinking. But all he saw in his near future was a scrambling sprint and a breathless apology.

He loaded the timetables on his watch, but with the backlog of passengers and extra stops, the next available seat would make him almost half an hour late. Devastated that his untimeliness would make him look unreliable on his first day, he considered walking all the way to the west side. But without the travelators he wouldn't get to the mall any earlier.

With nothing else he could do, he took a deep breath and joined the line. He stood beside an elderly lady wearing a transparent poncho. A fist-sized jade koi fish sat on her chest beneath the wet plastic of the poncho, looking like it rested underwater. Her gray eyes stared wistfully across the road at the barren district. Yoshi noticed the rainbow ring of a Lenz around her iris.

It must be wonderful, he thought, imagining what amazing scenery the Lenz was showing her. All he saw across the road was a row of generators and portable toilets lining the inside of the fence. And behind that, a ghost town of bland buildings and barren streets stretching three blocks to the drip-stained sea-wall. The dumped furniture that once littered the area had been stacked into piles outside the fence at the end of the street. Except for one lone, over-turned chair directly opposite him.

The chair moved, startling Yoshi, before he realized it was a seated man stretching his arms into the air. By the look of the stranger's sinewy frame, sun-darkened skin and tattered clothing, he guessed the man was one of the islander refugees. There'd been an article or two about them being displaced by the rising oceans, but he couldn't recall hearing any more about them.

An auto-bus pulled around the corner and zoomed through Yoshi's thoughts to pull up in front of the growing line. But the bus filled before he got near its doors.

He checked the time again—7:45 a.m.—and grit his teeth.

Come on.

As the bus drove away, the man across the road rose to his feet. His pants were shredded up to the knee, as if cut purposely, and he wore three singlets on top of each other. Even with the increasingly warmer winters, the temperatures were cool enough for jumpers. But 'Singlets' over there didn't seem bothered. With one eye on the line, he nonchalantly pulled aside a loose panel in the fencing behind him and entered the closed-off area.

Surprised by the blatant disregard for the law, Yoshi scoffed and looked to the others in line for mutual disapproval. But they all continued to stare into the air and swipe at things that didn't really exist. Singlets continued unchallenged, detaching the cables from one of the generators and maneuvering it through the gap in the fence.

"Aren't the sea-side sculptures beautiful?" said the old lady next to Yoshi. She pointed a bony finger directly at Singlets now wheeling the generator down the road. "I remember meeting my Makoto just there. A sea breeze snatched my hat, and this funny-looking fellow came out of nowhere and scooped it up from under me. The cheeky monkey let me chase him down into that underground parking area. Just down there, it was. Yes, right there."

The lady pointed further down the road to where the fencing and piles of furniture stopped at a rectangular, concrete shelter. Yoshi could just make out the large, faded letters of the words *South Ramp* on its side. Singlets wheeled the generator into the shelter and disappeared down the ramp into the underground that held the old lady's memories.

"I chased him down there," she continued. "He wouldn't give me my hat back unless I promised to meet him again the next day. Cheeky monkey."

Her words trailed off as she touched her cracked lips, her augmented vision having completely transported her mind to the past, and, perhaps, to a kiss she wouldn't speak of.

Blocking the ramp from view, another auto-bus came around the corner and drove up to the stop.

Yes!

But as Yoshi took a micro step forward in anticipation, the elderly lady remained staring at the empty ramp shelter.

"Excuse me," he said, tapping the crepe paper skin of her arm.

"Makoto?" she replied, turning and looking straight at Yoshi—her eyes suffered from the slight cross-eyed affliction Lenzers developed from focusing on the Lenz overlays. "Oh, excuse me," she said. The excitement on her face fluttered away, replaced by a blush of bewildered disappointment.

He smiled and nodded a bow, and he let her climb onto the bus first. After patiently waiting again for her to ease herself into the last empty seat at the rear, he found standing room beside her.

As the bus took off toward High Scape, he gripped the pole tight and imagined injecting speed into the engines. The bus beeped and jolted until it finally parked at the base of an elevator. Unseen mechanisms clunked onto its wheels and ferried it up through the transparent well.

The development area by the sea-wall spread out below, revealing its true size. A semi-circle as wide as High Scape stretched out from the esplanade's south end, enclosed the abandoned district, and curved back to the wall at the north end where it had left a cluster of old buildings and temples untouched. Although these structures had also been abandoned, they had survived the original tsunamis and were considered good luck for Shibido.

While the swarm of Sight drones focused on Maya's development, Yoshi's mind x-rayed the district in an attempt to imagine how the refugees could be living underground. But he knew so little about them, how many there were, or even how long they'd been in Shibido. What he did know was that they were more homeless than the homeless citizens.

He shuddered at what it might feel like to become so invisible, and all he could think about was not ending up living like them, the lowest of the low.

Because that's where the sea gets you.

The panic of his self-doubt returned, but his Grandpapa's voice arose in his mind.

"Shine your light."

An overwhelming gratitude suffused through him. His Grandpapa would say that phrase whenever Yoshi hesitated—before the old man's Outlook began declining and his words became less coherent. But Yoshi sensed his Grandpapa with him, and for the first time in his life, he felt thankful for being born on the Isle of Meti—the now-submerged island in the bay—and not some remote micro-nation like the ones the refugees had been forced to flee.

He glanced at one of the old temples on the north side of the district, imagined removing his shoes to kneel inside, and thanked his Grandpapa for raising him alone. He also thought of his parents, too, which he rarely did because it was impossible to remember their faces having lost them to the tsunamis when he was barely four years old.

Feeling a strange mix of both sadness and excitement, he promised himself, late or not, he would give the Santa role his all and make his Grandpapa proud.

"Memories are funny, aren't they?" said the old lady beside him, snapping him back into the moment.

"Sorry?"

"How do you know they're not just something your mind wished up and you forgot weren't real?"

Costume

The elevator jerked to a halt, and the bus zipped out across High Scape.

Making good use of the delay, Yoshi read up on how best to be Santa—grand and bold for the entry, kind and gentle for the photos. He listened to a cast about Santa facts, from what he did when faced with no chimney (he used magic dust to create one that disappeared after he left) to what he fed his reindeer (moss and grass, twice a day).

By the time the gleaming glass pyramid of Glasshouse Plaza came into view, he felt suitably immersed in Santa lore, ready to face any pertinent questions from the mall's young audience.

He checked the time—8:22 a.m.

Joyfully surprised by the early arrival, he sprang off the bus onto the drop-off platform next to the parking bay. Auto-pods zoomed in to unload shoppers, the festive-season excitement in their voices bouncing off the low concrete ceiling. In contrast to the merriment, however, a man in a black suit stood by the loading zone with his face almost touching the wall—a familiar glitch of companion *yujin*. A white-gloved lady, wearing an embarrassed expression under a bright yellow hat, patted the man's shoulder. Yoshi silently thanked the *yujin's* glitching for getting him a job.

Following Haru's directions, he cut through the pod bays toward the staff entrance. A rose-hued box-sign in the far corner, marked 'Plaza Staff Only', illuminated double doors beneath with an old theater glow.

He wove around the last row of parked pods and approached a half-opened tinted window. A security guard, wearing a short cape buttoned at the collar, looked up from a monitor. His right eye was brown, but his left eye was blue, and only the left wore the multi-colored ring of the Lenz. A waxy scalp glistened beneath his dark, comb-grooved hair, and a star-shaped name tag on his chest read 'Short-Term Security—Jin Chiba'. The guard's voice rolled deep as the ocean floor.

"Can I help you, then?"

"I'm Santa. I mean, I'm Yoshi Goto. Haru Hamada sent me. From Star Production."

Jin's eyes widened. "You're Santa?"

"That's right."

"Ain't you a little young to be Santa?"

"That's the magic of a great performance." Yoshi tapped the counter with impatience. "If you don't mind, I'm in a rush."

Jin turned back to his monitor, infuriatingly slow.

"Magic, huh? Mr. Goto, is it, then?"

"That's right."

"You're late, Mr. Goto."

"I know, I—"

"Says here you're to ride at nine, then."

"Ride? Don't you mean arrive at nine?"

"Nope. I mean ride." Jin slid a dark hand, the size of a large clam, under the window and held up a gun-like device. "Let's get you scanned in, then."

Not wanting to appear any more uninformed, Yoshi held back his questions and pressed his watch against the scanner.

"Okay, then," Jin said, pulling the device back through the gap. "Take the elevator at the end up to level five. The change room is second on the right. I'll let the Promotions Coordinator know you're here. You better hurry up, then. Wonderful Day."

The entry doors slid aside with a whoosh to reveal a long white corridor. Yoshi thanked the guard and hurried to the elevator. On the way up to level five, he checked Haru's message for any mention of what he was meant to be 'riding'—nothing. But he had read one thing wrong—where he thought he was to arrive at 9 a.m., Haru's instructions said he was to arrive *on stage* at 9 a.m.

He checked the time—8:38 a.m.

Ding! The elevator opened, and he rushed down the hall to the change room.

Inside, a bench lined the right, with a section protruding out in the middle between two sinks that created separate make-up bays. A back-lit mirror ran the length of the wall, information displaying in the glass:

Mall attendance: 86%

A Santa costume had been draped over the first bay's chair, wrapped in plastic. Although a large, green tote bag sat limp on the second bench, there appeared to be no-one else in the room.

He removed his clothes and pulled on the costume's bulky, velvet jacket and heavy boots, and faced the mirror. His growing paunch, and the deepening lines around his eyes, worked in silent alliance with the suit to add years to his appearance. He cringed at how he—Yoshi Goto, lead in the 2037 feature film *One Man Dreaming*—could have ended up in the role actors went to die in.

You know how you ended up here, his reflection shot back.

Woken by the inner voice, his doubt crept back in and the headache returned. He reminded himself of the promise he'd made on the bus, but that was made in the raw moment of seeing the refugee. Facing himself and the reality of his own life, he struggled to turn on a genuine shine in his heart; it flickered with false-starts, like one loose bulb in a string of cheap Christmas lights.

A muffled chorus of joyous squeals rose from the other side of the wall where hordes of excited children were no doubt filing into the atrium.

Shine your light.

He strapped on the costume's thick, black belt and yanked it tight. He rolled his shoulders to open his lungs and began his vocal preparation, starting at a low octave and working his way up.

"Ho-Ho-Ho-Ho-Ho-Ho-Hohhhhhh."

A knock sounded on the door, and a young, bespectacled man stepped through the gap.

"Mr. Goto? I'm Kai, Promotions Coordinator. Mr. Hamada said you might be late. I need you to sign this." He tapped the mirror. A standard employment form floated up to the surface. "And I need you to be on level six in fifteen minutes to fly."

"*Fly?*"

Yoshi almost barked the word. But his brashness retreated, struck by the intensity of Kai's hazel eyes— flecks of amber gave them the silky appearance of dark tiger's eye. They sat at odds with his boyish face. His hair had been bleached to the color of light ale, his simple-framed spectacles appeared to have no built-in mixed-reality, and the purple mall uniform was too big for him.

What an odd ball.

"You're flying the sleigh," Kai explained. "Didn't you read your brief? Ah, don't worry, it's all automated. The sleigh brings you down from the ceiling and lands itself by the tree. Holographic reindeer, and real fake snow for kids without Lenzes." Kai tapped his own spectacles.

"Of course, yes," Yoshi said. "Level six in ten."

He faced his Santa incarnation again and drew in a nervous yet excited breath.

I can do this.

Kai tapped the form in the glass. "And the form."

Flustered, Yoshi pretended to read the form in the mirror. A digital stamp from the Automated Contract Analysis service appeared in the top right, confirming it passed the ACA's real-time standard checker. *I wonder how many jobs that little bot replaced,* he thought as he signed the form with his finger.

"You look familiar,' Kai said. "Did you use to work here?"

"Ah, no," Yoshi replied, beginning another *Ho-Ho-Ho* in an attempt to mask his offense.

But Kai stepped between him and the mirror to fix a loose button on the jacket. A galaxy of freckles dotted his pale, luminous face, and a loose strand of hair curled out behind his ear like a piece of broken halo. He smelled of pine trees.

"This isn't the opera," Kai said. "You're Santa. You're meant to be fun."

Yoshi glared. "You obviously don't understand the importance of character immersion."

"Take it easy. They're just kids out there."

Calmed by Kai's friendliness, Yoshi lowered his facade.

"I had a difficult time getting here. And I'm struggling to get into character."

"Take a few deep breaths and let the Christmas spirit in."

Had too many glasses of that last night.

Kai tucked the padded Santa jacket properly through the belt.

"Remember, Santa inspires kid's imagination, telling them it's okay to dream and have secret wishes. They need that now more than ever."

Squeals beyond the wall spiked again. Yoshi pulled a face in the mirror, trying on a jovial, old man's expression.

"Do they even believe this anymore? Don't the channels give it all away?"

"Don't worry about that, they love going along with it. It brings out their generosity and their sense of magic. Even when they know it isn't true, they want to believe, sometimes just so they don't disappoint us adults. Don't you remember Christmas as a kid?"

But Yoshi didn't. His childhood memories were of his Grandpapa cleaning toilets and assisting sewerage bots before dementia dismantled the old man's mind and the cruelness of age took his body. By the time Yoshi grew old enough to get to know him, his Grandpapa's mind dwelled more often in another world. Yoshi couldn't even ask about his parents. It wasn't until he was much older when Yoshi realized that although the tsunami had taken from him a mother and father that he didn't remember, his Grandpapa had lost a son he'd raised and a daughter-in-law he loved. Christmas time was about hard work and not looking back.

But he didn't need to explain all that.

"My family weren't big on Christmas," he replied.

Kai scrunched one nostril upward, followed straight after by the other, in a sort of nostril wave, to push his glasses back up his nose.

"Well, think of it this way—Santa's a good alternative fact."

Yoshi laughed. "Thanks. I think that helps—"

"Hey," Kai said, his eyes sparkling with sudden admiration. "You're Joe Joe. From *Dream Man*."

"*One Man Dreaming*," Yoshi corrected, surprised by the recognition. "It was called *One Man Dreaming*."

"I *loved* that film. So bad, it was so good—no offense. It was just on the other night, on the *The Best Of The Zs*."

"Really?"

"Yeah. And you were great in it."

Yoshi filled with bittersweet pride, and Kai's invigorating scent. "Thank you."

Kai sat back against the bench and looked Yoshi up and down, seeming to forget the urgency.

"So, why's a famous actor like you being Santa in a mall?"

Yoshi didn't want to admit the depths of his desperation; he could barely admit it to himself. And he really needed to get back to his *Ho-Ho-Ho*.

"I've always wanted to do something for the kids."

Kai brushed the loose strand of hair behind his ear.

"Must be hard on your partner, though, with you always rehearsing and performing?"

A kaleidoscope of butterflies fluttered in Yoshi's stomach, but they were quickly lost to his pre-performance nerves. He *really* needed to get in character.

"No time for that." The lies just rolled off his tongue, and the return of his improvisation skills encouraged him.

Now, if he would just let me get on with it...

"Ah, the single life," Kai replied with a smirk and the cheeky air of someone suggesting alternative solutions. "I know what that's like."

Yoshi fumbled for an appropriate reply when a voice startled them both from the back of the room.

"Are you two finished? I'm trying to get into character."

A tall, lean-muscled guy stood up from behind the second bay that had been concealing him. He wore nothing but candy-striped stockings and a tortoise-shell hair clip holding back long, black hair. He stretched backward with a groan, his cut torso flexing like a living sculpture.

Yoshi turned away from the distraction. *Who's that?* he mouthed silently to Kai.

"That's Raiden. He's your helper." Kai cleared his throat. "Raiden, this is Yoshi Goto. He's Santa today. I need you both in position in ten."

Kai leaned forward to pull open the bench drawer and took out a bottle of breath freshener. "Um, I suggest you use this," he whispered. "If a parent smells that breath of yours, you're out."

Blushing, Yoshi hauled his defensive wall back up.

"Don't worry, as soon as I can get another job, I'm out of here."

Kai's eyes widened, and he poured his tone over ice.

"Oh, right, I thought you were doing this for the kids. I'll let you get back to your *great* acting techniques, then. Ten minutes."

Kai left and yanked the door shut behind him, leaving Yoshi's suit laced with the scent of pine, as if he'd been wrestling a Christmas tree. He jutted out his chin and locked his gaze with his reflection.

Finally.

But it was Raiden's turn to chat.

"Can't be easy pretending to be the biggest fraud on earth."

The words punched Yoshi in the stomach. Was he that transparent? He turned and smiled with feigned indifference.

"Excuse me, I need to get into character, too."

Raiden wrapped a hairnet over his head before slipping the clip out from underneath. His voice was rough, his tone cynical.

"Such a grand responsibility, keeping children distracted from the end of their world."

"Wow, you'd be fun at parties," Yoshi replied with restraint.

Raiden shrugged and attached two light wands to his belt.

"I'm just keeping it real. But I see you're like everyone else, blissfully and deliberately optimistic. Bet you're just itching for a Lenz, too."

Frustration struck a match down Yoshi's spine. All he wanted to do was immerse himself in character, but everyone and everything else seemed determined to distract him—including the lingering pine scent hinting at alternative solutions.

"So, what are you doing here, then?" he asked Raiden.

"A job's a job."

Another notification pinged in the mirror:

Santa arriving in ten minutes.

Raiden flicked his Santa's helper hat on Yoshi's backside as he headed out of the room.

"Bring the house down, Santa."

Ignoring him, Yoshi pulled on the wig and beard, and relaxed his stance. His posture and costume worked their rotund-old-man illusion like a charm. He took a few steps back and walked forward, the weight of the outfit pressing on his knees and restricting his movements. But he embraced the restriction—employing technique to fool his mind into thinking he was overweight—and the slow, hindered movements of an aged man came naturally.

"Ho-Ho-Ho!" he bellowed, patting his stomach.

Another cheer beyond the wall and a gust of fresh confidence flooded him, inflating the hope he could rescue his career. Again, thoughts returned of his

Grandpapa and all that he had sacrificed so that Yoshi could live a life above poverty.

He positioned the red hat with determination. The morning had thrown him hurdles, but he was on time and he was ready. This was his second chance, his turning point. He would bring a dimension to Santa that no one had ever seen before. He'd boom a *Ho-Ho-Ho* so jolly through the atrium every child would giggle with giddy joy, and their parents would reply with deafening applause.

"Let's do this."

Beard

At the end of the corridor on level six, he pushed open a hatch-like doorway embossed with a drone icon. A flood of bright light blinded him, and a symphony of echoing voices and electronic sounds streamed up from the atrium below.

As his eyes adjusted, he caught his breath at the sight of an ornate sleigh sitting on a platform. Exposed cogs, copper pipes, valves and pressure gauges adorned its front like it was something just arrived from another era. Circular cages at its base housed rotors that he guessed lifted and propelled the sleigh.

He grew dizzy with panicked excitement.

Beyond the platform, a ring of spotlights circled the atrium's pointed glass ceiling. Their warm glow kept at bay a miserable sky gorging on itself like a gargantuan mollusk.

"Hello?" he called over the mall's din as he approached the vehicle.

A lanky girl popped up from behind the sleigh, dirty overalls dangling from her bony shoulders.

"About time you got here."

Yoshi stammered an apology and hastily explained he hadn't flown a drone sleigh before. But the mechanic waved away his worry as she moved out from behind the vehicle.

"It's all automatic. Your job is to not fall out."

She swung the side door open for him, and Yoshi forged through his doubt to climb into the red-velvet interior. The mechanic latched a safety cable onto his belt and tested it with a yank.

"Let's get Santa airborne."

She stepped behind a metal lectern by the doorway and flicked switches on a control panel. Yoshi gripped the sides as the sleigh's engines revved and vibrated up through his boots. As artificial smoke burst out from vents and billowed over the platform, squeals and cheers exploded from below.

"Launching in ten seconds," yelled the mechanic through the roar of the rotors.

Yoshi gripped the rails tighter.

The mechanic saluted him and winked. "Three. Two. One. Lift off."

The sleigh jolted into the air, tossing Yoshi's heart up with it, and then hovered to stabilize. Floating sideways out of the platform enclosure, the self-driving vehicle lowered itself through the smoke. Shimmering blue rays shot out in front to materialize nine running holographic reindeer tethered to the sleigh by reigns of light. Their heads nodded and twitched as they galloped. Rudolf led them, his red nose glowing as he sniffed the air. Another reindeer—Vixen maybe—nipped her companion.

Yoshi still gripped the side rails, his knuckles glowing white. Having never visited the mall, his head swirled at the spectacle.

Under the glow of the circular skylight, the sleigh eased past the tip of a giant gold star and lowered through a web of twinkling lights that radiated out from a three-story high Christmas tree. Glass elevators slid up, down and across glass balconies circling the tree. Shoppers wove across each floor with hive-like activity, their gift-wrapped purchases stacked in robotic carry boxes trotting behind them on two legs. Sparkling with ever-reflected light, the atrium gleamed like the inner kernel of a mad jeweler's dream.

The reindeer dipped down, appearing to drag the sleigh with them.

Yoshi peered over the edge as the smoke cleared. Hundreds of shoppers covered the atrium floor, their heads cranked upward with eyes hungry for fantasy. A line of children snaked back from a cordoned-off area opposite the tree's base, next to a shiny, black prize auto-pod perched rear-end up on a display ramp. Oversized gift boxes, immaculately wrapped, spread out around the area like geometric algae.

Grand and bold for the entry, kind and gentle for the photos.

He waved and bellowed a hearty *Ho-Ho-Ho*.

The thousand-eyed monster belted out a scream so powerful from its unified lungs it almost knocked him out of his boots. There were so many of them, squirming, wriggling, laughing, and crying. He pulled back from the edge and waved at the shoppers crowding the balconies. Kai appeared, squeezing into a spot by the railing. Yoshi breathed in the festive pine-scented excitement.

Nearing the floor, the sleigh turned in preparation for landing. Raiden stepped around the field of presents and waved his glowing air-traffic wands in faux direction. The sleigh landed in perfect parallel with the prize pod, like the Plaza were testing to see whether nostalgia or promise would hold the crowd's attention the longest. The sleigh's engines shut down, and the reindeer holograms settled on the floor. A mass of short arms reached over the rope to touch the animals that weren't really there.

Relieved, Yoshi unbuckled his safety rope and stood to *Ho-Ho-Ho* again. He shook his belly with Pavarottian bravado and followed with a generous wave. Holographic snow materialized and rained over them all. Enraptured, the children *ooo-ed* and *ahhh-ed*. Intoxicated by the magnificence of the spectacle, Yoshi believed, in that moment, it was his performance enchanting the crowd.

"So, who's first to talk with Santa?"

"Me, Mr. Santa!" cried an excited girl, waving her arms from the front of the line. A red and white-striped shirt stretched over her gourd-ripe belly. He guessed she weighed 200 pounds.

"Well, come on up."

Raiden opened the cordon to let the girl through. She glanced back at her mother, who nudged her forward with a reassuring smile. Raiden led her by the hand up the sleigh steps and hefted her onto Yoshi's knee. He winced as the weight of a small fridge pressed down on his thigh. He gestured for Raiden to help him reposition the girl, but Santa's Helper had already turned and made his way back to the camera podium.

"What's your name, young lady?" he asked through a gritted smile.

"I'm Yumi."

"And how old are you, Yumi?"

The girl's eyes filled with a confused caution, and her lips twitched with suspicion.

"Aren't you supposed to know that?"

He couldn't let her see his own doubt. But the blood flow had slowed through his leg, and his heel began to tingle, throwing off his focus. Yoshi tried lifting her to his other leg, but the fridge didn't budge.

"Santa asks the questions, okay?"

"But, aren't you—"

"And what does a good girl like you want for Christmas?"

Yumi's eyes lit up.

"I want a Lenz, like Keira. She's only two years older than me."

"Well, maybe if you've been a good girl all year, you might get one." Yoshi cringed at how creepy Santa sounded. Suddenly, he felt like the fraud Raiden claimed he was, promising things he wouldn't deliver to a tiny human whose generation might be the last. Sweat trickled teasingly down his back. He steered the chat back on track to hurry it to the photo finish.

"So, what else would you like?"

Yumi's eyes widened further and sparkled with reflected Christmas lights as she listed three wishes. "But I have a question."

He clenched his teeth, all feeling in his leg gone. "Okay, one question, then it someone else's turn."

"Do you give to the homeless people? Daddy says they're lazy and shouldn't get handouts. But I think it's okay." She looked down, still twirling the end of the beard in her finger. "You can give them one of mine if you want."

A soft blast of true Christmas spirit hit Yoshi with the convicted power of a blessing. But Yumi twisted her mouth and leaned back, coiling a chubby finger around a curl of his fake beard.

"Your breath smells funny."

Instant beads of sweat broke out across Yoshi's forehead. The tingling had spread up his leg and morphed into a needling pain in his hip. He flexed his thigh in an attempt to relieve the pressure. Yumi suddenly screwed up her face again and twirled the beard tighter around her finger.

"And this doesn't feel like real hair."

Catching Yoshi off guard, she tried to pull his beard off.

"Hey," Yoshi warned, yanking his head away, terrified of being unmasked and ruining Christmas for the kids. But his action was bold instead of gentle, and his left hip jerked, flinging his numb leg sideways and throwing Yumi backward. She squealed, desperately clutching the beard. But her short fingers lost their grip—the beard snapping hard back into Yoshi's face—and she tumbled over the edge of the sleigh.

No! Yoshi screamed in his mind.

"Yumi!" screamed her mother.

A chorus of gasps lifted into the atrium in a puff of evaporated dreams.

Yoshi jumped to his feet, but his numb leg gave way. In a graceless collapse, he dropped over the opposite side, banging his hip on the prize-car ramp and plonking into the fake presents on the floor.

Cramping with pain shooting up his back, and mortified to his core, he clumsily clawed the crushed boxes out of his way. Yumi's hyperventilating mother stomping through the boxes to rescue her daughter. She glared at Yoshi with laser-burning eyes.

"Everyone stay calm," Raiden called out.

Relieved to see Yumi unhurt, Yoshi hauled himself up. But horror gripped him by the back of the neck as he saw the prize-pod ramp was empty. The tire-lock hung limp, knocked by his fall. He spun around to see the pod rolling directly toward the tree's base, squashing open presents in its path.

"Look out!" he yelled, pointing to the runaway pod.

The entire crowd—focused on Yumi until then—swung their gaze to the rolling pod. Raiden bolted through the presents after it, and Yoshi pulled himself along the edge of the sleigh in a futile chase, his numb leg dragging like a log.

Another collective gasp rose as the pod only bumped the tree and eased back to a soft stop. Yoshi's entire body locked, and all breath left him. The tree wobbled from top to tip with drunken carelessness, but remained upright just long enough for the entire atrium to exhale with relief before it toppled over as if in slow motion.

The pit of Yoshi's stomach dropped, and shrieks spiked the air. Branches crashed into the balconies, exploding an overwhelming burst of pine scent. The web of colored lights snapped from their balcony anchors with sharp pops and flung toward the fleeing shoppers in a sparking tangle. Yoshi and Raiden yelled out to everyone to get back, but the falling tree dragged to a stop before hitting the floor and slumped in a bend against the balconies. The dangling lights sparked and flashed overhead, just out of harm's way. Yoshi dropped to his knees among the broken presents, wrecked with guilted relief.

Yumi's mother, and the hundreds of other shoppers, were already whisking their children out the front doors. Raiden, too, was halfway across the atrium, ushering out another man. The holographic reindeer nipped at each other, oblivious to the spectacle.

Security guards arrived and closed in on the tot-tossing Santa who had brought the house down.

Glimpse

A string of flickering colored lights dangled outside the mall manager's office overlooking the atrium mess below. Their rainbow halo silhouetted her sharp-shouldered suit and helmet-shaped bob as she paced by the window, her heels click-clacking the floor. She halted and folded her arms, her hot breath steaming the glass as she hissed her words.

"Do you have any idea how much trouble I'd be in if anyone got hurt?"

Yoshi squirmed in one of the two matching guest chairs. The Santa suit's lack of ventilation marinated him in sweat and shame. Any optimism he had about his future lay on the atrium floor in pieces, right next to the fallen star of his confidence.

"Although it's not entirely your fault. It was the Promotions Coordinator's responsibility to ensure the pod was not left in neutral. But you have no idea how difficult it is to keep customers coming back here without some *fiasco* scaring them right out the front door at our busiest time. Mr. Honda at Shibido Midtown will be loving this—"

She stopped and pointed a pencil-sharp finger at Yoshi.

"Mr. Honda sent you, didn't he? He's been trying to undo me ever since we took the traffic away from his aging behemoth. I *knew* he'd find a way to sabotage me." She folded her hand into a fist, stood up straight, and looked out the window again. "It all makes sense. No one could be this unreliable."

Yoshi had no idea who Mr. Honda was, but he barely heard the manager's words anyway. He twisted the Santa hat, horrified by how much worse things could have been. White noise grew in his head as self-blame and reasoning fought for domination over any remnant of clear thinking.

Maybe I wouldn't have dropped the girl if I wasn't hung-over. But she was so heavy.

"Get out," the manager commanded.

"Mall Manager, I'm—"

"Get out!"

He rose and bowed deeply before retreating from the office, half expecting her to spin and launch at him. But it was only her voice that came after him, disturbingly serene.

"Oh, and Mr. Goto, you might want to get yourself a lawyer."

Wondering how he could afford one, staring at the floor, he hurried to the elevator and stepped inside

"Mr. Goto."

He jumped at the deep voice. Jin stood in the corner. A bucket-shaped hat now hid his thinning hair. Yoshi was struck by how ridiculous the *Short Term Security* uniform made Jin look, like some kid's comic train-driver.

"Excuse me," Yoshi said. "I didn't see you there."

Jin nodded.

"That's okay. You got a lot going on. But we got some things to do, so listen up. First, I'll be taking you to the changing room, and you're going get out of that suit. You're going do it fast, because I'm on two hours overtime. Second, I'm escorting you off the premises, and you're going to do that without a worry, because my wife's already mad I'm late home."

"I'm sorry," Yoshi said again, claustrophobic under the man's gaze.

Staring intently, Jin squinted, and bounced a pointed finger. "You..."

Yoshi's neck and shoulders clenched, fearing a berating, but Jin just chuckled.

"Yeah, that was you. In that crazy movie. *One Man Dreaming*."

Yoshi blushed and shrugged, relieved to have the focus shifted from the sink hole opening up beneath his life.

"Yes. Yes, that was me."

"Joe Joe. You're Joe Joe. Well, how's that, then."

"Guilty as charged," Yoshi said, laughing at the irony.

"My wife and I watched that on *The Zs* just last week. Well, I didn't think it was as bad as the reviews. No, I did not. I thought it was fun."

"Thank you."

Jin's eyes measured Yoshi in his costume, pity nestling in the contours of his face.

"Not much acting work out there, then?"

"I like to do odd jobs between roles, you know, do things for the kids."

Jin stared back, his face unreadable. "Technology replacing you, too, huh? Welcome to the future."

The elevator stopped with a *ding!*, and Jin led Yoshi down the hallway to the changing room door.

"I'll be outside here when you're done, Mr. Goto. Be fast, then."

Yoshi nodded and stepped inside to find Kai standing by the bench, Yoshi's jacket in his folded arms. The harsh neon light was unkind to his exhausted features, but it highlighted a resilience in the dark suns of his eyes.

"Looks like you were right about this being an interim job," Kai said. "For both of us."

"Kai, I'm so sorry—"

"What happened out there? You came down like you really *were* Santa. You had the whole mall enthralled. That little girl was loving you, playing with your beard, then you just flipped her out of the sleigh."

"I didn't mean it. I..." *I'm a fraud.* "It was an accident. And I hit the car lock by accident."

"That is my fault as much as it is yours. I didn't secure the pod. But maybe it could have been less of an accident, right?" Kai held up the bottle of breath freshener.

"I'm so sorry, about your job."

Kai waved Yoshi's apology away.

"I hated this job. I only took it 'cause a ticket vending machine took my last job at Roller Dome. I have no idea what I should be doing with my life, but it's not this. Are you okay?"

Kai's unexpected empathy threw a rescue blanket of calm around Yoshi that he hadn't realized he needed. The mall security had left him to sweat and overheat in his costume for half an hour while they yelled questions and accusations at him before he had to endure another thirty minutes questioning from the police, followed by the heated lecturing from the mall manager. No one had asked him if he was okay. He plonked down in the chair.

"I'm sorry, all sorts of sorry. But I didn't mean to hurt anyone. I was just trying to put food on the table." He held back a sob, almost cracking under the weight of guilt. "This isn't my ideal job either." *I'm Joe Joe, damn it.*

Kai's face remained soft but resolute as he passed Yoshi's jacket to him.

"So, what's next?"

"Good question," Yoshi said, as he stood back up.

Kai withdrew a gold lighter from his shirt pocket and held it out. Frowning, Yoshi took it and turned it in his fingers to see the words 'Shibido Connect' engraved on the back, with an address. It no doubt had more augmented information attached to it that he could see if he had a Lenz.

"What's this for?"

"It's a lighter. A waterproof one. You know, in case a wave comes over the wall. Just joking. But it is waterproof, a gift to the homeless from Shibido Connect. They hand out things like this, and food, to the homeless. They're out in the western warehouse districts. You could give them a call."

Yoshi filled with defiant protest. "I'm not homeless."

"I meant you can volunteer for them, because they give you food for your time. I've been doing it on the side, with Raiden. I know it's not a permanent solution, but it's food. And volunteering might get you cred, in case a judge is going to be deciding your fate sometime soon. Do something for the kids, you know?"

Embarrassed yet warmed by Kai's realism, Yoshi slid the lighter into his jacket pocket. "Thanks."

Kai winked and moved toward the door where he paused to give a farewell smile. In that moment, Yoshi thought he heard a distant drumming until he realized his heart was pounding hard and fast. The absurdity of the situation called to him to ask for Kai's number, yet it simultaneously screamed that it would also be totally inappropriate. The moment passed, and Kai opened the door.

"Good luck, Yoshi."

He slipped out after bowing, leaving Yoshi to face his sweaty, drawn reflection in the mirror. It wasn't pretty.

Exhausted by a maelstrom of emotions, he sighed with relief as he pulled off the heavy suit, but his body remained weighed down by his problems. His second chance had not only backfired, it had amplified his desperation. Would he be sued? At the very least he'd be labelled a danger. Could he ever work again with a record like that? Would Kai and Raiden be handing *him* food on the street? Was there such a thing as third chances?

He finished changing, grabbed his jacket and followed Jin through a maze of corridors that seemed to wind on forever.

"You look like you wear only one Lenz?" he asked, to break the awkward silence.

"My right eye keeps rejecting it. The view's a little distorted with just one, but, to be honest, I prefer to keep one eye on the real world. Saves me from going cross-eyed."

Yoshi considered asking for the spare.

They arrived at a nondescript exit that opened onto a side street running between the mall and the pod-park, far away from the main entrance. A sea of city noise swam into the corridor on a breeze cooler than the morning's humidity.

"My apologies again, and to your wife."

"Forget it," Jin said. "I've got her and a warm bed to go home to. A lot more than others have, right? You get home safe, then, Mr. Goto. That humidity promises a storm. I suppose 'Wonderful Day' would be improper right now."

Yoshi forced a smile and bowed a goodbye. As he stepped outside, the door banged shut behind him and echoed up the street. He glanced nervously in both directions before heading to the right.

At the end, concrete pathways radiated out, segmenting a sprawling urban park. Clouds— illuminated internally by the sun they were hiding— slow-twirled above as if vacuuming up any remnant of his dreams. He considered calling his agent, but he couldn't bring himself to face that conversation, so he took a travelator toward the Scape's southern elevators.

He passed a park on his left, where a pony-tailed girl in a pink tracksuit practiced Karate, probably following a guidance program in the Lenz. Behind her, a boy chased something in the air that wasn't there. At the end of the lawn, a small group stood before a giant, glowing screen, the photodiodes of their Lenzes recharging from the screen's optic signals while transmitting the secrets in their tears to Maya.

His watch vibrated, and Tora's bright-smiling face filled the screen again.

"Ho-ho-ho. How's the job going, Chief?"

"It's not."

"Hey, why you outside already?"

"Tora, I knocked the tree over."

"What you say?"

"I dropped a kid out of the sleigh, I fell out after her, and I knocked the giant Christmas tree over."

"Oh, damn. That's gonna be all over the channels."

"No one got hurt, but there's probably a pack of parents and lawyers after me." An image from an old American film rose in his mind of an angry, pitch-fork-wielding mob chasing after him. He picked up his pace.

"It might not be a bad idea to get outta the city for a while," Tora suggested.

"But it was an accident."

"That's not how the channels will tell it. Drama gets the Sight."

Tora was right; it was only a matter of time before the news picked up the story and amplified it to every Lenz, the spike in Sight sending a swarm of media drones to hunt him down. He'd get more Sight than he ever bargained for.

"But I don't think I can even afford a train ticket out of here—oh, crap!" Caught up in his dilemma, Yoshi missed the travelator's right lane that would have taken him south toward home. Instead, the walkway zoomed him east toward High Scape's bay side. "I just missed the turn off. I'll have to loop around. Damn it. It's like the whole day's against me."

"Or it's trying to tell you something. I'll search some options for you and get back. Remember, no matter how bad things get, what matters most is what happens next."

Tora's face vanished from the screen, a fading light stain left behind by his beaming smile. Yoshi sighed, wishing he could meet his only friend for a beer in the real world.

His watch vibrated again, and a bank alert popped up on the small screen:

Deposit received:
¥84,500
From Maya Technologies Inc.

Twin fireworks of disbelief and relief popped in his chest at the sight of his residual payment. Just being able to cover another month's rent reassured him the whole day wasn't completely conspiring against him.

He dared himself some excitement at the size of the payment—double the last.

And I've been recognized twice in one day.

He caught his thoughts. Since there were traumatized children out there because of him, he didn't think it appropriate to indulge in fantasies of fame and adoration. He tapped off the display.

But it was odd that *One Man Dreaming* was screening more often.

Who am I kidding? I'm probably going to jail.

Reaching High Scape's eastern side, he stepped off the travelator and crossed the road. A dashed stream of cargo drones flew low overhead with their coastal delivery of Shibido's technologies. He stopped at the rain-drizzled glass panels looking over the sea-wall to Shibido Bay. The mist still hid the island of his birth from sight, and rusted telescopic viewers hung limp on their mounts, neglected ever since the Lenz arrived in the citizens' eyes.

The solitude was perfect for him to gather his thoughts. He listened for the slow rhythm in the bay's white noise to focus on his reality, to hear if there was, as Tora suggested, a message he needed to hear.

The bay's shifting slate surface jittered like television static, tempting his mind into thinking it could detect shapes and objects. But the crashing waves grew in ferociousness, exploding against the top of the gargantuan concrete ribbon that divided life between before the Shift and after. Waves rippled through the low cloud base above, transforming the sky into a stormy sea viewed from underneath. Yoshi imagined the earth prototyping a new sea level frighteningly higher than anyone predicted.

Coming, coming, coming.

"Don't get lost in there," said his Grandpapa's voice in his head, a memory of whenever he caught Yoshi daydreaming.

Giving up on the desperate idea the universe might try to speak to him, he turned to leave. But just as he did, the clouds slid apart and revealed a patch of blue sky, and sudden sunlight ignited the sea-sprayed air in a hypnotizing display. Protruding from the bay, something large and faceted emerged from the vanishing vapor, and the dissolving mist revealed the strikingly geometric remains of the Isle of Meti.

Yoshi's breath caught in his throat.

But as fast as they had parted, the clouds reconnected, rendering Meti invisible again.

He blinked, unsure if he'd imagined the glimpse or not. He scanned the misty bay for any remnant of the island, but there was nothing, leaving his mind as murky as the sky.

An unfamiliar voice startled him from behind, vanquishing the vision from his thoughts.

"Mr. Goto?"

He spun to find no one in the immediate vicinity. An auto-pod had stopped by the road, however, as black and glassine as a rhinoceros beetle. Apprehension tightened his chest; the pod looked just like the one he'd sent rolling into the Christmas tree. He looked around, wondering if his imagination had grown a mind of its own and given him some sort of cerebral Lenz, one that exaggerated fears rather than dreams.

"Mr. Goto?"

This time he was sure the voice came from the pod. He took a few steps toward it, squinting at the windows, but they were too tinted for him to see through.

"Who's there?"

The side door pushed out with a hiss and slid aside, exposing a lush, white leather interior, but empty of passengers. A gasp escaped Yoshi like a little bark.

A smart pod.

"Hello, Mr. Goto. I'm Driver. I'm here on behalf of Maya Technologies."

Yoshi's heart pounded so loud in his ears he couldn't be sure of what he heard. A gentle rain fell.

"From where?"

"Maya CEO Mr. Tyler Gray asks to speak with you. Please, would you allow me to take you to Maya Studios?"

Dizzy disbelief filled his head like helium—the tech titan who created the Lenz was back in Shibido and wanted to speak to him? It had to be a prank.

"May I ask what this is about?"

"Tyler Gray is the Chief Executive Officer of Maya Technologies. He would like to speak to you about Joe Joe and *One Man Dreaming*."

Yoshi went as rigid as a hiding ninja, his instinct crouching in guarded anticipation. Raindrops counted seconds of silence in the puddles and tiny, twin oceans gathered at his boots. Could a smart pod even be impressed? He couldn't be sure, so he thought it best to present a professional composure.

"Is this about a role? Because I'm looking at a few right now, but I might be able to consider others."

"I'm sorry," Driver replied. "I am not authorized to tell you anymore. Mr. Gray has a lot he'd like to talk to you about at the studios. Would you please step inside?"

The interior light tinged amber, transforming the seat into a cozy escape from the drizzle.

"Well, I'll have to make some phone calls and rearrange today's appointments," he lied, and climbed in.

The door slid shut, and the plush leather hugged his shoulders like the hide of a Chieftain's conquest. The pod took off and the rain fell harder. Across the road, a couple holding hands scattered for cover.

As the pod headed back to High Scape's center, Yoshi thought again to call Haru, thinking the summons from the likes of Tyler Gray might soften the bad news about the mall. He tapped his watch, but his agent's number was engaged, and it didn't divert to voice mail. He tried again with the same result; perhaps Haru was being yelled at by the mall manager.

With equal parts excitement and trepidation, Yoshi's mind raced. Staring out the front window, he didn't see the rainy street. He looked back through time, back to the events that led him to shooting down both the set of *One Man Dreaming* and his career.

***

As far back as Yoshi could remember, a climate of disappointment dulled his Grandpapa's presence. But when Grandpapa Goto entertained Yoshi with one of his mad tales, the old man became more performer than narrator and shone in the moment. Interacting with his own shadow, he would stretch and hunch his body into all sorts of shapes and alter his mannerisms and voice through a vast range of different characters.

As Yoshi grew older, the stories became more like collections of random snippets, as if, during his growing absentmindedness, Grandpapa Goto wandered in and out of other people's memories. And the more he disappeared into that other place, the more memories of his own he seemed to lose.

By the time Yoshi started high school, the old man's dynamic storytelling had stopped, and communicating with him had become like talking to a stranger. His health worsened, too, and he had to be moved into Shibido South Aged Care, where subsequent medication hastened the deterioration of his Outlook. The old man's growing depression drew Yoshi in with whirlpool force, breaking Yoshi's heart into smaller and smaller pieces, like plastic in the ocean. Eventually, what remained of Grandpapa Goto's rambling sifted down to one persistent, urgent declaration.

"Coming, coming, coming."

An undercurrent of terror drove Yoshi to seek an alternate reality. But he couldn't afford a Lenz like most others at school. So, when the theater club asked him to participate in their annual production, he grabbed the chance to pretend to be someone somewhere else.

The stage's make-believe made all the sharp angles of the real world disappear, exposing him to a virtual reality he could afford. He spent every afternoon rehearsing and watching other actors, leaving him less time to visit his Grandpapa. Guilt plagued him, but there were no clear rules for how to balance caring for a loved one and nurturing one's own energy needs.

On the night of the play's performance, just before Yoshi was to go on stage, Shibido South Aged Care called with the news his Grandpapa's heart had given out. Yoshi didn't know how to handle the turmoil of heart break and guilt, and an irrational fear flooded him with the idea the ocean was coming for him next. He hung up on the call and headed to the portal of the stage.

Mimicking the greatly exaggerated gestures of his Grandpapa's story-telling, he completely detached from the world, and he lost himself in an alternate state where there was no ocean and nothing to fear, just an expansive sensation of shifting between layers of awareness—until a sharp whisper called to him through the ether, its urgency sucking him out of the supernatural sensation and drawing him back into his own body with a *whoosh*.

Stunned, he found himself back on the stage in front of a silent audience, an immeasurable time having passed from when he first began his lines. His fellow cast members glared at him and nodded toward back-stage. Dazed, he exited and returned to the change room with no memory of what he'd done. But by the time the play finished to a generous applause, someone had uploaded a video of his 'highly colored' performance—an overly intense interpretation of the role, totally out of alignment with the play's tone. But it was a *good* performance, so good, in fact, he made the others on stage appear faded, contrived, and drooping. The polarizing reaction to the scene-stealing high-school actor generated enough online noise to catch the keen eye of talent agent Haru Hamada.

Haru needed a cheap actor with a little notoriety to leverage, to play the lead in a low budget film version of *One Man Dreaming*. The Japanese graphic novel had garnered a reasonable and active fan-base, guaranteeing a profitable audience from a film adaptation.

Haru convinced Yoshi to audition. Yoshi buried himself in the novel's intricately woven tale of an insomniac coder who built a dream-design app, only to become trapped in his own dreams. Delving into the coder's complexities and sleep-deprived neurosis, Yoshi brought Joe Joe alive through vigorous and erratic mannerisms, wild eyed stares and a distinctive drawl—an overall exaggerated characterization to keep Joe Joe highlighted throughout the dreamscape's visually dominating scenes. By the time Yoshi auditioned, his performance style, youthful looks and fresh-faced naivety impressed the casting agent so much she just had to have him.

Sensing a potential explosion of interest in his budding new protégé, Haru negotiated any reuse of Yoshi's likeness as Joe Joe to require separate negotiations, ensuring Haru himself would remain in any future profit loop.

One Man Dreaming's production time and budget was super tight. For the ninety-days of rehearsals and filming, Yoshi had to channel the zealous and neurotic Joe Joe fourteen hours a day.

Meanwhile, word got out about the novel's adaptation, noise grew among sci-fi forums, and a large media network picked up the teaser snippets. Sight on the film's promo channel grew, and in a few short months, Yoshi found himself pulled deeper into a position that might catapult him into stardom.

A good performance was no longer good enough.

At first, his commitment to the role impressed the cast and crew so much the words 'Academy Prize' fluttered through the set. But he couldn't replicate the feeling he'd had in the school play, and his consistency wobbled between total metamorphosis and wooden caricature. Panic became his day-to-day vibration. The crew's doubts hovered, and the future tabloids in his head closed in. He resorted to taking micro doses of LSD to immerse himself deeper into the novel's surreal world until he no longer heard any doubts and believed his acting ability a sort of superpower that raised him above the boundary of any script. His improvisations confused the cast and crew, and an increasingly impatient director was forced to rewrite scenes or reshoot them quickly and creatively edit them in.

By the day Yoshi strode up the studio driveway to film the shooting scene, he had buried himself alive inside Joe Joe. Sometime between wardrobe dressing him in his canary-yellow t-shirt and red bomber jacket, and make-up applying Joe Joe's comet-shaped birthmark under his right eye, the prop gun was placed in his hand and the director called "Action!"

He strode onto the elaborate set of the Stratodel, where a giant rig of blue and green lights—representing a malevolent AI—was suspended by a web of ropes attached to the floor and ceiling. The crew stepped back in awe as Yoshi moved with exquisite believability, embodying a Joe Joe as real as the day. The director followed him in an impromptu one-shot, capturing the performance from Joe's Joe's distorted perspective and zooming in close for his catch phrase.

"Let's do this."

But Yoshi's weak connection to the present slipped with each moment, and the heat of the light rig above cooked whatever grip he had left. Untethered and lost in his psychosis, he mistook the azure glow above him for a giant wave *coming, coming, coming*. He stumbled backward and became entangled in the support ropes. The glowing rig above shook, and the crew scattered. Fearing he was drowning, Yoshi thrashed in panic, and his finger pulled against the gun's trigger. The blank shattered a rope, setting off a chain reaction of the broken ends snapping and whipping the support undone, and the massive light rig dropped to a thunderous and shattering crash.

The crew escaped unhurt, but Yoshi broke his arm, and the damaged equipment delayed production. While he recovered in hospital, the director quit, fed up with watching his own career be destroyed scene by scene. The film dropped behind schedule and flew over budget, and the studio 'could no longer wait' for Yoshi to return.

They appointed a new director who shot what remaining scenes she could, filming Yoshi's stand-in from behind and overlaying mixes of Yoshi's voice. She creatively edited existing footage and filled any remaining gaps with bizarre animation sequences in a scramble to deliver a final version on time.

The day Yoshi was released from hospital, the low-grade, abstract version of what *One Man Dreaming* was meant to be premiered without him. The replacement director's unrelenting psychedelia and tonal inconsistencies failed to capture the novel's essence, and reviews vomited on it. Fans were divided over Yoshi's performance—from "Experimental AF!" to "Who ordered the extra cheese?"—but they were united in their disgust at the mutilation of the novel's original sophistication. Box Office sales fell so far short of expectations the film was pulled from cinemas after only one week and sent straight to *The Best Of The Zs*.

Rather than receiving any prize, Yoshi was awarded a reputation as the most problematic actor in the industry. Struggling to secure work even as an extra, his roles dried up faster than his bank account. He dropped into a growing unemployment line, competing with machines and robots for menial jobs just like his Grandpapa had done to keep their heads above   water.

Offer

"We're here, Mr. Goto."

Snapped back to the present, Yoshi found himself returned with an undeniable epiphany—having screwed up the Santa job and landing himself in another knot of reputation and legal concerns, he'd fundamentally repeated the *One Man Dreaming* fiasco.

The pod stopped outside a gate securing five tall studios huddling around a cul-de-sac in front of a gleaming pagoda-styled high-rise. Maya's crossed-ringed logo sat half-way up the exterior, as big as a giant's shield. Excitement spread its wings in Yoshi's chest and beat back any further dwelling on the past. A guard stepped out from a booth by the gate and scanned Yoshi's watch before letting the pod through.

Numbers covered the windowless fronts of the five studios, and the pod stopped by a path running between 3 and 4. The tower entrance looked tiny at the end of the path, like a rectangular mouse hole.

"Take the walkway to the entrance to Maya Head Office," Driver instructed. "I'll be here for when you come back."

Yoshi took a deep breath of bravado, climbed out into the cold, and headed down the path.

Inside, warm air beckoned him down a long, wide corridor. Animated snippets of the studio's films flickered floor to ceiling across the walls on either side. He neared a round room at the end where an open elevator sat waiting.

"Hello, Mr. Goto," said a strikingly formal voice from his left. An immaculately groomed young man in a crisp, charcoal suit stood out from a steel desk and bowed. "Mr. Gray welcomes you. The elevator will take you to level eleven."

As Yoshi thanked him and stepped into the elevator, the host bowed again and repeated himself.

"Hello, Mr. Goto. Mr. Gray welcomes you. Hello, Mr. Goto, Mr. Gray welcomes you."

The man seemed to get stuck mid-bow as the elevator doors closed. The back of Yoshi's neck prickled.

A yujin.

He'd never seen the companion android's in public service before. And their physical perfection and precise politeness usually rendered them more performance artists than fully sentient beings. Their eyes, too, often gave them away, dull like cheap jewelry, rather than glistening with the organic wetness of human eyes. But if it wasn't for the host's malfunctioning… Yoshi feared it was only a matter of time before the *yujin's* glitches were ironed out making them employable for more than personal use.

Unsure if he'd been invited to his reinvention or replacing, Yoshi tucked in his shirt and finger-combed his hair, hoping he didn't look as disheveled as he felt. Wondering what he would say when meeting the enigmatic CEO, he ran a quick search on his watch.

Should have done this on the way.

Images appeared of a dark-eyed Caucasian man, thirtyish, skin like marzipan, and with a slick of jet-black hair sliced by a part as white as snow.

Tyler Gray (born 18 February 1992) is a British digital designer who is the Chief Executive Officer of Maya Technologies. A self-taught programmer, Gray developed and sold several successful Mixed Reality apps before moving to Japan in 2016 to marry Hina Abe, a Japanese seamstress he met while on a business trip to Shibido. Remaining in Japan, Gray founded Maya in 2020, which he grew into a leading consumer technology company by 2022. One year later he launched his industry-changing Lenz, enjoying its success until the Shift—

The elevator eased to a stop and opened onto a spacious, mirror-walled foyer overlooking the bay. An exquisitely dry and crisp air greeted Yoshi's skin. He crossed the floor—buffed to a gloss like the surface of a still lake—and his endless reflections in the mirrored walls appeared to walk on water.

Stopping at the window, he looked down on the lush lawns and stone pathways of High Scape. Below its abrupt edge, Maya District spread out like a giant mold bloom. Beyond, the sea-wall, Shibido Bay rocked gently. Light caught his reflection in the glass and superimposed clouds floating through his head. He squinted futilely for any sign of Meti.

A click sounded from behind, and he spun to see the left wall by the lift slide aside. Gray stepped into the foyer, his complexion wax-museum worthy and imbuing him with a celebrity presence. Filled with awe, Yoshi smiled and bowed, but Gray appeared not to see him. A pale ghost of a woman—with a familiar wave of silver hair and a white pants suit clinging to her lithe frame—followed Gray into the room. As the two conversed with lowered voices, Yoshi also recognized the woman—Mio Wada, Shibido's Mayor.

The pair bowed, and Gray ushered the Mayor into the elevator. As she disappeared behind the closing doors, Gray turned to Yoshi with a rambunctious clap and strode forward to bow.

"Thank you so much for coming. I'm Tyler Gray, CEO of Maya. Demonic of me to keep you waiting, I do apologize. It's a delight to meet you, Mr. Goto."

"It is an honor to meet you, too, Mr. Gray," Yoshi replied, bowing deeply.

"Please come this way."

Trembled by nerves, Yoshi followed Gray through the doorway and into a short hall.

"I must confess," Gray said over his shoulder, "I'm a tremendous fan of *One Man Dreaming*. When Maya obtained the film rights, I thought to myself, 'Wouldn't it be fantastic to meet *the* Joe Joe?' And now, here you are. Oh, yes, this is definitely the time to bring him back."

"Bring him back?"

But Gray didn't respond as he led Yoshi into a long room centered by an elliptical table. At its end stood two sharp-suited young men, twins, with identical goatees and eyes sparkling with entrepreneurship. Next to them was a stern-faced Caucasian woman, her stare arresting Yoshi. Thick, dark, semi-damp curls draped down her cheeks with octopus nonchalance, as if some amphibious creature had crawled over the sea-wall and made a home on her head. Yoshi squirmed under their gazes until Gray swept a hand at the twins to begin introductions.

"This is Reo Uchida, our Chief Financial Officer; his brother, Sora Uchida, from legal; and Lavinda Osbourne, our Communications Manager."

"Good afternoon," Yoshi said with enthusiasm, sweeping their unified gaze with one confident smile and bowing to each.

"Good afternoon," the three replied in unison, as they took out the business cards.

Yoshi froze. He'd completely forgotten to be prepared for the customary business card exchange—it had been so long since he'd been in any formal situation. He apologized profusely and took each of the other's cards with both hands, but their blinking smiles did not mask their disappointment. Lavinda sighed heavily and rolled her eyes toward Gray, but he maintained his gracious composure and gestured for Yoshi to join them at the table. Putting her un-Shibidoan manner down to foreigner's ignorance, Yoshi gave Lavinda a friendly glance as they sat.

Taking the seat opposite Yoshi, Gray tapped on the table. A *Non-Disclosure Agreement* form loaded inside it.

"Before we begin, Mr. Goto, I ask you to agree that what we discuss today cannot be repeated outside these walls."

It is. It's about a role.

Yoshi rubbed his clammy hands together under the table and waited for the ACA approval badge to appear in the top right of the form. He signed with a sweaty finger, and the form disappeared.

"Wonderful," Gray said, smiling and resting his hands on the table to make a pyramid. "Now, I'm sure you're simply bursting to know why I've called for you. But first, tell me, have you noticed an increase in your royalties over the last year?"

"I believe so," Yoshi said with feigned uncertainty. "From the film's run on *The Best Of The Zs*, I'm guessing?"

"Among other channels. Over the last year since *One Man Dreaming*'s lack-luster cinema release, the film has secured a regular run on *The Best of The Zs*, while dubbed versions have been played at independent cinemas throughout Europe, on campuses in the U.S., and in Australia. In a very short time, the film has developed somewhat of an international cult following of its own."

Yoshi had to chew his inner lip to contain his excitement as Gray continued.

"Now, to be honest, the fan's interest is a mocking one, a shallow love. We all know what a horrid tit of a film it was. What did the Times call it? 'Illogical, unhinged.' Nonetheless, while other more-established cinematic franchises decline, *One Man Dreaming*'s popularity grows. And as a consequence of this interest, Joe Joe himself is experiencing a kind of character renaissance. Admittedly, he, too, is ridiculed as much as he is loved, but such quibbling polarity generates great noise on the channels. And our algorithms predict that this growing noise guarantees a profitable outcome from a sequel, which we have titled *Dreams For All*. Did you ever imagine?"

No, Yoshi didn't, and for the second time that day, he wondered if it was his flawed Outlook that kept his potential limited.

"Imagine," Gray said, holding up a hand as if evoking images from the air, "it's been several years since Joe Joe saved the Dream world and returned to the real world. To atone for his meddling in other people's dreams, he has used his wealth to build a floating, forested Stratodel in the stratosphere, as an escape for people from the world's constant surveillance. But one night, he's approached by Leon Jerome—an inhabitant come from the Dream world itself—"

"Liveys are in this?" Yoshi interrupted before he could stop himself.

"Yes. Leon Jerome plays himself. His Sight is a steady 167 million. He guarantees us a substantial audience. Now, as I was saying, Leon warns Joe Joe that the Algorlines rebuilding the Dream world are out of control and will escape and start destroying the real world if they're not stopped. Joe Joe thinks Leon is another trick of the AI, but then the Algorlines escape the Dream world, forcing Joe Joe to help Leon get people to the Stratodel."

Yoshi cringed. The new commercialized narrative sounded nothing like the original Japanese novel, and vaguely linked by Joe Joe and the Algorlines. He noticed a framed original *One Man Dreaming* poster on the wall behind Gray where gnashing Algorlines chased Joe Joe through a kaleidescoping setting as he ran hand in hand with the enigmatic O. The forested city of the Stratodel floated in the sky behind them.

"What about O," Yoshi asked, "and the other original characters?"

"I'm afraid they don't have any audience draw. Otherwise, the algorithms would have suggested to include them."

"And what happens to Joe Joe?"

"Well—" Gray caught himself and smiled. "You sly dog, you almost had me giving out spoilers. Suffice to say, we're on a super-tight schedule to leverage audience interest, so this sequel is a short twenty-minute episode, an introduction to the launch of a much larger experience—the biggest, most seamless mixed-reality venue ever built. Maya District."

"One episode?" Yoshi said, back-tracking. "So, *Dreams For All* is a series?"

"No, no, just one episode. It's an introduction to Maya District."

Yoshi's excitement melted away like the last pieces of floating arctic ice.

"As you know," Gray continued, "films have to be more these days. People want *story worlds* to explore in real-world locations. Ever since we launched the Lenz, we haven't been able to keep up with audiences' demand for Mixed Reality venues. The wait for entry is murderous, the inside queues endless, all constant reminders of the invisible wall separating reality from the virtual. It's all so primitive."

"As I'm sure you've heard, we're transforming Shibido's esplanade into a Mixed Reality district—one of five around the world—a live, interactive theater, that will take full advantage of the Lenz's unique MR capabilities. As soon as a Lenzer walks into Maya District, their Lenz will automatically enter full-immersion mode and actors will draw them into a story designed to make them the star, creating a space between the real and the virtual where they can dwell for a while, or longer, or until they can't tell the difference. And when they've had enough, they simply walk out of the district, their story saved for their return. With access twenty-four hours a day, seven-days a week, and no gates or lines or advertisements, there will be nothing to remind them of the separation between reality and fantasy."

All Gray's talk of some over-the-top, role-playing theme-park boggled Yoshi's mind. The only reality he cared about was shining up his tarnished star.

"So, this district will be a remake of the *One Man Dreaming* world?"

Gray leaned forward.

"This is where it gets interesting. In the last eight months, approximately a quarter of Lenzers around the world have watched *One Man Dreaming* and interacted in the *One Man Dreaming* forums. Surely, you've seen the memes in the channels. On further analysis, we saw the majority are talking about—and re-watching—one scene in particular, which these users' Mirage mode has rendered into a filter. Best if I demonstrate. Let me show you a typical example of a Lenz feed."

Gray tapped the table again. A first-person point of view appeared, of someone walking down a street in High Scape. Advertising blinked on cracked walls, twisted tubes of neon flashed in signs on buildings, holographs extruded themselves from the sides of high-rises, and colossal graphics metamorphosed across the water-stained sea-wall in the background.

"Now, here's what the Mirage algorithm displays for *One Man Dreaming* fans—remember this is over thirty-seven million Lenzers."

Gray swiped the video and the advertising disappeared, the puddles vanished, and the city transformed into the floating garden city of the Stratodel from the Dream world. The stratosphere's stable, weather-free sky surrounded it, and stars twinkled above, seemingly within reach through the city's transparent dome. Through transparent viewing floors, the cloud-covered earth could be seen below, an occasional flock of high-flying Whooper Swans passing between the Stratodel and the cloud tops below.

"That's right, Mr. Goto, Maya District's first incarnation will be the Stratodel. This is, after all, what we all want—an escape from the troubled climate to a place of tranquility above, where we can forget about the past and the future. Maya District will recreate this environment for Lenzers to star in their own stories that they can share as cinematic selfies."

Great, more talentless competition. Yoshi shifted in his seat and cleared his throat. *Stay professional.*

"So, how can I help? I'd have to check my schedule if I can move anything for new filming work."

A proud smile spread across Gray's face.

"Oh, no, we've made the film, and we've almost finished post-production."

Yoshi's gut dropped like a faulty elevator.

"You've already made the film?"

"We made it in three weeks. That's the beauty of our Maya Media Generator—we feed in audience data, its algorithms produce a script with a cast that will appeal to the widest audience. Once we approve, the CGI program builds the scenes, and another program composes the sound and music. If we have a human element, such as real characters like yourself, we scan a character library from them, feed that into the generator, and then render. This scanning and rendering are all we need to do for *Dreams For All*, before the launch of Maya District on the 23rd December."

"The 23rd? But, that's barely three weeks away."

Yoshi's brain hurt with the rush and disappointment of it all.

They don't want me to play Joe Joe, they want me to hand him over.

"Ludicrous timing, I admit. But, as I said before, we have a small window of opportunity. We'll promote the film at the Nebulae expo on the 11th, before launching Maya District in sync with the other Districts in Germany, Great Britain, the U.S. and Australia; five portals opening across the world at once to bring everyone together with *Dreams For All*."

Gray paused and took a slow, deliberate sip of water before continuing.

"Which brings us to why you're here. We've recreated a CGI Joe Joe—"

"Why don't you just use me?" Yoshi blurted. He had mined his own personality to create Joe Joe. They were blood brothers. He had buried a part of himself in the character, like he'd planted a seed for something greater.

Gray slow-blinked and smiled. "That's what we want to do. But we're a technology company. Technology is what we know, it's what we can control."

"But you won't be getting the *real* Joe Joe, the spontaneity. *I* made Joe Joe what he is."

"Yes, you did. You manifested such charisma and nuanced complexity. That's why we want to scan you *being* Joe Joe, to capture his movement, his essence. With all our brilliant technology, it's the one thing that stops us deeply connecting with the audience, the one thing we struggle to reproduce—soul."

Gray tapped the table's surface and a new form appeared there.

"I'm offering you this princely payment for just the next few weeks of your time, and for your consent to use your image as Joe Joe ongoing."

Yoshi had to recount the zeros on the end of the payment to be sure he wasn't seeing things—he was looking at enough money to get him through the next year without working, even more if he managed it well, or less if the mall sued him. Either way, it was more than he'd make in years staying on his current trajectory. He regained his composure.

"It sounds exciting, but I need to give it some thought."

Gray ran a finger slowly around the edge of the water glass, the remaining liquid sparkling like stored magic.

"Of course, Mr. Goto. I can give you twenty-four hours."

Yoshi looked up, dumbfounded. "I need more than twenty-four hours. I need to speak with my agent—"

"Yoshi, the last time we checked—last night, was it Lavinda?" Lavinda nodded her calamari curls. "We know you haven't had a decent role since *One Man Dreaming*. And we all know that you won't get another one because the industry sees you as a risk."

Yoshi had to divert his eyes from Gray's brutal honesty, but only to look directly into Lavinda's steely gaze.

This is just negotiation. This is how things roll at this level. But Haru should be here.

"It's just the image rights issue I'm not sure about. My agent negotiated a particularly—"

Gray ground his teeth loudly with impatience.

"I'm sure this is all somewhat overwhelming, Mr. Goto, but the public's interest in *One Man Dreaming* will be short-lived. We race toward a closing portal, if you will, to grasp this lucrative opportunity. And you know how tight production schedules can be."

How could I forget? Yoshi thought, remembering hearing from his hospital bed that *One Man Dreaming* would continue without him.

"So," Gary continued, "let me put this matter of rights into perspective for you. Maya already owns all dimensions of Joe Joe, and yes, your agent secured the need for your consent for any new instance we use your likeness. So, this is a one-time reimbursement for all future use of your image as Joe Joe. You'll still own your own personal image and your own brand. I can transfer the first installment of the payment into an account of your choice today. Right now, in fact. All you have to do is sign."

Gray tapped the table again, and the contract enlarged like a manta ray swimming up to the surface. Yoshi's hand clutched at the air above it, temptation cramping his fingers. But sensibility shouted from the depths of his urge to snatch the yen he desperately needed.

"I need some time."

A cloud of silence froze the room. Gray ground his teeth again. He unclasped his hands and sat back.

"Of course. You need your twenty-four hours. Please, take them. And as a token of my good will, I want you to have this." He withdrew a polished, spectacle-shaped metal case from inside his jacket and slid it across the table. "That will last you one day. Enjoy it while you make up your mind."

Yoshi's heart tripped a beat, and a sudden exhilaration vaporized the seriousness of his situation.

A Lenz.

Barely able to show restraint, he reached for the case and fumbled it open. Inside, a black mask lay snug in the case's velvet lining. He lifted it to see a silver, thumb-sized vial underneath. He picked up the cool object and caressed the simple instruction engraved on its side:

Tap once for each eye

"Now," Gray said, standing, "let me see you out."

"Oh, yes, I'm sorry," Yoshi said, stuffing the mask and case into his pocket. He clasped the vial in his other hand. "Yes, of course."

As he jumped to his feet, Reo and Sora stood and bowed him farewell. Lavinda did the same, but her face remained as pinched as an anus.

"Twenty-four hours, Yoshi," Gray said, as he ushered him through the corridor toward the elevator. "I understand it's a rush, but I think you know which option will do us both the best."

"Yes, yes, thank you," was all Yoshi could manage as he tried to pull his attention away from the cold metal in his grip.

"Driver is waiting downstairs to take you where you need to go. The pod, too, is at your disposal until we meet again, here, noon tomorrow, unless you come to your senses beforehand."

Yoshi finally managed to reign in his excitement.

"Thank you, Mr. Gray," he said, with more formality. "Thank you, so much. I'll see you tomorrow."

Gray clasped his hands in front and narrowed his eyes, his pristine character suddenly seeming a little oily.

"You know, not only could that much money see you live very comfortable for a while, but an alliance with Maya Technologies can also help resolve any lingering troubles."

A cold sweat broke out across Yoshi's body. *He knows about the mall.*

Gray pushed the elevator call button.

"Until tomorrow, Mr. Goto. I must leave you now," he bowed and disappeared down the corridor.

The implications of Gray's words bounced around Yoshi's head like a ball in a roulette wheel, until realization fell into place—the twenty-four hours was a mere courtesy. Whether the contract was solid or not, he really didn't have a choice.

At the very least, then, he needed representation, and a professional opinion on the contract. Since he couldn't afford a lawyer—there were so few for such small jobs since the virtual lawyer bots proliferated—he searched online for an automated service offering some sort of free trial. The first result was ACA, the same online review service that stamped its badge on Maya's non-disclosure form and on the mall's employment form—four stars, good reviews, accurate and reliable, enough to have been referred to in a court case. Okay, so that was for the personalized analysis, which he couldn't afford. Still, it sounded like the free, standard summary would, at the very least, identify any glaring issues.

He loaded up the contract and then turned his attention back to the only agent he wasn't completely invisible to. Haru would be furious about the mall, but Yoshi hoped if he could dangle the contract in front of him, Haru might just reconsider. But when Yoshi tried to call again, Haru still wasn't answering.

Fine, Haru. I'll come to you.

He decided to head home first to freshen up and look his most reliable. The elevator arrived and he stepped inside.

Satisfied he had the scaffolding of a plan, he looked down at the silver vial he'd been twirling feverishly between his fingers.

He could no longer contain himself.

Lenz

He twisted the base of the vial, and a small hole opened at the bottom. He held it above his right eye and tapped, and a translucent liquid splashed into his eye with a glacial chill. Squinting against the freeze, he could almost feel the nano-bots colonizing the Lenz over his iris. He dosed the other eye and blinked them both open.

A semi-transparent Maya logo floated in the air an arm's-length away, then faded as a menu of icons aligned in his semi-peripheral. A message prompted him to blink to grant access to his online profiles, his watch, and his earpiece. Then a twinkling matrix overlaid everything in his sight as the Lenz scanned the real world. After a few seconds, the matrix faded, and an animated tutorial floated in the air.

Welcome to the Maya Lenz experience.

THE BASICS

Navigating the Lenz–look at an icon and blink twice to select.

Navigating the Real World–take care traveling while you adjust to the visual enhancements.

Stay Charged–the Lenz charges itself via kinetic energy, but you can also boost its charge by staring at one of the many charging light panels located throughout the city. Watch your favorite Livey while you charge!

Nighty Night–the Lenz auto-detects when your eyes are resting and dims itself to Sleep Mode.

Love your eyes–with all our screen time, eye problems are part of modern life, so take care of your optics by regularly visiting a Vision Bar.

TOOLS

Navigation–Don't know where to go?

Information–Looking for a bar, restaurant or store?

Guidance –Need to fix a tire? Use a new tool?

Fitness–Track your steps and read your tears.

Social–Looking for a date? Forgot that person's name?

Companions–Virtual versions of your partner, pet, or even a passed loved one.
Night View–See better than a cat.

FUNCTIONS
Avatars–Choose how others see you.
Filters–Choose how you see others and the world. Try Maya, X-ray, or any one of the many exciting themes.
Entertainment–Stream movies and music on the go.
Livey channels–Stream your favorite Livey star into your everyday life.
Mirage Mode–Let the Lenz track your viewing behavior and auto-filter your view to the way you most want to see the world.

Yoshi's mind raced with what his Mirage might show him. How did he want to see the world if he could choose? He'd never thought about it. He blinked on the icon:

> *The Lenz is evaluating your profiles.*
> *Your Mirage will activate when ready.*
> *In the meantime, why not explore*
> *the 6.3 million Channels*
> *and over 1700 Filters?*

Rather than disappointing him, the forced wait heightened his excitement, and he choose the *Random* filter. The Lenz set itself to *Wildlife*, but the elevator remained unchanged as it stopped at ground.

Checking the settings, he stepped out into the foyer, and a roar shocked him backward. A polar bear reared up on its hind legs by the desk, its massive jaw dripping with saliva. Yoshi's pounding heart almost beat itself out of his chest before he realized it was just the *Wildlife* filter on the *yujin*.

"Wonderful Day, Mr. Goto," the bear said.

Yoshi chuckled nervously at the mental alarm still ringing in the primitive part his brain. He kept his distance anyway as he passed the bear illusion to get to the corridor.

Reaching the end, he exited the building and the filter changed to *Utopia*. A silky glow brushed the slate sky with soft peaches and apricots. Heading back along the path toward the cul-de-sac, he passed through a giant temple of muscle-bound statues and sparkling waterfalls where the studios stood before. A squawk sounded from above—the Lenz also enhancing sound through his earpiece—and a giant eagle spread its glorious wings as it glided between the buildings.

Drawn into the device's immersion, he stumbled sideways into the side of the temple. With his brain struggling to resolve his true spatial awareness, he kept one guiding hand along the wall until he reached the cul-de-sac. The road had been transformed into a clearing of flowering grass where butterflies danced around the waiting auto-pod.

Driver greeted him as he climbed inside, its voice modulating as if seeking the right pitch and tone to suit the filter. "Welcome back, Mr. Goto. Where would you like to go?"

"Home, please, the container yards in the south districts. But drive around High Scape first, just for ten minutes." He decided some experimentation on the way wouldn't hurt.

As the pod hummed into life and took off, his own face featured in advertisements playing across the city's buildings, weaving his social media photos through their narratives. On the side of a passing auto-bus, a video played of him drinking a frosted bottle of beer at some restaurant he'd dined at a year or so prior, reminding him to "Enjoy again the refreshing sophistication of Asahi!"

The bus moved out of the way, and a bright, green line zigzagged through the southern districts in the distance, mapping his old jogging route, probably tracked and recorded by his watch. His worn shoes transformed into sleek running shoes and a gritty male voice promoted "The Maverick—our most innovative new runners."

He marveled at the exquisite flawlessness of the Mixed Reality, a million times more immersive than his broken MR goggles at home. But an overwhelming array of "Buy now" prompts quickly polluted his vision. He tried turning off the promotions but found he had to pay for the ad-free experience.

Ignoring the adverts as best he could, he experimented with more filters and chose *Streeter*. The filter dressed every pedestrian in oversized caps and tracksuits, and adorned them with gold chains, gargantuan rings and gold dental grills. Fashion labels branded walls and vehicles. A melodic sampling emerged from pedestrian noise, pod-engines revving, billboard audio snippets, and the engines of passing cargo drones overhead. Entranced, Yoshi tapped the arm rest to the beat.

"Driver, pull over where you can, and then meet me back at my apartment."

The pod let him out by an open square. He blinked off *Streeter* and strolled to take in the circus of other Lenzers adorned with outrageous virtual personas—a Red Riding Hood and wolf hybrid; a schoolgirl Darth Vader; a gold dragon; many dog and cat people; and others appearing as light or floating, morphing shapes.

Still not fully trusting his sense of space with the Lenz, he blinked off the avatars so he could walk safely while exploring the Livey channel.

Curious about his competition, he searched the Livey Legends. Each one wore a badge for surpassing a following of 150 million. He cursed the 'nobodies' streaming their 3D selves, sucking the Sight out of traditional celebrities and stealing roles from real actors; they were the black hole to his potential star. But he couldn't stop staring at their shine.

'Myth' caught his eye first, a floating woman made of thousands of the same shape, enlarging and shrinking in sync with a subscriber's breathing, helping them meditate. 'Ferno,' a horned, female demon with a body of fire, could be summoned to appear above the user to hurl virtual flames at everything in sight, a popular form of stress relief. 'Marbles', an interactive wombat-like creature, appeared in a floating slingshot that could be pulled back with a hand gesture to catapult into walls, exploding the rotund animal into hundreds more Marbles—a children's favorite.

Jealousy corkscrewed through Yoshi as he scrolled through the list. He fumed at the lack of meaningful talent he was forced to compete with, a complete and utter bunch of nonsense distracting a quarter of the world's population every day—

A pair of striking cobalt eyes stopped his thoughts in their tracks. They stared out from a demandingly handsome dark-skinned face—Leon Jerome, Lenz Legend Number One, sent Yoshi into school-boy giddiness.

Leon Jerome (born Leon Jerome Davis, January 17, 2018) is an African American professional basketball player, actor and Channel influencer. After a successful basketball career in the United States, Jerome rose to international fame via his slapstick pranks on his Lenz channel, earning him a starring role in Maya's web comedy series 'Me Be Like'. With his Sight reaching an all-time high of 167 million, Jerome is considered a model for achieving Livey stardom. In 2039, Jerome launched 'BIMA' (Best Influencer Management Agency) for aspiring teen Livey celebrities.

Actor? Yoshi scoffed, but he eyed Leon's Sight with envy. That's what his reinvention needed, a presence in the Lenz to keep him relevant in the real world. *Sight makes you present, Sight pays your bills, Sight keeps you from disappearing.*

He loaded Leon's Livey, and a voice to his right startled him.

"Hey, bro, what's up?"

Leon walked beside him, as real as the road, gazing at Yoshi with his stellar blue eyes. From Leon's subtle facial expressions and skin imperfections to the interplay of his shadow on the ground, the Livey's realness was stupefying.

"Are you live right now?" Yoshi asked.

"I'm as live as you want me to be, bro."

But a slight delay in the Livey's response betrayed its algorithms calculating a response. Still, Yoshi could imagine how the millions of fans willfully suspended their common sense to believe the stunningly athletic 3D chat bot was real and just with them.

"We're all here for you," Leon said, waving to the buildings and streets around him where replications appeared in various locations. In the corner of the square, Leon played basketball, a sports brand's logo spinning above his head. A group of Leon avatars danced atop a building across the road. On the side of buildings, photos carouseled showing him in various shirtless poses, a tattoo of another logo animating on his sculptured body.

Thunder clapped above, and rain dropped in a sudden heavy shower. Flustered, Yoshi turned Leon off and scanned the square for cover. The Lenz flashed a green arrow above a low-walled opening on the far side. He darted through the moving crowds to the entrance and merged with a group of other shelter-seekers to file down a stairwell.

Descending under the Scape, he blinked at the shift from the dark overcast sky to the bright, artificial lighting of Low Ground. The wind dropped and city noises clicked and beeped from below. Low Ground stretched out like a well-lit subterranean base. Taller high-rises connected the ground to High Scape's underside, while shorter towers created a stubbed grid of varying heights. Below, brightly lit roads veined off several main arteries and weaved through the honeycomb vastness, giving Yoshi the impression he descended into the molecular architecture of a leaf.

Reaching ground, road works detoured him from his attempt to head east into a labyrinth of twisting streets. Atop an old low-rise building stood a faded, peeling billboard, promoting day trips to an island in a sunny bay:

Escape is just a boat ride away.

Yoshi stopped, recognizing the forested island as The Isle of Meti from before the Shift. As if reading his thoughts, the Lenz suggested the *Forest* filter. His curiosity accepted.

Giant vines with broad, waxy leaves tentacled around the billboard and spread out across the buildings all around him. The buildings themselves became giant cedars, the gutters their buttress roots, and wild grass sprouted underfoot. The metallic traffic noises transformed into a symphony of insect and bird sounds. In the distance, the glass and steel pod elevators shimmered like waterfalls. Inspired, his imagination ignited the musty air with the sweet smell of pine and the energizing fragrances of wildflowers. He kicked a stray can, and it transformed into a tossed acorn as it bounced along. A large, wild boar bolted by, Yoshi almost forgetting the illusion was a passing auto-pod.

Entranced, he lost track of time and direction. He wandered out from under High Scape, but on the bay side. The rain had slowed to a drizzle, but he was so immersed he thought the forest filter had morphed into rainforest. The path slanted downward and led him into an avenue of arching trees that ended in a curtain of run-off.

As he stepped through the watery veil, the forest scene flickered and vanished, and he found himself standing in a concrete tunnel. The Lenz's scanning matrix overlaid the walls but stopped, incomplete. Disorientated, he blinked on the menu to open Navigation, but it failed to load. A faded sign on the wall—*To Esplanade Parking Garage*—pointed forward to a T-junction, where tendrils of vivid graffiti disappeared around the corners. He looked behind to see he'd come down a ramp under the main roads—he'd wandered as far as the edge of District Maya.

The rain fell hard again and splashed the entrance, forcing him back. Out of curiosity, and while he waited for the rain to ease before heading back out, he approached the junction to find the tunnel opened out onto the abandoned parking area. Thick, circular pillars stood like sentinels in the residual light and disappeared into the shadows. A distinct, earthy scent emanated from the left, a burning spice or herb trying hard to mask an underlying miasma of mildew, rust, and damp concrete. He wondered if the Minaki were close, and what they did down there with their time.

To the north and south, safety lights embedded low along a sloped wall lit the immediate area—a malfunctioning light to the south flashed spasmodically. Shadow shapes of bins, and what looked like garbage piles, hulked by the walls in either direction.

Remembering the access ramp near the bus stop from that morning, he considered taking the tunnel toward the south and calling Driver to pick him up from there. A playful breeze brushed against his skin from the right, suggesting the way to the south ramp was clear. A wariness that he was entering the refugees' space stalled him, but his unusually strong curiosity drew him in. After glancing back at the rain-drenched ramp entrance, he headed down the tunnel.

Staying close to the sloped wall on his right, he kept an eye on the ledge at the top where thick, square pillars connected to the ceiling. Rubbish and broken furniture poked out from the deep shadows between the pillars. Contrasting styles of graffiti stretched up the slope and across the ceiling where some street-artist

Michelangelo had sprayed their random words and symbols.

Further along, the air thickened with a musty warmth. Staggered plips and plops echoed through the cathedral silence, and broken glass winked along the ground like rubies and emeralds. As he neared the malfunctioning safety light, the flashing exposed the mad color of the graffitied walls in snap shots. A large outline of a stick-torch dominated the slope on the right, its strobed image pulsing into his brain.

A sudden whoosh from behind startled him, and he spun on his heel. His left ankle twisted, and he slammed backside-first onto the cement.

"Get back!" shouted a small voice.

A young boy circled him—maybe six or seven years old, hard to tell in the flashing light—and swung a long stick in figure eights.

"Settle down, kid," Yoshi shouted. "You're going to hurt someone."

But the anger in his voice betrayed his fright, as the reality of his predicament struck him with a sudden, sharp clarity—he'd let the Lenz distract him, and now he was walking alone in an abandoned underground garage when he should have been home getting ready to see Haru.

He pushed himself up while trying to get a good look at his young assailant. The boy wore red shorts and a baggy, fluorescent orange shirt, both of which accentuated the scrawniness of his frame. A blue cast tinged the pale skin of his bony arms and shoulders, making him almost holographic in the strobing light. With his fair skin and jet-black hair, he didn't look islander at all, and he was too young to be in the underground on his own.

Yoshi glanced around, hoping a worried parent or sibling would appear.

"Are you here on your own, kid?"

The boy stopped pacing and stepped back into a squatted stance, his stick held forward, and blocking the way south. The flashing light started to give Yoshi a headache.

"Look, kid, I need to get home, and you should, too."

He took a step forward to go around the boy, but his tender ankle forced him to limp. The boy side-stepped and swung his stick.

"Get back."

"Hey, take it easy," Yoshi growled with impatience.

"Get back!"

Clenching his fists, Yoshi winced as he stepped in the opposite direction. But the boy swiftly cut him off again, and Yoshi's tolerance snapped like a breaking bone.

"Get the fuck out of the way!"

His words ricocheted through the tunnel and hurled his echo back at him from all around. A sudden shame dissipated his anger, but the boy ignored him anyway and returned to his battle stance.

Yoshi wiped sweat from his brow. "Look, kid—"

A high-pitched clicking startled him from behind and echoed across the ceiling like bird warnings through a canopy. He turned, careful of his ankle, and froze at the sight of a tall man walking toward him through the flashing light.

"You lost, mister?" called the man.

"No, I'm fine," Yoshi called back. "I was just telling this—"

But when he turned, the boy was gone. He scanned the immediate area and the top of the slope, but the boy was nowhere to be seen.

He turned back to the approaching stranger, and his gut clenched. It was Singlets—the generator-stealing refugee he'd watched disappear into the tunnel that morning. The man stopped a few strides away.

"You are lost, I can see it." His accent made his sentences melodic.

"I am a bit," Yoshi admitted, unsure if he should mention the boy, unsure about a lot of things. "I'm trying to get to the south ramp. Can I get out this way?"

Singlets didn't move, his demeanor unreadable. "That is the way."

"Okay, thanks. I'll just keep going then. Thanks."

Yoshi gave Singlets a bow and hastily limped away. He glanced back once to see the refugee unmoving in the strobing light, the boy still nowhere to be seen. The stick-torch symbol flashed its stain into his mind from the slope. Eager to put more distance between him and the refugee, he hurried toward an arch of light ahead.

After a good five minutes, the pain in his ankle eased to a dull ache, and he picked up his pace. As the light ahead grew closer, he found himself passing neat piles of discarded possessions— futons rolled up like giant sushi, appliances, bookcases, chairs, and lamps. Arms and legs of broken toy robots—the type that were popular years ago—stuck out from some of the piles, creating a macabre still-life. His imagination began conjuring some primitive ritual of the refugees, but he told himself the islanders were probably not allowed to work and were finding things to do.

Leaving the odd piles behind, he followed the sloped wall for what seemed like another thirty minutes, until the cool breeze returned with the sweet smell of precipitation. Finally, he spotted the trapezoid of light marking the southern access, and he ran up the ramp.

The rain's tribal beats grew louder as he stepped through a twinkling curtain of run-off to see the bus stop across the road. Small lakes dotted the road, blooming from backed up drains, but the rain was trailing away toward the mountains. The sight and sounds reassured him where he was, a balm to his raw nerves.

Dodging the puddles, he crossed the road to move away from the underworld's entrance. The Lenz menu flickered back on, and he heaved a huge sigh, still annoyed at himself for letting the Lenz side-track him so much. He blinked off all its overlays and summoned Driver, determined to make sure Gray's contract was tight as he said it was or do his best to get Haru to make it so.

By the time Driver arrived, an exhaustion of his mind and body surprised him. He climbed into the pod and banished any further thoughts of the boy, Singlets, or the strange piles of debris, and imagined himself on stage at the Nebulae Expo in front of a roaring crowd.

Choice

The coral crunch of gravel under tires announced the pod's arrival at the container district. Abandoned with the loss of Shibido's port, and replaced by the cargo drone system, the shipping containers had been repurposed as cheap housing. Towers of stacked, rust-stained containers lined both sides of the street, and the aged mechanics hauling cage elevators up and down their exteriors rattled overhead.

Exiting the pod, Yoshi rode up the side of his tower to a jolted stop at his level. Shutting his apartment door behind him, he slumped against it. A dominating red glow beamed through the shades from the Real Toy Robotics sign across the road, and a slow, steady leak dripped loudly from the bathroom. The previous night's empty whisky glass sat on the coffee table looking forlorn for a refill next to his broken MR goggles. Outside, two dogs barked blindly at each other from opposite sides of the district. The comforting normality filled him with a gratitude he never thought he'd feel for his crappy, leaky home.

He pushed himself out of the moment and soaked in a warm shower for as long as the restricted hot water allowed. Freshened, he dried and searched his wardrobe for something suitable to wear. A red, leather jacket and yellow t-shirt seemed to shimmer in response from the wardrobe's shadowed corner. He'd kept the items of Joe Joe's costume as a sort of self-bestowed 'Prize for Best Effort'—a reminder that even though he'd messed up *One Man Dreaming*, he had earned the lead role in the first place.

Joe Joe's costume might inspire Haru to get excited about my return to the role.

He slipped into the shirt and jacket—the back and arms of both tighter than he remembered—and turned to the mirror behind the front door. A gust rattled it from outside, ruffling the edges of two yellow-edged photographs tacked to the mirror's top corner. They made Yoshi think of the notes he had to place strategically around the apartment to remind his Grandpapa to close the fridge and switch off the hotplate.

Pushing the memories back, he turned side-on and sucked in his slight paunch. The deconditioned Joe Joe looking back didn't inspire him as much as he'd imagined.

Another gust, and the two photos fluttered to the floor like suicidal moths. He snatched them up and stuck them back on the glass, glancing at them as he tried not to. In one, a thin, dark-haired woman held a baby next to a shirtless man fishing from a dilapidated jetty, both of them laughing in the spray of a wave hitting the jetty's edge; in the other photo, the steep-sided geometry of Meti, pre-tsunami, protruded from Shibido's choppy bay like the bow of a sinking ship.

He pulled his gaze away, not because of what they made him feel, but because he didn't feel anything. Trying to remember the day the tsunami came was like trying to imagine something that happened to someone else. There was a time, when he was very young, he wondered if his parents even existed, or if they were just another one of his Grandpapa's stories. Of course, he grew to know better, and he'd tried to own those memories for his Grandpapa's sake, but pretending to remember a depressing story told to him from the unraveling mind of a crazy, old—

He caught himself, disappointed by his own disrespect for the man who'd raised him.

Dementia, the doctor had called it. But Yoshi knew it wasn't dementia that had claimed his Grandpapa, not really. It was the growing uncertainty of the ocean that got into the old man's brain, slowly flooding his perspective with hopelessness until it dragged his Outlook under for good.

Still staring at the photographs, Yoshi heard his Grandpapa's voice:

"Don't get lost in there."

His Grandpapa would say that when he caught Yoshi daydreaming. But a vivid imagination was really all Yoshi felt he'd been left with after large chunks of his reality had been washed away. Yoshi now wondered if perhaps his Grandpapa had been talking to himself.

Outside, a loud moan from the sea-wall honked across the city, as if the world's largest ghost cruise liner had arrived, demanding to dock at a wharf long since gone.

Weighed down by his solemn reflection, he tapped his watch to request a call-back from Tora. The unreliable app didn't respond immediately, ironically making Tora feel more like a real person.

He sucked in a gut full of courage and pulled open the mirrored door to return to ground level. Seeing the black auto-pod waiting with its door open, a wariness made him pause under the awning. Having been so distracted by the Lenz, he wasn't sure about indulging in any more of Gray's 'gifts'.

Star Production was at World Square, on the south side of the city, only half an hour's walk away. He looked to the west where the morning's dark cloud armada butted the steep, forested mountain range. To the east, rows of altocumulus arched over the bay, too white and ethereal to hold any rain. If he took the travelators, he wouldn't even break a sweat.

Declining the ride from Driver, he headed out of the industrial district and alighted a city-bound travelator toward High Scape. He began preparing his first words to Haru, when a voice startled him from behind.

"No way!"

A short girl—with black lipstick, many nose piercings and wearing bulky MR goggles under a hooded jacket—stood so close he had to take a step forward. A cable dangled from her makeshift headset to a backpack under her jacket. She stared up at Yoshi through the goggles' tinted glass.

"You watching this Santa thing?"

Prickled by apprehension, Yoshi pretended he didn't hear and turned forward again to appear busy in thought—*Oh, look, another one of those black boxes going up on a light pole.*

The girl continued, oblivious to his rudeness.

"Can you believe it? They won't release his identity, so some innocent guy got swooped and trolled."

A dreaded curiosity got the better of Yoshi, and he loaded a news feed in his Lenz. A shaky video showed children and parents running out of the Glasshouse Plaza atrium. The headline at the bottom of the video bolted Yoshi with panic:

Mystery Santa Ruins Kid's Christmas

The video stopped and zoomed in on a blurry image of Yoshi's bearded face. As the report continued, the flickering dots of a facial recognition program tried to match him with a citizen identification, but the beard seemed to thwart the attempt. The report cut to a studio newsreader with a mustache so thick he looked like a human walrus.

"With the video going viral, a Lenz user shared a possible face-match they'd found for the mystery Santa. Reacting to public attention, the media drones connected with streaming CCTV footage to track down the innocent suspect and swarmed him walking home alone. The man handed himself into the police where he was cleared of any involvement. The mistake has since quelled the growing hysteria, but many are still fixated with discovering the identity of this mysterious Santa who ruined their children's Christmas. We'll let you know more as soon as we hear it. I'm Ken Morita, and, remember, no matter what happens, it's been a Wonderful Day."

Maybe for you and your ratings, Mr. Morita.

Yoshi wished he'd taken the pod.

"Crazy, isn't it?" asked the girl from behind him.

"It is crazy," Yoshi replied, shrinking back into himself. "People shouldn't get so caught up in these things."

"Well, excuse me, but I'm living for this. He actually looks familiar to me, reminds me of someone I've seen recently, maybe on TV or—"

But the girl suddenly yelped with pain. Startled, Yoshi spun to see her rip off her goggles and throw them to the travelator floor. Unsure if she was immersed in a game or needing help, he stumbled backward. Bald as a bowling ball, her head glistened with sweat, and her brow was blotched from the goggles.

"Are you alright?" he asked.

"Something zapped my goggles. My vision's all blurry."

Her voice was panicked, and she rubbed her eyes.

"Just give it a second," he suggested.

Swearing again, she clutched the rail to steady herself and squinted up at the passing buildings.

"A stupid scrambler, that's what it was. Do you see one anywhere?"

With no idea of what she was talking about, he looked around and spotted another black box on a light pole disappearing behind them. He glimpsed the crossed gold rings of Maya's logo on the box's side.

"Are they black? Attached to the light poles?"

"Yes!"

"I think we just passed one."

"Damn it. They're everywhere, now. Hacking the Lenz channels is getting harder."

She picked up her fried goggles and slipped them into her backpack. Her eyes were bloodshot, and the goggles had left a faint outline on her face.

"Are you sure you're okay?"

"I'm fine, just a little shaken." She nodded to the walkway ahead. "Turn-off coming."

Yoshi faced forward again to see the walkway split, one path veering right toward the sea-wall, the other continuing to the city.

"Thanks," she said, stepping to the right just before the walkway verged. "Wonderful Day."

Although frazzled, Yoshi exhaled a sigh of relief with the girl gone. But the attention on the 'Mystery Santa' made accepting Gray's offer seem even more inevitable.

He alighted the walkway at the edge of World Square and headed to the tower where Haru had his office. But when he reached the foyer entrance, he found the glass doors locked. He ran his fingers through his hair and cleared his throat before pressing the intercom, but no one answered. He tried calling Haru directly again without success. Getting desperate, he banged the glass, hoping he might catch the attention of someone, but still nobody responded.

Now what?

A lone drone buzzed overhead. He dipped his head for fear his face was being scanned and pressed the intercom one last time. A deep and familiar voice spoke in response.

"Do you know how many calls I've had to dodge?"

"Hey, Haru. I've been trying—"

"Do you know what this is costing me to keep both our names out of this? They're after you, Yoshi, and it's only a matter of time. And when they catch up with you, you're on your own. If I were you, I'd get out of town."

"I'm so sorry for the mall, Haru, but I'm not here to make excuses. Maya Technologies have offered me a contract. They've bought the options for *One Man Dreaming*, and they want me—"

"Maya?"

"Yes. Their District experience will be based on *One Man Dreaming*. Can you believe it? And they've offered me a contract for digital acting work."

Haru paused so long Yoshi thought he'd hung up.

"Haru?"

"What exactly have they offered you?"

"It's just a three-week contract so they can scan me for a digital Joe Joe. But I get to do some promos for the film and for the district launch. This could be huge for me, for us." Yoshi swallowed a growing lump in his throat. "They do also require me to sign over my image rights and royalties as Joe Joe, but for a great compensation, and—"

"Are you deranged? Your royalties for scanning and promos? When they're about to reboot the franchise?"

"But you know how fast trends change now, Haru. We've got to think long-term. Gray can suppress the mall incident, and I'll be able to network again, bigger opportunities. If you just look over the contract—"

"You do realize I get commission from your *One Man Dreaming* royalties?"

"Ah…" Yoshi had forgotten that detail.

"You know, Yoshi. When I met you, I saw something unique, a passion, a determination. I'm not seeing that anymore. I don't see Yoshi Goto anymore. You do what you want. Wonderful Day."

Yoshi stared at the silent intercom. Inside, he floated away like a lantern down a river, before a bell chimed in the distance, calling him back to his body. Another chime, coming from his earpiece, and a notification appeared in his view. He blinked it open to see the Maya contract returned from the Automated Contract Analysis, its badge of approval stamped in the corner of the first page.

Not expecting such a fast response, he took a deep breath, and focused on the report.

ACA CONTRACT ANALYSIS
The agreement set out in the supplied document states that you, Yoshi Goto,

understand and accept that Maya Technologies can use your image, as Joe Joe, for any future projects. This agreement also means the studio has the sole rights to use your image, as Joe Joe, in any other ancillary uses, such as video games, toys, etc. In the case of your death, the studio owns all rights to continually use your image for the Joe Joe character, to assure the character's continued appearance. The studio will only ever use your image to represent the character of Joe Joe, and never to represent yourself, Yoshi Goto. In return, you will be paid the one-time compensation payment as per the contract, no royalties will be owed to you by the studio, and you agree to:

1. Never dispute the arrangement

2. Never hinder the studio's use of your digital image as Joe Joe

3. Never partake in any behavior that may degrade the Joe Joe character

There is… 1 Highlight:

As explained above, the signatory forfeits royalties to all media productions and any related marketing/ancillary items related to the Joe Joe character.

Please note this is a generic summary only. For a detailed, personalized assessment, based on the Signatory's specific circumstances, please sign in with your Wallet.

So, there it was—the contract was just as Gray said. Still, the risk of signing without a personalized assessment weighed heavily, but he wasn't going to get one with the few yen he had left after rent.

His watch vibrated, and Tora appeared in the right of his vision.

"Hey, Chief, how you traveling? Sorry for the delay in getting back to you. I got some options for you—"

"Tora, I'm freaking out. Word got out about the mall, a video's in the channels—"

"Okay, Chief, slow down. What's happening?"

"People are trying to find out who the mall Santa was."

"Oh, that's not good, my friend."

"But Maya Technologies have offered me a great one-time compensation payment to scan me for a few weeks so they can own my image as Joe Joe."

"Well, that sounds good, doesn't it?"

"But I'd have to give up my residuals, which is a gamble considering they're rebooting. But the payment is really good. And Maya can make the whole mall issue go away." He knew he was trying to convince himself as much as Tora.

"Could you live off the residuals?" Tora asked. "Would they be reliable?"

"No. And the reboot may fail."

"You haven't had any decent acting work since before the mall, besides those karaoke videos. And how much do you have saved?"

Yoshi cringed at the mention of both the videos and his bank account. He bit his lip as he blinked through the menu to show his balance in view.

Tora whistled. "Well, that's a lot to some people, but not you. When's your next residual?"

"I just received one, but it went on rent."

"And what can you do with this great one-time payment?"

"Well..." Yoshi paused, realizing he'd been so caught up in the excitement he hadn't fully imagined the change in his future. "I can invest that money back into my training. I could hire a marketing team to drive up my Sight. I could take back control of my career." *I could make Grandpapa proud.*

"And if you don't accept?"

Yoshi's silence did all the answering.

"Exactly, exactly. So, what are you worried about?"

"The contract. I've put it through this online thing, and it checked out, but the analysis isn't personalized."

"What does that mean?"

"Well, the summary analysis can't guarantee me the best deal, but it did clear the contract of any ambiguity."

"Exactly, exactly. You may not get the best deal, but you get the mall issue and your finances sorted out. You got to appreciate what you got. Good luck, my friend. I'll check in later."

Tora's face zapped off screen.

Good to chat, my friend.

But he hadn't voiced the emotional struggle that swirled underneath the rights issue—how could he explain that to an algorithm? The thought of signing away his connection to the only thing people knew him for still filled him with an irrational dread that he might be signing himself out of reality.

Stop imagining things.

He headed back across the square. As his mind re-ran the pros and cons of signing, he spied the shiny, black auto pod waiting by the road like an escape vehicle, its engine humming and door open.

He clenched his fists and jutted out his jaw.

Quit being a coward.

He strode over to the pod and climbed in. As the door shut, Gray's face materialized in the front window.

"Yoshi, I trust you've seen the news. This mall business is reaching a point I can no longer do anything about. I promised you twenty-four hours, but you need to decide now."

The contract appeared in a smaller screen on the dashboard. Yoshi sucked in a lung full of courage and exhaled his doubt.

"Let's do this."

He swiped his account details from his watch to the dashboard, and Gray's face lit up.

Let's do this. Let's do this.

As he held his hand over the form, his sensibility shouted one last time. But the persistent drum of Joe Joe's catch phrase drowned out any last remnants of indecision. He drew his signature on the screen and the contract vanished.

"Wonderful," Gray exclaimed. "Welcome back to showbiz, Yoshi Goto. You start tomorrow."

"Thank you," Yoshi stammered, exhilarated by his own daring.

"Driver will take you to New Gate Towers, where you'll stay for the next three weeks at our expense—we can't have our stars living in such…remote districts as yours. And I've set up credit for you at the lobby stores—get yourself some new clothes. Do you need anything else from home?"

"I… I guess I don't."

"You can always have them picked up for you after if you do. Go and relax now. Oh, and Yoshi. Stay out of trouble. Wonderful Day."

Gray's face disappeared from the window revealing a clear view of High Scape ahead. As the pod zoomed off, he felt catapulted into his future.

The pod made its way to the elevators and wove through High Scape to eventually pull into the unloading bay out the front of New Gate.

"Call for me whenever you need me," said Driver. "I'll be here tomorrow at 8:45 a.m. to take you to the studio. Is there anything else I can get for you now?"

Declining, Yoshi climbed out and paused to gaze up at the shining tower. Entering the foyer, he passed through a short corridor into a grand, high-ceilinged lobby, where a two-story Christmas tree stood in its center. Its twinkling lights reflected in a shiny, obsidian floor as if it floated in space. Still raw from the mall incident, he kept a wide birth of the tree as he passed. After checking in at reception, he rode an elevator to his apartment.

Exhausted, he stepped into a stark-white room, opulent in its crisp minimalism. A wall-to-wall, floor-to-ceiling window overlooked High Scape and the bay. An armchair covered in cow hide sat on a large white rug, like a lone calf in a snow field. He dumped his bag on the floor and helped himself to a whisky from the stocked bar. Calming down in the tail of the day's whirlwind, he slumped into the armchair and nestled into its hide.

Taking a generous sip of the delicate, honeyed-orange spirit, he let its warmth suffuse through him. He tried to put some form to the day's events from his excitement of landing the Santa job to the disaster of the falling tree to his sudden reversal of fortune and the unexpected bonus of a Lenz, all leading to the reboot of his career—it didn't seem real.

Now the networking starts.

The warmth unlocked the tension in his muscles as it made its way to his brain where it revealed the true depth of his exhaustion. He rested the glass on the floor and let his eyes shut for an afternoon nap. The events of the day slipped from his thoughts, leaving behind a flickering gif of the homeless boy swinging his stick.

As both the boy and the world dissolved, he was only dimly aware of a notification popping up before the Lenz set itself to sleep mode:

Your Mirage is ready.

PART TWO

The Portal

Schedule

A pulsing penetrated his sleep and drew up the shades of his eyelids. Although a hazy morning sunlight blinded him, his Lenz menu appeared crisp and close. He recalled waking at some unknown hour in the cowhide chair—neck stiff from his head hanging back at an awkward angle—and stumbling to the bedroom.

Another pulsing on his wrist, and Driver's caller ID showed in his Lenz. He coughed away any morning croak and blinked to accept.

"Morning, Driver."

"Good morning, Yoshi. This is your 7:45 a.m. wake-up call. ETA: 1 hour. I'll wait for you at the front of the building to take you to the studio."

He sat up and stretched, shocked by how long he slept. Outside, a breathlessly cloudless sky stunned the day, bright and childlike. Muted by the apartment's pristine quiet, a string of cargo drones flew silently over the sea-wall. The low sun illuminated gusts of spray on the choppy bay, and Meti's ghostly shape peeked through the mist.

Feeling the sun's warmth, he inhaled deep, expanding his body so there was more of him to enjoy the photon bombardment from space.

Shine your light.

He jumped to his feet and almost danced across the floor to the bathroom. He didn't normally shower or eat in the morning, but he wanted to start his new future looking and feeling his best. As the warm water massaged his body, he began his expression exercises, pinching his face into a squished raisin, then spreading his eyes and mouth wide open before pinching them back to raisin again.

By the time he dried and dressed himself, he felt more awake and alive then he had in years. He foraged fruit and boiled eggs from the fridge and watched the news in the corner of his vision as he ate.

"In world events, supplies for the Mars 1 Colony have been delayed again by China's ever-reaching claim on orbit access. The South American Union have made another withdrawal from the world's bio-diversity vault as the New Amazon struggles to recover. And Greta Thunberg—"

Yoshi blinked to a different channel where the reporter with a giant mustache touted more exciting local issues.

"—an always-open augmented reality district, inhabited by actors who will lead you into a movie designed about you. Not only that, you'll be able to stream your movie-selfie *live* to the channels. Full report tomorrow. I'm Ken Morita, it's a Wonderful Day."

It certainly is, Ken.

Following a quick pep call from Tora, Yoshi jumped into the shiny elevator—a quiet dream compared to the cage rattling down the side of his container tower. He strode out through the lobby into the main corridor to discover it was actually an arcade through a Vision Bar. On the right side, customers laid back in reclined seats while Lenzists tapped screens beside them. On the left, in a dark spherical room, video walls showed elements of the eye's structure and how Mirage Mode worked with the eye and brain.

A vague memory awoke of his Mirage resolving, and he blinked on the icon to activate it. With a spring in his step, he exited onto the street and scanned the streets and buildings. Although the city gardens looked thicker and greener, and the buildings looked sharper and cleaner, the world looked the same. Disappointed, he decided to check the settings later and climbed into the waiting pod.

"Good morning, Mr. Goto," Driver said as the engine hummed to life. "I hope you are excited about today. I'd like to share with you some information about your fellow cast members."

Four avatars appeared in the pod's window, all of them wearing a Legend badge—Bamboo Run, a horned satyr; Suzy Lee Bingo, a schoolgirl Kung Fu champion; Dhven, a many-armed cyborg monkey; and Leon Jerome. A short video introduced them all.

Bamboo Run, a bare-chested, satyr-like girl with antlers and the legs of a Sika deer, led subscribers on 'spiritual' running courses, drawing her 155 million subscribers. Then there was Suzy Lee Bingo, a primary school girl with platinum blonde hair and an armored school uniform, who challenged other Liveys to virtual Kung Fu bouts, subsequently defeating every foolish opponent and gaining herself a Sight of 162 million. Yoshi couldn't be sure what 'Dhven' did—a Hindu-god-like cyborg monkey with twelve arms—but the robo-deity's Sight had reached 152 million.

A thrill raced through him and unsettled his nerves at the same time. He quickly reminded himself that he was the only real actor in the project—the *star*. But, as he looked through the Livey's popularity, he begrudgingly surrendered to the fact he needed to learn from them about building a following in the channels.

The pod arrived at the studio's gated entrance and the *Short-Term Security* guard stepped out from the booth, scanner in hand. The pod's window lowered, and Yoshi recognized the security guard from Glasshouse Plaza.

"Mr. Goto," said Jin, "we meet again."

"Mr. Chiba, what are you doing here?"

"There was a staff reassignment after yesterday. I think they might be trialing a *yujin* guard at the mall, can you believe it, then? I'm sure the thing will glitch and I'll be called back. Anyways, I'm here for now."

"Ah, I'm sorry to hear that."

"Well, it's much more interesting here. Maybe Head Office thinks I'm star material."

Yoshi laughed. "Well, you do wear that outfit well."

"Tell that to your director, then, before the *yujin* put me out of work for good."

"You and me both," Yoshi replied, laughing, but not because it was funny.

The scanner beeped and Jin slipped it back under his cape.

"Okay, then, Mr. Goto, you're on your way. Wonderful Day." He tipped his hat and stepped back to wave the pod through.

Yoshi climbed out at Studio 5 and pushed through double doors into a large room. Four people sat silent around a table, all staring into the air, their eyes flicking through whatever their Lenzes showed them. Next to an empty chair, a muscular man stretched back, his clinging body-cloak rippling at its edges from some Lenz effect. Yoshi's gut fluttered with excitement.

Leon Jerome.

Yoshi guessed the other three had to be the other Liveys flown in from overseas, but they looked nothing like them—a pale, teenage Chinese boy with heavy teal eye shadow; a dark-skinned girl, perhaps twenty-one, with an extraordinarily angular face and long, muscular legs; and a stocky boy, barely twenty, his body a gorilla ball of bulging, hairy muscle.

As Yoshi approached, Leon looked up. A halo of black roses floated around Leon's head, advertising some hair product that Yoshi had once used. His skin was darker in person, almost black, and his left eye looked inward more than the right. Yoshi wondered for the first time how long it would be before his own eyes began developing strabismus.

He let the thought float away as he drank in every captivating aspect of Leon's facial architecture from his sharp, muscled jaw to his generous lips. Leon smiled a reef of stony teeth, and Yoshi recalled reading somewhere how big teeth alerted a human's primitive brain to the presence of either a strong mate or a dangerous foe.

"Hi. I'm Leon."

Yoshi's ability to speak took a couple of awkward seconds to make its way back from the other dimension he'd been spun into.

"Hi," he finally managed, "I'm Yoshi."

Leon offered a handshake. As their hands clasped in naked embrace, a tingling fire zipped through Yoshi's skin. Leon eyed him up and down.

"It's a shame you die in the first scene."

Yoshi's jaw dropped. "What?"

Leon guffawed and slapped Yoshi's hand away.

"Just messing with you, bro. I haven't read the script either. Doesn't really matter though, does it? What I mean to say is, that's why we're getting paid so lush, right?"

"What do you mean?"

The front doors swung open and Lavinda strode in. The other Liveys blinked away their distractions and sat up. Lavinda stopped by Yoshi's side, her thick, black hair as damp as the day before, as if she'd slept on the sea-sprayed wall.

"Thank you all for coming today. We've got a lot to cover, so let's get straight into today's agenda. First, I'll be explaining how both the Nebulae expo and the premiere event will play out, and then we'll run through your schedule for the next few weeks before we do an intro session in the Immersion room. Let's start with introductions. Mr. Goto?"

Clearing his throat, Yoshi faced the others.

"I'm Yoshi Goto. I played Joe Joe, from the original *One Man Dreaming*."

But the blank faces and blinking eyes staring back at him showed no sign of the awe he had been expecting.

"Anything else?" asked the long-legged girl.

Yoshi smiled meekly, annoyed by his own desperation to impress.

"Oh, yes. I've done some commercials."

"Well, dude," interrupted the teenage boy in make-up. "I hope you don't do to this film what you did to the original."

A chuckle rippled through the group, and Yoshi shrunk down into his seat.

One by one, the others stood and introduced themselves. A halo of information appeared above their heads as they spoke revealing their Livey identities.

The first to stand was the long-legged girl, Jenya. Her Livey was Bamboo Run, the horned satyr. After Jenya, the smart-ass teenager introduced himself as Dax, his Livey being Suzy Lee Bingo, the schoolgirl Kung Fu champion. Otis stood last—gorilla-boy. His Livey was Dhven, the twelve-armed cyborg monkey.

At first, Yoshi couldn't comprehend why Maya wanted to scan the odd balls sitting across from him. Then he realized each one of them used their own face for their Livey and performed or behaved in ways unique to their bodies—Jenya's long, muscular legs for Bamboo Run's running; Dax's androgynous and lithe frame for Suzy Lee Bingo's sharp agility; and Otis's hairy bulk for the cyborg monkey. Like Yoshi himself, they had each created an augmented character Maya wanted to own.

Leon stood last, slow and deliberate.

"Hi all, I'm Leon Jerome. What I'm sayin' is, you might know me from my Livey channel, Leon Jerome."

Although he added nothing else, he returned to his seat to a round of applause. Yoshi filled with jealousy and adoration. As the clapping died down, Lavinda rose and addressed them all.

"Now that we're all on a first name basis, let me take you through what we are working towards. On the 23rd December, Maya will premiere *One Man Dreaming*, and introduce the ultimate in immersive entertainment. All Lenzers will be invited to the premiere event at Maya District, where they will watch the first screening of *Dreams For All*. The film will be projected onto the sea-wall in an ode to the traditional cinema experience. A select group of VIPs will also be invited to watch the film from a closed-off area by the sea-wall. The film itself will be a short, thirty-minute sequel to *One Man Dreaming*, as a segue into the feature experience of the evening."

"As the film ends, the VIP area will transform into the final scene, seamlessly immersing the VIPs *into* the film. Actors will enter and engage the VIPs, leading them into a storyline designed just for them, while giant screens, projected onto the sea-wall, will share the VIPs' experiences with the audience. The immersion will last approximately twenty minutes."

"So," Jenya said, "this will be like an introduction to how the whole district will work when it's open?"

"Correct. Maya District will be open for the event, but only the VIP section will be activated. Attending Lenzers will be able to wander the empty buildings and streets—which stretches four blocks back from the esplanade to the sea-wall—and watch the VIP's experience via the projections on the sea-wall. When Maya District opens to the public on 5th January, the entire district will be ready to transform into every subscriber's personal movie."

"So, if I don't subscribe," Jenya asked, "and I wander through the area when it's open, what do I see?"

"The augmentation of the district will remain invisible to any non-subscribers, and their Lenz, or our actors, will direct them away."

"Okay," Jenya said, scratching her nose and looking like Lavinda's answer gave her ten more questions. "So, if—"

"Don't worry about the details right now, it will make more sense as we go along. Let's talk about the schedule. For the next two weeks, you'll be performing in immersion orbs so we can scan your character's mannerisms. The orbs will immerse you in various emotional and physical situations, to provoke your character's behavioral essence. You'll also be doing verbal exercises and interviews so we can graph your voices. These scans and recordings will form your character's emotional libraries that we'll feed into your CGI characters for the film, and for ongoing appearances in the district. Due to the tight schedule, we'll be compiling and uploading your scans daily."

"On the 11th," Lavinda continued, "we have a stage at Nebulae Expo to show a trailer, to introduce your new characters, and to share a teaser of our technology. Following that, scanning and character infusion will continue, giving us time to render the film in time for the premier on the 23rd. Your work will be done by the 17th, but you're contracted until the 22nd in case there are any last-minute issues."

The finality of her words reinforced how little time Yoshi had to network. Short film, short production time—the path toward his permanent separation from Joe Joe was speeding up. His head spun with tactics. The main opportunity for exposure—to make an impression on fans who might pump up his Sight— would be the on-stage panel and autographing session at Nebulae.

"Right," Lavinda continued. "I've sent you all a copy of the schedule with more detail. Submit any other questions via the chat portal. Now, before I share the script for *Dreams For All*, we'll recap *One Man Dreaming*. Get comfortable, people, I need you to concentrate."

A screen appeared in Yoshi's vision as a voice-over narrated a short re-edit of the original film.

"*One Man Dreaming* told the fantastic tale of Joe Joe, an insomniac coder who longed to dream. Plagued by accidents and mistakes caused by insomnia, the cynical Joe Joe locked himself away from the world and created an AI-based app that allowed users to design their own dreams. With access to his customers' night fantasies, he watched the play of their fears and desires, trying to imagine his own abstract mind-tales. But he soon became obsessed with a mysterious user named O. After his accidental meddling in one of his customer's dreams caused a real-world mishap, he decided to shut the app down. But when he succumbed to O's allure one last time and used the app to say goodbye to her in her dream, he became trapped in the Dream world."

"Creepy guy," said Jenya.

"He's meant to be flawed," Yoshi said, "it's more realistic."

Jenya rolled her eyes as the narration continued.

"Unable to wake up from the surreal dimension, Joe Joe found himself chased by Algorlines—mangled looking machines chewing up the dream world—forcing him to discover that he could move between other people's dreams. Assisted by the mysterious O, he used all he knew about his customers to manipulate their deepest fears and desires in the hope that when they awoke, they might go and wake him up in the real world. His efforts sparked a series of comedic real-world events that, combined with his adventures through fantastic dreamscapes, kept the audience—and Joe Joe himself—wondering if he was still alive in a coma, or dead and in purgatory."

More chuckles rippled through the group at the experimental animations and editing. Yoshi cringed at his own acting.

"After discovering that the Algorlines were manifestations of his own app's algorithms, Joe Joe discovered the AI had deliberately trapped him in a dream state to prevent him from ever turning it off. But that meant he *was* still alive in the real world. With O's help, Joe Joe fled the Algorlines and journeyed through other people's dreams to face the creation of his own doing. When he reached the center of the Realm, he found the AI residing in the 'Stratodel', a garden island floating in empty space, left untouched by the Algorlines."

The whole shemozzle started to hurt Yoshi's brain.

"Succumbing to the island's hypnotic force, Joe Joe almost lost himself in his fantasy of falling in love with O, forcing him to choose between staying in his ultimate dream or saving everyone else's ability to dream. But when he discovered O was just a ruse built by the AI, Joe Joe tricked the AI into flipping its programming to make the Algorlines rebuild the dream world, and to wake him up back in reality.

"Returning safely to wakefulness, Joe Joe discovered his insomnia cured, but he had to keep the AI activated to allow the Algorlines to rebuild the Dream world so the world could dream again."

The cast laughed as they applauded, but Yoshi squirmed in his seat.

"So," Lavinda said, "that leads us to the sequel, *Dreams For all*. I'm now sharing with you the script, if you can bring that up in your Lenz."

Finally, Yoshi thought as he enlarged it in his view.

"As you know," Lavinda continued, "your Liveys will be new characters who are being introduced as anchor characters for the Lenzers' stories in Maya District. You have all come from the Dream world, and your motivations are simple—get people to the Stratodel. Let's go through the storyline."

As Yoshi listened, he quickly realized there wasn't any more to *Dreams For All* than what Gray had told him. Five years after *One Man Dreaming*, Joe Joe had used the millions from his app to build a floating Stratodel in the real world as an escape for people from the privacy invasion and information overload of modern life. But on the day of its opening, Leon arrives through a portal from the Dream world to warn Joe Joe that the Algorlines will escape. But Joe Joe thinks Leon is another trick of the AI, and Joe Joe traps him. As Dhven, Suzy Lee Bingo, and Bamboo Run arrive to rescue Leon, the Algorlines escape through Leon's portal, leaving Joe Joe no choice but to help Leon and his friends evacuate people to the Stratodel.

Formulaic crap.

"What's that, Yoshi?" Lavinda had stopped and the others were all were staring at him.

"Sorry?"

"I thought I heard you mumble something."

Did I say something? "No, nothing, not me."

She narrowed her eyes and continued.

"Right. Well, as I was saying, as the Algorlines corner you all on a skyscraper roof, the film ends. At this point, the event's focus will shift to the VIP area, and the district's interactive setting will come alive. Actors appear and prompt the VIPs into exploring the setting to reach the Stratodel."

After a thirty-minute Q&A, Lavinda stood and lead the group to another set of double-doors at the rear of the room. A sign above read *Immersion Orbs*.

Leon licked his stony teeth. "I been lookin' forward to this."

Inside, a trapezoid of light shone through a skylight and spot lit two rows of semi-transparent black spheres, six in all. Their bases glowed a neon blue, and they vibrated with a subtle energy in a collective *ohm*.

The Lenz displayed each character's name above each orb.

At the back of the room, a tall woman in a black coat swiped on an interactive table. Next to the table stood five fridge-sized, matt-black machines, lights blinking on their side, like futuristic coffins.

Fine hairs rose up along the back of Yoshi's neck.

The woman looked up and stepped into the center of the room to meet Lavinda in the middle. The downward light ignited Naomi's pale face under her short, silver hair. Her large eyes beamed, and whisper-thin lips exposed fleshy gums; she looked like a kept fiend. Yoshi imagined Lavinda hugging her awkwardly alone in the room, feeding her kelp she untangled from her own wet hair, while making Naomi promise to keep the orbs in pristine condition.

The women bowed and Lavinda turned back to the group.

"Everyone, this is Naomi, our Head of Technology. She'll be running the scanning sessions."

"Hello, and welcome," Naomi said. Even her voice was ghoulish, slow and gravelly like a body dragged across a floor. "Well, I'm sure you've all seen MR rigs before, hmm? Anyone here not been in an MR rig before?"

Yoshi raised his hand, alone, and Lavinda rolled her eyes. He stammered an excuse.

"I mean, I've done MR before, but nothing like these orbs."

Naomi waved his concern away with a bony arm and stepped closer to the group.

"They take a bit of getting used to, but you'll be fine. However, moving a virtual body while your physical body remains still can play havoc with some people's vestibular system. This medication," she said, withdrawing a small container from her pocket to hand everyone a translucent capsule, "will minimize any disorientation you may experience during and after the immersion. Shall we get started, hmm?"

"Alright people," snapped Lavinda. "In the orbs."

After a quick examination of the capsule, Yoshi swallowed it and headed over to Joe Joe's orb on the far side of the room.

Up close, the orb appeared to be made of many small, glass hexagonal panels which gave it the transparent appearance. A harness, goggles and gloves hung from the interior's ceiling, and a flat base rose up at the edges, like a large round tray. Nervous with excitement, Yoshi slipped on the goggles and haptic wear and adjusted them for comfort. As Naomi checked everyone's fittings, her voice spoke through the orb's speakers.

"The orb goggles will override your Lenz view. When your display is blue, you're offline, and so is your avatar, rendering both you and your character invisible in the virtual world. When your display is full color, your avatar is active and fully visible."

Yoshi pulled on the goggles and the orb vibrated. His view of the room transformed into a vibrant, monochromatic blue version of itself, and a green grid replaced the orb around him. He reached out to touch the grid with a virtual version of his hand, and his heart skipped a beat—the hand was more callused than his own, with fingertips stained yellow. Looking down, a body more toned and muscled than his wore a red jacket and yellow t-shirt.

Hi, Joe Joe.

Looking around the room, Yoshi could no longer see Lavinda or Naomi. The other cast members stood where their orbs had been, but appeared as their Liveys—the horned satyr, the many-armed cyborg monkey, the armored schoolgirl, and the sculpted athlete. Excitement raced through him as Naomi explained how the orb worked.

"Multiple lasers and cameras contained in the shell will scan the minute details of your mannerisms and expressions as you control your character's avatar in various virtual scenarios. To simulate the experiences of walking, running, falling, etc., the motion pad will speed up or slow down, and the orb may turn itself and you. Everybody strapped in, hmm? Get yourself into character, and let's start with some simple walking."

Yoshi felt like a product pushed along a conveyor belt; clearly no one understood that great character immersion took more than a few seconds.

"Yoshi," Naomi pressed, "start walking."

He took a slow first step, afraid he might fall forward into the orb's shell. But as soon as he did, the motion pad moved, forcing him to take another step, and another. The room disappeared, replaced by a plain blue floor stretching infinitely in all directions along a mirrored wall reflecting the group.

Watching Joe Joe's reflection move through the surreal space, Yoshi clenched his fists and channeled Joe Joe's distinctive, vigorous stride. The orb's grid remained at a safe and steady distance, helping him develop a sense of spatial awareness. He merged in line with the others as they followed a green line on the floor.

"Now," Naomi said, "stop and face the mirror."

Between them and the mirror, a faceless man appeared, wearing loose, white jacket and pants. He stood with his legs apart and knees slightly bent.

"So far," Naomi continued, "your brain is interpreting your avatar as something novel, a toy to play with. Guide, here, will help you deepen your connection, so your brain thinks of your virtual character as its real self. Follow Guide's actions and stay focused on your breathing."

Guide pressed his hands together in a prayer motion before leaning gently to one side and raising his opposite arm in the air, hand pointed down. Slow and graceful, Guide led them on a sort of Tai Chi sequence. Yoshi mimicked as best he could, connecting with his reflection, trying to believe Joe Joe's younger, fitter body was his.

"Doing great, people," encouraged Naomi. "You're getting ultra-high resolution rendered every second, hacking your perception system faster than any home MR goggles. Your brains are already starting—and wanting—to believe you're really what you see. So, let's take it up a notch, hmm?"

Guide dissolved, and with him went the floor and mirror. Yoshi's head lightened as he found himself standing on one of many small platforms floating in a vast blue sky above a patchwork of city streets far below.

A counter in the top-right of his vision began counting down from five as Naomi gave final instructions.

"Follow the prompts and make your way through the course."

The counter reached zero and a platform to Yoshi's left flashed green, signaling to him to jump to it. He took a step forward, but he balked at the giddying drop below, even though he knew it wasn't real.

His platform vibrated and began crumbling from the edges. He took a deep breath, stepped backward, and then leapt forward to the other platform. The orb snatched him off his feet and flipped him horizontal to mimic his diving. He just caught the platform by its edge, and the orb simulated the physical experience of him dropping before jerking to a halt. Below, Joe Joe's legs—his legs—dangled over the dizzying elevation. His heart pounded with real fear.

After hauling himself up, he had to hold his arms out on either side to maintain a sense of balance. Around him, Leon, Bamboo, Suzy, and Dhven leapt from platform to platform as they raced ahead on their courses.

Another platform to Yoshi's left flashed green, further away than the first. Sweat trickled down his temples and into his eyes. The platform beneath him crumbled into the abyss below. His brain began to feel like it was swimming around inside his skull.

"Remember to breathe," said Naomi's disembodied voice.

Yoshi drew in a few deep breaths—*Let's do this*—and jumped. But his destabilized inner-GPS conflicted with the virtual motion, and he spun sideways. Blood rushed to his head and he flailed wildly. He heard a snap, and his goggles ripped off, tearing himself out of the virtual scene as he crashed into the orb floor.

"Goto!" Lavinda yelled, storming across the room. "What are you doing? Did you take your pill?"

Panting and sweating, he sat up and pressed against the orb, hoping the sideways-falling sensation passed. A rising acid tickled his throat.

"My visual went haywire," he lied, refusing to admit to motion sickness for fear it might disqualify him from participating. "You need to make sure these things are safe. I could have broken an arm."

Lavinda scowled and shot a demanding look at Naomi, who shook her head and shrugged. Lavinda spun back, her nostrils flaring as she leaned forward to whisper.

"I knew things would be difficult with you." She scowled at the mess of the orb and turned back to the group. "We need to do some debugging, people. We'll pick this up again shortly."

Dax groaned aloud as he pulled off his goggles. He shot Yoshi a filthy look. "Thanks, Goto, I was just getting into that."

"We all were," snapped Jenya.

Although the spinning in his head slowed, Yoshi's stomach rocked like the sea. He clenched his abdominals, trying to settle what was inside.

"You're a jinx, dude," Dax said over his shoulder as he left the room.

"You a *yujin*?" Otis asked. "Cause you glitch like one."

Yoshi pulled himself up onto legs as unsteady as a newborn deer's, but he held his head high like he'd done nothing wrong.

"Don't worry about me, guys," he said sarcastically. "I'm fine."

But the others just shot him wary glances as they exited the room, as if they thought his failure to be contagious.

Acid tickled his throat again, and a sudden sweat broke out across his body. Sensing Lavinda's eye on him, he gulped back the curdled taste of vomit and headed to the exit.

"Hey, Dizzy Man," Leon said, appearing by his side. "You don't look so good. You need some fresh air?"

"I'm fine, but fresh air sounds good."

"You'll be okay."

Leon patted him on the back as they walked back into the front room. Jenya, Dax and Otis were already seated again and staring into the air. Reality seemed to be the place they spent the least time in, using it as a portal from one mixed or virtual experience to the other. Yoshi envied their ability to switch realities so fluidly.

As soon as Leon pushed the front doors open, a hot and sour flush hurled up the remains of Yoshi's breakfast. He ducked to the side and vomited on the ground.

"Whoa," Leon exclaimed, stepping back.

With his stomach empty, Yoshi stood upright and wiped his chin. "I'm fine."

Leon laughed again and wrapped a strong arm around him, his muscles vibrating against Yoshi's body as he spoke.

"Take a few breaths, Dizzy, reconnect."

His legs still weak, Yoshi leaned against Leon's hard torso and drew in a few slow breaths. As his nausea abated, a message from Lavinda flashed in his Lenz.

Orb recalibration will take 3 hrs.
Continue familiarizing yourself with the script,
and return to the Immersion room at 1 p.m.

The studio doors swung open, and Yoshi had to peel himself away from Leon. Dax glanced in their direction, but, seeing Yoshi with Leon, his dislike for Yoshi seemed morph into one of wary curiosity. As the others headed across the cul-de-sac toward the cafeteria in Studio 2, Leon poked Yoshi's chest.

"Looks like you got us the morning off, Dizzy. Nice one. What I'm saying' is, let's get outta here."

"Sure," Yoshi said, astounded Leon wanted to associate with him.

"Great, let's take my pod."

After wiping sweat and embarrassment from his brow, Yoshi followed Leon toward the front gate. Leon's athletic physique bulged through his clothes, his back muscles and buttocks rippling with captivating synchronicity. Yoshi noticed, too, the road and buildings shimmered with a surreal luster, and the edges of his vision had crystalized ever so slightly. In the gardens by the gate, the leaves appeared as translucent as jade, and above, a subtle opal sheen slowly unfurled through the sky.

Leaving his embarrassment behind, Yoshi followed Leon through his Mirage as if in a dream.

Detour

A replica of Yoshi's pod pulled up, and Leon let him climb in first. Plonking in by his side, Leon slapped a brief grip on Yoshi's thigh.

"You hangin' in there?"

Yoshi nodded, his nausea replaced by a new thrill. A sweet, musk infused the interior, but it wasn't the pod's fragrance.

Leon tapped the dashboard to open a compartment containing bottles of minted water and offered one to Yoshi. While Yoshi swished his mouth, Leon made gestures in the empty air in front of him.

"Excuse me a sec," he said, "just checking my feeds."

"Is that your channel?"

"Sure is. Here, I'll share my view."

He made another few swipes and a virtual, three-dimensional dashboard of screens and spheres floated in front of him. Multiple screens showed various video and photo feeds—even videos about the making of Leon's videos, and photo shoots capturing his photo shoots.

"This lets me track all streaming of my channel and allows me to go live into one particular stream, like for someone's birthday or whatever. I keep a mini version of this in the corner of my view all the time, too."

Yoshi's eyes widened at the blueprint to his future. In the top middle, big and bold, shone Leon's stellar Sight.

"Could you show me how that works?"

"Sure, I can give you an intro. Is there a quiet place we can go? I'm staying at New Gate."

Leon's words hinted at showing Yoshi more than his dashboard. Yoshi reminded himself of his goal—to network and learn, as much as he could, as fast as he could, before the portal closed on the future he was just beginning to glimpse.

A tap on the pod window startled them both. Jin smiled from outside.

"You boys movin' on, then?"

Leon looked at Yoshi for an answer.

"Sure," Yoshi said, wondering how far he would go to achieve his goal. "I'm staying at New Gate, too."

Leon gave the pod their destination and turned back to Yoshi.

"Lavinda showed us the original *One Man Dreaming*. When you introduced yourself back in the studio, I was like, 'Wow, how'd he *do* it?' It's like you became someone else."

"Immersion techniques," Yoshi replied, trying to sound the senior by drawing on the little he'd learned on his quick rise to fame. "I spent weeks exploring Joe Joe's back story, how his residual emotions came through his everyday actions; walking, leaning, sitting, drinking. Once I got into his head, and lived his lifestyle, his mannerisms emerged naturally."

"So, what happened, on set, with the accident?"

Yoshi flushed with embarrassment but remained composed.

"I lost myself in the Fourth Wall," he said, embellishing the truth.

"The what?"

"It's this wall actors imagine, between the stage and the audience, to forget anyone is watching, to immerse themselves in the character and scene. I got *so* immersed I forgot the wall wasn't real, I started believing Joe Joe was the real me. Does that make sense?"

Leon nodded, his eyes wide with fascination.

"It's a powerful thing," Yoshi continued, remembering his out-of-body experience from the school play, "channeling a complete experience worth of emotions. Some actors become almost possessed by the characters they play. In the past, they were often considered sorcerers with the power to influence people's thinking."

"So, acting's a kind of magic."

Yoshi laughed. "Not sure about 'magic.' More an immersive illusion. But…" He paused, daring to show any doubt. "I wonder if the audience care for it anymore, now they have the Lenz."

Leon gave Yoshi's thigh another cheeky squeeze, sending a magic of his own into Yoshi's groin. The pod throbbed as it accelerated.

"The studio hired me because I'm popular, but they brought you back because of your acting."

"You've spellbound a lot of people, too," Yoshi said, spellbound himself by Leon's chest stretching open his shirt.

"What I do is just eye candy. I know it. I don't nourish anyone's soul, I just feed 'em snippets to keep them comin' back. That's all they want, an immediate fix, so they don't even have to think or imagine. And that's all Maya wants—an immediate audience. All hail the FOF."

"The what?"

"Future Optimal Following. You don't know this? Maya takes Lenzers' viewing data from the Lenz and uses algorithms to determine the films that most people want to see—the genre, the storyline, the cast, right down to the timing of release. They don't make a move without the algorithms telling them to, because the algorithms predict when people, like you and I, will peak in popularity. That's our FOF. Mine's in nineteen months. That gives Maya about a year and a half to make the most of my rising interest before Leon Jerome is done."

"They can't know that for sure."

"They know everything. If they haven't offered to buy your ID, then I'd say your FOF has been and gone. I just made the cut, I think. They don't consider anyone taking too long to peak because of the, you know, uncertainty of our time."

"They want to buy your actual identity?"

"They already bought it—my name, my history, my past, and, most importantly to them, my near future. They want to own and control everything to maximize immediate profits. That orb thing learning my personality and mannerisms, it's all a hand-over of 'me' to them. Once I wrap this up, I'll be someone no-one knows and celebrating on one of those Tianjin pontoon resorts. And I can tell you, I am ready for some anonymity. Burnt out at twenty-two isn't a good thing."

A pinball of panic ricocheted through Yoshi's plan. He'd finally gotten a ticket on the fast train to success and now Leon was telling him the tracks were running out.

"How accurate is this FOF thing?"

"Maya's profits rely on them. They wait for the kids—desperate for Livey fame—to do all the work to build a following, and then Maya buy them out. Makes more business sense to Maya to build an emotion library of them and feed it into their CGI. No more huge investment to make sure the kid celebs remain stable. They can program the digital Livey for as many films, shows, and games as they like. All residuals, and all profits from ancillaries, become Maya's."

Yoshi's head raced with the implications.

"So, if I don't have a FOF, my career doesn't have a future?"

Leon nodded. "You can still do some extra work, I guess, but—"

"But I just signed over my royalties for a chance to get back into the industry," Yoshi said more to himself.

Leon wiped his lip slowly before he spoke again.

"Maybe you put too much into Joe Joe 'cause looks like he's gonna outshine you. Why you so desperate to get back in, anyway?"

Yoshi looked out the window at the bustling city and the ominous dark shape of the sea-wall behind it. With his plan seemingly falling apart, he shook with an irrational fear of the vast liquid mass barely contained by the ribbon of concrete and steel.

Coming, coming, coming…

He turned the questioning around. "Did Gray buy everyone's ID?"

Leon smiled at Yoshi's avoidance and nodded. "Our Liveys are us. We are our Liveys."

"But, how could you sign away your own identity? And what about all the work you did to build that agency for aspiring Liveys?"

"Look, Dizzy, maintaining a presence in the Lenz is relentless. If you don't feed the fans consistently, if they start to drop off, even just a little, you lose the algorithms' favor and your entire income, your livelihood, starts diving. You start to disappear from the world. And that's when you see the fans don't really care about you. They only care about the thing you let them project upon you. And, eventually, they get over you and need another fantasy. And when they're done, you're done—done as the polar bears. That's the truth of the FOF. What I'm saying is, get what you can, while you can, and get out."

"That's not a very Shibidoan Outlook, Leon. We should think more positively."

Leon laughed again, but it was shallow and forced.

"My manager wants me out before I stream one of those 'Burnt out at 22' breakdowns and show my Livey hanging itself from every building."

The fire in Yoshi's groin fizzled. The Legend he thought was some beacon of fame and fortune had turned out to be nothing more than a has-been battling an Outlook bleaker than Yoshi's own.

He looked out the window again and willed the Lenz to show him something wonderful, anything to distract his mind. The sun shone like a gold diamond, the sky opalized, and the buildings twinkled in the Mirage's immaculation, but there was no warmth coming through the window.

Leon shoulder-nudged him. "You still there, Dizzy?"

Before Yoshi could respond, the pod interrupted.

"Sir, there appears to be a disturbance ahead at your destination."

The pod slowed to a stop just before New Gate's entrance. A large group of people, young and old, marched back and forth past the front entrance, holding placards, and pumping their fists in the air as they chanted.

"Turn off! Wake up!"

A drone projected the same words halfway up New Gate's front side. Leon leaned over to look out the window, his chest pressing against Yoshi's.

"What's goin' on out there, Dizzy?"

But Leon's scent had become suffocating, the sudden claustrophobia sucking all the air from the pod and squashing Yoshi's lungs. He tapped the open button and jumped out onto the foot path, gasping air while pretending to have a closer look at the protest.

Leon stuck his head out the doorway. "You okay, Dizzy?"

"I'm just… I'm still a bit nauseous from the Orb."

"Did you want me to get you through the crowd and upstairs?"

Yoshi hesitated. In the fresh air, he didn't feel so doomed by predictive algorithms, giving his mind room to believe he could still turn a FOF. But Leon's jaded perspective was playing havoc with his own Outlook. What he really needed—

"Yoshi?" a familiar voice called from behind.

Kai pushed out of the marching crowd, eyes wide and blinking from behind his spectacles. A white, sleeveless t-shirt showed off his lean, muscular arms. Yoshi's heart did a little jig. Maybe it was the Mirage, he thought, but Kai seemed to shine and the world around him softened, as if tinted by a subtle vignette.

"Kai? What are you doing here?"

"I thought that was you," Kai said, catching his breath. He gestured to the protest. "We're blocking people from getting into New Gate. Maya owns it. We're protesting that district of theirs. It's forcing the homeless out, and they got nowhere else to go."

Yoshi froze, the situation thickening with hazard. He really didn't need Leon finding out about his Santa fiasco, and he certainly didn't want Kai to know he was working for Maya—he wasn't sure why it mattered what Kai thought, but it did.

"Has this been going on for a while?" he asked, stalling.

"About an hour, but I've got to head off. I've got community work now with Shibido Connect.

Remember them, the volunteers I told you about? Hey, why don't you come along, see what we do?"

Kai twitched his nose, popping his glasses back up onto the ridge.

"Ah, hi there," interrupted Leon.

Kai turned, only just noticing Leon staring at them from the pod's open door.

"Kai," Yoshi stammered, "this is Leon. Leon this is Kai."

Leon smiled like a commercial. Kai returned a brief bow and smile and faced back to Yoshi.

"So, you wanna come?"

"Well…"

Flustered, Yoshi felt stuck between dimensions and momentarily lost the ability to speak. But Leon broke the awkward pause for him.

"Hey, Dizzy, it's cool. We can hang out later. You should spend time with your boyfriend."

Kai burst out laughing. "I'm not his boyfriend."

"No, no," Yoshi almost shouted. "We're not boyfriends."

Leon shrugged. "Sure. My bad. What I'm sayin' is, I'm gonna high-tail it to the gym 'till all this calms down. Hope you feel better, Dizzy. Wonderful Day."

Leon winked as the pod closed its door and took off.

"Yoshi, are you okay?" Kai asked. "You're acting weird." He spoke as if they'd met more than once before. "What are you doing here, anyway?"

Stealing a glance at the protest, Yoshi fumbled for an excuse.

"We saw the crowd and just stopped to see what was going on."

"Okay," Kai said, frowning. "So, you wanna join me, then? Now's a good a time as any, right? Unless you found another job already?"

Yoshi really just wanted to crawl back into the safety of the apartment. But his heart beat loud and eager, like a dog's tail thumping the floor when it thinks it's going for a walk. With a few hours until he was needed back at the studio, he let daring get the better of him.

"Sure, okay."

Kai surprised him by taking his hand and leading him away from the chanting crowd. The tiny balloons of delight set off through Yoshi's body were of a calmer thrill than his flirtation with Leon. He held on to Kai's hand firmly, wondering if not saying anything about Maya could be considered lying.

Connect

As they left New Gate behind, Kai turned back and looked Yoshi in the eye.

"I see you got a Lenz. How is it?"

Yoshi blinked self-consciously. "It's good. I'm still getting used to it."

"Aren't you worried about the effects?"

"Well, eye problems are just part of modern life."

"Wow, you've really bought that narrative, haven't you?"

"There's a lot of benefits with the Lenz, you know?"

"Benefits, side-effects—they're all affects. You'll end up seeing more illusion than reality."

A shout from ahead called Kai's name. A short girl, with sharp tufts of pink hair, waved him over to a small group peeling away from the protest. Kai introduced her as Lily. She gave Yoshi an odd glance before wrapping an arm around Kai. The others chatted boisterously, charged with the energy of their marching and chanting. Yoshi trailed behind to let Kai catch up with his friends.

The group slowed at a pod-charging station, and Lily led them to an older model auto-van with 'Shibido Connect' hand-painted on its side. She yanked the door open and Kai climbed through, pulling Yoshi in.

"How far are we going, Kai?"

"Just down to Low Ground, not far."

They squeezed into the back corner, and the others climbed in after. Kai didn't let go of Yoshi's hand.

As the van took off into the traffic, the motion rolled a megaphone from under the front seat down to Yoshi's feet. Lily snatched it up and stuffed it back in its place.

Yoshi leaned close to Kai and kept his voice low. "Have you been involved with this for a while?"

"Just a month. So, who's Leon?"

Yoshi froze at Kai's sharp reversal of questioning. He tried to stem the blood rushing to his face, but he blushed even more.

"He's just a colleague."

Kai squeezed Yoshi's hand and smirked. "Is he as good an actor as you?"

"He's an actor friend."

"Fair enough. So, how long have you been acting?"

"About three years, since high-school."

"That's it? And then you got the lead in *One Man Dreaming*?"

"My agent saw a video of me from a school play. He needed someone who fitted the character from the novel. Just lucky, I guess."

"What got you into acting in the first place, then? You don't seem like the fame-chasing type. You seem the opposite. Reclusive, even."

Yoshi squirmed under Kai's analysis, unable to tell if his questions were genuine or mocking.

"You wouldn't understand."

"Oh, I see, too high-brow for non-thespians, is it? Well, let me guess. You use it to escape feeling in reality."

Unable to think of a retort, Yoshi could only scoff, but Kai's words hit surprisingly deep.

Kai looked out the window, not seeming to expect a reply, or perhaps to give Yoshi a moment. A speck of fluff flashed in the light, floated across the landscape of Kai's face, and entangled itself in his eyelashes. He blinked, like he was sending Morse code to the clouded sky. And that's when Yoshi realized what drew him to Kai—his ability to talk right on the borderline between candor and brutal honesty made Yoshi feel more present, and the world more real.

"I guess it is an escape," Yoshi admitted, following Kai's gaze out the window.

"From what?"

The question awoke a familiar guilt in Yoshi, but the rocking of the pod eased him into a pause, allowing him to reflect on the last two days' relentless pounding against the inner wall around his past.

"My Grandpapa brought me here when I was really young, from Meti."

"The island in the bay?"

"Yeah. He and I survived the tsunami, but my parents didn't."

Kai turned back to Yoshi, his brow knotted. "I'm so sorry. That must have been hard."

Yoshi shrugged.

"I was only four, I don't remember them, or Meti. My Grandpapa and I were looked after when we got here with housing and education assistance, like most victims of the Shift. But it wasn't much, and he had to raise me on his own. He'd tell me these crazy stories to keep me entertained, act them out like a performer. But his Outlook declined as he got older, until he had to go into care. The medication really messed with him, depressed him. Watching him deteriorate was... We just became more like strangers every day.

"Then the school theater club asked me to participate in the annual play, and I thought it would help keep my mind off things. So, I gave it a go, and it helped me forget about things. In a way, I think my Grandpapa wanted me to do it, to tell stories with performance."

Kai rubbed a thumb across Yoshi's knuckles. "Thank you for sharing that."

Yoshi felt like he'd dumped a bag of rocks that he never knew he'd been carrying. He squeezed Kai's hand in return.

"And what's your story?"

"Nothing interesting, unfortunately. Been here my whole life. My parents moved west a few years ago, but I stayed and did a degree in event management. Went through a few jobs, all a bit soulless. I'm hoping to go full-time with Connect, but if that doesn't happen, I'll have to move back west, where the rent is cheaper. I'm luckier than some though, right?"

The auto-van pulled into a transfer lane and steered itself into an elevator tube. As it lowered down to Low Ground, Yoshi looked out over Maya District and lost his breath. The entire district and sea-wall were gone, replaced by a lush island frontage, dotted with small houses. Wooden jetties poked out onto the calm waters of a sea level much lower and calmer than he ever remembered seeing. The Mirage's serenity spoke so directly to his psyche he could almost let his mind believe it was real.

"Hello," Kai said, calling him back.

"Sorry, what did you say?"

"I said, that's where we're going."

Kai pointed to a cluster of huts nestled in the foliage by the water. Not used to the way the Mirage so heavily altered the world, Yoshi put the mode on a five-minute pause so he could see what Kai was pointing at. The calm sea disappeared behind the re-emerging water-stained sea-wall, and the island coast faded, replaced by Maya District's immaculately featureless suburb. The huts Kai had pointed to revealed themselves as the 'lucky' buildings and old temples left untouched outside the District's fenced perimeter.

Several other Connect vans sat at the edge of a small park just before the old area.

"What do you do there?" Yoshi asked.

"We hand out hot meals to the homeless, and to the Minaki." Kai smiled at Yoshi's confused look. "They're refugees. The rising ocean displaced them from a group of islands in the North Pacific."

"So, they just came into the city and stayed?"

"They used to sail to a headland market here to trade, but after that went under, they disappeared for a while. Then, about eight months ago, the officials noticed they'd set up camps with the homeless in the old esplanade buildings. They could have been here longer, no one really knows. That's the Lenz for you.

"Anyway, when the officials eventually realized, they approached the Minaki for identity and health checks, and allowed them to remain while the Council worked out what to do. But the international legal system still doesn't recognize people displaced by the Shift as refugees, so the government isn't legally obliged to do anything. The Mayor talked about exploring a new visa that would allow them to work, but that was months ago, and the Council's initial support dried up. Connect's been providing food and assistance, while others in the group lobby the council for a resolution. But since the public has forgotten about the issue, it doesn't have any political value, so the Minaki are just floating here in limbo. Then Maya District forced the homeless back into the city, and the Minaki went into that group of buildings behind the park." A mischievous smirk spread across Kai's face and filled Yoshi with unease. "We got to lobby harder."

The elevator eased the van to ground level and zipped out toward the park. As they neared Connect's gathering, Yoshi noticed a long, rectangular concrete structure with the same torch symbol spray-painted on its side as the one he'd seen in the underground.

Lily parked the van next to the others, and Kai led Yoshi out into a buzz of activity. Volunteers placed utensils, bowls, hot tea and candy on foldable tables, while others filled large metal pots from a container in an open-sided truck. The rich, aromatic smell of hot beef stew wafted through the air. Over a hundred men and women, layered in disheveled clothing, stood at the perimeter, lured out of hiding. They kept their heads down, their postures slumped from a shame they no doubt felt from being seen as lacking self-reliance.

"Other volunteers come along and donate medical services," Kai explained as they walked. "It's a place for people on the streets to meet others, and we let them help us if they want to. There's a tech kiosk as well. The Minaki don't use it, though, they just take the food and disappear back into that building over there, the one with the big torch on its side."

Kai stopped them at the truck with the metal chambers inside and passed Yoshi a large empty pot.

"Can you give me a hand with this?"

Kai's passion for the work glowed on his face and sparkled in his eyes. Out of the purple mall uniform, he brimmed with a more confident and volatile energy. Something stirred in Yoshi—admiration. But, also, a little caution.

They filled two pots full of the piping-hot stew and carried them to a table set with bowls.

"We hand out food here so the shoppers up there might see." Kai put down the pot and pointed behind them toward High Scape.

Two blocks back, a busy sky-bridge connected two shopping towers below the edge of High Scape. Shoppers rushed back and forth across the glass bridge, followed by bi-pedal carry boxes loaded with purchases. A five-story-high screen graced the side of both buildings—in full view of those crossing the bridge—showing a celebration of a newborn panda at the Ueno Zoo in Tokyo. Yoshi's Mirage finished its pause and transformed the buildings into clusters of giant bamboo, and virtual pandas began climbing out of the screens and up the building sides.

"Those shoppers are too busy to notice anything down here," he said, following Kai back to the truck.

"Normally their Lenz would block us from their preferred view. But we're working on a way to make them see the homeless."

Kai handed him a heavy pot of steaming rice and they returned it to the table. He wiped a forearm across his brow and nodded toward the street leading out from the old buildings.

"Here come the Minaki."

A bird-like clicking emanated from down the street, like it was coming toward them. But Yoshi couldn't see anyone.

"Where?"

Kai pointed to the empty street. "Right there."

Yoshi squinted, but he still couldn't see anything. The clicking grew louder, like many people were flicking their tongues from the roofs of their mouths.

"I can hear something."

"Yeah, they do that when they first turn up. It sounds like birds alerting each other."

Then Yoshi saw something, fifteen or so yards away—the air above the road shimmered. Vertical slivers of color slit the blur, distortions that grew into ethereal figures. As the Minaki took full form in

Yoshi's view, the severity of his Mirage's alteration of reality shocked him. The clicking sounds grew even closer, and more Minaki emerged, solidifying in detail as they neared, as if his Mirage auto-dimmed its effect in response to anything moving directly at him.

He glanced around the area, blinking, wondering what else the Mirage might be hiding.

"You alright, Yoshi?"

"I'm fine," he lied.

"I've seen that look on a Lenzer's face before. They also didn't admit they couldn't see things."

The Minaki stopped their clicking noises and joined the lines. As Kai and Yoshi served the steaming rice and stew, Yoshi took a better look at the city's unofficial guests.

Island life had frizzed their hair and bronzed her skin, and they wore the same purposely cut, brightly colored pants that Singlets had worn. Their faces looked drawn, and their dark skin grayed from lack of sunlight.

"How many are there?" he asked Kai.

"A few hundred. Some think Maya is trying to remove them from our Sight, to help us forget about the Shift. Not sure about that, but they've definitely been forced further out of view. First the rising ocean, then politics… must be terrible living in constant fear of something always coming after you."

Kai's last words scratched a nail down Yoshi's spine.

Coming, coming, coming.

Worse still, he felt himself sinking deeper into his dishonest silence about working for Maya. Avoiding the subject, he nodded at more islanders coming from the old buildings.

"I'll get more rice," Kai said as he headed back to the van.

A familiar voice from the other side of the table startled Yoshi.

"Still lost?"

Yoshi halted, recognizing Singlet's sun-weathered face.

"I'm sorry," he said, continuing to serve the stew again. "I didn't see you there."

"Yes, this happens."

"Did you want rice as well?" Yoshi said, as he filled the man's bowl. "We're getting more rice."

"We are not the refugees."

"I'm sorry?"

"We are migrants. We are all migrating, we are all in transit. The shore has not gone, it has moved. This place, this time, it is a portal."

Yoshi felt the walls of his dishonesty closing in. Singlets bowed and walked off. Yoshi breathed a sigh of relief and served a woman stepping forward with her bowl held out.

"Here we go," said Kai, placing the refilled pot on the table.

"How long did you say you've been with Connect?" he asked to mask his unease.

"I told you, a couple of weeks. I feel like it makes me see the world more clearly." Kai's handsome features grew solemn. "I know it isn't very Shibidoan to talk about it, but that's the problem, we never *do* talk about the past, or our *real* Outlook. I don't think we properly processed the Shift. After all the changes the world made, to be turned inside-out by the compounding effects of what we'd already done… the Shift took our hope and sense of control. But instead of our awareness growing, we made our distractions more sophisticated. We've been turning further and further inwards ever since, hiding in the channels, inside this limbo between a reality we refuse to look at and our Outlook's useless wishful thinking."

"It's important to be optimistic," Yoshi argued, "to nurture positivity and hope." But, even to himself, his words sounded like they confirmed Kai's point.

Kai lifted his chin and smiled.

"People think it's futile to be heartbroken by the state of the world, to think about how many have suffered. But our despair we hide from, this is what we need to feel, it's alerting us to what really matters, it's guiding us on how to respond, to reimagine the future by changing what we *do*. If we don't let ourselves feel the sadness, we'll miss its message, and we'll get the future we're all silently fearing. How do you want the future to be, Yoshi? How do you imagine it?"

A cave silence hung in Yoshi's mind—he'd never really thought beyond getting his career back on track. Kai saved him from saying something stupid.

"I imagine people not waiting for others to do something but engaging with each other about what they *really* care about, and putting their visions to the test, not just passively hoping for change. I know it's emotionally draining to look beyond Maya's distraction, but people who fight for their own vision are brave, because they have to believe in it a long time before others start to see it."

He smiled at Yoshi as if he directed his last words at him. But Yoshi didn't *want* to think about life without Maya; he wanted to be *in* Maya.

"Enough," snapped the homeless woman he was serving.

Yoshi had over-filled her bowl and spilled hot stew onto her fingers.

"I'm so sorry."

After a forced "Thank you," the woman moved away, and Yoshi put down his ladle.

"Look, Kai, I want to be straight up with you. I respect what you're doing, but I'm not an activist like you. I'm just trying to get ahead, you know? Acting is all I have, so—"

But before he could complete his confession, a brash shout from behind cut him off.

"Fucking pandas."

A familiar rangy-limbed, long-haired guy strode toward them, pointing at the giant screens by the sky bridge.

"Is that Raiden?" Yoshi whispered, recognizing him from the mall.

Kai nodded. "He introduced me to Connect."

Next to Raiden walked a sturdy young man carrying a green tote bag slung over his shoulder—not very bright looking, but eyes sparkling with keen daring.

"Look at them," Raiden continued, pointing to the pandas, or possibly the shoppers. "Dumb as holes in the ground. So self-absorbed they can barely look after themselves, let alone their young. But the world ensured pandas survived because they're dumbness is so kawaii. Meanwhile, we let the polar bears starve to death because tenacity in other beings intimates us."

Kai laughed and nudged Yoshi. "Don't you love how he just says what he thinks."

"Maybe he thinks too much."

"Better than thinking too little." Kai stood up and threw a hug around Raiden. "You remember Yoshi? From Glasshouse?"

"Oh, yeah. The Santa of children's nightmares."

Yoshi dipped his head, fearing someone might identify him.

"I'm sorry about that," he replied quietly, forcing a smile.

"I'm just stirring you. And don't worry, I'm not a snitch. It was an accident. I should thank you, actually." He slapped his companion's chest. "I met Akio that day thanks to you. And he's been all sorts of good luck."

Yoshi recognized Akio as the one Raiden assisted out of the mall atrium. Akio slipped the green bag from his shoulder and pulled a drone from the tote. Kai's eyes widened with uneasy surprise.

"We're doing this today?" he asked Raiden.

"Yep," Raiden said. "Right now."

A prickle ran up Yoshi's back. "Doing what?"

Kai mouthed "I'm sorry" to Yoshi, and then raced away to the van they'd arrived in.

Raiden called out to the volunteers. "It's on, people."

Suddenly, anyone who wasn't dishing out food or tea scuttled to the vans. Akio had the drone flying toward the sky-bridge as Kai returned with the megaphone and handed it to Raiden.

Yoshi grabbed Kai's arm. "What's happening?"

"Raiden's got a way to make the shoppers see us, and the homeless."

Akio let out a *whoop* as he hovered his drone in front of the skybridge. The giant screens on the buildings below flashed with static and then displayed the drone's view of the shoppers. They stopped, lured by the sight of themselves on the screens. Media drones flew in, their camera eyes driven by what the shoppers' Lenz's were focusing on. and flew the drone backward, fast, until it hovered near the vans, filling the large screens with the congregation of the homeless.

Yoshi's skin iced. Fearing what he was getting caught up in, he hid behind the nearest van to scan the area behind for an escape. But Lily ran out to stand among the homeless and held up what looked like a flare gun. She fired. A flare shot upward to explode in the dull, overcast sky and tinged the homeless with its bright, pink light. Alarmed confusion contorted their faces as they covered their eyes from the glare.

More media drones flew toward them, streaming the drama to millions. Raiden climbed onto the roof of the van hiding Yoshi, and he switched on the megaphone. An electrical squeal pierced the air as he shouted.

"It's time to wake up and *see* the true situation of homelessness in Shibido. See what your denial hides from you. Turn off your Lenzes and wake up to reality. Turn off and see!"

The protesters erupted into chanting, but the shoppers appeared to lose interest, stepping away from the windows one by one. Raiden swore.

"It's gonna take more than words to wake them up," he called to the others.

Thinking the protest was over, Yoshi's racing heart began to slow. But as he dared to step out from his hiding spot, sirens blared from the street under the sky-bridge. Red and blue lights flashed across the buildings as police pods blazed toward them. The shoppers stopped again and returned to the windows, and the drones swarmed back in. Raiden stepped down from the van's roof as the other protesters gathered around him.

Yoshi peered around the van—any way back to the city was being televised by the drones. Behind him, the refugees fled back toward the concrete structure with the torch painted on its side, and—

He squinted, uncertain of what he saw. The boy from the tunnel appeared at the end of the warehouse, holding his stick-torch. As the Minaki reached the torch building, they raced past him and disappeared around its side.

Yoshi's watch vibrated, snapping away his attention. It was Tora. He swiped off the call to concentrate, but he struggled to think with Raiden's voice rising in anger.

He looked around at the protesters again and spotted Kai standing firm by Raiden's side. Yoshi fumed at being led into the volatile situation, but Kai's fidgeting fingers betrayed his nerves. Yoshi didn't want to leave him, certain Raiden was leading Kai's best intentions astray. He glanced back at the torch building where the last of the refugees disappeared, and then he ran over to Kai.

"Kai," he whispered. "Do you wanna end up in jail?"

"We can't just do nothing," Kai said, a fearful determination in his eyes.

"Well, I'm not staying. I didn't ask to be a part of this."

Guilt flashed across Kai's face. "I'm sorry, I didn't know this was happening today."

A voice boomed out from up the road where a silhouetted policeman stood by his parked pod. Yoshi froze.

"Attention protesters. This congregation is in violation of Shibido's anti-disturbance laws. Discontinue immediately, dismantle all tables, and move on. The drone pilot must come forward and surrender themself."

"And where do the homeless go?" Raiden yelled back through the megaphone. "What about the Minaki?"

The policeman paused to look up at the swarm of drones before replying.

"Negotiations are underway for alternative lodgings—"

"That's crap!" yelled Raiden, the megaphone screeching again.

The others cheered and pumped their fists in the air.

"Turn off! Wake up!"

But as more police arrived, three volunteers bolted, and two others took off in a van. The doors of the police pods opened and slammed shut as officers jumped out and held their Tazers forward.

With one last glance at Kai's stern face, Yoshi ran toward the torch building where the Minaki, and the boy, had disappeared.

Debris

Reaching the concrete structure, he ducked around its corner and skidded to a halt. A faded sign above the entrance read *To Esplanade Parking Garage*, and a stairway disappeared down into the underground. Hesitant about going into the underground again, he peeked back around the building to see the police catching the scattering protesters. They were everywhere, blocking the way back to the city. He swore at his predicament and jogged down the stairs into a wide corridor, and he crouched behind a large, rectangular garbage bin.

Resting his head against the cold metal, he tried to slow his heart as it pounded in his ears.

What was I thinking?

But he knew the answer to that—he *hadn't* been thinking, not with his brain. He'd let himself get swept away by his immediate chemistry with Kai. Maybe his Mirage exaggerated his own intentions and influenced his decision making. Perhaps new romance itself is the greatest augmentation of reality.

He recalled the last time chemistry had sparked between him and another. It must have been over year since he met a guy online. Rei, or Ren. They spent two weeks talking online non-stop. It seemed like a real connection. When Yoshi asked to meet in person, however, Ren stopped responding, and eventually blocked Yoshi's further requests for an explanation. As for other lovers, they had come and gone like common colds.

Yoshi reminded himself what he had decided back then—the sea was full of fish that would never come out of the water.

Maybe I should get a companion yujin from that Good Time Adult Store.

His heartbeat settled, and he laughed at how foolishly he'd underestimated the bravado behind Kai's cuteness. But sweet-faced trouble was the last thing he needed.

He checked the time—11:10 a.m.—plenty of time to get back to the studio if he could get through the parking area. He tried loading a map, but the Lenz menu had grayed out again in the underground.

With his vision fully adjusted to the dim light, he peered down the tunnel. He figured he just had to reach about midway through to the access ramp where he'd come down the previous day. Then he could make his way back to the stairs or find an elevator up.

A distant shout outside snapped him to attention. He peeked around the bin to check the way was clear and then hurried into the open parking area.

The same distinct earthy scent of incense and spice from the day before filled the air, barely masking the dank smell of mold. But the combination appealed to him as the dense, organic stench of a forest floor. Further along, thin wisps of smoke appeared and coalesced upward in arcs, immersing the way ahead in a mystical haze. The half-lit graffiti stretching overhead stirred his imagination, and he saw tree-like shapes reaching up the walls and over the ceiling. They seemed to form one harmonic tapestry, as if each individual piece was part of a collective landscape.

Stop daydreaming.

Passing piles of frayed, upturned furniture, he kept by the sloped wall. As he neared a well-lit area ahead, a murmur arose, and he slowed. He could make out the silhouettes of the islanders, some standing, some sitting. A meme came to him as he approached the dispersed group—*Everyone smiles in the same language*—so he smiled and acted normal.

The first to notice him—a group of girls sitting on cardboard—began their clicking noises that repeated through the underground. His back tingled, but the clicking died down and the Minaki showed no threat to him; he passed through groups of the them without challenge. Chatting and lively, they seemed to have put the drone ordeal behind them.

They took great ceremony in their interaction, gesturing for another to speak and bowing in response. A group of boys sat by the gutter, drawing the torch symbol on the back of old posters, while some passed blankets and clothes to others on the ledge at the top of the slope. Some wove rope from scraps of smaller ropes, like they were still mending nets on the shore of their island home.

The light, he noticed, came from many dented Vitamin-D lamps powered by the stolen generator. Groups huddled around the light, the glow painting their closed eyelids with gold.

He found himself searching the crowd for the boy, but unsurprisingly, he wasn't among the Minaki.

At the edge of the settlement, the smoke thinned. A boy and a girl dismantled one of several cupboards and tables piled together. They worked with a gentle synchronicity, passing tools and furniture parts between each other with a steady ebb and flow.

A humble dignity had etched lines in their faces that Yoshi hadn't noticed in them outside—perhaps, he thought, it was just because he now gave them more Sight. The space the Minaki had created for themselves brought a surprising liveliness to the underground—it no longer seemed like a damp passage through neglect, but a simplistic resting ground where the unassuming islanders remained, in an abstract way, in charge of their lives—not in need, but in a state of reflective preparation. But where would they go?

Yoshi's stomach clenched into a fist of guilt, and he struggled to accommodate the inconvenient empathy into the psychological map for his reinvention.

After fifteen minutes or so, the sounds of the islanders ebbed into the distance, and he could see ahead the section with the flashing light. For an instant, he considered looking for the boy to check on him, then he spied the T-junction and his eagerness to get back to ground flicked the idea. But when he turned into the tunnel leading out, he found the access ramp had been blocked off from outside.

"Fuck!"

Resigning to walking all the way to the south exit, he clenched his fists and headed into the flickering light. As he kept an eye out for the boy, he spotted the torch symbol on the slope and a dusty red sleeping bag poking out from the ledge above it. A coolness blew through the humidity, and Yoshi's instinct made him spin around in time to see the boy behind him.

"Get back," the boy said, swinging his stick again.

But this time Yoshi kept his balance and remained calm.

"Hey, there. Why aren't you with the others, down the other end?"

The boy's frail shape seemed to shimmer in the oscillating light with a fierce, yet fragile, glow. An awful helplessness welled in Yoshi's heart. He took a step back, determined not to lose his temper.

"Are you here with anyone?"

But the boy didn't reply, and there was no sign of anyone else sleeping on the slope nearby.

I should take him back to the others. But what if he doesn't want to go? Maybe I shouldn't get involved.

Although the flashing light made it hard to see detail, the boy looked paler than before, and his actions seemed strained. Yoshi removed his jacket and held it out.

"Here, you need to keep warm."

The boy stopped swinging.

"It's coming."

Yoshi's back prickled. "What is?"

"It's pushing us all back together." The boy ran up the slope, over the torch symbol, and disappeared over the ledge.

Crap. "I didn't mean to scare you," Yoshi called out.

No reply.

He climbed the slope and stopped short of the sleeping bag. Unable to see anything, he lobbed the jacket into the darkness.

"You can keep it."

Still no reply.

He checked the time again—11:23 a.m.—and he ran back down the slope. Promising himself he'd report the boy's location to Social Services, he mentally logged the torch graffiti as a marker and hurried on.

Continuing south, he passed more of the odd stockpiles of furniture. But these had been broken down into parts and sorted into neat rows, from chair legs, tabletops, couch frames, and cupboard doors, to bottles, tools, plates, cutlery and trinkets. As he passed through the deconstructed possessions of lives gone by, questions unrelated to his self-driven agenda infiltrated his thoughts.

Where would the Minaki go if Maya closed off the underground completely? Was he really contributing to their mistreatment by being involved with the District?

I can't quit the first proper-paying job I've had in two years. And I don't want to protest with Kai. He scared the life out of the very people he was protesting for. And Raiden, he's just preying on confused and vulnerable people like Kai. Did they even ask the Minaki what they wanted?

He tried to stuff the questions back into the crack they'd sprang from, to stop them from sabotaging his own good fortune. But a heavy empathy lingered in his heart.

Finally, he reached the south exit. He ran to the top of the ramp and gasped a lung full of fresh air. A line of people waited at the bus stop across the road, making him momentarily wonder if he might have fainted waiting in line the day before, and everything else had been a dream.

He summoned Driver to take him back to the studio early, so he could try to patch things up with Lavinda before the others arrived.

"Certainly, Mr. Goto. ETA 10 minutes."

He crossed the road, eager to move away from the underground entrance, in case its persistent magnetism pulled him in again. The Lenz menu flickered back into its active state. His Mirage replaced the sea-wall and Maya District with the island shoreline and calm bay. A luminous sheen suffused the gray sky above, the light drizzle transformed into strings of tiny diamonds, and a soft blur shimmered the edges of his vision.

But as inviting as the illusion was, a burr remained on Yoshi's heart that he struggled to ignore.

What's wrong with the Lenz helping me forget depressing things I can't do anything about? Worrying doesn't change anything, and it certainly doesn't help my Outlook. I need to stay focused on the wonderful potential of my immediate future!

Interrupting his thoughts, a twinkle in the trees opposite caught his eye—a lit stick-torch, embedded in the ground, flickered by the doorway of a hut, right where the ramp entrance was. Reminded of his promise to call Social Services, he searched in his Lenz for the number and blinked to call.

"Hello, you've reached the Department of Social Services. How can I help you today?"

"I want to report a... an underage person sleeping homeless."

"Okay. So, you want to report a person for sleeping on the street?"

"Yes, but the homeless person is a child. Maybe six-years-old."

"I'm sorry, I didn't get that. Please answer the question again. Did you want to report a person for sleeping on the street?"

Damn, a phone-bot.

"I want to report a child is homeless and sleeping in the underground parking garage under the esplanade."

"Okay. So, you want to request an investigation into a potential victim of youth homelessness."

"Yes, that's right."

"Okay, great. Let's start with the child's first and last name."

"I don't know his name. I don't know him. I just saw him in the underground." Yoshi blinked open a map and zoomed in around the area he'd entered the day before. "There was an access ramp just beyond the east side of High Scape somewhere. But that's closed off now."

"Okay. Is there any way we can identify this person?"

"He's about three and half feet tall, very pale skin. Black hair. He sleeps near the closed ramp entrance, just inside, near a T-junction. There's a large torch graffiti thing on the slope where he sleeps. He might be wearing a red bomber jacket with Joe Joe on it—I gave that to him."

Static hummed through the call.

"Can I have your name please, sir?"

Stay out of trouble.

Gray's words flashed through Yoshi's mind, and he froze.

"I'd like to stay anonymous, thank you," he said, even though he knew the department would have already recorded his number.

"We value your privacy, sir, and you can hear our Privacy Policy by saying *Hear policy now*. Otherwise, please state your full name—"

Crap.

He blinked off the call.

Believing he'd done all he could do, he silenced any further thoughts about the Minaki, or the boy or Kai, or anything else other than networking his way back into the industry and establishing a damn FOF.

The pod arrived, and as it drove him back to the studio, he strategized how to win over Lavinda's tough front, and nurture his delicate connection with Leon. The morning's events ebbed away like a dream being forgotten. By the time he reached the studio, his meditation on his goal had forged a focus as sharp as the horn of a unicorn, ready to nail the afternoon's orb session—and Leon if he had to.

Progress

After Jin scanned him through the gate, Yoshi headed straight to Studio 5, hoping he might also get some immersion practice before the others arrived. But as he approached the double doors of the Immersion room, he heard voices from inside.

Naomi tapped on her table at the back. Leon and Dax stood by the strange, fridge-sized machines next to her. As Yoshi neared them, he could see the machines were open, and, to his great shock, each one had a *yujin* standing inside it—and each *yujin* was one of the film's five characters, including his own look-a-like Joe Joe.

"What are these for?"

Naomi looked up from her work and gave him a forced smile, clearly still annoyed from the morning.

"Hey, Dizzy," Leon called, wrapping his arm around his doppelgänger. "Two for one deal."

But Yoshi couldn't take his eyes off his own clone, a creepiness spreading through him like runaway mold. Although Joe Joe had been altered and refined according to the studio's ideal, the *yujin* was fundamentally just a younger Yoshi with the comet-shaped birthmark below its right eye.

"Please don't touch them," Naomi said.

"But what are these for?" he repeated.

"They're actoids, *yujin* actors, for the district experience. They'll learn your character's mannerisms, too, so we'll have both real and virtual representations."

While Leon and Dax seemed amused by being completely replaced, Yoshi's imagination raced into the future. Would people be able tell the difference between him and his clone? Could Joe Joe have his own channel? Would that be good or bad for his own FOF?

"But they're glitching," Dax said, leaning in to take a closer look at Suzy Lee Bingo. The actoid faced the inside of its container. "It's so weird how they just face walls for no reason. She looks depressed."

"They don't get depressed," Naomi quipped with increasing annoyance. She tapped Dax's shoulder to move out of the way, then opened a panel behind Suzy's ear to tinker with the internal mechanics. "If you all wouldn't mind giving me some room, I need to continue working on these problems."

"I had a Chow Chow that did that," Dax continued. "Damn dog just faced a wall and pressed its head against it. Turned out it had some sort of dementia."

"Dementia doesn't make people face walls," Yoshi said defensively.

"*Dogs* with dementia *do*."

"Maybe," Leon offered, feeling the bicep of his actoid replacement, "they're sad 'cause they're conscious enough to know they don't have a soul."

"Maybe," Dax added, his voice rising with the excitement of the analysis, "they're so depressed they don't *want* to be conscious."

"They're not *depressed*," Naomi snapped, slamming the Suzy's neck panel shut and spinning around. "And they don't have *dementia*. They're a highly developed AI that's advanced beyond its own hardware. I'm running out of time to balance them out, as well as scan you lot, so can you all just please let me do my work, hmm?"

Yoshi and the others glanced at each other in surprise.

"I'm sorry," she said, blushing and smiling apologetically. "I'm under a lot of pressure. If you could just get in your orbs so I can check the calibration, that would be most helpful."

She pulled the container of nausea pills from her pocket and handed them out. When she got to Yoshi, she gave him two. He noticed her take one herself when she returned to her worktable. He wondered if she worried about developing the technology that might one day take her own job.

Coming, coming, coming.

The double doors swung open and Lavinda strode in, the other cast members following. Thanking them all for their punctuality, Lavinda ordered them into their orbs to get into character.

Pushing aside his unease about the actoids, Yoshi donned the harness and pulled on the goggles. The world around him morphed into the orb's monochromatic blue version. He started his breathing techniques and lowered himself into Joe Joe's persona. As he let the emotions manipulate his posture, he overheard Lavinda talking to Naomi.

"Is this the new lot of actoids?" she asked.

"Yes, from that little company the studio just bought. Real Toy Robotics, you know it? Their hardware is superbly reactive. I've never seen—"

"Do you know what the problem is or not?"

"I... I think they *may* have a sort of depression. A kind of resignation syndrome, perhaps."

"Robots get depressed?"

"Figuratively speaking, it's possible. Their empathy facility might be overloaded and need some adjustment. I'm not sure, but I think I'm onto something. I'm feeling hopeful."

"I need more than hope, Naomi. I need working actoids, ASAP."

Lavinda's footsteps echoed as she moved into the center of the room.

"Listen up, people. This afternoon we'll dive into the parachute drop scene. Naomi ensures me there will be no more hold-ups. Are you ready, Yoshi?"

Shadows flooded Yoshi's view, and his surroundings morphed into the cylindrical inside of a cargo drone container. The walls and floor rattled, and a roaring engine noise filled his ears. The details—the fine fraying of dangling straps, random scuff marks on the floor and walls, erratic wind noises—imbued the virtual scene with undeniable realism.

The spherical grid in Yoshi's view disappeared, and he braced himself. Naomi's disembodied voice was his only reminder of the real world.

"Your parachute release button is on your left thigh. Follow the instructions in your Lenz. Get ready to jump in ten."

A loud clunk from the wall in front reverberated through Yoshi's body. Instinctively, he reached out to hold the wall as the rear door jolted open. The orb's immersion mechanisms rattled him to his bones and pounded him with a buffeting, roaring wind, as if he was really standing in an open cargo drone thousands of miles above the earth. He blew a few short breaths to keep control and glanced over his shoulder to check his parachute was there. The others had lined up behind him—Bamboo Run pawed the floor with a hoof, Suzy Lee Bingo's armored uniform remained unmoving in the buffeting wind, Dhven stood with his twelve arms outstretched, and Leon, an obsidian Adonis, stood chilled as a whisky and soda on ice.

"Ten—nine—"

He stepped to the edge, the gusts rioting against his body. Far below, the stark ribbon of the wall divided Shibido's glinting geometry from the ocean's vastness.

"Two—One—Jump!"

He gulped back his fear—*Let's do this!*—and threw himself into the void. The orb's harness jerked him into a horizontal position and blasted him with an upward wind that crushed his lungs, but Naomi's extra pill kept him calm.

"You're all at total immersion, using the same parts of the brain as you would in real life. You are no longer watching, you are *experiencing*. Release your chutes in five, four—"

Yoshi reached down to his thigh.

"Three—two—one."

He slammed the virtual button, and the opening chute jolted him upright with a *whoosh*. As he settled into a float, he could hear the others whooping from somewhere above.

The tops of High Scape rose up toward him. Below, a blue light pulsed around a large cube structure nestled in between taller buildings. An information banner appeared over it:

High Palace Exhibition Hall

"Use your body to steer toward the exhibition hall and aim for your marker on the stage." Naomi's voice had moved into his mind, the virtual world now reality.

As he floated down to the cube, its ceiling slid open. A blue target appeared on a spot lit stage and he dropped toward it. As a swarming, cheering crowd came into view by the stage's edge, he steered himself to land right on his marker. A thunderous applause burst from the crowd, forcing him to take a step back as his parachute collapsed behind him. Exhilaration rushed through his veins. He lifted his arms, and the crowd roared again.

The others landed beside him, their arrival whipping the crowd into a frenzy.

"Well done, people," said Naomi, "a great first pass."

The stage and crowd flashed and disappeared. Ripped out of a universe his consciousness had decided was real, Yoshi found himself standing in an unfamiliar living room. He swayed with discombobulation, but the orb's perimeter re-appeared, and his spatial awareness adapted.

"We'll run through that again tomorrow, but now you'll spend the rest of the afternoon in a normalized domestic setting, so we can capture your character's everyday movements and actions."

Yoshi looked around to see Dhven, Bamboo Run, and Suzy Lee Bingo standing in an adjacent kitchen area. Bingo brushed aside her black, windswept hair and nodded to Yoshi in acknowledgment of his improvement.

"Nice one, Dizzy," said Leon, appearing by his side. "Your boyfriend would be proud."

"I told you, he's just a friend."

Leon chuckled. "Joe Joe's kinda cute when he gets flustered."

"We're still scanning," Naomi interrupted. "Stay in character, hmm?"

Yoshi spent the next three hours in the virtual house with the others, all in character, sitting, talking, eating, drinking, and interacting normally with the house setting so Naomi could capture their character's daily micro behaviors.

By the time the house dissolved and returned them to the immersion room, he was already getting the hang of slipping between realities. After a debriefing from Lavinda, he returned to the chairs in the front room and plonked down to fully allow his body and brain to re-synchronize.

"You did alright, Goto," said Dax coming out of the immersion room with Otis, Leon and Jenya behind him. "Coming for some food?"

Yoshi jumped back to his feet. "Sure."

"Walking isn't going to make you sick, is it?" Dax stirred.

Yoshi gave him a mock punch as they stepped outside into the cul-de-sac. Lustrous vines covered the studios, silver-green grass covered the road, and the soft blur at the edge of his vision now fractured like crystals.

"Maybe," Jenya teased from the behind, "it was just Leon's looks that made you sick the first time."

Leon elbowed Jenya playfully with feigned offence. "Don't be jealous of my genes, girl."

"I don't wanna go anywhere near your *jeans*, *gurl*."

The others laughed, and the comradery warmed Yoshi. But as he followed Dax into the cafeteria, his splintered peripheral made him misjudge the width of the entrance, and his shoulder banged against the doorway, knocking him backward.

"Hey," Leon said, catching him. "You alright there, Dizzy?"

"Yeah, yeah, all good. Just wasn't looking."

Yoshi continued inside but stayed alert, frustrated he wasn't mixing realities as well as he thought. He joined the others at a table overlooking the grassy cul-de-sac and ordered a ramen, hoping a decent meal might help ground him. But as he reached for a glass of water that Jenya handed him, he knocked Leon's all over his shirt.

"Damn, Dizzy! What's up with you today?"

The others chuckled, but a frown on Dax's face showed his initial distrust of Yoshi was returning.

Yoshi apologized, and Jenya joked about Leon not ever winning a wet t-shirt competition. While Yoshi laughed along with them, he tried looking directly at the crystalized edge of his vision, but it moved. Uncertain if it was part of the Mirage or a Lenz fault, he blinked off his Mirage. The edge-distortion disappeared, and the return of the real world's subdued atmosphere settled his confused sense of space. He leaned over to Leon and whispered.

"Does your Mirage ever get too intense?"

Leon shrugged. "You're probably still adjusting. You should take a perception session. You got the care goggles, right?"

Yoshi nodded, remembering the pair that came with the Lenz.

"Just put 'em on and load up the virtual Lenzist. It's like an automated eye-examination, but with adaptive, personalized responses."

"Okay, thanks."

Eager to conquer his aversion to switching realities, he left the group at the cafeteria and summoned Driver.

Meeting the pod at the studio entrance, he climbed inside, and pulled the goggles from the glove box. As he slipped them on, the snug device beeped, and a dark overlay covered his vision. After a safety warning displayed, another message followed:

Welcome to Lenz Care.
Please wait while we load your profile.

Promotional facts displayed as the goggles prepared his session:

Did you know over 67% of device users develop
short-sightedness from overuse of screens?
Vision change is part of modern life,
but Maya's Lenz can help you adapt.

———

Like a spiritual third eye, Mirage learns
from your social media, and from your
day-to-day viewing behavior, and
alters your view with a personalized filter.
Activate your Mirage for specific occasions,
or stay immersed for continuous
positivity and beauty.

Another beep and two aperture-like shapes appeared directly in front of his eyes, twisting into alignment with the speed of robotic safecrackers.

"Wonderful Day, Mr. Goto," said a perky, male voice from Yoshi's earpiece. "Thank you for using

Lenz Care today. I see this is your first visit. It's only been two days since you activated your Lenz. How are you enjoying the experience?"

"To be honest, I'm a bit disorientated at times."

"Did you watch the welcome video? Did you know you can adjust your settings?"

"I've played around with those. But the resolution at the edge of my vision is too strong, or maybe it's deteriorating."

"I see. I'm just going to check your eye's structure and pressure, so I can analyze these while we talk. Please keep your eyes open and look forward. Are you ready?"

Yoshi consented, and a bright, pin-prink of light flashed in each eye, followed by a soft blow into each one.

"I think it's just my Mirage," he suggested. "Maybe it needs recalibrating or something?"

"I see. Your eye structure and pressure are normal. Please tell me more about what you're experiencing?"

"Well, when my Mirage first resolved, everything looked beautiful, clean and sharp, like the world had been airbrushed. And then everything started to look more forested, like the city was a giant island. It's beautiful, but the effect is blurring the edge of my vision, and it's making me bump into things. Is this normal?"

"I see. Let me explain how the Lenz works with your eyes. Although most objects you see day-to-day are a distance away from you, the Lenz generates an overlay that sits close to your eye, so the eye constantly switches between long and short focus. This can cause dizziness, or visual discomfort, and take a little while to adjust to. Your Mirage increases how much of your view is overlaid, replicating more of the real world. So, it doesn't just brighten and enhance, it adds detail that it creates itself, which does require more focus on the overlay close to your eye. Adjustment takes from two to three weeks. After six to seven weeks, if you ever deactivate your Lenz, decompressing from this view can take a while. That's why we recommend keeping your Lenz, and your Mirage, continuously activated."

"But is my Mirage just going to keep intensifying? It's not quite what I imagined it would do."

"So, it's not showing you the Mirage you expected? How do you imagine the world should be?"

Reminded of Kai asking him a similar question, Yoshi's frustration began to simmer.

"I just expected the Lenz to show me, without me thinking about it. Isn't that what the algorithms are for? So we don't have to imagine it ourselves?"

"The Lenz Mirage is very powerful. It deeply analyses your online profile data and merges it with your viewing behavior to understand what you really want to see."

"I know how it works, but I'm pretty sure I don't envision the world disappearing."

As soon as he said it, Yoshi realized his Mirage showed him exactly how he feared the world would be—a repeat of his island home slowly succumbing to a determined nothingness, as if being eaten by invisible Algorlines.

"Look, I just want the whole deterioration thing to stop."

"Certainly, Mr. Goto. I can help you with that today. I have reset your Mirage to a lower influence and slowed its increase to give you more adjustment time. Also, I'm sharing with you some recommended daily Lenz-based exercises. Please follow these for one week. Would you like me to reactivate your Mirage now?"

"Okay."

"Your Mirage mode has been reactivated. If your issues persist, please visit a Vision Bar to consult a human Lenzist. Thank you for using Lenz Care today."

The aperture graphics vanished, and the dark overlay dissolved. As he pulled off the goggles, a notification appeared in the top right of his Lenz, and the eye-exercises downloaded. Outside, the world was again lustrous in color and shine, but the island effect was gone, and the blur with it.

****

The next day, Naomi showed the cast the CGI version of the parachuting scene with a test-infusion of their characters. Then, Lavinda went into more detail about how the film and the Maya District experience would work together.

"At Nebulae, we want to give the audience a tantalizing hint of the district's mixed-reality potential. The final scene of the trailer will be the parachuting scene. As your characters land on stage, the trailer will end, and the actoids will step out from behind a cloaked wall as if they just parachuted in."

Yoshi's mouth went dry. "The actoids are going on stage at Nebula?"

"Of course."

"But what about us, the cast?"

Yoshi looked around at the others, but no one seemed to care they weren't getting an appearance. Naomi looked to Lavinda for support.

"Nebulae panels are short sessions," Lavinda explained, "and we have a strict agenda. We want to keep the focus on the technology."

"But Nebulae was… I thought that was when I, or we…"

The foundation of his plans crumbled beneath him, but he refused to give up hope. While the actoids continued to malfunction, he had a chance. It was all he had.

Over the following two weeks, and much to Yoshi's great glee, Naomi continued to struggle with the actoids, the pressure of fixing them draining her face to a gaunt mask. During one session, she fed the cast's performances directly into the actoids, so that they moved around the immersion room like remote-controlled people. But the very next day, the Dhven actoid stalled.

Inspired by the persistence of their glitching, Yoshi immersed himself in the gamut of emotional performance, like an understudy secretly praying for the lead to be hit by an auto-bus. He looped scenes of *One Man Dreaming* in the corner of his Lenz each day and obsessively rehearsed Joe Joe's mannerisms.

Day-to-day life took on a numb but promising cast as he surrendered to the acting-for-scanning and its relentless schedule. He began to enjoy not having to think or choose. He just had to do as he was told and stay focused—like an actoid that didn't glitch.

Although his dialed-down Mirage gave him less trouble, he practiced a few of the exercises anyway, setting aside twenty minutes a day. The island-ification didn't return, and the Mirage's effect remained limited to painting the world with its surreal sheen.

His friendship with Leon grew. But Leon refused to believe there wasn't something going on between him and Kai. He replaced his flirtations with an uncomplicated, brotherly mentorship, allowing Yoshi to focus on learning how to set up his channel. Both grateful and disappointed, Yoshi soaked up Leon's experience.

In his limited spare time, Yoshi reached out to agents. Although he gained no in-person exposure, the growing marketing for *Dreams For All* bumped up his Sight, and Leon shared videos of himself with Yoshi on his own channel, driving Yoshi's Sight to almost 20 million. Yoshi still had to define a unique angle, since he couldn't use the Joe Joe connection, but, eventually, an agency on the west side responded to his queries and said they'd consider representing him if his Sight reached 50 million.

Tora's calls grew less frequent. As much as Yoshi missed his virtual *yujin's* personality and banter, he viewed the fewer calls as a good sign for his Outlook. And, he thought, perhaps it was time he made more friends in the real world.

Exactly, exactly!

Maya completed its pristinely, monochromatic suburbia by the sea-wall, but there were no more protests at the sky bridge or New Gate. The few times Yoshi's mind strayed to Kai, he told himself to let sleeping dogs lie.

By the morning of 15th December, the day before Nebulae, he received word from Gray that the Santa issue had been 'taken care of.' His Sight sat just shy of 50 million, and, to his great delight, he arrived at the studio to find the Joe Joe actoid facing the wall. Lavinda had no choice but to book Yoshi and the others for Nebulae.

That night, lying in bed, he imagined walking onto a real stage, in the real world, and to real cheering. The exposure would surely ramp up his profile and catapult him back into the industry's consciousness.

Proud of how far he'd come since the Santa incident, he imagined his Grandpapa acting out one of his stories until he drifted to sleep with a smile on his face.

Nebulae

He woke early, tiny maracas of nervous excitement shaking under his skin. As he pulled on Joe Joe's yellow t-shirt—trying not to think how much better it would fit his actoid doppelgänger—Tora's bright, smiling face appeared in his Lenz.

"Hey, Chief. Today's the day!"

"Exactly, exactly!"

"How are you feeling?"

"I'm excited."

"You deserve this, Yoshi. You didn't give up and there you are. Just remember that."

"Thanks, Tora."

"You look good. You look fresh."

That was an AI lie and he knew it. He saw the evidence in the mirror—stubborn dark circles under his eyes from late nights in the orbs. But nothing would tarnish his Outlook. After more pep talk, Tora wished him good fortune, and Yoshi headed to the lobby.

As he made his way outside to the waiting pod, he played a scene from *One Man Dreaming* in the corner of his Lenz. He tensed his back and shoulders, moving in rhythm with Joe Joe in the video. So immersed in the dynamic swagger, Yoshi's shoulder collided with someone passing by, knocking them both sideways. Catching his balance, he looked over to see a familiar, sun-weathered face.

Singlets.

Yoshi flushed with embarrassment and stumbled out an apology. Singlets appeared unperturbed, as if waiting for Yoshi to be silent. In one hand, he held what looked like a stack of flyers. He pushed one into Yoshi's open palm.

"Oh, no thanks," Yoshi stammered, pushing the flyer back.

But Singlets closed Yoshi's hand over it and walked off. The wind rose and the flyer fluttered in Yoshi's fist like a trapped bird. He unfolded the crumpled paper to see a sketch of the stick-torch with a hand-written message underneath:

Ceremony of Luma,
Underground Parking Garage,
December Full Moon.
Shine your light.

The last words lit him up with a lighthouse flash, like his Grandpapa had spoken from beyond the grave. He peered through the crowd again, but Singlets was gone. Joe Joe shouted from the video player in his

Lenz, and he stuffed the flyer into his pocket to weave through the pedestrian traffic to the pod.

"Good morning, Mr. Goto," Driver said, as Yoshi climbed in. "Wonderful Day."

The pod pulled out from the curb, and Yoshi paused *One Man Dreaming* to have another look at the flyer. The flame of the torch appeared to move as he pressed out the creases. A check of his calendar told him the December Full Moon fell on the 23rd—the same day as the premier.

Good luck getting any Sight that night.

But the synchronicity of the events, and his Grandpapa's words on the flyer, filled him with curiosity.

"Driver, can you tell me anything about a Ceremony of Luma?"

A column of search results listed in the pod's window, mainly 'luminescent' beauty products and services, but nothing related to the islanders. He searched directly for 'Minaki refugees', and a small article displayed with a map of an archipelago.

ABOUT THE MINAKI

The Minaki, translating roughly to 'sea light,' are a resilient and private people of the Agushi Archipelago, a micro nation in the North Pacific Ocean. Surviving the Shift's tsunamis, the Minaki remained on the higher grounds of

Agu-shi. In 2039, however, the continuing rise in ocean levels forced them toward mainland Japan where they are currently seeking refuge.

It is believed the Minaki once lived permanently at sea, but their exact origins remain unclear. They were vehemently private when on their archipelago and denied all anthropological visits to better understand them. However, during trading, they spoke openly about their beliefs and enquired as much about others.

While inhabiting Agu-shi, the Minaki lived a harmonious and self-sufficient lifestyle as fisher and crafts people and were diligent traders even as the shorelines changed. They spent four to five hours per day working to ensure their survival and traded only for what they needed for food and shelter. Although they resisted the use of modern tools or technology, they showed a great knack for understanding electrical equipment when assisting stranded vessels.

Their own language is distinct, yet, from their years of trading and interacting with other cultures, they developed a basic understanding of various other languages.

DAILY LIFE & BELIEFS
Their social structure appears egalitarian, with importance placed on kinship and reciprocal labor rather than following any formal authority.

The Minaki have expressed a rich culture of ritual and ceremony, the heart of which is the shore, "where the sea trades with the land." Trading itself has been an important ceremony to the Minaki—not only for the benefits of exchange, but as a means for the transference of what they call *luma*. They describe *luma* as a form of 'soul energy' which 'flows through time as well as space and between life and death'. Maintaining the flow of *luma* between others, they believe, can be an antidote to grief and rivalry.

Even the Minaki's leisure activities and daily rituals appear to have a ceremonial quality about them, for they believe respect and gratitude for each moment helps *luma* flow. They do not recognize borders as walls, or death as an end, but both as passageways for *luma* to migrate in all directions.

There is a type of shamanic role, known as the *Taka*, that conducts ceremonies believed to be for various purposes including reconciliation, healing, and connecting with the dead—but always, essentially, to maintain the flow of *luma*. The role of *Taka* is constantly rotated through each tribe member, including children of a very young age, as "everyone must be *Taka* at different times."

Yoshi ran a finger over the creased torch again. Thinking of the peaceful faces he'd seen in the underground and the energy he'd felt from them, he held a new reverence for the city's unofficial guests. Oddly, knowing more about them surprised him with a humbling calm, rather than filling him with guilt for being involved with Maya. He folded the flyer with ritualistic care and returned it to his pocket.

With a clear mind, he turned his attention to his artistic preparation. He performed several rounds of facial exercises, followed by vocal warm-ups. By the time he had his vocal chords vibrating like bee wings, and his jaw pivoting like a well-oiled hinge, Driver announced their approach to High Palace.

"ETA, 2 minutes."

Through the front window, the three-story high cube loomed ahead, nestled among taller, gleaming towers. His heart beat like a drum. But as the pod veered left into the entrance road, it was forced to slow due to a thick, flowering bush that appeared to have grown across the road.

"Obstruction ahead," announced Driver. "Slowing to pass safely."

An angry murmur emerged from outside as the pod neared the out-of-place bush. Yoshi suspected an effect of the Mirage just as a branch thumped the window. The bush illusion dissolved into a chanting group of sign-wielding protesters spilling onto the road. Another sign banged the window and pressed against the glass.

"Turn off! Wake up!"

The sign pulled away to reveal an angry and familiar face.

Raiden.

Yoshi banged the window in return and shouted at Raiden what to do with his sign.

"Please don't be alarmed, Mr. Goto," said Driver. "The doors are secure, and the glass is tinted to protect your privacy. We'll be through in a moment."

The pod slipped out from the group and left the chanting behind. The flowering bush illusion returned as if the group was never there. But Raiden's bang on the window echoed in Yoshi's mind.

Fraud. Fraud. Fraud.

Furious that Raiden had upset his morning serenity, Yoshi forced himself to breathe deep and slow. The pod wove up through the exhibition hall's tiered parking garage until it settled into a vacant spot. Yoshi climbed out and took a calming moment.

"Yoshi?" called Gray, standing by an open emergency door. A neon sign above illuminated the part in his hair with albino scar translucence. He waved Yoshi over. "Ready for the big day?"

Yoshi pushed Raiden out of his mind and nodded with enthusiasm. "Let's do this."

"Good man. I'm taking the scenic entry. Walk with me."

Gray led him through a series of corridors to another emergency door. As he pushed it open, light splashed through with a booming roar. Yoshi followed him out onto a metal walkway overlooking the main hall and was struck by absolute awe.

Thousands of attendees, dressed in outrageously exaggerated character costumes—both real and augmented—wove through a vast, three-level, transparent maze of walls, floors and stairways. Through the center of all three levels rose a giant glass column where Cosplayers posed mid-air, kept aloft by wind machines, while media drones buzzed around them like flies.

On the ground level, dense pockets crowded the many viewing platforms and merchandising alleys. Mechanical antennae, sharp wings and giant swords bumped against each other among virtual smoke, flares and magic spells. Security rovers on exo-stilts—costumed as some sort of panda-human hybrid—kept a watchful eye as they giraffed through the crowd.

"Look at them all," Gray said, leaning his elbows on the rail and making his familiar finger pyramid. "Thanks to Shibido's technological advances, this is now the largest pop culture convention in Asia. Hundreds of thousands flock here to immerse themselves in fantasy. But they don't just copy characters, they evolve them, merge with them. They blur the line between audience and fantasy and dive straight into the blur. And they can't get enough. They want the magic all around them, every day, not just in their vision, but here,"—Gray banged the railing—"intertwined with reality, so they don't have to return to the disappointment of real life."

"Maya District will give them that," Yoshi said, cringing at how greasy his kowtowing sounded.

"And that's why they'll stay for the launch. But they'll tire of the Stratodel concept and want more."

Yoshi felt compelled to add something more intelligent to the conversation. "Perhaps they want more… meaningful stories, not so formulaic."

Gray's face twisted into a mask of disgust.

"Are you unhinged? People follow formulae so they don't have to think or remember. I'm talking about Maya District adapting and evolving into whatever story a Lenzer's Mirage mode resolves specifically for them. The district will be a holographic universe of multiple worlds existing simultaneously in the one place, all changing over time. What more could they want?"

The mayhem below danced its colors in his eyes. Yoshi suddenly wondered what Gray might have lost in the tsunami. As if sensing his mind being probed, Gray clapped his hands together with a bang.

"Oh, listen to me, getting ahead of myself and missing the moment. There's no time for that. It's Nebulae!"

He took off along the balcony. Yoshi raced to keep up as he followed him down a circular stairway. They came out into a long corridor, Leon's laughter echoing from an open room at the end. Gray wished him good luck, and then he took off in the other direction.

Entering the small room, Yoshi found Leon and the others sitting around a table littered with water bottles and wrapped sandwiches. The waterfall murmur of the expo's crowd came through a closed door on the back wall. Excitement bat its wings in Yoshi's chest.

"Ready for the big day, Dizzy?" Leon said, greeting him with a hug.

"So ready."

As he greeted the others, Lavinda burst through the door.

"Great, you're all here. We've had a change of schedule. We're on first."

"What?" demanded Dax, a freshly unwrapped sandwich in his lap. "*The Badminton Vampires* and *Sherlock and Hyde* are meant to go on before us."

"There's a protest on the talent's entry road, and the Vampires have been held up. Attendance at the stage is at full capacity, and we've been told to go on."

"Let's get it over with," said Dax, tossing his sandwich onto the table.

Lavinda pushed open the door at the rear of the room, and the crowd noise that flooded in vibrated the air. She ushered them into a long, narrow room, and Yoshi's skin tingled.

Finally, a chance to reconnect with an audience, to reignite my shine—

But what he saw inside the room snuffed out his excitement.

A shimmering one-way holo-wall to his left separated the room from the stage, where a seething crowd hoarded at its edge. But between him and the screen stood the five actoids, facing the crowd, ready to walk through the holo-wall. And on the right side sat the five orbs.

Leon play-punched his shoulder. "You okay, Dizzy?"

"I thought we were going on stage," he whispered.

"This is as real as it gets, bro."

"But that leaves us just the autographing session to connect with fans."

Naomi handed them their anti-nausea pills and again gave two to Yoshi. Swamped by disappointment, he closed his hand over them like a robot, unable to stop staring at Joe Joe's back.

A clap behind startled him, and Lavinda's tone sharpened.

"Right, everyone, a serious note. Before we begin, I must remind you all of the confidentiality terms of your contract. If you find yourself struggling with your role in assisting Maya today in presenting the actoid technology as ready, I ask you to dig deep into your sensibilities and remind yourself that your final payments are tied to your adherence to the non-disclosure agreement. Does anyone have any issues fulfilling their obligations today?"

No one vocalized any and Yoshi's head still reeled as he tried to pivot from his shock. Lavinda positioned herself by Naomi and clapped her hands again.

"Right, then, everyone in the orbs. We're on in fifteen. This will be just how you played it out during scanning. After Gray shows the *Dreams For All* trailer, ending on the parachuting scene, you'll walk your actoid through the holo-wall and onto the markers. From then, follow Gray's lead. When question time comes, I'll feed you the replies. Repeat them as I tell them, and we'll get through this just fine. For those of you experiencing any nerves, just remember that character is more important than talent."

Yoshi didn't find Lavinda's words as reassuring as she seemed to think they were. In fact, for a split moment, he almost gave into his frustration and stormed out. But his climbing Sight—now 52 million—glowed in the corner of his vision. He gulped down the pills and trudged through the mud of his setback to climb into the orb.

Strapping in, his view transformed into Joe Joe's perspective of a blue, monochromatic view of the seething crowd.

"Any problems for anyone, hmm?" Naomi asked, her voice slightly quivering. "No? Start bringing out those characters."

Yoshi forced himself to focus, mining deep to transform his disappointment into Joe Joe's forceful stride. After several minutes, a small screen appeared in the top left of his view showing Gray walk on stage and past a long table to stand in front of the holo-wall. A thunderous roar vibrated the floor and orbs as the fans cheered, rebooting Yoshi's excitement. Behind Gray, the words *One Man Dreaming* displayed on the holo-wall.

"Wonderful Day to you all. Thank you for coming. As you know, the *One Man Dreaming* franchise has had a revamp. But this is just part of a whole new dimension of immersive entertainment that you'll soon get to escape into. But first, what you've all come here for. Let's do this."

The crowd cheered as the lights dimmed, leaving the title *One Man Dreaming* floating in darkness. The words shimmered and then reformed into *Dreams For All*. The crowd whooped and hooted, but they quickly settled as the trailer began.

After several minutes of loud action and snappy one-liners, the trailer reached its crescendo with the parachute scene.

"You're on-stage in thirty-seconds," Naomi advised.

Color flooded Yoshi's view of the room, signaling his actoid was active.

"Forward in five," Lavinda continued, as Gray introduced the cast.

"And now," shouted Gray, "for the first time ever —"

"—four—"

"—the next generation of actors—"

"—three—"

"—and your guides to the Maya District experience—"

"—two—"

"Maya's actoids."

The holo-screen showed the five characters landing, and the crowd erupted. Yoshi's heart pounded double-time, drumming out any remnant of his disappointment.

"—one."

Yoshi stepped his actoid through the Joe Joe in the holo-wall. The crowd's whistling and clapping went berserk, the power of their raw excitement shaking the stage. Swing-cameras on the ceiling zoomed up and swung crazily overhead.

Overwhelmed by the fans' number, and their fervent welcome, a faint dizziness teased Yoshi's balance, but he stood firm.

As Gray boasted the actoid technology, the crowd calmed down and gazed in wide wonder. Intermingled among the front row were fans wearing virtual Joe Joe masks, three different versions of Batman, and a familiar glistening bald head—the punk girl from the travelator whose MR goggles got zapped by the scrambler.

Gray wrapped up the intro and gestured to the cast to take their seats at the table for question time. A sea of hands shot up. Gray pointed to the punk girl in the front row.

"Hi, I'm Nina Fuji. This question is for Leon. If you're playing yourself in a fictional world, how much of your character is really you?"

As Leon answered with something about becoming stuck in the Fourth Wall, a tall woman squeezed into the front row next to Nina. Costumed as Ripley from Alien, complete with curly wig and navy jumpsuit, the woman eyed Yoshi from behind an alien-crustacean mask. The back of his neck itched.

"Thank you, Nina," Gray said, as hands returned to the air. "You there, Batman."

"Hi," the three Batmen replied in chorus, much to the crowds' amusement.

"I'm sorry," Gray replied. "I meant the Batman from Batman Begins."

After the right Batman expressed how much he hoped "the sequel doesn't suck," Gray took another fifteen minutes of questions and comments. As they flew out from the eager crowd like paper airplanes, Lavinda fed the cast their answers just as fast.

"Okay, we got time for one more." Gray pointed to the tall woman. "You there, Ripley."

Although muffled by the mask, the tall woman's voice held a disturbing familiarity.

"I'm just wondering why you made this Joe Joe as stiff as the original."

The crowd burst into laughter. Paranoia rushed blood to Yoshi's head so fast he felt like he'd been microwaved.

"Hey, hey," Gray interjected. "That's not Nebulae. We respect artists and each other here."

"Laugh it off, Goto," commanded Lavinda.

But Ripley wasn't finished. "Well, how do we know these robots aren't remote controlled?"

Yoshi froze, and Joe Joe with him. He feared the whole crowd could see through Joe Joe's eyes and spy him puppeteering from the orb. Their laughter became cackles, and the lights reflected in their glaring eyes transformed them into a ravenous cat people, reminding him how devotedly they could love, and how terribly they could turn.

"Just laugh, Dizzy," Leon whispered, nudging Joe Joe's back.

"Hello?" Ripley heckled over the awkward pause. "You in there?"

Raiden.

Sharp anger twisted Yoshi's insides and snapped him out of his paralysis.

"How 'bout I come down there and show you just how real I am?"

The crowd exploded into cheers. Raiden's eyes narrowed, but the crowd was too loud for him to respond.

"That's not what exactly I meant," whispered Leon, "but they seem to like it."

Gray quickly regained control of the crowd by touting the source novel's achievements, as if they could be attributed to *Dreams For All*. Then he wrapped up by teasing the audience one more time about Maya District.

"Before we go, my friends, I'd like to leave you with a thought. Imagine, one moment you're walking along the street in Low Ground, the next thing, Joe Joe appears, or maybe it's Leon, asking you to help them get to the Stratodel. For fun, you accept, and within minutes you are being chased by mysterious strangers, solving impossible conundrums and exploring fantastic landscapes. Logic tries to remind you that what you see and feel is not real, but your heart is pounding and your skin tingles with adrenalin. You choose to stream your experience live, or you have it recorded and edited into your own film. And you come back, again and again, and soon you don't know or care what's real or what isn't, because there's no longer any difference. That, my friends, is Maya District, premiering with *Dreams For All* on the 23rd December. We do hope you'll join us."

Gray bowed to the final applause as the lights dimmed.

Leon nudged Yoshi. "That's our queue."

As Yoshi followed the others, he glanced back into the dispersing fans. A gap formed, and there Raiden stood, smiling from behind the crustacean mask. He turned and headed toward the main exit and was swallowed up by the crowd.

As soon as his actoid was behind the holo-wall, Yoshi yanked off the goggles and harness and jumped out of the orb. Lavinda appeared like black magic in front of him.

"Why didn't you do as I say? Why didn't you just laugh?"

"What is your problem with me?" he snapped, having enough of her constant, whiny negativity.

"You're going to ruin this for all of us. Again."

"What do you mean, 'again?'"

"You ruined *One Man Dreaming* for the whole crew. I was part of that crew."

Face to face with his past, Yoshi's breath stuck. But he was so damn sick of feeling bad about it, that, for a wild moment, he almost punched Lavinda in her face. But Dax broke the tension.

"Nice work, Yoshi," he said with genuine admiration.

"Nailed it," agreed Jenya.

"Great work, Lavinda," Leon added.

Yoshi clenched his fists and dug his nails into his palms. Lavinda glared at him until she finally huffed, spun on her heel, and headed over to Naomi.

Leon appeared by Yoshi's side and patted him on the shoulder. "Don't let it get to you, Dizzy. It's never easy in the virtual."

But getting acting advice from a damn Livey was the last straw. Yoshi's taut hold on his anger snapped, and he stormed out the side door to the main floor.

"Dizzy," Leon shout-whispered, "don't be stu—"

But the door swung shut on the rest of Leon's warning.

Trouble

Too mad to realize he was dressed as Joe Joe in the yellow t-shirt from the original film—and therefore risking drawing attention—Yoshi shoved his way through the crowd toward the main entrance, hunting down Ripley with predator determination.

The swirling crowd thickened into a moving wall, forcing him to meerkat over the sea of costumes. On the other side of a knot in the crowd, a big, black, curly wig bobbed between merchandising stalls, but was slowed by the congestion. He force-squeezed through the bottleneck and gained ground.

"Raiden!"

The wig spun around, and Raiden's eyes shone bright with surprise from behind the alien mask. Yoshi lunged for his jumpsuit, but Raiden darted sideways and slipped like a snake back into the seething crowd. Yoshi pushed in after him, following the bouncing curls as his prey diverted toward the corner of the hall. Suddenly, the wig vanished, and the current of the crowd forced Yoshi into a queuing area by the toilets.

"Hey, you," shouted a voice from high behind. "No line jumping."

A panda-man rover on exo-stilts lurched toward him. Yoshi nodded an apology and headed in the opposite direction, hiding behind a first-aid shed. Behind him, the rover lingered, peering across the crowd in his direction.

Damn.

The abrupt end to his chase cooled the flare of his anger, but he'd lost his bearings. He scanned the vicinity for a way to get back to the change room before he got himself into trouble.

To the left of the shed, a short alley ended at a set of stairs leading up to the viewing balcony, but its gate looked locked. He loaded the hall's floor plan in his Lenz to get directions, when a gap in the crowd opened up in front of him. But as he stepped toward it, the rover lurched toward him again.

"Hey, come here."

Crap!

He pulled back in behind the shed and glanced at the stairs again. A flash of fluorescent orange caught his eye as a short figure ducked under the stairs and pulled open a door hidden in the shadows. Yoshi did a double-take.

Was that the boy?

Escaping the rover, he darted down the alley to find the door easing itself shut. He pushed it open into a dimly lit concrete hall that stretched back to where a *To Pod Parking Area* sign pointed around a corner. Air rushed loudly above through exposed ventilation pipes in the ceiling. He let the door auto-shut behind to look down the other direction, and he froze. Twenty yards away, someone—*the boy?*—crouched by an opening in the wall. But they were too big to be a six-year-old, and the orange Yoshi had glimpsed wasn't the boy's bright shirt but some sort of high-vis overalls. Yoshi blinked, thinking his Lenz was playing tricks. A pair of large cutters clunked to the floor next to the stranger. When the stranger turned to reach for them, their face moved into the light, and shock knocked Yoshi back a step.

"Kai?" He had to shout, his voice almost disappearing in the din of the ventilation.

Kai squinted as he casually hid the cutters inside the wall opening. His eyes widened with panicked disbelief.

"Yoshi?"

Curiosity—and gravitational remnants of their initial attraction—moved Yoshi's feet forward.

"What are you doing here?"

"I'm doing maintenance, it's my new job."

Yoshi snorted. "How can you suddenly have a maintenance job?"

Kai stood up and faced Yoshi with a nostril-wave.

"How can you suddenly have a job with Maya?"

Yoshi blushed hard. "I'm just doing it to get ahead."

"Raiden said you'd say that. That's what everybody says."

Yoshi fumed at hearing Raiden's name. He stormed up to Kai to see what was in the open panel — two floor-to-ceiling computer mainframes sat at ninety-degrees to the wall, lights twitching across the bays. He glanced at the cutters Kai was trying to hide.

"What is this, Kai?"

Kai seemed to lose the ability to speak. He just stood there, his fingers white with their grip around the cutters.

"Did Raiden tell you to do this? Are you trying to sabotage my film?"

Kai snapped out of his paralysis and rolled his eyes.

"Your film? The world doesn't revolve around you, Yoshi."

"I didn't mean that, I meant…Is this seriously how you think you're going to make a difference?"

Kai lifted his chin defiantly and stepped closer to Yoshi.

"Is that what you think your little movie will do? Make a difference?"

Something metallic clunked behind Yoshi, startling him to glance back. Kai smirked.

"You're in trouble again, aren't you?"

"*You're* trouble. You're—"

Another clunk, followed by a metallic squeal as the door swung open halfway. Kai ducked inside the opened panel and yanked Yoshi in next to him. He slid the panel shut, forcing them to squeeze into the tight space between the servers, their cheeks only a breath apart. The humming circuit boards vibrated through their muscles, syncing their bodies with a jiggling buzz. As Kai slipped a hand free and put a warning finger to the bow of his lips, his familiar pine scent stirred Yoshi inappropriately. Flustered by erotic claustrophobia, he wriggled to get comfortable, but stopped abruptly as his crotch rubbed against Kai's. It was excruciatingly awkward and wonderful.

"Stop that," Kai whispered.

"Stop what?"

"You're squashing me. I can't move."

"I can't move either."

The approaching clunk-clunk of boots on concrete—barely noticeable over the ventilation noise—froze them both. Their hearts pounded at each other through their chests, like two prisoners trying to communicate through a common wall.

As Kai stared intently at the panel and waited for the footsteps to pass, the red and green power lights showcased his handsomeness. Involuntarily, Yoshi's eyelids snapped like a paparazzi's camera. He turned away, but he could see, in his peripheral Kai glancing back at him. Their breathing grew heavier, and Kai's chest pressed against Yoshi's like a set of waves against the sea-wall.

"Stop staring at me," Yoshi said after the footsteps had passed by.

But Kai didn't look away, and his eyes drew Yoshi deeper into the booby-trapped moment with tractor beam intensity.

"Your heart is racing."

"Be quiet. They'll hear us."

"What are you scared of?" His hot breath stroked Yoshi's lips.

"I'm not scared."

Kai glanced at Yoshi's mouth and then back into his eyes. Yoshi did the same. A smile teased the corner of Kai's lips, and Yoshi's pores tingled. Sweat beaded across his skin, and Kai's too, as if their bodies had decided some sort of lubrication might be required.

"You like me because I'm trouble."

"I don't need any more trouble."

"Then why do you keep running after it?"

A twitch in his groin, or was it Kai's?

"I don't, I…"

Kai stunned him with a kiss. His glasses pressed into Yoshi's cheek, but the marshmallow softness of his lips melted Yoshi into the moment and shot signals of surrender through his body. Their breathing synched—Yoshi in, Kai out—their chests riding each other, breathing through the one lung of the absurd, passionate moment. With every tremor, every slow deep inhalation, their bodies pressed further into each other's, vaporizing any negative space between them, and lulling them further into careless trouble.

The footsteps returned and stopped right outside the panel. Their lips froze mid-pucker. Yoshi could almost feel the guard's presence only an arm's length away. But the ventilation system in the corridor's ceiling masked their micro-sounds, and the footsteps moved on. Seconds later, the metal door down the corridor squealed open again and then banged shut.

Their lips parted with a glacial withdraw, and Kai's bottom lip snapped back with a jiggle. He smiled and twitched his nose. Yoshi inhaled his scent deeply again, staring into his eyes, and leaned forward for another kiss. But Kai's watch flashed a startling white light into their eyes. They both jerked in response and bonked heads.

Kai shoved the panel door aside with his free hand and squeezed out. Yoshi stumbled out after, struggling for something to say, when a message from Leon appeared in his Lenz.

Where are you? Autographing about to start.

An incoming call icon from Leon flashed at the same time.

"Crap," Yoshi said, holding up a finger to Kai, asking him to wait a minute. But Kai was staring at his own watch, his face filled with concern.

"Where *are* you, bro?" said Leon.

"I'm on way," he lied, glancing down the hall in both directions. A sign at the corridor's corner behind him read *To Backstage Area*. "I'll be there in five minutes."

"What were you *thinking*, Dizzy?"

Kai paced in a circle, his watch flashing a second and third time, and his frown twisting with panic.

"Leon, I gotta call you back—"

"What if someone saw you come out where the actoids went in? You weren't part of that security issue, were you?"

Yoshi eyed Kai. "What security issue?"

"Some protesters caused a fight at the front gate. Lucky for you, 'cause it delayed our autographing session, but it's starting soon. You gotta get back ASAP."

Kai looked up and mouthed four words silently:

I've got to go.

His eyes seemed to say something else that Yoshi couldn't decipher. Then he winked and ran down the corridor and past the *To Pod Parking Area* sign. Instinctively, Yoshi ran after him, but Leon's voice called him to a stop.

"Yoshi, you there?"

As the kissing bandit disappeared around the corner, a small sphere of emptiness opened inside Yoshi, as if Kai had run off with a treasure they'd only just unearthed together. His skin and lips still tingled, and his heart banged his chest to chase the invisible force that made it beat faster. Surprised by his intense response to the kiss, he lingered in the thrill, afraid that letting it go might damn any future impossibilities.

"You there?" Leon shouted.

"I'm coming, I'm coming."

He peeled himself away from the sticky moment and raced in the opposite direction.

"And just to give you a little motivation to get your ass back here faster," Leon said, "check your profile."

"What?"

"*Check your profile.*"

As Yoshi raced around the corner toward the backstage area, he blinked to open his personal actor profile—his Sight had reached a mad 88 million.

"People streamed the trailer and panel," Leon explained. "Joe Joe's response—*your* response—got so much attention, new fans started digging into the film's history. Ripley did you a favor. All that in the last twenty minutes."

Yoshi couldn't believe it. It was happening. But what good was it now if he had to compete with actoids?

Leon swore. "Lavinda's asking for you. We're going on in five."

"Crap." Yoshi skidded to a halt at an unsigned intersection. "I think I'm lost."

"Just hurry *up*," Leon shout-whispered and ended the call.

Yoshi took a deep breath, gambled on right, and ran as fast as he could.

As he left the noise of the ventilated area behind, he tried to reconcile the maelstrom of emotions swirling inside him. His heart refused to apply rational thought to accidentally running into Kai for a second time, but his pride knew only anger to protect itself against the indignity of Kai running off. And too many embers burned throughout his body for logic or ego to extinguish—he had to force himself not to think about what would have happened had they been stuck in the cupboard much longer. Even if they could barely move in there, he knew, given another minute, their sweating bodies would have Houdini-ed something.

The corridor took another sharp right and left.

He sensed the distance stretching between him and Kai, sling-shotting them back to the ends of their opposite trajectories. That was a fact he couldn't deny. And another fact—his life had been in a whirlpool since meeting Kai, with Kai always in some antagonizing cameo appearance in some different drama.

Logic was formulating a damn good argument.

Anyway, how many second chances can someone get?

He had this one chance, and somehow, he was doing it, he was pumping up his Sight. If the sea had taught him one thing, it was don't look back, because there wouldn't be anything left.

His angry, proud mind won out, and his heart let out a final whine as it curled up on its lonely bed.

An incoming call from Lavinda popped up in his view as another unmarked intersection appeared ahead. He swiped to decline the call as he went left and spotted a neon exit sign above double door.

Yes!

Racing to a halt at the door, he paused to hear muffled voices from the other side. Desperate to not miss the autographing, he eased the door open and peered out into a large hall filled with costumed attendees. Messy queues lead toward the opposite wall, and to his left, the main stage beckoned through an opening at the end. If he could get to the stage, he could slip back through the side door into the change room and find his way to the autographing hall.

He wove through the crowded lines toward the opening—at least the room's ceiling was too low for any stilt-walking security. Halfway across the room, a guy as tall as a road sign—wearing gold-plated goggles and a leather aviation cap—stepped in front of him.

"Is that an original Joe Joe shirt? Can I get a pic with you?"

"Ah, sorry, I'm in a hurry," Yoshi began, then automatically sucked in his stomach as the man leaned in for a selfie anyway.

"Nice one," the stranger said.

Yoshi turned to move on, but a short, middle-aged woman shuffled in his way. With her orange bob and bandage-style costume barely holding her dignity in place, she looked like a Leeloo from *The Fifth Element* who had let herself go. She gazed up at him through eyes bronzed with black and orange eye shadow.

"I just gotta ask, are you the *real* Joe Joe? You look… you look like he would look now. Like, *real*."

Steampunk guy turned around.

"Yoshi Goto? I was just reading about you."

The woman squealed with delight.

"It *is* you!"

As she snuggled into Yoshi's side to take her own selfie, Steampunk Guy bombarded him with questions about *One Man Dreaming*. Yoshi remained professional while looking for an escape, and he noticed the words *Dreams For All* gracing the pillars on the back wall. He suddenly realized what the crowd was lining up for—he was already in the autographing hall.

"Wonderful Day to you both," he said, slipping away toward the front of the lines.

"Bye, Yoshi Goto!" Leeloo called after him.

Another man, wearing Princess Leia's slave outfit from *Return of The Jedi*, cocked his head at hearing Yoshi's name.

"It's Yoshi Goto," said He-Leia to his friends, "the original Joe Joe."

Within seconds, a throng of the curious and eager surrounded Yoshi. Appeasing the first few demands for autographs, he squeezed his way toward the front, when a hand grabbed him by the shoulder and yanked him out of the crowd. A muscled security guard pulled him under a rope and into a cordoned-off area.

Leon and the other cast members sat behind a waist-high bench, film posters and pens in front of them. They looked up in unified shock—and admiration.

"We didn't know you were coming in that way, Mr. Goto," said the guard, directing him to the others.

Yoshi took his spot by Leon. The actoid smiled proudly at him.

"Damn, Dizzy, that entrance was genius. What I'm sayin' is, you learn fast." Leon guffawed and slapped him on the back.

The crowd reached back fifty-persons deep. Arms hung over the barriers, reminding Yoshi of the children at the mall. But this time the audience wanted to see *him*. He wished his Grandpapa could see him there, too.

The security guard let the first wide-eyed fan through, and Yoshi's heart stopped—a young boy walked forward, wearing a red, leather Joe Joe jacket, just like the one Yoshi had given to the homeless boy. But the kid smiling up at him was a solid boy, with longe hair. Yoshi breathed again. As he signed the boy's poster, he had a déjà vu of signing the contract in Gray's office.

Nina Fuji, the bald, punk fan, stepped up to Leon with adoring eyes. She glanced once at Yoshi, a brief look of familiarity on her face, but she didn't seem to recognize him from the travelator.

Halfway through the autographing session, Gray appeared at the end of the table. He announced that thirty lucky Cosplayers would join the VIPs at the premier. He randomly selected winners from the crowd—an excited Nina squealed with delight as Gray chose her—then he disappeared backstage again.

After another draining but exhilarating hour, Yoshi and the cast were led backstage. Leon wrapped an arm around him and steered him down the corridor. He frowned and sniffed at Yoshi.

"You smell like a Christmas tree."

Yoshi goose-bumped but didn't reply.

In the back room, Lavinda thanked them all for a job well done, but she didn't approach Yoshi and seemed to avoid eye contact.

"I'd say they're reassessing their plans about you, Dizzy," Leon said. "I'd watch my back if I were you."

But Yoshi was less fearful and more excited by the challenge, as if Kai's kiss had breathed some of his feistiness into him.

At the same time, Yoshi's watch vibrated with a call from Social Services. He almost answered but Leon patted him on the backside.

"Let's celebrate. We're all going to *Unusual Business*."

The call ended, and he followed Leon instead.

***

Over the next five days, activity slowed down at Studio 5. The scanning sessions consisted of minor repeats of small actions and mannerisms. Lavinda never confronted Yoshi about his behavior at Nebulae, and Gray didn't call him in. Yoshi never admitted his arrival at the autographing was an accident, and Leon was certain Gray was waiting to see the effect of Yoshi's 'stunt' before he decided what to do.

Although Yoshi became more focused over the remaining time of his contract, thoughts of Kai had set up camp in the backwaters of his mind. But when Yoshi indulged a peek, his memory of Kai's face was a little blurry. He quickly found reason to forget about

Kai when the actoids disappeared from the orb room, their *yujin* anomalies apparently unresolved.

Tora didn't call over this time—a notification mentioned something to do with a high load on the app's server.

Something to do with crappy tech, more like it.

Leon shared more videos of himself with Yoshi, driving Yoshi's Sight to a staggering 95 million. Media drones followed them around on several occasions, requests for interviews increased, and the west side agent interested in Yoshi locked him in for a meeting after the holidays.

As he raced toward a future full of possibilities blooming over one another like clouds in a time-lapse, his Sight catapulted to 101 million.

On the morning of the 21st December, one day before his expiring contract would free him to speak to agents, a message appeared in his Lenz:

Please attend a priority meeting at 9 a.m., Studio 5

Terms

After a brief hello to Jin at the front gate, Yoshi ran through a sudden downpour to the studio, certain he was about to face the repercussions of his actions at Nebulae. Had he gained enough Sight to secure himself a FOF? What would he do if Gray offered to buy his identity?

Inside the studio, Leon, Jenya, and Otis sat around the table in their customary position—head-back and eyes focused on invisible things. They waved hello at Yoshi without looking up. Dax peeked through a gap between the doors to the immersion room.

"The orbs are gone," he announced, coming back to the table.

"Maybe the whole thing's been canned," Otis joked, but an underlying unease about the 'priority meeting' anchored his kidding.

Lavinda walked in and everyone stood.

"I have good news, people. The scanning is complete. Naomi's patch on the *yujin* has passed all reliability tests; they've assimilated their character libraries beautifully. Your work is done, and the future is here."

Yoshi's gut dropped. "They're fixed?" he asked, his voice squeaking.

"What was wrong with them?" Jenya asked.

"Naomi could better explain it, but, in layman's term, they just thought about everything too much."

"Told you," Dax said to the others, "they were depressed."

"Do we get to see them," asked Otis. "Our clones? Can we see them in action?"

Lavinda shook her head.

"I'm sorry, they're in ongoing preparation for the premier. Now, on behalf of Maya Technologies, I want to thank you all for your hard work. You've done a great job, and you deserve this early finish. The wrap party will remain on the 22nd, but we understand some of you may be leaving the country earlier, now that you can."

"Leaving the country?" Yoshi said, looking round at the others.

"Thanks everyone," Lavinda concluded. "I'll be in touch about the party." She stepped up to Yoshi. "Goto, you did good. You did really good. Gray wants to speak to you in his office."

Stumped by the unexpected praise, and dumbfounded by the abrupt ending to the contract, Yoshi could only stand there and watch the others say goodbye to each other, until Leon came over and hugged him.

"Good luck, Dizzy Man. Maybe we can meet up after the no-contact period."

"What is going on?" he said, pulling back.

"We're all outta here. Part of our contract. My advice to you—take the deal."

Leon squeezed his shoulder and turned to hug Dax. Otis hugged Yoshi at the same time as Jenya ruffled his hair.

"It's been fun, Yoshi. All the best with what's next."

"Yoshi," called Lavinda from the doorway. "I'm sorry, but this is important."

Stuttering goodbyes, he dragged himself away to catch up with Lavinda under the outside awning. He pressed her for more information, but she told him it was a private matter for him and Gray, then she hurried off through the rain.

Pulling his jacket over his head, he crossed the cul-de-sac to the main tower and stepped into the long corridor. Videos on the wall showed the original trailer for *One Man Dreaming*. Joe Joe's face—his face— flashed all around him. As he neared the elevator foyer, the immaculately-dressed *yujin* host stepped from behind its counter.

"Hello, Mr. Goto. Mr. Gray welcomes you. The elevator will take you to level eleven."

No glitching.

The elevator settled to a stop on level eleven and opened with a burst of light. Yoshi stepped into the mirrored foyer, and the panel in the right wall opened, beckoning him down the corridor. He walked through and into the long boardroom, where Gray stood at the far end of the table.

Naomi—looking extremely pleased with herself—sat next to the goateed Uchida twins, who wore the same jackets and shirts they'd worn at the first meeting. Paranoia whispered in Yoshi's ear they might be *yujin*, too.

"There you are, Mr. Goto. Please, come in, take a seat."

Yoshi sat down across from them, and Gray joined, resting his elbows on the table and making his finger pyramid. Another non-disclosure form appeared in the table's glass, and Yoshi signed as Gray began.

"Congratulations on a smashing job, and on your extraordinary Sight. You proved yourself to have some decent pull, beyond what we expected. We, too, have had success. Naomi here, our new Head of Operations, has rectified the issues with our actoid's AI."

Gray paused for Naomi to take some recognition. She blushed and brushed a strand of silver hair from her pale forehead.

"It was simple, really. The *yujin* constantly project future scenarios, based on the probabilities of the present situation, so they can answer questions and act realistically. But they were projecting too far ahead, and the results were too much for their processors to cope with, so they were shutting themselves down. I just limited their projections to more immediate scenarios."

"They were depressed," Gray said, throwing his hands up. "Can you imagine?"

Naomi didn't look Yoshi in the eye.

"Brilliant, my dear," Gray continued. "You got us back on schedule. And Yoshi, your unpredictable Sight rise has made us rethink our own projections. Your popularity will steadily increase over the next sixteen to twenty months, securing you a decent FOF. So, let me get straight to the point." He tapped on the table, and a new document floated up under the glass surface. At the top sat a payment with many zeros. "I have a new offer for you. I want to buy the Yoshi Goto identity."

The room seemed to grind to halt as if it had been moving. So, it was true—the FOF *was* malleable, his future not tied to his past. Yoshi glanced back and forth between Gray's serious smile and the ridiculously generous payment.

Gray coughed into his hand.

"I'm sure it's ghastly overwhelming; Leon wore the same stupefied expression. But he signed. And, so too, did the others. So, take a moment to open your mind to the possibility of *starting again*. A new First Chance. Did you ever think it were possible? All you have to do is choose a new name and a new place to live. Maya will do all the administration. Adapting, Yoshi, that's what the future is all about. That's what we're doing, you and I, right here, right now."

Still dumbfounded to his toes, Yoshi couldn't speak.

"I'm sure you're concerned about the detail," Gray said, "So Mr. Uchida here will summarize that for you."

One of the Uchida twins cleared his throat, and Yoshi surrendered to the tidal wave of information.

"On signing over your identity to Maya Technologies, Maya Technologies will acquire the rights to your name, accounts and online profiles. You will be required to change your name and leave Shibido. In return, you will receive the generous payment as per the contract, in addition to your payment for the scanning. All costs related to your identity change and relocation will be covered by Maya Technologies, in addition to your payment. Due to the sensitive nature and timing of the contract, you will be given two days to consolidate your belongings and depart Shibido. Forth going, you may never act again, or engage with any activity directly connected to the entertainment industry, and you may not contact the other cast members for a period of twelve months.

And, finally, you may never again speak of your past life."

"But then, why would you?" interjected Gray, spreading his hands wide. "Not when you're sipping an Island Melt on a sunny pontoon in Tianjin."

Mr. Uchida continued to systematically list the contract's terms and conditions, then summarized what changing Yoshi's identity would really mean—no credit or employment history, no record of education or special training, and so on.

Yoshi eyed the payment again—there was a future in it, that was certain. Everyone had a price, and he wondered if he was staring at his. But thoughts taunted him of his doppelgänger performing all manner of activities in his likeness, perhaps creating new memories, new friends, and eventually becoming more Yoshi Goto than he ever was.

"I need to think about this Gray. I've got agents interested." *I defied your algorithms.*

His watch vibrated, but he swiped the call away.

Gray tapped the table.

"You're thinking you can profit from the rise of your popularity, maybe even extend your FOF. It's true, FOFs are malleable. But you must think about the logic, Mr. Goto—you can't sustain or manage your career. You ruined it before, and you almost did again with your reckless chase at Nebulae. You must see you're stuck in some perpetual cycle. If we remove that one erratic variable—*you*—we can really make something great of the Yoshi Goto brand, and you could be retiring on the balcony of your own hinterland estate in the south of Australia."

Yoshi's mind raced like a rat in a maze. Unable to fathom how Leon signed his identity away so easily, he stalled.

"Why do you have to own everything, Gray?"

Gray blinked slowly, like he'd heard the question many times before.

"When I first gave the Lenz to the city, I felt like Santa Claus himself, perpetuating the magic of imagination, just when the world had become as depressing as a tree stump. But it's more than entertainment, it's an escape from the very awareness that made us the dominant species, because, deep down, we know that to be too aware, too empathetic, is to be cursed. It's nigh impossible to live in the moment when what's ahead and behind us looks as bleak as it does. Some memories are stubborn. They require a grand, undeniable, *persistent* illusion. The Lenz is just a portal. Maya District will be the entry point. But Maya *City* is the destination."

"Maya City?"

"Once the district proves its financial success, the Mayor will have no reason to object to Maya District expanding over all of Shibido. Imagine, Mr. Goto, every second of every day orchestrated to your personal story, infinite versions of the city overlaying each other. To manage something on that scale, I *need* to control every aspect. I can't risk the unreliability of human actors ruining the 24/7 illusion."

Yoshi's mind filled with a fantastic vision of a kaleidoscoping city, filled with actors, and everyone pretending—perhaps even believing—they were in their own movies. But moths of doubt nibbled at the edges of the fantasy. Perhaps Kai was right about Gray wanting to erase the Minaki from people's minds—the Minaki, the homeless, the wall, maybe even reality itself.

His watch vibrated a second time—Social Services. The homeless boy's pale face shot into his mind with a force that almost projected itself out of his skull and into the room. A sudden, dull ache throbbed in his frontal lobe, so heavy with presence he felt a crack in his being, as if a tectonic shift pushed his beliefs to match his words and actions, urging him to challenge Gray's disregard for reality. He rubbed his forehead so hard the skin burned.

"Are you alright, Mr. Goto?"

"I don't think I can do it."

"Nonsense, of course you can. It's just a thing, a costume of sorts. The real 'you' is inside—no one can take that from you, right?"

Gray's sense of urgency irked him, like Maya already owned his identity. But something new and precious was at stake. For the first time in his life he could really see a Yoshi Goto beyond the immediate future.

Crap, even I'm talking about me as if I'm not me anymore.

With his shock subsiding, he noticed how differently he saw Gray compared to their first meeting—not an enigma, just another man.

"I suppose this is one of your now-or-never deals, Mr. Gray?"

"No time like the present."

"I'm not signing this now."

Gray's smile faltered.

"Oh, come to your senses, Goto. This dream of yours, I'm sorry to say, is over. All you really have left is your name. You have no family. Your best friend is an app. You've basically wiped yourself out of the world. What more perfect opportunity could there be for you, than to completely reinvent who you are? Take the offer and we both win."

The ache in Yoshi's forehead became a drum.

"I *said*, I need time."

"Yes, I presumed you'd need your twenty-four hours. Certainly, by all means, have a think about it. Have a *good* think about it. But remember, there are undertows that move us forward in directions that aren't always our first choice. It's just best to go with the current." He stood and looked down on the sea banging its head against the wall. "You know the way out."

A brutal silence hung heavy in the room. Naomi and the Uchida twins bowed their heads and looked down at the table.

Yoshi bowed and returned to the elevator as fast as he could, feeling Gray's offer creeping after him along the walls and ceiling, eating everything in their way, like Algorlines eating dreams.

***

The road crunched under his feet as he headed to the studio gate. A golden sun shower sparkled down around him from a blue sky, but an underlying electricity laced the air with sulphur. The crisp smell of rain—and a thunderbolt icon in the corner of his view—warned him of a storm approaching. He summoned Driver.

The headache had spread through his temples and seemed intent on planting itself along the back of his neck. A faint blur had returned to the edges of his vision.

A notification popped up, confirming Gray had sent through the contract. He immediately loaded it up to ACA and paid for the personalized analysis. He struggled to fill in the form with his head thumping, but he couldn't see what surprises there could be. As grandiose as the deal was, it was pretty clear: his whole identity—past, present and future—in exchange for a lot of cash so that he could buy himself a new one.

Jin stepped out of the booth, his friendly smile twisting into a frown.

"You don't look so good, Mr. Goto. Everything okay?"

Yoshi almost asked for Jin's thoughts on the deal but caught himself as he remembered he couldn't discuss it. He stood there trying to think of how to word a question that wouldn't give anything away, but no words came.

"That bad, huh?" Jin said. "I know the feeling. It's my second last day here."

"They fired you?"

Jin shrugged. "Less people gonna be here from next week, is what I'm hearing. More robots is what I'm thinking. Less people needs less people security. Probably getting replaced by a box of cameras and wires no bigger than my lunch box. So, what you got to be so down about, then?"

"Not too different to you, my friend. But I tell you what—if I suddenly come into a lot of money and need some security, I'll be calling you. So, you just hang in there, alright?"

"Why not?" Jin said with a shrug. "Crazy crap happens. You take care, then, Mr. Goto. That typhoon is picking up."

Yoshi glanced at the Mirage's blue sky, knowing if he had to leave Shibido he couldn't fulfil his promise to Jin, but he still meant it. Perhaps he would send Jin some money just to help him out.

He climbed into the pod and sat back into his thoughts as Driver took him to New Gate. He wondered how many actors and Liveys the studio planned to replace. He suspected every one of them. It did make some kind of twisted sense. Actoids wouldn't require a contract, food, accommodation, royalties, or a stunt double. They could be immediately repaired or replaced should they prove unreliable or do something stupid like break an arm. He envisioned his doppelgänger giving interviews and receiving awards. But how far would it go? The studio could control how they looked and aged, what lovers they took, how many children they had—their whole lives designed according to audience interest to make the studio a mountain of fast profit far beyond the Box Office.

His headache had become a skull cap of pressure, and the blurred edge of his vision shimmered. He took two aspirin from one of the pod's compartments. As they started to work their magic, he tried to rationalize the absurd choice before him by itemizing the areas in his life it would affect. His first thoughts steered to what he might lose, but a disheartening void stared back.

Gray had been right. All his family were gone. As for friends, he never had many, never felt the need for them. He never returned messages from his school friends, and no one from the industry reached out to him after *One Man Dreaming*. And with the no-contact clause, he couldn't say a proper goodbye to Leon and the others. There was, in fact, no one who would be touched significantly by his abrupt disappearance. To his surprise, he'd made himself as invisible as if the ocean had already claimed him.

Diving deeper into self-reflection, he wondered if he so feared vanishing without a trace—just like his parents—that he'd let the notion infect his mind, influencing his day to day actions over the years, so he sabotaged everything he did until his greatest fear finally manifested in his disappearance.

Maybe, it *would* feel good to rid himself of all of his past. His total reinvention was just waiting for him to say yes.

How would I decide a new name? What would I do?

He really needed to talk it out with Tora. He thought it strange that his erratic biorhythms hadn't generated a call. *Maybe Naomi could fix that crappy tech, too.* He blinked on the *yujin* app icon to request a call back.

Startling him, his watch thrummed in return, but it was from Social Services again. He hesitated to be distracted, but a relay of questions took off in his head—*Did they find the boy? Is he all right?*. He decided taking a break from thinking about his decision might help ease his headache.

"Hello."

"Hello. This is Social Services. Is this Mr. Goto?"

"Yes, it is."

"I am responding to your recent call regarding a homeless child in the underground parking garage."

"Yes. Did you find him? Is he alright?"

"In accordance with the Shibido Housing Act, our officers checked the reported area, and the missing persons register, but we found no trace of this child. It is possible the child you saw was just playing in the area."

"No parent would let their kid play down there for days. And I saw where he sleeps."

"We spoke to some of the homeless living in the parking garage, but no one corroborated your story."

"They're called Minaki. Did you even know they were down there?"

"We can confirm all illegal arrivals have been documented, and their movements are tracked while their situations are assessed."

"And how long is that going to take? They're disappearing, you know? You can't even find one boy."

"I'm sorry, sir, was your initial call about a missing person or council processes?"

The depth of his concern for the Minaki surprised him, like a geyser of empathy had sprung out from his cracking headache. The pain pushed through the aspirin and pressed a sharp point against the inside of his forehead, as if the boy himself hid there and was now determined to push his way out with his stick.

"I'm just concerned, alright? Do you understand *concern?*"

"The Shibido City Council takes these matters very seriously and asks that should you see this child again that you call us immediately."

"But I've called you already, and you're telling me he doesn't exist. How many other people are lost—"

"We thank you for your enquiry. Wonderful Day." The chat-bot ended the call.

Bastard.

But the bot's explanation made a frustrating sense. It was his sightings that seemed a mix of real and unreal—a pale boy, clearly not an islander, that Yoshi had only seen close-up in flickering light; then again among the abandoned buildings, but from a distance; then at Nebulae, ducking under the stairs, only that turned out *not* to be him.

He rubbed his forehead again, the pain's intensity increasing with every thump. The blur on his vision's edge had formed into coalescing crystals. He couldn't think straight anymore, couldn't get focused on the biggest decision of his life. Rising above all other thoughts, pushing out of the headache like the remainder of Meti reaching out of the sea, speared a thought he hadn't dared to recognize: *Did I imagine the boy?*

A light sweat broke out across his skin and the ache immediately ebbed back.

The pod arrived at New Gate, and as he passed through the Vision Bar arcade, he paused. A lady climbed out of a recliner and thanked the Lenzist. The lady left, and the Lenzist turned to Yoshi and smiled—a short, round girl with tight, black curls and a face as spotty as a bad banana.

"Can I help you, sir?"

He rubbed his forehead again, massaging the internal bruise, afraid to know what other inconveniences laid inside.

It's probably just the Lenz.

"Yes, I'd like a check-up, thanks."

"Certainly, sir. I'm Ami, your Lenzist today. Please, take a seat. If you could review and sign the consent form, I'll pull up your personal details."

Yoshi sat back into the recliner and accepted the consent request appearing in his vision. Ami tapped on the screen by his head.

Tap tap tap.

"I see you've had some past concerns with your Mirage. Blurred vision, wasn't it? How's that going?"

"That did calm down, but it's back now. But maybe it's my migraine. Anyway, that's not why I'm here. I think I'm having some… perception issues." His mouth went dry as he spoke, the words feeling like a shameful confession. "With what's real and what isn't."

Tap tap tap.

"Oh, I know, isn't it amazing. I can't wait for Maya District to open."

He ground his teeth as loud as Gray.

"No, I mean, I see this boy, he's five or six-years-old. I've seen him four times now. He's always on his own and swinging this torch-thing. But no one else has seen him and Social Services can't confirm he exists." He swallowed back his discomfort at what he was about to suggest. "Is it possible the Lenz can invent a person?"

Tappity tap tap tap.

"Well, I've never heard of that happening before."

"But it hides people with filters, right?" Yoshi pressed. "It hides the Minaki. Do you know that?"

"The what?"

Yoshi sat up to face Ami.

"The islanders in the old esplanade parking area. I was cutting through there, that's where I first saw him, the boy. I've seen him twice in there."

Suspicion laced Ami's eyes. She bit her lip and leaned forward to speak in a hushed tome.

"Did you give him money?"

"Money? No. I gave him my jacket. He looked cold."

Ami's eyes widened and her mouth dropped open. "You gave a gypsy your jacket?"

"He's not a gypsy, he's a kid."

"My boyfriend says don't go near the wall because the gypsies can act invisible and steal your things. This boy's probably been following you, hoping to get you for more."

Yoshi sat back, startled by the thought he could have been targeted. But, at least, that would mean the boy was real and he wasn't losing his mind.

Tap tap tap.

"Let me run a few tests on your Lenz," said Ami.

A goggle-shaped machine lowered from the ceiling and angled in front of Yoshi's face. Lights flashed and short bursts of air blew into his eyes. Ami took him through various eye exercises and then tapped the machine to send it back up to the ceiling.

"Well, I'm not seeing anything irregular in your eyes or your Lenz."

"So, it's me? I'm imagining things?"

"The Lenz algorithms decide what you want to see based on your data. Is there a reason you'd want to see a boy playing with a stick? Do you have a younger brother maybe, or a nephew?"

Yoshi shook his head. "I don't know any children."

"Then, I think there's your answer. You've got to be careful of those gypsies."

"But he didn't steal from me or ask me for anything."

Ami frowned with sympathy. "Mr. Goto, this boy holds you up with a stick in an abandoned parking garage, until you give him something. Then you catch him following you—"

"He wasn't following me, and—"

"And Social Services have no record of him. That spells g-y-s-p-y to me."

Another hotel guest walked in and waited at the edge of the room for his turn. Ami lowered her voice.

"Look, I'm no psychologist, but I've heard that sometimes stress can make us imagine alternate realties, like, to escape the issue. There are channels to help you deal with channel fatigue, too."

"No," Yoshi said loudly, and sat up straight. Ami glanced at the man waiting but Yoshi's mouth ran loose. "The Lenz is doing something to my brain."

"Mr. Goto," Ami said, louder and more assertive. She swung the screen around in front of him as data charts displayed. "The analysis shows your vision, and your Lenz, are functioning normally. You don't have a vision problem." She leaned forward and lowered her voice again, sincere concern in her eyes. "You have a *belief* problem. A *focus-of-the-mind* problem. You've got to be able to discern what's real from what isn't. That is your part of the user agreement."

Yoshi's ears flushed with embarrassment, as Ami looked over at the waiting customer again and smiled. "Won't be a moment." She swung the screen back in front of her.

Tappity tappity tap tap tap.

"I'm sending you a new round of daily eye exercises, and I'm complimenting you a course of Maya Vision Supplements."

She opened a drawer in the back of the chair, drew out a white pill bottle with Maya's logo on its lid, and handed it to him with a smile that confirmed they were done.

"Wonderful Day, Mr. Goto."

Yoshi looked her in the eye, the Lenz's vibrant-colored ring coiled around her iris like the tail of a parasite. He was sure it was already telling her brain to un-see him. He snatched the bottle.

"Is it, really?"

Ignoring Ami's shock, he stormed back outside for fresh air and slumped against the building. Everywhere he could see, people walked by as if in a dream, oblivious to the grayness of the world they wandered through, blissfully distracted from the past's museum of disappointments and the looming future of cliff edges. He looked back through the glass doors, at the man talking to Ami, holding his hand to his cheek to make his own little confession.

Maybe we're all having the same problem.

He was more confused about the boy than before, but he didn't know why it mattered so much. There he was, faced with the biggest decision of his life, and yet he couldn't stop thinking about someone he didn't even know existed or not.

But he *had* to know. Finding out if the boy was real or imagined would tell him who *he* really was, because these thoughts, these feelings, this debris, this is what he would be left with, this would be *him* when his name and past were gone.

It was beyond any logic, but there it was, washed up on the shore of his consciousness—*where the sea trades with the land.*

He summoned Driver and directed the pod to the abandoned buildings near the skybridge, where there was a certain singlet-wearing Minaki he needed to speak to.

Answer

The pod sped across High Scape toward the elevator, through a Christmas Lenz filter that transformed the city into a forest of illuminated pine trees. Relieved that at least his migraine had gone, he sat back and itemized the facts:

The times I saw the boy:
- *Twice in the underground.*
- *Once at the building near the sky-bridge.*
- *Once again at Nebulae, but not really, but for a second I may have.*

Possible explanations:
a) *The boy is some glitch of the Lenz, but the Lenz didn't work in the underground, so that rules that out.*
b) *The boy is real, Social Services just couldn't locate him, and I imagined*

*him at the expo. Totally possible.
Tidy.*

c) *The boy is all my imagination.
Worrying.*

d) *The boy is some unpredictable
combination of random variables that
no algorithm can ever map out. Not
acceptable.*

Although number three tinged the situation with a supernatural hue, his instinct orbited it and number two in a figure eight.

The pod locked into an elevator and dropped down to Low Ground. The island shore Mirage began to emerge, but he dialed it down. A bell-bottomed storm front, the size of a small country, rolled over the sea toward the city. Unseen waves assaulted the sea-wall, their colossal spray exploding down on Maya District's lifeless suburb.

He made a vow that if he couldn't find evidence of the boy's existence, he would accept that he'd imagined him and put the mystery to rest, with no more questions asked. Because what he did next, his future, depended on what he believed.

Reaching the north end of Maya District, a newly fenced-off area outside the district forced the pod to stop a few blocks back from the old buildings. Behind the fence, a flurry of people and vehicles buzzed around a huddle of polar-white, temporary buildings spread out like a mini Mars colony. Security guards—dressed in the short cape and bucket-shaped hat of the *Short-Term Security* uniform—guarded the perimeter.

Yoshi swore, realizing he'd have to use the south entrance and then walk back through the underground to find Singlets. But then he'd pass the boy's sleeping spot, too.

"Driver, we need to go to the south side of the district."

An army of raindrops assailed the windows as the pod sped around the district's circumference. Even with the beatification of the Mirage, the featureless buildings looked like relics underwater.

Arriving at the bus stop, the pod pulled up across from the ramp entrance—another stick-torch had been sprayed on its side. The rain fell harder. Gusts of the approaching typhoon flashed through the area, and the fencing around the district shimmied.

Let's do this.

He pushed the door open, dashed across the road and ran down the ramp. Skidding to a halt inside the damp underground, he flicked sterling studs of rain from his hair. Warm, musty air greeted him.

He moved further in, and the walls and ceiling came alive with graffiti color. Silver ribbons of water trickled down the slope on his right, twinkling like the flashes of tiny cameras in a stadium. The Lenz menu did its bothered flicker and dropped into dormant mode.

Okay. I need to rationalize this. There's no city record of the boy, missing or not. Boy isn't real—1. Boy is real—0. But I saw him here, twice. Not real—1. Real—2.

The logical thinking grounded his nerves.

Deeper inside the parking area, the neat piles of discarded furniture had disappeared. He pressed on, looking for the flashing light. But, instead, a glow emanating ahead silhouetted tall, distorted shapes reaching up to the ceiling.

What is this?

As he neared the strange structures, they appeared like giant origami creations frozen in their unfolding. They ran in two parallel lines and arched over to form a tunnel.

Drawn toward the surreal, geometric forest, he slowed his approach. D-lamps sat at random intervals among the structures, projecting sharp shadows on the graffitied walls and ceiling. Up close, he realized the structures were made from the piles of broken-down furniture. The beams of cupboard frames had been roped together to form the shape's tree-like architecture, while smaller parts—arms of chairs, lamp shades, sheets of plastic and fabric—had been tied taut between the frames and woven out into branches.

Sensing he walked among a sacred space, Yoshi guessed the tunnel of structures were part of the Ceremony of Luma. As he continued through, a sliver of a cool breeze sliced the mugginess. The structures quivered, blurring their edges. The shadows on the walls and ceiling shuddered, making the graffiti appear to shape-shift, confusing Yoshi's depth perception. He stopped, lost in a moment where the tunnel disappeared and the space around him expanded, transporting him to another place full of life and color.

Then the breeze dropped, the movement stilled, and the visual distortion vanished. He hesitated, unsure what he'd just experienced. Adrenalin set him on alert and quickened his heartbeat.

This place is fucking with my head.

He hurried on until he emerged out of the tunnel into the open parking area where the lone safety light flashed ahead. His arms goose bumped. He slowed again as he entered the flickering light, his eyes wide as UFO lights. He spotted the torch symbol on the slope, and above it, the red sleeping bag. A shiver zinged up his spine. He climbed the slope and peeked over.

In the strobing snippets of light, he could make out the red sleeping bag covering a small, dank space, dotted with old plates holding melted candles. Bunches of dried flowers laid on the bag, but not the elite varieties from a city florist—these spindly branches looked like flowering weeds gathered from the roadside. The boy's stick-torch rested against the back wall. In front of it lay Yoshi's red jacket, in a crumpled, dusty heap, as if untouched for weeks.

Another breeze brushed past him.

He picked up the jacket, its leather slippery with dust that spun off and twinkled in the air. He gave it a light shake, and something fell from the pocket to clang on the concrete. As if whistled to like a dog, his heart jumped to its feet and wagged its tail at the sight of Kai's lighter.

"What are you doing up there?" a voice startled him from below.

He spun around to see Singlets approaching the base of the slope. Instinctively, he shoved the lighter into his pocket and steeled himself for the confrontation. Singlets scaled the slope in a few strides, then stopped to catch his breath.

Yoshi held the jacket forward as evidence.

"This is my jacket. I gave it to the boy who was sleeping here. You saw him, right?"

"You telling stories?" the man asked through small gasps.

"He was here, the boy, a couple of weeks ago, remember? He blocked me walking through here, just before you came along. Four-foot, dark hair, six or seven-years-old. You saw him, right?"

The man eyed Yoshi with serious suspicion. "Our children don't come to this place."

Not real—2. Real—2.

"But, I *saw* him here, twice," Yoshi insisted, shaking his jacket in front of him. "He was down there, swinging that stick around. And yesterday, at the Nebulae expo. And—"

"And did you see him floating though the sky as well? You people get crazy in your eyes."

"Whose things are these, then?"

The man's face softened.

"Many things were in this place when we arrived. There is a sadness in them that tries to speak. Perhaps those who need to hear will come."

The hairs on Yoshi's arms sprung up. "What are you talking about?"

Singlets nodded at the structures back down in the parking area.

"These items, they want to speak to the citizens of Shibido. The Ceremony of Luma will open a portal to share their message with the city. If they come. But it's hard to hand out an invitation when people don't see you."

Yoshi's head spun as he struggled to make sense of the man's words. But he wasn't leaving without answers.

"What do you mean 'portal'?"

"*Luma* cannot flow here. This place, this time, it is a portal, but sadness has made it a wall. The ceremony is a collective meditation, to open the portal, to let *luma* flow again."

Yoshi suddenly recalled a game he once played at school with others, where they tried to summon the fox spirit, Mr. Kokkuri.

Great, I'm inside some urban legend.

He shook his head from frustration and pointed to the stick-torch leaning against the wall.

"What does that mean? That's a torch, right, like on your flyer, and on the ramp entrances? The boy had a stick, like that torch."

The man's eyes narrowed. "This boy you saw had this?"

"Just like that." Yoshi ran halfway down the slope and pointed at the symbol. "Just like this. What does this mean?"

Singlets hesitated.

"*Taka* use the torch to guide others on their journey through the portal."

Yoshi threw up his hands and climbed back up the slope to face Singlets.

"What does that even *mean*? *Taka*, portal, ceremonies! There was a kid here, I saw him, or I didn't, and I *need* to know which!"

The man dipped his head. "I have seen this boy."

"What?"

"The boy is one of those who needs to speak."

"*What?*"

Yoshi's grip on reality shuddered. Singlets doubled, and the walls and ceiling seemed to bend. Dizziness swamped him, his legs wobbled, and he stumbled sideways. But Singlets caught him by the arm.

"Easy, now," he said, and helped Yoshi sit down.

Yoshi clutched the jacket, as if it were the last remnant of reality, and his world came back together. He didn't like what Singlet's words suggested, or the way they blew his tally apart. He took a deep breath before saying his next words.

"Are you saying this boy is a *ghost*?"

Singlets looked away, the strobing light flickering his face like white campfire.

"He is a message. And he has come to you for a reason."

Yoshi looked up at the graffiti on the ceiling, his sense of reality reeling.

"I don't know what to fucking believe."

"Come to the ceremony," Singlets said, resting a warm hand on his shoulder. "At the full moon. Bring your friends. It can help you be sure about what you believe."

Have I been hallucinating? Am I having a mental breakdown?

"No. That's crap."

My life has finally got some order. I'm letting this gypsy get into my head. He didn't see the boy, he just said that off what I said. This is all crap.

Remembering his vow to make a decision no matter what answers he did or didn't get, he sucked in another deep breath and decided what he believed—he had imagined the boy in the underground, perhaps from some subconscious thing to do with his own past, to be carefree again like a child, or to forget things, or one of any number of psychological reasons some doctor could pull out of an ink blot. And after first imagining the boy, his thoughts had generated some kink in the Lenz's algorithm that echoed his imaginings in the real world, making him think he saw the boy at the old buildings and at Nebulae.

That's perfectly possible, no ghosts required. The boy isn't real. Case closed.

"Thank you. I'm sorry to have bothered you." Strength returning to his legs. He stood and eased down the slope.

"Remember the ceremony," Singlets called out. "It will show you more than that thing in your eye ever will."

Yoshi didn't look back. He marched southward, his hand gripping the jacket all the way. Reaching the end of the strobing area, he ran the through the forest of creepy structures and down the tunnel until he reached the ramp.

His thighs burned as he came out of the exit, and he leaned on his knees to catch his breath. The waiting pod by the bus stop in the rain looked artfully composed like a movie scene. The Lenz menu flashed as it reloaded. The rain transformed into a sun-lit shower twinkling across a glorious, clear sky that stretched over a gleaming metropolis.

He hurried to the pod and climbed in, steeling his mind against a niggling doubt about his decision. He slammed the door shut behind him and sat back to enjoy the rain's applause on the roof. He made a new vow—to also forget about the underground and the ceremony and the islanders.

As if proving to himself he could do it, he closed his eyes and willed a white light to blast through the Lenz' algorithms that vaporized any abnormalities.

You warned me, Grandpapa, not to get lost in my imagination. But I hear you now—I need to use it better, focus it on a new me.

He believed it as hard as he could.

Friend

"Is everything okay, sir?" Driver asked.

"It is now. It's a Wonderful Day."

"Where can I take you?"

He needed a quiet place, with a whisky on the rocks, where he could remember what it was like to be no one.

"Driver, where's a bar open now, close by, a quiet one."

"I found these results."

A short list of bars appeared in the windshield, all in the south districts. Yoshi recognized the name of one, a nondescript bar he'd passed many times but not the type he would ever go into.

"The Undertow. Take me there."

"Certainly. ETA, 9 minutes."

The ramp disappeared in the rear vision screen. More heavy-bottomed clouds rolled in over the wall, dragging in another downpour. Lightning flashed overhead and a wicked crack of thunder whipped through sky.

As the pod turned into the southern districts, he spotted the bar's easy-to-miss lantern sign, right next door to Good Time Adult Store.

The Undertow
Est: 1987

Pulling the jacket over his head, he climbed out of the pod and pushed through the windy rain bombarding him like rubber bullets. Entering through the door below the sign, he stepped into a dark foyer where an iron staircase spiraled down to a green and orange glow. Faint music rode up the stairs on spiced smoke and eased the tension in his body.

He hung the jacket on a drying rack and descended into a dark, low-ceilinged fire-hazard of a bar. Small, round tables sat underneath low-hanging, UFO-shaped lamps, their downward cones of smoky light spot lighting disembodied hands holding colored drinks. The walls seemed dark emerald, drawing focus to the bright, amber-lit bar tucked in an alcove at the rear. Jim Morrison's voice sang from old speakers on the ceiling about finding an island in someone's arms and a country in their eyes.

Yoshi wove through the tables to the bar and ducked under the low archway where more UFO lamps hung over a long bench. A flaking mural of the world's ocean currents covered the back wall above shelves of multi-colored bottles—mirrored walls at either end made the bar and mural seem endless. The alcove muffled the music from the main room, and a small box-TV sat directly opposite Yoshi, its screen threaded with static.

He perched himself on a split-leather stool at the far end and ordered a whisky. As the barman's silhouette waved in acknowledgement, Yoshi admired the mural to clear his head. Arrows swirled around the world's continents, but the land masses and currents were probably out of date since the Shift. By the shelves below, faded adverts of Shibido from its pre-wall days hung on the wall, showing a bustling town edging up to a busy promenade lining a calm beach.

The barman returned, placed a glass on a white napkin in front of Yoshi, and poured a honey-colored ribbon. Yoshi licked his lips at the delicate splash over ice. As the barman returned the bottle to the shelf, Yoshi took a generous sip. Its vanilla-kerosene kick struck the back of his throat like a match and filled his insides with warmth.

The bartender banged the top of the TV, and the static jolted into aerial footage of High Palace. As Yoshi gulped the rest of his whisky, he recognized Ken Morita's excitable, mustache-muffled voice-over.

"...announced an exciting line-up of new films coming next year. The biggest news is a short film sequel of 2037's box-office flop, *One Man Dreaming*.

Maya Technologies are showing great confidence in the failed film's rising cult status by using it as the lead-in to their game-changing, always-open, fully-immersive arena. Sound confusing? It's meant to be. Maya promises you won't know what's real and what isn't." The footage cut to Morita back in the studio, but static swallowed up the transmission again.

"How about another?" Yoshi said, his voice catching on the after burn of the first.

The barman grabbed the bottle and poured again.

"Forgetting the past or the future, my friend?"

"Thinking about both, unfortunately."

Yoshi took another gulp. The world around him softened, and the mural appeared to twinkle from flecks of some metallic material catching the light. He welcomed the effect. The day had left him raw, as if he'd been swept out over the wall and shipwrecked on Meti. He tapped the glass for another refill and gulped that, too, then pointed a finger at the TV.

"They're using clones now, you know, in films. Actoids, they call 'em."

The barman, standing with his back to Yoshi, didn't respond and continued to turn a dish towel inside a glass.

Squeak, squeak.

Yoshi talked on anyway, glad to at least have someone to talk *at*.

"I mean, can a robot really convey emotion, with human nuance and spontaneity? You know what I mean? That stuff that comes from within a *person,* in the moment, *unprogrammed.*"

Squeak, squeak. "It does seem a shame."

"It's a crime, is what it is. Can a damn algorithm know what it's like to get drunk?"

Yoshi put his face into the light of the lamp and squinted up at the back of the barman's shadowed head.

"Do I look stupid to you?"

"No, sir," the barman replied without turning. *Squeak, squeak.*

"Well, I am," Yoshi confessed, sitting back. "They had me in this big virtual-bubble thing, scanning me, to give my doppelgänger *my identity.* What did I think was happening?"

The barman froze, and Yoshi took it as recognition.

"Yes, that's me, Yoshi Goto. The *original* Joe Joe. Well, I *was.* Goto, that is."

Yoshi tapped his glass a fourth time, enjoying marinating in the mourning of his lost dream. The barman turned, keeping himself in the shadow as he poured with haste. Yoshi gulped another mouthful of liquid fire and then sat back to watch the room's edges become even fuzzier. Or was that the Lenz? Did he even care anymore?

The aloof barman turned his back again as Yoshi threw down his fourth shot.

And now I'm seeing double of you, my shadowed friend.

"At least I still have the satisfaction of knowing my acting was the foundation for that. Some people don't make the difference between actors and their characters. You know the Fourth Wall?" He poked his chest. "I'm stuck in it, stuck in the blur between what's real and what isn't."

"Yes, sir." The barman said, retreating toward the other end of the bar.

"Oh, *excuse* me," Yoshi called out. "You're *so* busy with your *cleaning*." He rose his glass in mock toast to the barman's dutifulness before taking another gulp.

"Exactly, exactly, my friend," the barman replied.

Yoshi halted the glass just before his waiting lips.

"What did you just say?"

The barman hunched and snatched another glass to polish. Yoshi grabbed the lamp shade above him and twisted it up to spot the back of an unfamiliar head. But on the wall behind him, Yoshi recognized the shelf of bottles from the *yujin* app. Unable to comprehend what it meant, he dropped the light and tapped on his watch to send a call request to Tora. The barman's watch flashed.

"It can't be," Yoshi said, still struggling to process what his mind was saying was true.

The barman scrambled to shut off his watch but dropped the glass to the floor with a smash.

"*Tora?*"

"That's not my name, Chief, I mean—"

"You're a *real* person?"

The barman bent under the bar to sweep up the broken glass.

"I think you've had too many, sir. Time to leave."

Momentarily sobered by shock, Yoshi slammed both hands on the bench and leaned over.

"I know it's you, you fucking fraud!"

Tora stood up and held up his hands in placation, glancing out into the main area in case anyone heard. The lamp's swinging cone of light revealed his embarrassment in swaying snapshots.

Yoshi studied the barman's face, still not quite believing. But he could see the Tora avatar had been face-tuned from the barman's own features—the dark eyes, the big smile—while blurring the sun-weathered lines and frizzy hair.

But it was Tora, real as the bar itself.

Tora grabbed the lamp to stop it swinging.

"Hey, Chief."

Yoshi plonked back down into his seat.

"Holy crap. *Why* would you do that, pretend to be an avatar pretending to be a person? How... How could you lie to somebody like that?"

"It's just a job, Chief," Tora said, twisting his hands in each other. "They offered, I took. Desperate times, you know?"

"Who's 'they'?"

"This little start-up. Their AI kept getting into arguments with customers, so they started using people as pretend avatars until they fixed the problems. But they couldn't, so they kept us on. I know how that must sound, but you know what it's like to be desperate, don't you Yoshi?"

Yoshi sat up straight and pointed a finger.

"Don't you do that. Don't use what I told you about me to defend yourself." His spike of sobriety dipped as everything he'd confessed to Tora created a whirlpool in his immediate thoughts. "What about my privacy?"

"Oh, no, Chief, privacy is guaranteed. I gotta hand back all my pay if I ever break that—"

"*That's* no guarantee."

Tora shrugged. "Come on, Chief, you don't really care about privacy. You're an actor, and you let the Lenz track you all day."

"Oh, my God," Yoshi said, spinning around to look at the other patrons. "Is *everybody* acting?"

"Chill, Chief. Chill. That Lenz is messing with your mind."

Yoshi shook off the paranoia and tapped the glass. "I need another drink."

Tora poured again.

Yoshi really wanted to be mad at him, at *someone*, but he was more thankful the closest and only thing he had to a friend was real and right there in front of him. In any case, he realized, Yoshi Goto's privacy wasn't going to be his for much longer.

Tora rested the bottle down on the bar.

"Look, Chief, I don't want any trouble. I work three jobs. This one, I get no money, but I get a room to sleep in, so I don't have to sleep on the street like the rest of my tribe."

Tora's words barely made it to Yoshi's brain as pieces of explanation fell into place—Tora's call inconsistency, his delay in call-backs, the flickering digitization of his face from the real-time face-tuning.

"Wait a minute. What do you mean, 'tribe'? You're Minaki?"

Tora's grip on the bottle tightened. "You gonna report me?"

"No, no, of course not. I'm just in shock. To be honest, I always wished I could have a drink with you, and just, you know, talk in person."

Tora smiled and bowed. "I'm Mico. That's my real name."

Yoshi bowed his head in return with drunken gusto.

"It's really good to meet you, Mico. Please, have a drink on me."

"Ah, I'm not supposed to drink on the job."

"You work here on your own?"

Mico nodded and glanced around the tavern before pouring himself a generous glass.

"To a better future," he said, clinking Yoshi's glass.

"It's a Wonderful Day," Yoshi replied.

They drank, and Mico poured two refills.

"So, Yoshi, I owe you a few calls. What's the update?"

Yoshi leaned forward.

"Well, I'm not meant to talk about it, but the Studio want to buy my *actual* identity. They want to control every aspect of the business. I have to change my name and move away. Never act again. Can you believe it?"

"But you love acting, it's your... what do you call it here? Your *ikagai*!"

Yoshi looked down into the empty glass.

"The world doesn't need actors anymore. And you want to know something else? *I* don't need acting anymore, either. I hid in it because I couldn't handle being in a world where everything was taken from me. And I got lost in it. I'm just a fraud. Maybe I *need* an audience, so I can suck up their energy, like a vampire—"

"Okayyy," Mico interrupted, pouring Yoshi a water and sliding it over to him. "Let's step back a bit. You done some good as an actor. Same as me being a virtual *yujin*. We make people feel, good or bad, but we help them feel and retell their story to themselves in a way that makes it easier to deal with. Maybe even heal."

Mico's words opened a window on Yoshi's darkened spirit, but regret quickly rushed in. He shook his head.

"I shouldn't have signed that first contract."

"My bad," Mico said, admitting to his original advice on the subject. He refilled Yoshi's water. "I guess you don't know what they're gonna do with this Joe Joe character, or how people might associate you with any of that. What differentiates you from him will disappear." Tora stood up and raised his hands into pantomime claws. "And only one of you will survive."

Yoshi crunched on an ice cube. "I liked you better when you weren't real."

Mico gave up his foray into acting and leaned on the bar.

"You asked that I help you stay positive. But I've always told you like it is, 'cause that's what you responded to. So, as much as the odds say you should take the money and run, I say why give it all up now?

You've been fighting for this for a while. Okay, so the last hill just got a little higher. Doesn't mean you abandon the race."

"It got more than a little higher, Mico. It's a giant fucking wall."

Mico's nostrils flared with a sudden, fierce excitement, and he pointed a finger at his own chest.

"I work three jobs, illegally, and still go without food more than I eat. When I have nothing to eat, I steal it. I'm a criminal here, because the city doesn't want to remember we exist. You got the system on your side, and you want to give up when it gets a little tough? Sell your identity, then, like it's a piece of old furniture. You don't know what it's really like to fight to be visible."

Mico's words stumped Yoshi for a response.

Mercifully, a clear transmission burst through the static on the TV. Ken Morita stood in front of a three-dimensional 3D weather model, its clouds animating over a map of the east coast. Morita seemed to shout from beneath the small TV.

"Typhoon No. 33 is expected to be right on top of Shibido within the hour. Although the wind and rain are increasing, this is a fast-moving storm and will have moved north by the morning. All commercial aircraft have just been grounded; however, Cargo drones remain cleared for flights until further notice. The Japan Meteorological Agency advises everyone to stay indoors, close all windows, and listen for updates. I'm Ken Morita, and this has been a Wonderful Day."

"That storm's getting serious," Mico said.

Yoshi crunched another ice cube. He really wanted to just drink and chat with his friend, but with less than twenty-four hours to make the biggest decision of his life, he couldn't risk being trapped in The Undertow. He tapped his glass.

"One for the road?"

Tora shook his head but poured anyway. Yoshi threw back the last defiant gulp—it tasted like hard truths.

"Well, thank you very much, my friend," he said, hearing his own words slur. "It has been a pleasure to meet you. I wish we had longer to get acquainted."

Mico looked Yoshi in the eye. "You better fight, Chief."

"If only it was as easy as that."

"I'll call you tomorrow to make sure you did."

"Goodbye, Mico, and all the very best to you, my friend."

Warm and floating, Yoshi waded around the obstacle course of tables toward the staircase.

"You better fight," Mico called out.

Hammered, Yoshi reached the top of the stairs with a gasp and wrestled on his jacket out the door.

Ancillary

A whoosh of windy rain wrapped around his legs and spun him in a clumsy dance along the footpath. In his drunken fog, he forgot the waiting pod, and he rushed to get out of the rain in the direction of his old container apartment. Keeping close to the store fronts, he bounced off the windows as he tried to walk straight.

"Watch your back," barked a voice from behind, startling him. A short man zoomed past pushing a hand-trolley laden with a coffin-sized box.

"Hey, watch it!" Yoshi called.

But the man zipped through the red-lit doorway of the Good Time Adult Store ahead. Realizing where he was, Yoshi glanced at the window's contents: five scantily clad companion *yujin* stood in a row, posed in anticipatory positions.

"Well, hello, ladies and gents," he shouted through the wind. "I see you are all new here."

Maybe I'll treat myself—

His drunken gaze pulled focus on the middle *yujin's* face and his thoughts froze solid. Staring back at him through his own reflection was a younger version of himself with a comet-shaped birthmark below his right eye.

"What the—"

The Joe Joe companion *yujin* moved its mouth and spoke three words.

"Let's do this."

Yoshi jerked back so hard he stumbled to keep his balance.

"Are you kidding me?"

With his thoughts still blown by disbelief, paranoia rushed in. Thinking he was a joke character in a badly written novel, he looked skyward, as if he might catch a glimpse of the reader's face behind the letters. But raindrops bombarded his eyes. He wiped them away and stormed through the red-lit doorway into the Good Time Adult Store.

Neon white ceiling light glared back at him and glistened off all manner of plastic-wrapped sex-toys hanging on the walls. Halfway down the store, a counter poked out from the left where a short, sparrow-faced lady signed the delivery guy's tablet.

"That's the last one. I'm getting out of this weather," the delivery guy said, unloading the tall, wet box next to two others. Joe Joe's face—Yoshi's face—gazed blankly from behind a window in the box's front panel.

"Son of a bitch."

The storekeeper and delivery guy looked up in unison.

"Son of a bitch," he repeated, slurring, and storming toward them.

The storekeeper pointed a bony finger at him. "Hey, you. Remove your shoes."

Yoshi pointed at the boxes and bellowed with all his Santa practice.

"You take them outta the window, right now!"

The lady pointed harder back at him. "You go home and sober up, right now!"

He reached the first container and banged a fist on its side.

"This is me! I didn't authorize these!"

The storekeeper glanced back and forth between Yoshi and his *yujin* likeness. She started chuckling. "This one got the looks, huh?"

Yoshi turned to the delivery man and banged the box again. "Take them outta here, right now."

"Don't you touch that!" shouted the storekeeper. She zipped out from behind the counter and swiped Yoshi's arm off the box. "You get out of here, right now!"

"And you," Yoshi said, pointing a dangerous finger at the storekeeper's face. "You get me out of the window."

Twin fires lit up in her dark eyes, and her jaw shot forward. "You don't tell me what to do, mister."

"Ok, I'm outta here," said the delivery guy as he pushed his trolley toward the doorway.

"Oh, no, you don't," Yoshi snapped, grabbing him by the shoulder. "You take all these back to where they came from."

The delivery guy knocked Yoshi's hand away with one swift motion. "Easy, man. You need to do as the storekeeper says and go home."

The delivery guy disappeared out the door, but Yoshi wasn't done. Furious, he stumbled after him and back into the rain.

A door slammed shut to his right—a small truck parked by the footpath, water up to its hubcaps. He yelled at the van as he ran toward it.

"I didn't authorize this. Do you hear me?"

A hand shot out from the driver's window and gave Yoshi the pinky, before the van revved and took off down the road, spraying him with gutter water. Wiping rain from his eyes, Yoshi caught sight of the familiar name across the back of the van:

Real Toy Robotics

The storekeeper yelled at him from under the store's awning and pointed to Joe Joe in the window.

"I bet he gets more action than you, too!"

She broke into a cackle, the five *yujins* standing in the window behind her like a silent cheer squad.

Fueled with blind rage, and oblivious to any danger, Yoshi chased the van down the road. The storekeeper's maniacal laughter followed him, but one word drummed through his mind, louder than the storekeeper's cackle.

Fight, fight, fight.

Turning the corner, he glimpsed the truck's lights disappearing into the rainy gloom. Soaked to the bones, he stumbled to a nearby building's alcove entrance and fell against the door.

Gray, you son of a bitch.

Catching his breath, and close to buckle point, he blinked fiercely to call Gray.

"Answer, you—"

A click cut off the ringing tone. For a split-second, Yoshi thought the call had been deliberately diverted.

"Tyler Gray speaking."

"You son of a bitch."

"Sorry, who is this?"

"You know damn well who this is. You recall every one of those freakin' sex dolls, right now, or I'm gonna sue the pants off you."

"Calm down, Yoshi, calm down."

"Don't you—"

"Yoshi! You're drunk. I can hear it. Let's talk about this tomorrow."

"But, it's me! It's my face. You don't have the right to—"

"We have all the rights. You signed them over, remember. The companion yujin is an ancillary item."

Realization fell into Yoshi's drunken mind like a pinball down a gobble hole.

"You're making sex dolls as merchandising toys?"

"Oh, for heaven's sake. We've given children action figures from movies for years. Why can't adults have them too?"

"What are you talking about? This is my identity."

"No, it's Joe Joe's identity. You still have yours, remember? And sounds like your trashing it, surprise-surprise. I'm about to connect to a long-distance conference. Let's talk about this tomorrow, after you've sobered up."

"Now, you listen to me—"

"Get home safely, Mr. Goto. And, please, don't do anything stupid, or you might not have an identity worth selling."

The line clicked dead. Rain bombed the street.

Directly ahead, peeking over the building tops from a few blocks away, the Real Toy Robotics sign glowed in the rain, the word 'Real' flashing. Whisky-fueled fury burned Yoshi's eyeballs and blasted his rationale.

With no clear plan but to reclaim his image, he launched out of the alcove and charged down the street toward the factory. The rain bombarded him from every direction, spraying off the road and walls. Hell-bent on his vague mission, he ran all the way to the industrial district.

Lungs bursting and thighs burning, he came to a gasping halt outside the Real Toy Robotics' driveway. Whips of silver lashed the neon sign, its glowing red letters pulsing like both a welcome and a warning.

The delivery van sat at the end of the driveway with its rear doors opened onto a raised garage, next to two other trucks. The wind rose and dropped with shrieks and menacing howls. No one was in sight.

He ran to the garage and hefted himself up onto the ledge. Dripping small puddles behind him, he strode across the docking bay and pushed through double doors into a high-ceilinged warehouse. Aisles of stacked boxes on carts towered up to a scaffolding-lined ceiling that arched over like the belly of a whale. Tall, rectangular auto-lifters on wheels followed white lines on the floor, scooping crates and zooming through the double doors back to the garage.

Wide-eyed with adrenalin, his heartbeat drumming in his ears, he crept sideways, looking back and forth like a frantic crab, ready to dodge an auto-lifter if it zipped toward him.

Halfway along, the stark neon light beaming down sobered him just enough to lay his craziness bare. A momentary doubt gripped him, and he glanced back down the aisle, the docking entrance seeming miles away. But a Joe Joe staring back at him from inside its box across the aisle snapped him back into his frenzied fury.

He continued to the end and looked left and right up the corridor. He could see some sort of packing room through glass doors on the opposite wall, but a red light above showed the room was secured shut. To the left, crates of stacked *yujin* boxes rolled out of the packing room on a conveyor belt where an auto-lifter scooped them up. He snuck down to the conveyor opening, waited for a break between crates, and scrambled through the curtain of plastic strips.

Inside, he followed the conveyor belt backward, ducking under mechanical arms that swung from the ceiling to stack the boxes on the crates. Longer black arms plunged up and down as they plucked the androids from another belt and laid them in their boxes. As he reached a doorway at the rear, he glanced at the second conveyor belt to see Joe Joe's face—his face— staring up at the ceiling.

After a flippant, sneak peek to see just how accurate Joe Joe's anatomy was, Yoshi huffed, and slipped into the next room. A torch light flashed across frosted doors at the back. He ducked between machine cabinets along the wall as the doors squeaked open. Footsteps walked through and the torch's cone of light scanned the room. After glimpsing a uniformed man leave via the front doors, he ducked through the back doors and into another manufacturing chamber.

Another Joe Joe *yujin* slid along the conveyor belt as robotic arms prodded its skin and joints. Farther back, more robot arms sprayed synthetic skin over a complex, metallic skeleton. The last room stank of burnt rubber and hot oil, where the androids were mere hydraulics connected to a scaffolding. Yoshi felt like he'd watched himself being dismantled.

He scanned the room, looking for some angle of attack, some way to strike at the heart of the production line. He spotted a single frosted door in the rear corner, almost hidden at the end of a row of machine cabinets. A green glow flickered behind the clouded glass, so he approached slowly. Three words were printed across the door:

Artificial Emotional Intelligence

His alcohol-addled thoughts twisted like a possessed Rubik's Cube, and a delusional idea of sabotaging the *yujin's* programming billowed in his drunken mind. He eased the door open.

Inside, a row of monitors sat on a long desk, a green cube slowly spinning on each of their screens. Opposite, a single row of *yujin* stood naked. Joe Joe was closest, but there was something different about him, different from the others on the production line. Yoshi's pickled mind couldn't put a finger on what it was, so he walked up and looked Joe Joe in the eye. An undeniable human presence stared back. Then it hit him like a slap across the face—the *yujin* in front of him didn't have a birthmark, because it wasn't Joe Joe.

"Holy crap."

The whole row of *yujin* were clones of the cast as themselves—Dax, Otis, Jenya, Leon... and Yoshi Goto.

A muffled voice from outside startled him out of his skin. He darted to the desk and squeezed underneath it, pressing himself into the shadowed corner. Torch light flicked across the frosted door and footsteps approached. He sucked in his breath and squeezed deeper into the corner. Two silhouettes stopped just outside the room.

"Have you seen a delivery guy around here?"

"Nah, been quiet as a graveyard."

"Well, there's wet footprints all the way through the packing hall. They dried up at the back, but someone's been through there."

The other guard's reply faded as they walked away.

Yoshi slid out of the tight space and gasped for air. A slow-returning sobriety nudged him to flee before the guards raised the alarm, but one glance at his naked doppelgänger summoned back his anger. His vague mission found its purpose.

Adrenaline raced through his body as he hefted his double onto his shoulder. Staggering sideways under its weight, he steadied himself and carried it out past the metal skeletons receiving their guts. He hurried past the skin-sprayers, ducked under the robotic arms, and made it back to the packing room.

After a brief pause to catch his breath, he unlocked the main door and pushed it ajar to check the way ahead was clear. He darted down an aisle, dodging an auto-lifter. By the time he reached the bay with the *yujin* on his shoulder, his lungs burned and his head throbbed like a sumo's hemorrhoid. An auto-lifter drove in from the factory and stacked a crate into the open rear of the remaining truck.

With no further plan but to escape to his nearby old apartment, he paused to shift the *yujin* onto his other shoulder to prepare for a dash through the rain. But just as he poised to leave, a guard in a hooded raincoat climbed up onto the bay ledge from outside. Yoshi pushed back against the wall, keeping in the shadow. To his horror, another guard stomped in from the warehouse.

"See anything?" The second guard asked his drenched partner.

"Nothing. But trucks have been coming in and out all night. It's hectic for everyone with the dismantlers coming tomorrow."

The waiting truck's rear lights lit up, illuminating the bay and Yoshi. Looking around for somewhere to hide, he ducked behind an auto-lifter rolling through the door and partnered it to the back of the remaining truck. But the guards hadn't moved, and the auto-lifter dropped its crate in the truck and pulled away. With nowhere else to hide, he darted inside the truck and crouched behind the crate. He kept the *yujin* on his shoulder, ready to run as soon as the guards disappeared.

After a few more words to each other, the first guard stormed back into the factory and his partner walked off to the side. Yoshi waited a few seconds and then rose to exit, but the truck's engines roared to life, rattling the cargo and toppling him backward. His clone crashed on top of him as the rear door shut with a loud clunk, and all light vanished.

No, no, no.

He pushed the clone off him and ran to the locked doors, scrambling for an opening mechanism that wasn't there. The truck jerked into motion and rolled away into the roaring rain.

No, no, no.

He slammed a fist on the nearest *yujin* box, cursing his bad luck. He turned back to the cabin and tapped his watch to light up the dark. All around him, Joe Joe, Leon, Suzy Lee Bingo, Bamboo Run and Dhven peered out from behind their windows, shimmying with the motion of the truck. He was suddenly sober as a monk.

The truck turned a corner and rattled over uneven terrain. Rain pelted the roof as options scrambled in his head for a leader.

If he called someone for help, he'd have to explain what he was doing in the cargo with a stolen *yujin*. If Gray found out, he might pull the whole deal and press charges. So, he dared to wait until the truck arrived at its destination, where he'd try to sneak out. He had nothing to lose trying.

His clone laid on its side on the floor as if relaxing. He slumped down next to it and checked his Lenz's GPS. The truck was heading down the main artery and turning again. He zoomed in on the map looking for a possible destination—another mall or a wholesale outlet—but he couldn't spot anything that made sense.

The truck braked, turned again, and slowed to dip downward before coming to a stop.

He jumped to his feet and dragged his clone behind the boxes nearest the door—he still intended to take his hostage. Crouching in anticipation, he listened through the rain for any sound of approaching footsteps. But a loud groaning roared from above, and a series of deep clunks echoed as unseen things attached to both sides of the roof. Exquisite terror gripped him.

A cargo drone.

Forgetting about any consequences, he threw his clone to the floor and banged on the door, yelling for help. The container jerked upward, then lifted smoothly until it jerked again and locked into place in the drone's belly. He screamed and banged furiously, but the drone's engine roared into life and swallowed his small noises. The thrumming of rotor blades began and increased in pace, and the container jerked sharply again as the drone lifted off. Yoshi gripped the side for stability, the container's rattling vibrating through his body. In the dim light of his watch, the *yujin* jiggled in their boxes as if excited to be flying.

Recovering from his initial panic, he blinked to call the police, but the Lenz popped up a no-connection message. Fearing being stuck in the container for days—possibly being found unconscious or dead next to his naked clone—he shuffled around the tight spaces between the boxes, trying to pick up a signal, but nothing. Overcome by hopelessness, he plonked onto his knees and dropped his head into his hands.

What the fuck have I done?

The drumming rain intensified to a roaring white noise and the wind screamed along the container's side, invading his ability to even think. He took massive breaths in and out to pull himself together, but the container suddenly lurched and slid him sideways with the cargo. He braced himself on his knees and held the boxes in place on either side of him. The standby light on his watch faded off, dropping him into darkness. He stayed like that, peering into the howling black, for an indiscernible time, until a piercing crack of thunder shuddered the metal walls and the drone dropped to its left side. The engines squealed as the drone struggled to right itself.

I'm gonna die in here, he thought, growing weak with terror.

Another thunderous lash, followed by an explosion somewhere outside. The container dropped to its right, toppling him to the other side and crushing him with boxes. Pinned to the spot, he gurgled as his legs struggled to push the heavy boxes away.

Another gust, bigger and stronger than all the others, slammed the drone with the strength of a giant. Rising terror chased all his thoughts away. A mechanical scream pierced the air, followed by the whipping sound of cables snapping and banging the roof. The container dropped at its rear, and the boxes slid away and slammed into the back doors. Released from their crush, Yoshi scrambled for something to grab in the dark, and his hand found a rail on the wall. A loud explosion rocked the container, and its rear burst away in a shower of sparks. Yoshi screamed, his feet slipping on the tilted floor. The boxes spiraled out below into dark, manic curtains of rain. Freezing cold terror shot through his body as he gripped the rail with all his life-force. Gusts bustled in, buffeting him to the side. A monstrous flash of lightning lit up a thrashing ocean below, as the last box dropped into the choppy waters.

Holy fuck this is it I'm gonna die right now right here.

Overwhelming horror squeezed the air out of his lungs and shrank his testicles into balls of pain. A final sharp, ear-cracking scream, and the whole container dropped, plummeting Yoshi into the sea that he always feared would get him.

Boat

A rising, exotic trill called him from the darkness.

Cold, wet stone pressed painfully against the heaviest points along his body. He swallowed, wincing at his cracked, dry throat.

The pitter-patter of a gentle rain extended his awareness to a soft crash of waves tumbling close behind. A cool sheet of water rushed over his legs and puddled at his torso before ebbing back. Licking dry lips, his tongue retreated from the salt. With tremendous effort, he turned his head slightly, the grit of sand scratching his cheek, and he opened his eyes.

Mist pearled the atmosphere. He had to squint to pull the world into focus. Nouns began to attach themselves to things around him.

A primeval shore of high grass and dark, wet rock slanted steeply upward. He arched his head up to see the grass gave way to a forest of thick-trunked trees reaching a peak. To his left and right, large rocks and half-submerged trees disappeared around a corner. His head thumped back at him like an angry giant woken mid dream, but the sight of the calm shore filled him with equal relief and disbelief.

As he moved his head, he became aware of symbols floating in the corner of his vision. His foggy brain took a moment to recognize the dormant menu of the Lenz.

The trill sounded again from the canopy, echoing in the calm absence of city noise. Another wave rushed up through the grass and over his legs. He flexed his fingers and toes, and slowly engaged his back muscles to roll over and sit up.

Muted daylight dulled the ocean surface into a vast, ashen membrane, its mercurial hem laced with the turquoise shimmer of luminescent plankton. A rectangular container floated just beyond the shore, stuck on the something just under the surface. He squinted into the distance, but the grayness hid anything further out.

He pushed himself to his feet and stretched, awakening an army of aches up his back. He leaned his head back so his dry mouth could catch what rain drops he could. Silent lightning flashed through the clouds and a memory flashed so vivid it overrode his vision.

A storming ocean, screaming, plummeting.

Shocked back into standing straight, an explanation for what happened formed in his mind—lightning hit the drone barely ten minutes after take-off and it crashed into the sea. By some miracle of chance, he'd been washed ashore.

But where?

He turned back to the sheer hill face. Recognizing its geometric shape, an astonished familiarity struck him—he'd been washed up on what was left of Meti.

He gripped the tall grass to be sure it was real, that he was real, that he wasn't dreaming. He swallowed on his dry throat again to feel the tiny cuts, and he drew in the deepest breath he could, expanding his lungs until they hurt. The waist-high grass hissed around him. It was real; he was real, alive and real and saved by his island birthplace that he once had to flee.

A wondrous gratitude filled him with breath-taking lightness. He touched his chest with a new, humble appreciation of the bloody organ beating inside him that connected him to the world.

A cool breeze brushed his cheeks and rustled the grass again, drawing his attention to the right. Spying something long and bent protruding from the rocks, his stomach clenched—an arm.

He waded through the grass toward it and another body came into view further up, and then another, resting in awkward positions with their limbs twisted or missing.

He reached the first *yujin* to find Joe Joe staring up at him from among the broken remains of its box. The shock set off more fast snippets of memory—Gray's offer to buy his identity; his drunken theft; the lightning blasting away the container door. A great dread brought him to his knees, and he clutched his head in both hands.

What have I done?

The invisible bird in the forest repeated its high-pitched vibrato, calling to his survival instinct. He wiped away his tears and checked his watch—although undamaged, it had no connection. Thinking of the GPS inside the *yujin*, he tried turning it on, but it didn't respond. He turned it over, exposing a charred, artificial brain showing through a gaping hole in its skull. A wave rushed up and tried to drag it back to sea. He hurried to the next, but it was also too damaged, and so was the next. He slumped down into the long grass when a familiar voice startled him from behind.

"Hello."

Yoshi spun around. Tangled in the branches of a half-submerged tree, his own doppelgänger wriggled and nodded. Yoshi scrambled to its side and pulled it free. One arm and both legs were missing, and wires protruded from the wounds. Repulsed and fascinated, he winced at the sight of his limbless self.

"Hello, can you hear me?"

"Hello. How are you today?"

Although irked by the perfect rendition of his own voice, just hearing the *yujin* speak spiked his hope.

"Where are we? Is this Meti?"

"I'm sorry, I cannot calculate my location."

"Can you connect at all?"

"My communication systems are intact, but I have no reception to activate my distress beacon. I may be able to connect GPS from higher ground."

Yoshi surveyed the forested slope behind him. The rain fell harder, and a spark flashed from the *yujin's* wound where its left arm use to be. Panicking the *yujin* may short-circuit, he hefted it onto his shoulder and hurried to the tree-line. Stumbling over thick roots intertwined like lovers' limbs, he entered the canopy's shelter and headed toward the peak.

As far as he could see, spears of green leaves crossed black trunks and branches. He searched his thoughts for any memory of his short childhood on the island, but the mass of green only reminded him of a documentary he'd once seen, about how early humans could identify more shades of green than any other color to find the edible and avoid the poisonous. His stomach growled at the thought of food.

The rain's murmuring through the branches replaced the soft crashing of the waves, and the forest's rich, organic funk mingled with the salty atmosphere. The rain trickled through gaps and collected in mercurial puddles in the boughs of giant leaves. As he stopped to gulp mouthfuls of the cool refreshment, ants as big and gnarly as popcorn marched up the wet trunk in front of his face.

He pushed on up the steepening ground. The thickening canopy blocked the light, changing the prehistoric-looking leaves to silver, and a symphony of sonic whips and clicks emerged. The rain's drum grew louder, bending branches down and releasing heavier streams of water. Reminded of the leak in the bathroom of his container apartment, he longed to be back there where the Red Toy Robotics sign flashed its warmth through the windows.

The *yujin* grew heavy, and his legs began to quiver with each step. He rested against a vine-strangled trunk to shift the android onto his other shoulder, and he noticed he stood on an overgrown path. He tried to imagine himself as a five-year-old boy running along the trail, but any true memory of the island remained teasingly out of recall.

He followed the trail until he stumbled into an area where the trees thinned, and light fell in. His sight locked on a moss-blanketed, oblong shape on the other side, looking out of place among the lush foliage. A wisp of familiarity blew across his mind. He held onto it and stepped slowly toward the shape.

Pushing aside leaves the size of elephant-ears, he exposed the remains of an up-turned boat, about five meters long, propped between the bough of two trees. Branches had been stacked together to make walls, and fronds tightly woven to thatch holes in the hull. Next to a wide opening in the make-shift hut's side, a stick-torch protruded askew from the ground, just like the one in the homeless boy's shrine. Yoshi's weary mind struggled to make sense of any connection. He stepped over a large puddle at the entrance and carried his wounded clone out of the rain.

Although open at both ends, the hut welcomed him in with a surprising dryness. He lay the *yujin* next to a circle of rocks forming a small pit in the center, and he slumped to his knees by its side. Exhaustion tempted him to lay down and sleep, but he held the *yujin's* head to check the beacon.

"Are you still working? We're higher now. Can you connect?"

The *yujin* stared blankly at the ceiling.

"Acquiring GPS…"

"Come on, come on."

"GPS acquired."

"Yes!"

"Connecting to satellite network. Connected. Distress message and location sent."

"Fuck yes!"

He slumped onto his back and let all the fear, worry and panic evaporate out of him. He thought of the city—the pods, the travelators, the safety of the wall—and gave silent gratitude until exhaustion began to claim him. But the persistent danger of his situation demanded he stay alert.

Forcing open his eyes, he was surprised by unfamiliar symbols painted on the underside of the boat, and across the frond-thatching. The strange, tribal-looking hieroglyphics covered the entire ceiling like constellations.

"Where am I?" he asked aloud.

"You're on the Isle of Meti," replied the *yujin*. "Zero-point-eight-eight miles from Shibido."

Yoshi pushed himself up onto his elbow. "You can access the net as well?"

"I am fully connected to the internet via satellite."

Yoshi rolled back to look up at the symbols again.

"Do you know what this hut is?"

"I cannot find a match for the craftsmanship, but the symbols on the ceiling appear to those used in a *Taka* hut, a place of ceremony built by the Minaki tribe of Agu-shi."

Ceremony of Luma.

"But what is it doing here?"

"It is presumed the tradition was brought to Meti by visiting Minaki."

Yoshi's breathing slowed, and a warmth crept over him. Light from the large puddle by the entrance reflected faint ripples of light and shadow across the ceiling. Remembering Singlet's flyer, a strong sense of déjà vu washed over him, like he'd fallen *through* the flyer and into a dream. He chuckled at his exhausted thoughts, and thunder rumbled in the distance. He had to fight his body's demanding need to sleep. He wished his Grandpapa was there to tell him a story.

"Tell me more about the *Taka* huts."

"On Agu-shi, each village had an older *Taka* who would build a hut in a sacred place, enter a trance, and paint symbols on its ceiling. The *Taka* would then bring tribe members to the hut at times of trouble or conflict, a sign they were ready to become *Taka* themselves. The *Taka* would light a small pit, scented with herbs, to permeate the air and induce relaxation."

Yoshi's frazzled mind imagined the smell of the smoke pit burning. He could almost feel its heat as if the cold stones had reignited. In his growing delirium, he thought the *yujin* was his Grandpapa telling him a story.

"The participants laid down and focused on the symbols while the *Taka* led them on a vision ceremony."

A light sweat broke out across his skin with calming release, and his mind continued to wander the symbols above. The shifting light and shadow seemed to give life to them, and his exhausted mind transformed them into more recognizable shapes. He spotted what looked like a small boat by an island shaped like Meti.

"When they were finished, the participants would know if they would be *Taka* themselves."

The sensation of warmth grew stifling, and the apparition became more vivid. A lone figure appeared by the boat and pulled it ashore. They then dragged it up a steep peak and turned it over to make a hut. As Yoshi tried to focus, the figure enlarged, appearing to come to the foreground. The hut extruded itself backward, giving the basic shapes of his vision more dimension and perspective. The figure grew even larger and more detailed, until they stood over Yoshi, a stick-torch in hand, and a face that instantly calmed him.

"Grandpapa?"

The face and shapes blurred, and the heat intensified, pushing Yoshi to the brink of unconsciousness. His eyes fell shut and he sensed his very being floating upward into darkness, detaching from the weight of his body. The boundary of his curiosity expanded, like the mind of a child. A light emerged ahead, and he aimed for it. The light grew until it engulfed him and blinded his mind's eye. A bird trilled over the sound of lapping water.

Sensing his body again, he opened his eyes to find himself looking down at his toes. He wiggled them against the weathered wooden planks of a jetty. Raising his head, he blinked at pink rays of a sun setting over a still sea. Hazy afternoon sunlight warmed his face. A soft hand squeezed his.

He looked up into a woman's face, and he knew it was his mother's. A man spoke to her, and he knew the tall, lean man was his father. He laughed, his mind empty and enjoying the moment—nearly four-years-old, standing on a jetty in the sunset with his Mama and Papa.

"Where's Grandpapa?" Papa asked his mother.

"I think he's gone to his hut."

"The fool's getting too old to go up that hill."

"I'm worried about him," agreed his Mama. "Things are missing from his room, photos and clothes. I think he's moving up there. This morning he was so agitated, he just kept saying 'coming, coming, coming.' You need to talk to him."

"He doesn't listen to me. He's still angry at me for not picking up the torch."

Their voices bounced over Yoshi's head, speaking as if they thought his young mind could not understand. But he knew Grandpapa was getting funny in the brain. He spent more time in his hut at the top of the hill than he did in the house. Yoshi always wondered what Grandpapa did there, but his Papa wouldn't allow him to go.

His Papa kissed his Mama goodbye, and then ruffled Yoshi's hair before climbing off the jetty into a fishing boat. Yoshi hated his Papa going fishing all night, but the darkness meant the boat spooked the tuna less. Something had been stirring them to the surface over the previous few days and his Papa wanted to make the most of an easier catch.

After waving goodbye, his Mama walked him up the jetty, across the road, and through the sunflowers in their front yard. He looked up, and it felt like he was seeing for the first time the watermelon-colored roof tiles and black-potted plants along the stone porch. As his Mama led him inside, she asked him to plant the leftover vegetable seeds. Being the gardener made him proud, and he loved digging his hands in the dirt.

"Don't go too far," she warned as he ran down the steps into the back garden.

Like all the houses by the shore, Yoshi's backed onto the base of the island's steep hill. The final rays of the disappearing sun set the peak ablaze with bright peaches and purples. A sudden light-headedness assailed him, as if the world had slipped a little in its spin. He swayed on the spot, but the sensation passed as soon as it had come, and he thought nothing more of it.

But he didn't feel like planting seeds any longer. He glanced back at the house to make sure his Mama wasn't watching from the window, and then he ran up the hill.

Long grass whipped his bare legs as he scrambled up the slope, growing longer and thicker until it gave way to a forest of towering trees. He followed a faint path weaving through gigantic leaves hanging in the way.

Nearing the top, he smelled sandalwood burning and heard chanting. He spied a boat overturned in a clearing and propped up on branches. Faint smoke curled out from both ends of the funny-looking hut. His Grandpapa appeared at one end, swaying a lit wooden torch in the air with exaggerated gestures.

Excited with curiosity, Yoshi stepped out of the trees and crept closer, the sandalwood growing stronger. Inside, people laid around a small smoke pit. His Grandpapa moved the torch over them to create shadows on the ceiling, as if leading them in a story only they could see.

Struggling to make sense of the game, he grew bored and headed back down the path to finish his chore. A deep navy had spread across the sky from the east, chasing the last light. He grabbed a stick and whacked the fronds blocking his path in imitation of his Grandpapa with his torch. The world dropped into an eerie silence.

Halfway down, a flock of birds burst from the branches around him, shattering his make-believe. He whacked the grass again, when shouting began from below—a few voices at first, then many, panicked and fearful. People ran along the shore, yelling and waving, while others hurried away toward the nearest buildings.

Dread filled him.

The shore didn't look right. The tide was lower than he'd ever seen. Boats lay on their sides on exposed sand, like shipwrecks. Confused, he wondered how his father had gone out in the boat if the tide had been so far out.

A hare sprung from the grass, startling a yelp out of him, before it bolted back into the bush. Wishing he'd stayed in his backyard, he raced down the hill toward home, but a terrible scream stopped him in his tracks.

A long, dark wall had appeared out in the sea, wider than the island. He couldn't remember ever noticing a wall in the sea before. His heart pounded in his ears as he struggled to process what he was seeing. Then the wall shimmered, and a great fear struck him—it was a wave, a giant wave, coming closer, and fast.

His legs shook, and he dropped the stick. He feared running down to his house, but he couldn't turn away. He could only stand and watch as the wall raced toward the island, bringing with it a beautiful rushing noise.

It all happened so unbelievably fast.

The wave rushed over the sandy ground exposed by the low-tide and swept the stranded boats toward the jetties. Yoshi looked desperately for his Papa to appear in his boat and save them. Screams pierced the silence.

To his terror, the wave ploughed the boats into the jetties, smashing them into the trees along the shore and swirling all the debris over the road. The force swept cars off the ground and drove them into the beach-front houses. Something popped loudly, followed by a slow, excruciating rip, like the noise the big tree made when it fell in the storm last summer and just missed their house. Lights sparked out of windows and flames burst from the insides of buildings as the flood inundated the entire shoreline. The popping and ripping continued until a rumble trembled the hill and the rushing white noise engulfed the screaming.

Shaking with shock, Yoshi fell to his knees. A wet warmth bloomed over his crotch and down his legs. He screamed out for his Mama, so sorry for not listening, for not staying in the garden, for not being with her now.

The water below kept coming and submerged the entire sea-side town, swallowing it whole, until it was nothing more than a churning mess of houses, cars, trees and garbage.

And still, the water kept coming, inching up the slope and overflowing into Yoshi's traumatized mind. Everything he knew had been obliterated right before his eyes. He never doubted his parents would always be with him, but now they had been wiped from the world. His young, terrified mind struggled to frame the disaster, what it meant, what it meant for tomorrow, but the edges of the world blurred, and he swayed on his knees.

Strong hands plucked him from the rising darkness. Bobbing up and down on a bony shoulder, he recognized his Grandpapa's sweet, smoky smell.

"Don't look back," his Grandpapa said through gasps.

Yoshi looked anyway, but he no longer recognized anything, all strange, dark shapes floating like weird symbols in a vast sea. The world looked like it was sinking, and still the water came.

His Grandpapa wheezed and stumbled, but he didn't stop. Yoshi's head grew heavy again, and everything went as dark as the sea below that was still *coming, coming, coming*.

PART THREE

The Gift

Invisibility

Roaring engine noise barraged his ears, and gusts buffeted his body. The air pulsed with the throb of rotor blades. He tried opening his eyes, but a glare forced them shut again.

A shadow moved across his eyelids, and a voice shouted through the din.

"Can you hear me, Mr. Goto?"

He tried again and managed to open his eyes. A young woman leaned over him, wearing polished aviators and a yellow helmet. A golden lock of hair hung over her forehead, but a faint, dark mustache betrayed her as a true brunette.

"Yoshi Goto, can you hear me?"

He nodded—at least he thought he did—and he tried to sit up, but straps restrained him to a stretcher.

Random snippets of memory flashed through his mind, like a flicker book with missing pages and the rest out of order: a weather reporter on a small TV warning about a storm; his shoes splashing through a rain-deluged street; himself standing naked in a dim factory office.

"Where am I?" he asked, his voice snatched off by the wind.

"We picked up your *yujin*'s beacon. You're on Supa Panther 2, one of the Special Rescue Team's helicopters. And you're on your way home. You're a very fortunate man, Mr. Goto."

He mumbled something about becoming stuck in the cargo trailer, and the paramedic relayed his status through her helmet communicator.

"Pulse 120 and thready. Blood pressure 85 over 58. Ringer's Lactate running. Says he's a Real Toy Robotics employee, got trapped in the downed cargo drone. Most fortunate human being!"

Yoshi rolled his head to see out the window. At first, he didn't recognize the world. The storm clouds had thinned to gossamer ribbons dissolving across a pink sky, and the sea's aquarium stillness stretched on forever.

"Was there another Shift?" he asked, his mind confusing itself. The paramedic patted him on the shoulder.

"Everything's going to be just fine, Mr. Goto. The typhoon has passed, and it's a Wonderful Day. You're nearly home."

Below, the wall's ribbon of concrete came into view before they passed over a patchwork of buildings and streets before lowering onto a building top. While the rotors still spun, two nurses appeared by his side, their white coats flapping in the wind like wings as they unloaded him into a waiting elevator.

He watched ceiling tiles overhead zoom past as he was transferred through a busy ward full of voices, astringent smells and beeping machines. After he was parked inside a shared dorm, a doctor visited to advise he'd be kept overnight for observation, then left him with the nurse who checked his hydration drip. Finally, the fuss ended, and he was left to rest behind a closed curtain.

In the private, sterile oasis, he sat back into a flood of more memories, from stumbling drunk out of The Undertow to waking up on Meti and finding the hut; the tsunami, his parents, and his young mind collapsing under the weight of it all. A great sadness, an *old* sadness, welled up through his heavy soul, and with it came a new awareness—he had blamed himself not just for his parent's death, but for everyone who died on Meti that day.

He bit his quivering lip to hold back tears, but two escapees trickled down each side of his nose. He wrapped his arms around his shoulders and hugged his childhood self, a young boy who found the instant vanishing of everything he knew so terrifyingly difficult to fathom, and a guilt so colossal, that he'd let the tsunami take his memory of that day, too.

He held the unearthed sorrow in his chest until it receded further, exposing the wreck of his acting career as a failed attempt to hide from his fear, a world he'd created to escape to but lost himself in.

Soft voices and footsteps beyond the curtain formed a gentle background soundscape.

He imagined his four-year-old self kneeling among the wreckage on Meti, and he summoned the faces of his parents to his mind. Feeling the depth of what had been taken from him, he held their memory close; his mother's soft but firm grip, his father's hand ruffling his hair.

I know, now, there was nothing I could do. And I know you'd want me to live a happy life with an open heart.

Thank you, for all that you did for me. I promise to live that happy life you wished for me. I won't forget you again.

He unwrapped his arms and voluntarily set adrift the grief that had locked him out of a happier future, the scars of its final passing becoming shapes and symbols on the inside of his heart. A pressure released from his body like steam.

He laid back again in the cloud of pillows, noticing an island calm nestled in his chest, as if some lost idol had been returned to the chamber of his soul. Released from his permanent state of tension, he sensed a new energy growing in the space created by the experience in the hut. He wondered if the *coming, coming, coming* that haunted him all along, wasn't the fear of the ocean out to get him, but the memory calling out from the deluge of his trauma with a truth that would transform him.

Without warning, the curtain whooshed back, and a pristinely dressed young woman strode in. Slicked, black hair and a focused expression pulled her face tight. She wore a Maya badge tagged to her chest.

"Hello, sir, I'm Yuna, the resident Lenzist. I check Lenz performance for anyone involved in serious incidents. Are you having any problems with yours?"

He noticed his Lenz Menu was still dormant, so he tried blinking it on.

"I see the menu, but it's not activating."

Smiling maternally, Yuna pulled a glove from her pocket and wiggled in her fingers. Alarmed, Yoshi squirmed in his bed. But Yuna held up the gloved hand, palm forward, revealing a symbol on each fingertip.

"Tell me, what do you see?"

"On your glove? I see some symbols."

The Lenzist frowned. "No augmentation? No floating animals or swirling patterns?"

"No."

Disapproval furrowed her brow. To Yoshi's great relief, she took off the glove, before withdrawing a familiar silver vial from her pocket. "Tilt your head back, please."

But as Yuna poised the vial over his eye, he grabbed her wrist.

"Wait."

She gasped and he let her go. She pulled her hand to her chest and allowed the matronly smile to return.

"It's okay, Mr. Goto. I'm just restoring your Lenz."

But the thought of any more distortion of reality disturbed the idol of calm Meti had left in him.

"I'm fine for now, thank you."

The Lenzist scrunched her face and gave another disapproving frown.

"Well, I see you've worn the Lenz for only a couple of weeks. Your regular vision shouldn't be so impacted that it would need any rehabilitation. But don't leave it off for too long, please, or you'll have to go through any adjustment period again, alright?" She patted him on the leg and disappeared behind the curtain.

Left alone again, Yoshi laid back to sleep. But a muffled urgency called him away from the temptation, as more fragments of his life flashed through his mind like a lighthouse gone mad; the prop gun going off on the set of *One Man Dreaming*; the prize pod hitting the tree in the mall; the scream of lightning exploding the cargo drone open—all accidents. But stealing his clone was a deliberate crime. The rescue team would have scanned his face, and the police were most likely informed. It was only a matter of time before they contacted Gray and turned up at the hospital for a statement

Just check out, walk home, get some thinking time.

He lowered his legs over the side of the bed to test his mobility. His muscles pinched in return, but after a few steps he felt fine. In fact, he felt lighter than he remembered, as if he'd been wearing a backpack full of weights all his life. A new energy simmered in his core. He could run if he had to.

He reached over to pull the IV drip out of his arm, but another rustle of the curtain made him jerk his hand back and turn around. His gut dropped.

"Hello, Mr. Goto."

Tyler Gray stepped inside the curtain and slid it shut behind him. He carried a black tote and wore a look of concern.

"Thank heavens you're alright. As soon as I heard that one of my *factory workers* had been trapped in a container, I just had to make sure they were okay."

A maelstrom of emotion swirled inside Yoshi. He gripped the side of the bed to steady himself.

"You had no right to build a *yujin* of me *before* I'd made my decision."

Gray maneuvered around the bed as he spoke.

"I understand. You were intoxicated and angry, and you lashed out. I'm sure you weren't of sound mind when you *broke* into the factory and stole and damaged my property. I'm sure, just like before, we can work something out."

Yoshi's instinct reared up like a cobra. "What do you mean?"

"I suspect it won't be long before the media hear about this and the Sight drones swoop in. I *could* let you leave now and corroborate your story, as a factory worker, and not press charges. Just as I helped bury the mall issue. All this I can manage."

Gray placed the tote on the table and faced Yoshi. His thin veil of politeness slid aside, revealing an utter contempt that had been sitting inside all along.

"Maya District is at a critical point. I can't have you screwing up our product with your unpredictability. Like you did to *One Man Dreaming*, like you did at Nebulae, like you did yesterday. You're a damn Ground Hog Day pest. You must be annoying even to yourself."

Anger flared through Yoshi, but he could no longer deny he'd made all his own choices. Admitting that instantly cooled his internal reaction, his new inner calm already beginning to infiltrate his life.

Gray's posture softened, too. He drew a tablet from his pocket and placed it on top of the tote, the new contract glowing under the glass.

"You can detach yourself from all of it, Yoshi—your messy past, your uncertain future—and give yourself a new name, a new you. Anything you choose.

You can just *vamoose,* without any responsibility, and into the role of your choice forever. All it takes is a signature. I'll even still give you the generous payment. You see? I'm not a monster after all. I'm just a businessman with a passionate vision. So, Yoshi, are you ready to play your most convincing role, the *new you?"*

Gray's watch flashed. He held up one finger, mouthing the words 'One minute,' then he stepped out behind the curtain. As his pacing silhouette rippled back and forth across the pleated curtain, snippets of his conversation interwove with Yoshi's thoughts.

—"Ceremony of Luma? Never heard of it. We booked the area two months ago."—

He's right, I've done it again—One Man Dreaming, the mall, and now this.

—"We have permission to set up there, do they? And the council notified the public days ago about no access to the old area tonight."—

If I've been trying to be someone else my whole life, was any of it even real? It was just a costume of sorts. For the first time, I know what I'm not.

—"I hardly doubt anyone has even heard of this ceremony. Move them on. Leave the Mayor to me."—

Maybe this is my real second chance, to break the cycle and have the future my parents and Grandpapa would've wanted for me.

Gray whisked the curtain back aside. "Please excuse me, that was urgent—"

"It's okay. I get it."

Gray clasped his hands in front with monk grace and remained silent.

"You're right," Yoshi continued, "I've been chasing a fantasy. It's time I let it go."

Gray nodded and nudged the tablet toward Yoshi.

Certain he was answering the call of his new energy, Yoshi traced his finger across the tablet and signed away the costume of his name.

An odd clucking noise escaped Gray as he retrieved the tablet. He disappeared the device into his jacket with magician deftness and crisped his posture.

"Doesn't that feel *liberating*, Yoshi? Now, when you're ready, Driver will be downstairs to assist you in finalizing things. The police are on their way."

"What? But what do I say to them?"

"*You* won't need to say anything to them. But the *new* Yoshi Goto will. The *yujin* you stole from me was not the only version. The new Yoshi Goto will speak to the police and the media tomorrow. Now," he said, patting the tote, "get changed, and we'll help you slip out." Gray stepped behind the curtain to let Yoshi change.

Yoshi pulled the drip from his vein with a wince and opened the tote to see the costume of a fugitive— black cargo pants, a white t-shirt and a gray hoodie.

Not wanting to leave any trace of himself behind, he stuffed his old clothes into the bag after changing. Something metal clanged at his feet—Kai's lighter.

"Are you ready, sir?" asked a new voice from behind the curtain.

Yoshi slid the lighter into his pocket and grabbed the bag as the curtain opened again. One of the Uchida brothers waited for him, but Gray was nowhere in sight.

"This way, sir," said Mr. Uchida.

Yoshi followed him through an obstacle course of moving beds, crisscrossing nurses and wandering patients. Reaching the elevator, they rode down to ground in silence and exited the building to where Driver waited.

"Good luck, sir," said Mr. Uchida. "Driver will take things from here."

Mr. Uchida bowed and gestured for Yoshi to climb into the pod. By the time the door shut, the Uchida twin was gone, leaving the pick-up zone empty except for an elderly man in a white gown in a wheelchair by the entrance—face a maze of wrinkles, hair a cloud of white, and waving at someone unseen.

The pod pulled away, jerking Yoshi back. Driver seemed to be in a hurry.

The absence of his Lenz had returned the world to its dull, bronzed grays. He flexed his focus on the buildings furthest away, testing his vision for any Lenz-induced short-sightedness, but it seemed fine.

As the passing shadows of buildings flashed afternoon light on the pod's windows, he sensed a delicate lace of new beginnings shimmering under the day. He shut his eyes and looked forward to soaking in New Gate's pristine bath.

"Sir," said Driver, "I'm taking you home to get your possessions in order. On the way, I can assist you in initiating the identity change process."

As Driver explained the next steps, Yoshi's watch vibrated with a message from Haru Hanada.

Subject: New Role

He scoffed at his ex-agent's nerve and swiped to delete.

"To initiate the process," Driver continued, "please grant me access to your digital ID. I can draw your documents from there and autofill all forms. Maya Technologies has clearance to fast track your documentation and has prescheduled a hearing for tomorrow."

"Tomorrow?" Yoshi's voice squeaked.

"Before we can begin, you must choose your new name. The studio has compiled suggestions to assist you in your decision. Adopting a generic name will help minimize any chance of future scrutiny."

The act of choosing a new name seemed significant, like it should have meaning. A list of bland names displayed in the pod's windshield, but he had no idea what would suit the new him.

"I need time to think about this."

"Certainly, sir. Take the next two hours to read the tips we have prepared, and you can decide while you pack your things."

"Two hours?"

"Tonight, you'll stay at Mountain Station, and remain there for two to three days until you receive your digital documentation. Then, you'll travel by train to stay at the airport hotel until your passport is issued. You can use that time to decide where you'd like to go. The studio will purchase you a one-way ticket to the destination of your choice."

Maya's fast-tracking made it clear to Yoshi they wanted him out of Shibido before the premier. He noticed, too, Driver already only referred to him as 'sir'.

The pod slowed at the turn to New Gate, and Yoshi again imagined laying in the bath, perhaps where his new name would come to him. But the pod turned right and slipped into a lane heading toward the southern elevators.

"Where are we going?"

"We're going to your home, sir, so you can organize your belongings. I've arranged for your clothes and personal items from New Gate to be sent to the hotel."

New Gate disappeared behind him in the rear-view monitor as the factory tops of the industrial district peeked out from the south.

He couldn't shake the feeling he was going in the wrong   direction.

Farewell

The pod slid into a glass elevator and the southern districts stretched out ahead. Streets flooded from the storm had formed moated blocks, and garbage lay strewn across the dry roads like ocean debris regurgitated from the bellies of whales.

Reaching ground level, the pod headed toward the main southern artery. Yoshi read through the tips for choosing a new name.

1. Choose a name that you'll feel comfortable using and being called.
2. Practice introducing yourself in a mirror or with strangers to see how it feels.
3. Practice signing your new name to develop a natural signature.

As the pod turned into the industrial district, the Real Toy Robotics sign came into view. But the neon was off, and the letters R, E, A, L had been pulled down by a crane that now reached for the Y. As he passed the factory, a string of delivery trucks pulled out, passing a sign on the fence:

Acquired and relocated by Maya Technologies.

Yoshi cringed at how berserk with drunken anger he must have been to attempt his foolish raid.

The pod turned into the street opposite and stopped outside his container tower.

"Please remember, sir, we require your new name in two hours. I'll be here when you're ready with your belongings. Bring only what you can carry on a plane. We'll look after the rest for you."

Butterflies took flight in his stomach—the name-changing process sped up with every passing minute.

Dodging puddles to the elevator, he struggled to recall what possessions of any real value he owned, as if the process was downloading and deleting his memories. Reaching his level, he pulled the front door open, and ankle-deep water washed out and over his feet. Swearing with surprise, he sprang up on tippy-toes and stepped back ballerina-style. He stared with disbelief at the sight of the flooded, storm-wrecked interior.

He took a few steps inside and looked around. A torn blind fluttered by a broken window that framed the crane outside lowering the Y. His wall screen had fallen and smashed on the coffee table, its shattered glass twinkling on the floor under the water.

Checking the bedroom, he surprised himself by how little he had of value, sentimental or monetary, like his existence hadn't mattered even to himself. The wardrobe lay face down, one arm of a jacket poking out from underneath like a squashed cartoon robber.

Looking for anything worth salvaging, he spotted one of his Grandpapa's photos drifting past the doorway. Picking it up by its corner, he turned it around to see Meti on a calm bay. Water dripped from its edges, as if his woken memory of the tsunami had somehow released a flood from the photo. The soaked image's weight tore itself from his fingertips and it fell back to the water.

He surprised himself again with how little nostalgia or sadness he felt about not returning. A sudden urge compelled him to decide his new name before leaving the apartment. Any significance of the choice had gone, just an item to tick off a to-do list.

He looked around, certain he could draw something from the debris, and he spied the empty Jack Daniel's bottle by the sink. He faced the mirror.

"Hi, I'm Jack. I'm Jack, nice to see you."

He always wanted an English sounding name.

So, he just needed a surname.

He cleared his mind and thought of how it all started, two and half weeks ago, when Haru called him to play Santa. Saint Nick. Nicholas. No, not that, his surname had to be Japanese to save him explaining himself. Tanaka, then. Common enough, but perhaps too common. Kobayashi. Jack Kobayashi.

"Hi, I'm Jack Kobayashi."

He felt nothing, but at least the name didn't feel uncomfortable.

That'll do.

Done with the surprisingly dispassionate business, he took in a deep breath and left the apartment without looking back.

As he exited the elevator on ground floor, his watch vibrated and Mico appeared on the screen. The sight of his only friend strummed his heart.

"Chief, where you been? I've been worried."

Yoshi opened his mouth to explain everything but caught himself. Mico was not going to like his decision.

"I got a bit swamped."

"Why don't you come to The Undertow and tell me about it? I'll buy you a water."

Yoshi realized he was just going to have to face his friend's disappointment if he wanted to say goodbye.

"Yeah, sure. I need to shower first. I'll be there in thirty."

He climbed into the waiting pod and asked Driver to take him to the nearest capsule hotel.

"Certainly, sir. And have you decided on your name already?"

"I have. Jack Kobayashi."

Saying the name felt quite natural.

"Well done, Mr. Kobayashi. If you could sign the form on the screen, I'll initiate the process. I imagine this must be quite exciting, re-installing yourself."

He didn't hesitate and signed *Yoshi Goto* for the final time.

"Thank you, Mr. Kobayashi. I shall now initiate the process to officialize your new identity."

As the pod passed the Real Toy Robotics factory, the crane lowered the Y onto the ground.

Determined to think of himself as Jack Kobayashi by the time the documents came through, he brought up a blank screen and practiced his new signature. The name flowed easily, and he developed a comfortable version before he reached the hotel.

After Driver checked him in under a Maya account, he waited his turn for the communal shower. When he finally stood under the warm water, his thoughts and worries melted away, and he had to drag himself out. Redressing in the clothes Gray had given him, he headed to The Undertow.

As the pod slowed by Good Time Adult Store, he kept his face turned away until he ducked inside The Undertow's entrance. Heading down the spiral case, he found the front area almost empty.

Yoshi spotted Mico behind the bar at the rear. Weaving between the empty tables, he prepared to say goodbye to his only friend.

"Chief," Mico said, pouring two whiskies. "Tell me you fought."

Yoshi waved away Mico's question. "Let's toast the future."

Mico slid him the drink. They chinked glasses and gulped, then gasped together as their throats burned.

"You *look* like you been fighting," Mico finally managed. "You gonna tell me what happened or do I gotta use persuasion."

He poured them both another drink.

Yoshi laughed and shrugged. "Sorry, Mico, I just… you wouldn't believe me if I told you."

"Chief, it don't matter if I believe you or not. What matters is you say it out 'loud."

Chink, gulp, gasp.

Yoshi wiped his lips and took a deep breath.

"I sold my identity to Maya. In a couple of days, it'll be official—Maya will own Yoshi Goto, and I'll be Jack Kobayashi. I can't ever act again, and I have to leave the country. But I've been paid plenty to go anywhere I want and create the life I really want."

Mico blinked spasmodically, like Yoshi's words were spit in his eyes.

"Why would you do something so *stupid*? I told you to fight."

Yoshi took another deep breath.

"Because I did something even more stupid. The other night, after I left here, I went to the robotics factory and stole a clone *yujin* they'd made of me." He paused for Mico's reaction, but his friend remained stunned and mute. "I got stuck in a cargo drone. It crashed, and I ended up on Meti."

Mico's eyes shot wide, almost throwing his eyebrows off his face. "You *crashed* on *Meti*?"

"Sort of. A rescue team found me in a hut. I must have stumbled onto it; some parts are vague." He scratched his head and looked up at the mural of outdated ocean currents, hesitating at what he was about to say. "I had a vision in that hut. I saw… I must have been dehydrated or had concussion or something. But I saw my Grandpapa, I saw my parents, and then I saw what happened the day the tsunami hit Meti. I always thought I didn't remember it because I was so young, but the hut, it showed me."

Mico crossed his arms and looked away for a moment, then looked back at Yoshi.

"That sounds like a *Taka* Hut. I didn't know there were any on Meti."

Yoshi rubbed the edge of his glass. "I think my Grandpapa built it."

"Your Grandpapa was Minaki?"

The stick-torch symbol flashed in Yoshi's mind, and his Grandpapa's face came back to him from the vision.

"He was a citizen of Shibido, like me, but I've never seen his birth certificate, so, I guess it's possible. Or maybe his Papa was Minaki, or his Grandpapa. But I believe he was practicing this *Taka* thing on Meti. Maybe he was the only one." *He's still angry at me for not picking up the torch.* "My father didn't believe in it."

Mico nodded.

"Not everyone takes to being *Taka*. It's not easy carrying the burden of the light's source so others can benefit from its shine."

Pour, chink, gulp, gasp.

"But what does a *Taka* do?" Yoshi asked.

"The *Taka* provide communion with spirit to unblock energy in people. They are like pressure valves for soul energy, between the living and the dead, the past and future. And once someone goes through a ceremony, they can take on the *Taka* role, illuminate others by sharing what they learnt from facing their own struggle. So, maybe you are *Taka* now."

A bark of incredulousness escaped Yoshi. "My Grandpapa never took me through any ritual."

"But, maybe, now he has, in the *Taka* hut."

"My Grandpapa went craz—he struggled enough with just being present, he couldn't even tell a proper story."

Mico leaned down again.

"The crazy *Taka* are often the most powerful. Most *Taka* can hold full awareness for only a short time, and then they must pass it on. If they spend too much time going between here and there, they get stuck in the portal they hold open, like that Fourth Wall thing you think you got stuck in. They lose their mind. But some remain lucid deep in their madness, and those ones, they can do some real magic."

Yoshi rolled his eyes. Mico returned a mock bark of unbelief and poured another round, but Yoshi didn't drink his. Mico gulped, and his words began to slur.

"You know, you city people think these sort of experiences are the mumbo jumbo of the magicians and witches in your movies. Your technologies leave no room for *luma* to flow. But *Taka* ceremonies can alter people's consciousness, they are a sacred technology passed on to those who believe in the crazy things that start happening in their lives. Anything unusual happen in your life lately, Yoshi?"

"You mean besides falling out of a cargo drone with my doppelgänger and waking up on the island I was born on? I've had the craziest few weeks anyone's ever had."

Mico winked and poured himself another. "And have you met any unusual people?"

Yoshi thought of the boy, and Kai, but he shook their images out of his mind. Mico smiled warmly.

"You had a vision that reminded you of who you are. Then you came back and you were stripped of who you were trying to be. That is *Taka* magic."

Yoshi rolled his eyes again. "Magic?"

"You don't believe in magic? You're acting is like *Taka* magic. You work in the imagination. You enter an altered state, bridge the here and there, and take the watchers to another place. *Taka* are the ancestors of actors, like your Grandpapa is of you."

Mico's drunken words were starting to craft the crazy into a weird kind of sense. But Yoshi didn't *want* them to make sense. He'd made his decision, and he feared if he started believing in magic, he might also have to believe in ghosts.

"Well, I'm not an actor anymore. I'm not even Yoshi Goto."

Mico shrugged, poured himself another drink and gulped it down. His eyes grew glassy and his words slipped on his slurring.

"You said it's not official yet, right? Two days, right? You're still you, Yoshi."

Yoshi pushed his glass away.

"I'm not Yoshi Goto, I'm not Joe Joe, and I'm not *Taka*. In fact, until I get my documents, I'm nothing. I'm a refugee."

Mico's eyebrows arched, and Yoshi cringed with instant shame.

"Sorry, Mico, bad choice of words. I'm just saying, I need to focus on one future, one reality. In a few days, I can start again. I'll be Jack Kobayashi, and I'll be able to go wherever I want. I can't mess this chance up like I've messed up everything else. I'm breaking the cycle."

"Okay. You keep telling yourself this ridiculous story, *Jack Kobayashi*."

"*My* ridiculous story? You want me to believe my dead Grandpapa came to me in a vision on a sinking island to make me a *shaman*? To do what? Levitate the city and fly us all away to a Stratodel?"

Mico frowned. "What's a Stratodel?"

Yoshi groaned aloud. He stood and held his watch to the pay terminal.

"Mico, my friend, it's my turn to call time out."

"I was just getting into that discussion," Mico said, scrunching his face. "Shine your light, my friend."

"My Grandpapa used to say that."

"You know what that means?"

"Shine the brightest."

"No. It means *illuminate the most*."

"That's what I said."

"No," Mico said, placing a palm on his chest. "It means to shine your true self, but not to shine brighter than others, to *illuminate* them. Light, hope, *luma*, this is what our true selves give to each other."

Yoshi reached over the bar and hugged his good friend. They held tight.

"I'm glad we got to meet."

"Me too, Chief. You take care of yourself."

They patted each other's back and let go. Yoshi finalized the farewell with a deep bow before weaving back through the spot-lit tables and up the stairwell.

Stepping into the afternoon chill, he let the door shut on shamans and portals and talking dead people, and he summoned Driver. Trying not to look behind at the companion *yujins* in the next-door window, he gazed up. Cobalt-tinged clouds streaked a pink afternoon sky, and he wondered what the sky over the Tianjin Pontoons looked like. He shoved his hands into his pockets, and his knuckles hit cold metal. He pulled out Kai's lighter and twirled it in his fingers until the pod arrived.

"Are you ready to go to the station now, sir?" Driver asked as he climbed in.

Sitting back, he stared at the lighter before answering. But he didn't see the tarnished gold, or Shibido Connect's address on its side. He watched a replay in his mind of snippets of Kai, badly edited by a memory ill-prepared for the unexpected recall—the twitch of Kai's nostrils each time he shifted up his spectacles; Kai holding Yoshi's jacket in the mall change room; his excited smile as he came out of the protest crowd in front of New Gate; the warmth of his hand in the van; their bodies pressed against each other in the server cupboard; their tongues wrangling like oiled-up Turkish wrestlers.

Surely a chemistry like that was worth a more proper goodbye than a wink in a maintenance corridor.

"Mr. Kobayashi? Is there anyone else you would like to say goodbye to?"

Perhaps it was the natural and ancient desire to capture another kiss that made up his mind, if only for the last kiss' sake. Or maybe it was just to be the one who walked away first. Regardless, Yoshi told himself Kai was his last loose strand in Shibido that he should tie off.

He stopped twirling the lighter, so the address faced him, and he read it out to Driver.

"Certainly, sir. ETA, 13 minutes."

As the pod zoomed toward the south-west districts, Yoshi emboldened himself to thank Kai for opening his heart. But the more he rehearsed it in his mind, the cornier it sounded. Perhaps he could just pretend he was returning the lighter.

Buildings receded and thinned out on either side as he traveled along the interchange before shooting out to merge with the highway traffic. A giant billboard loomed over the road, showing a video of a mother in a park lifting her baby into the air as sentences faded in and out below:

In this technological age,
our youngest should get
the earliest possible start in learning.
After all, connecting is everything.
Lenz for our most precious,
for their best start in life.

Yoshi shook his head as the billboard disappeared behind him. *Kai's going to love that one.*

After ten minutes, the pod exited the highway to weave deep in among a tight warren of streets. Becoming more nervous, he decided to let the farewell conversation with Kai just happen.

The pod found its way to a stop outside an orange, two-story warehouse.

"We're here, Mr. Kobayashi. Should I wait for you?"

"Yes, thanks."

His heartbeat sped up as he crossed the street, and he broke into a light sweat. As he wandered down the side path, a dog barked at his footsteps from behind the fence. The building stretched far back, and seven or so doors dotted the exterior. No sound came from inside, but a powerful chemical odor rode out on a gentle breeze from the rear.

He checked the address details on the lighter before walking down to the fourth door and knocking. No one answered, so he thumped politely, but still no response. He ran his fingers through his hair with a sigh and resigned to the fact he'd gotten so caught up in the excitement of seeing Kai again that he hadn't really thought it through.

"Hey," called a familiar voice from above. Kai's freckled face and naked shoulders poked out of a window on the second level. His bespectacled smile seemed to activate some anti-gravity function around Yoshi's body. "What are you doing here?"

Yoshi held up the lighter. "I was packing my things to head off and found this in my pocket. Thought I'd say a proper goodbye since we didn't get to last time."

Kai's smile dimmed a little, and Yoshi's antigravity sensation wavered.

"I'll meet you around the back," Kai said and disappeared inside.

Sensing disappointment, Yoshi headed down the path to an open space at the rear where the funk of soldered metal, paint, and burnt glue wafted out from an open garage door. Gold and red body parts of some sort of robot costumes hung from the ceiling. Partly hidden by the suspended limbs, a man with a scarf wrapped around his head, and wearing a respiratory mask, held a welding iron to a gold helmet. Yoshi recognized the Cylon helmet from the old Battlestar Galactica reruns on *Flixy*.

The man suddenly stopped and pulled his mask down. Yoshi's back tightened into crocodile skin as his eyes locked with Raiden's.

"Oh, hi," Raiden said casually, before calling upstairs. "Kai. Fun Police are here." He pulled the mask back on and continued welding.

The suspended costume parts quivered on the right and Kai emerged, shirtless and his pale skin glistened with the shine of a light sweat.

Yoshi parked his anger at Raiden. "Hey."

"This is a surprise," Kai said, stopping an awkward distance away.

Yoshi fumbled for the words he wanted to say, but Kai's aloofness got the better of him. He gestured to the costumes.

"What's all this?"

"We're protesting—" Kai stopped himself short. "What are you doing here? I thought you didn't need any more trouble."

"I'm leaving Shibido, and I just wanted to say goodbye."

Kai squinted through his glasses and took a step closer. "You've taken your Lenz out. You've either lost everything or you found yourself."

Yoshi couldn't hold back from smiling at Kai's frankness.

"Kai," called Raiden from inside, pushing a suspended red arm out of his way. "We gotta get this costume done ASAP if I'm gonna have both ready."

Behind Raiden, a sketch of Maya District had been tacked to the wall, an aerial view, with a grid drawn over the top of it. The back of Yoshi's neck tingled.

"You're protesting *One Man Dreaming* again?" he asked Kai.

"We're protesting Maya District," Kai explained.

"Nothing personal, Yoshi," Raiden added. "Your film is just a casualty in this."

Yoshi ignored him and lowered his voice. "A *casualty*, Kai? Sounds a bit serious."

Kai folded his arms. "Maya are seeking approval to spread across *all* the districts in Low Ground. The homeless will be completely forgotten, and the Minaki will have nowhere to go. People need to be reminded of what's real."

The talk had veered far from the private and personal chat Yoshi had imagined. But the depth of Kai's empathy for issues bigger than himself resonated with Yoshi more than before.

"I know, Kai, it's wrong. And it's brave of you to do something, but—"

Grunting sounded from the side path. Akio stomped into the backyard, lugging the same large green bag he had hid the drone in. But now the bag's sides bulged with something much larger and heavier than a drone. He nodded at Yoshi and Kai and hauled the bag into the garage where he unzipped it and pulled out two black boxes.

"What are you doing with scramblers?" Yoshi demanded.

Kai jutted his chin. "You better go, now, Yoshi."

"This looks like *more* than trouble."

Kai looked away, struggling to speak, and Raiden called out on his behalf.

"We're going to shut off the Lenz and remind everyone of reality."

Yoshi's head spun. "Are you crazy?"

Kai held up his hands to placate Yoshi's shock, as he called back to Raiden. "How about we keep things more private?"

"There are other ways to make a point, Kai," Yoshi said, "safer ways."

"Like what, Yoshi, a petition? People aren't going to change their behavior unless their comfort is challenged. They need to be convinced that a change is good for them. It needs to *feel personal*."

Kai didn't look as convinced by his own words as he seemed to think he was.

"Lobby the council, then, I don't know. People could get hurt."

The crunch of gravel underfoot quietened them both as Raiden walked up. Yoshi stepped back, every muscle in his body tensed.

"No one's going to get hurt," Raiden said, looking at Kai's worried face. "The estimates for attendance are low, just about everyone's streaming from home. We're just going to break the spell long enough to fuck up the Sight."

"The Lenz is the problem," Kai said to Yoshi. "It distracts everyone from reality."

"And the council is loving the tourism Maya's bringing, so they won't be jeopardizing that. They're passive terrorists."

"No," Kai said, shooting Raiden a sharp look. "They're stuck in the hopelessness from the Shift. We all are. We worry today's kids might be the last generation, don't we? That's what we think, right, that another Shift is imminent, a worse one? But it's too depressing to even mention. We just self-medicate our despair with a constant flow of alternate realities. And the Lenz is making us lose the ability to perceive which one is real."

"People are responsible for their own decisions," Raiden argued. "Gray is helping them do it, but they choose not to care."

"He loves the challenge of profit," Yoshi said, "but I think he genuinely believes he's giving people a kind of hope."

Raiden stepped forward. "How close are you to him?"

Yoshi flushed with guilt. Kai's eyes lit up with whatever idea Raiden was suggesting.

"Help us, Mr. Big-Time-Actor," Raiden said, "with your great acting skills and contacts."

"Yes," agreed Kai excitedly. "You could help us get into the VIP area."

Yoshi backed away. "There's no way I'm getting involved in this."

"See, Kai, he's the same as everybody else, just cares about himself."

Yoshi ignored Raiden's taunts and looked him in the eye. "Can I speak to Kai alone? Just for one minute?"

Raiden huffed and stormed back into the garage, swiping aside the limbs. Yoshi turned to Kai.

"I didn't come here to argue. I just—"

But Kai took his hand and silenced him.

"We're the same, you know. You just don't see it. But I saw it when we first met. Everyone else gave up on their hopes after the Shift. They stopped trying. But not you, Yoshi. You kept chasing yours. You believe in a future."

Surprised by Kai's impression of him, Yoshi rubbed Kai's fingers and took a breath of courage.

"I was deluded. But you started to make me *think*. That's why I'm here now, to thank you for that. For making me more real."

Kai grabbed Yoshi's other hand.

"Then help me make others more real. Or are you still worried about Yoshi Goto's image?"

Yoshi dropped his head, caught off-guard.

"Yoshi?" Kai pressed.

Yoshi really didn't want to say anything, but he'd learnt silence was a lie.

"I'm not Yoshi Goto anymore."

"What?"

A whirring buzz squealed out of the garage as Akio drilled parts of the Cylon costume together.

"I sold my identity to Maya," Yoshi shouted.

"You *what*?"

"I have to change my name and leave Shibido."

"Are you crazy?"

"I did something stupid and Maya were going to press charges. I'd go to jail."

"Why would they want *your* identity?"

"My profile's getting Sight again, and it's rising. Maya want to own that and all their actors."

Kai threw his head back and roared with laughter. "You really are trouble, Yoshi Goto, or whatever your name is now."

Yoshi couldn't help but laugh with him. Then Kai gave Yoshi's hands a squeeze and let them go.

"Look, I'm really happy you came to say goodbye, but I'm in the middle of something that's a lot more important than you or me."

"I get it. But this is dangerous. People mightn't be ready for this awakening. Maybe they need the delusion, like kids pretend to believe in Santa. Remember? You might wreck the only way they know how to hope. And you might get hurt."

"Raiden is right," Kai said, shaking his head. "Sight rules everything these days, and people aren't going to change unless they really see, and feel, they're in danger, too."

Raiden stopped drilling and called out. "Come on, Kai. I need to see how this fits with the rest of it."

Inside, Akio had assembled the red Cylon costume, while Raiden wired MR goggles to the golden helmet. The district map behind them suddenly made more sense to Yoshi. A gold flag stuck out of the northern edge, and a red flag stuck out of the south. At the top of the map was written and circled 7:45 p.m.

Red coming in from the south, gold in from the north—like a war strategy.

Yoshi grabbed Kai's arm and nodded toward the garage.

"Raiden thinks things aren't going to get better unless everyone is as angry as he is. He's dangerous."

Kai shook off Yoshi's hold. "We believe in what we're doing. Can you say the same?"

"I don't have a choice."

"There's always a choice. Go with the easy option, like everybody else. Or fight it."

"It's not that simple." Yoshi fumed at Kai's stubborn black-and-white perspective. "And what's wrong with being like everybody else? What's wrong with wanting to *not* think about things, to have some enjoyment now while we can?"

Kai's face shuttered through shock and anger, before locking into disappointment.

"Not everyone takes easily to the truth."

Without a goodbye, he turned and headed back in among the suspended robot costumes.

Furious Kai got to walk off first again, Yoshi briefly considering calling the police before deciding he didn't want to seem like a jaded admirer.

Kai slipped an arm into the gold Cylon costume as Raiden placed the helmet over his head. He gave Yoshi a final glance through the tinted glass of the MR goggles, and then he looked away.

Yoshi couldn't discern if what he saw in Kai's eyes was growing excitement or fear. He tore himself away and skulked back up the lane. Unable to get Kai's eyes out of his mind, he suddenly recognized the look on his face for what it really was—denial. Kai had built his own Maya delusion, made himself a hero in his own movie, and got himself in too deep to admit it.

Swamped by disappointment, and certain there was no place left in Shibido for any magic he could believe in, Yoshi looked forward to vanishing for good.

Perspective

A cool ocean breeze blew across the city to the slopes of the mountain range, skimmed through the branches of stepped pine trees, and eddied inside a glass and concrete hotel room on the fifth level of Mountain Station Hotel.

Yoshi woke shivering to find himself face-down on a leather couch, his body contorted from a restless slumber. He wiped spittle from his cheek and checked his watch—4 p.m., 23rd December. He'd slept twenty two hours.

Stretching out the stiffness, he sat up. Two black totes sat on a marble table surrounded by four Ghost chairs. He opened one to see his clothes from the hospital, and in the other, his unwashed clothes from New Gate. He zipped the bags closed and walked over to the window to take in the afternoon view.

The sun-lit pine trees sliced the city view into pieces, their tips aflame with brilliant orange from the unseen sun dropping somewhere behind him. Through the branch's sharp gaps, High Scape glistened atop

Shibido like a crown, the sea-wall her dirty dress. The pre-dusk smelled like things disappearing.

He pressed his forehead against the cool glass. The distant perspective gave him thinking room to reflect upon the blitz of the last few weeks—being catapulted from the leaking corners of his old apartment to the opulent heights of New Gate, with regained celebrity status, then thrown by some cosmic force back to Meti and his past, to finally be escorted out of the city to a future of his choice. He still couldn't believe it.

Crazy crap happens.

The sadness of the day the tsunami took his parents hovered in the background of everything, but the new energized calm that appeared in its absence filled him with a sense of wholeness. He knew who he was, beyond a role, beyond a name. And although his dream had changed, surviving the drone crash had humbled him with a belief that things worked out how they were meant to work out.

He tapped his watch to check his account; Maya's payment had been paid in full. Overlaying the account details, a notification popped up—one missed call and one voice message from Haru Hamada. He played the message out of pure boredom. Haru's tone sounded polite, friendly, and a little desperate.

"Yoshi, you there? I know we had words after Glasshouse, but that's water under the bridge, I hope. I was wondering if you're up for a job tonight. I'm supplying extra talent at the Maya District launch, and I need some last-minute MR character pilots. Give me a—"

Yoshi swiped the message into oblivion.

Wondering what he would do while he waited for his documents, he grabbed a cola from the fridge and voice-activated the room's entertainment wall. Its edges illuminated a pastel orange and pulsed with the AI's words.

"Good morning, Guest. I hope you enjoyed your sleep. Tonight's forecast is clear with a high of thirty-two Celsius here in the mountains and thirty-six in the city."

Yoshi slumped on the couch, threw his feet up on its arm, and opened the cola with a *tssss*. "Where's a warm and isolated place to live somewhere overseas?"

"Looking for somewhere warm and off the beaten track? You could try the higher Northern Rockies, Canada. Glacial reduction has exposed a beautiful barren landscape contrasted by fields of luscious grasses, offering a quiet and safe wilderness experience."

The wall played a video of a grizzly bear rolling on its back through patches of post-winter snow to land among a field of yellow avalanche lilies. The bear lazily munched on a juicy, slender bulb as a solo hiker trekked by—a beautiful, romanticized Lenz theme, since there were barely any grizzlies left. Yoshi wondered if that might happen to the Minaki, ignored into existence, then rendered by the Lenz as some Maya-fied filter.

He gulped a mouthful of cola and belched. "Anywhere else?"

The wall offered a stream of options, but Yoshi stared blankly at the videos, his thoughts drifting to a destination he would never reach called Kai. He caught the thoughts, stopping them before they dragged him into the abyss of regret. He imagined Kai from the first time they met, freckles like fallen stars across his brave face. He froze the memory in black and white, shrank it, and then let it fall away in a far corner of his mind.

Needing to escape the confines of the room, he decided to explore the hotel. After splashing his face and slicking back his hair, he headed down to the reception level and crossed the polished wooden floor to the busy bar at the end.

Made of glass walls on all sides, the bar appeared to float in between the army of pine trees on the east side and the wet, black mountain face on the west. Ten train tracks began in the station underneath the hotel and led into the rectangular tunnel bored through the mountain. Rivulets in the rock sparkled around the tunnel's entrance, like a velvet curtain studded with diamonds, and flickered shards of light across the bar's floor and ceiling.

He ordered a light beer and found a table overlooking the platform. A bell rang somewhere behind him—a Santa roamed the reception lobby, ringing a gold bell and crying Ho-Ho-Ho. Yoshi raised his glass to the past, then turned back to watch the activity on the station. By the time he'd drank half of his beer, a familiar voice startled him from behind.

"I guess we're breaking the no-contact rule already."

Gulping away the mouthful in surprise, Yoshi plonked his beer on the table and jumped to his feet to hug Leon.

"What are you doing here?" He almost knocked a pair of black-framed spectacles from Leon's face.

"Been here since we finished, Dizzy. I just checked out of the onscn retreat next door. What I'm sayin' is, I'm zen, I got my docs, and I'm heading out in twenty." He took the seat opposite. "So, did it take you long to sign the deal?"

"Let's just say, I didn't have much of a choice."

A knowing smile spread across Leon's face.

"Gray got something on you too, huh? Yeah, he's a cold-blooded bastard. Still, he pays well, can't complain about that. So, what's your new name?"

"Jack Kobayashi."

"That sounds cool."

"It's not cool, but it's fine. And yours?"

"Landon Zachary."

"*That* sounds cool."

"Landon was my father's name, Zachary my Grandfather's. God rest both their souls."

Yoshi took a deep sip of his beer, taking a moment to study Leon's face. As well as spectacles replacing his Lenz, the ex-Livey looked different in a way Yoshi couldn't put his finger on.

"So, you removed your Lenz, too?" he asked.

"Yup. Compulsory to do the retreat. Not putting it back in for a while either. Got 'Lenz-induced exotropia'. You removed yours, too?"

"Yeah, I just want to see things as they really are for a while, you know? At least until I choose where to go. You still headed to Tianjin?"

Leon shook his head. "The pontoons seem too hectic now. I feel like some sort of... quiet celebration. I'm heading to Canada. Pristinely solitary since the melt. Gonna get back to basics. Do some fishing."

Brakes squealed out from the tunnel below as a train eased in. Information boards along the platforms lit up in synchronization:

Welcome Lenzers. Maya District premieres tonight.

Train doors slid open and passengers poured out, many dressed as Joe Joe, Leon or one of the other Liveys. Leon and Yoshi both dipped their head to hide their faces as the crowd filed up the escalator to the foyer. Another train pulled in beside the first.

"Looks like the premier's going to be massive," Leon said, nodding to the crowd. "Shame to be missing it."

Yoshi looked down at his near empty glass and twirled it slowly, arcing a sudsy orbit of froth along the inside. "Not really."

"Don't tell me you don't wanna see your work on show; the actoid, and the CGI version of you. They're you, Dizzy."

Yoshi shook his head. "They *replaced* me."

"But you're the *person* all their actions are based on. You're their *soul*. And now there's more of you gonna lead people back into their imagination."

Yoshi sculled the rest of his beer, popped the empty glass on the back of a passing bipedal waiter-tray and accepted its offer to bring another. He took a moment to take in Leon's unexpected perspective—he'd really Zenned out in just two days of a retreat.

Below, a third train unloaded more costumed arrivals. They joined the constant stream from the platform heading up through the reception hall to where they boarded auto-buses waiting outside.

"Look at them," Leon said. "They all got that little light in their eye, distracting them from the guilt they're really feelin'."

"Guilt?"

"We inherited a huge burden to fix the world and we failed. They know they're hiding from that behind their Lenz, and they feel guilty about that too."

Yoshi frowned. "Sorry, *who* are you?"

"I told you, I been on a retreat."

"It was just two days."

"What I'm sayin' is, it's much easier to choose an experience from a menu then deal with the ones life gives you."

Leon's somber turn reminded Yoshi of Kai's words:

Not everyone takes easily to the truth.

"Don't be too hard on them," Yoshi said. "Even when we see the truth it takes a while to act. Or we wait for someone else to act first, and then it's too late."

Leon looked Yoshi in the eye. "Things didn't work out with your boyfriend, huh?"

"I wasn't talking about him, I just meant…"

"I could see the chemistry between you two. And you can't argue with chemistry."

The fear-strained excitement filling Kai's eyes stared back at Yoshi in his mind. A sudden understanding arose in his awareness—why he'd hidden in acting, why Kai rebelled, why the city hid in the Lenz, why Raiden wanted to slap the city awake, why Gray was mad for control, and maybe, even, why the uber-aware *yuijn* faced the walls.

Heartbroken by the state of a world.

"It's more than guilt, what we're all feeling. It's a collective broken heart. The Shift was the world's heart attack. And the aftershock of overwhelming disaster stories and images left us fundamentally heartbroken and *afraid* to feel anything anymore."

Leon sat back, surprise glinting in his eyes. "Spoken like a true wounded soul."

But Yoshi's revelation was not done with him. Kai's face was replaced by the memory of Gray in his office, talking about empathy as a curse.

"And if we don't feel, we can't *imagine*. We've got sensors replacing our senses, reminders and GPS dulling our intuition. We've outsourced our imagination—and our connection to whatever other spiritual or higher-conscious layer there is—to the Lenz. We can't see any other future than the one coming because our hearts are blind."

An image of the boy swum up into Yoshi's mind, swinging his stick and wiping away the already-fading image of Gray—*it's pushing us all back together*—until Yoshi saw nothing more than Leon sitting opposite him and staring.

"Yep," Leon said, "you really liked Lover Boy."

Another train squealed in below, and a news video filled the glass walls of the bar showing tens of thousands of people wandering through Maya District's stark, monochromatic landscape.

A sharp fear spiked in Yoshi's core.

The news continued, showing *Short-Term Security* guards patrolling the VIP area at the base of the wall and ushering a small protest away. The scene cut to a wide-eyed young man reporting from the edge of the district, the crowd swelling behind him.

"With an estimated physical attendance of 300,000 Lenzers—and rising—emergency fencing and extra crowd control has been put in place. It's going to be a wonderful evening."

The bipedal returned with Yoshi's beer, but he couldn't take his eyes off the mass of people flooding into the district.

"He's going to get hurt," he said aloud, without thinking.

"Who?" Leon asked, helping himself to the waiting beer.

Yoshi sucked in his lips as if he could recall his words, but Leon's eyes went wide with realization. "You mean Lover Boy?"

Yoshi nodded. "He's protesting."

"By the look on your face he's doing more than that."

"He doesn't realize how many people will be there. Or Raiden lied."

"What is he doing?"

Yoshi shook his head, fighting a rising sense of responsibility.

"That bad, huh?" Leon said. "Maybe you should try talking to him, let him know about the crowds."

"I tried talking him out of it, but he's caught up with these dangerous people."

"Why don't you go to him?"

"I already did that, too. He thinks he's going to fix things."

Leon leaned forward. "I did a lot of reflecting during my time in the retreat—"

"Leon, it was two days."

"I know, I know. But I did a lot of reflecting in those two days, and if there's one thing I see now, you gotta follow your unpredictability. There's too much logic and algorithm in the world. No mystery can get through, no surprise."

"I told you, I already went to him."

"Everyone deserves a second chance. Sometimes a third. Sometimes it takes many tries to get it right. If there's something there you really care about, or someone—"

"I don't even have his number. I'd have to go to Maya District." Yoshi snatched his beer back from Leon for a gulp and wiped a stratocumulus from his top lip. "Anyway, I can't afford any more trouble. I'm not sabotaging myself again."

Leon eyed him.

"You're too hard on yourself. It's all about perspective. Maybe it wasn't sabotage, but your instinct rescuing you just in time to steer you toward your true path." He leaned forward. "You still have a day or so 'til your documents arrive, right?"

Yoshi threw up his free hand. "Why is everyone telling me to risk the one good thing in my life?"

"Up to you. Only you know how much danger he might be in, and all these people."

Yoshi glared at the blatant guilt trip. But Leon ignored him as he stood and slapped him on the back.

"I gotta pee."

From further down the corridor, Santa rang his bell again, the chime almost lost in the din of the crowd. But the vibration of its *Ding, ding!* made it to Yoshi's brain, and an idea sparked, a tiny flash of light that disappeared just as quick but burned like an ember determined to cause a fire.

No, that's stupid. Don't even think about.

The information boards above the train lines below changed in sync again and displayed the standard safety message for public spaces:

Remember: If you see something, say something.

He forced his brain to think logically, desperate to protect the last opportunity he'd garnered himself. But the idea refused to stay quiet, and his imagination ran free without the Lenz telling it what to imagine.

Joe Joe appeared in the cinema in Yoshi's head. Wild-eyed, like he hadn't slept for days, he threw open a plan across Yoshi's thoughts and stabbed a finger on it.

Now, listen up, Yoshi, cause I'm only gonna say this once. That denial in Kai's eyes was despair. He's feeling it more than anyone. He wants to let go of his sense of burden, but he needs a good enough reason to do it. He needs someone to prove to him others won't give up, so he can stop trying so hard. And you know it's you. I know you don't wanna hear that, cause its damn inconvenient, what with your new life awaiting you. But Leon's right, you're the only one that knows. As crazy as fuck as it sounds, you could use the role from Haru to get into the event, find Kai, warn him how many people are coming, and, just maybe, stop him doing something more stupid than you or I ever did.

But Yoshi remained unconvinced by the flaky plan. Even if he did manage to get into the event, how would he find Kai in the crowd?

Stopping him mid-thought, he recognized the map on Joe Joe's plan.

That's right, Yoshi. You've seen Raiden's map on the garage wall. A red flag in the south, and a gold flag in the north. Raiden was fitting Kai into the gold Cylon costume. Kai will be on the north side, near the event control area. You just gotta make your way there and find the gold Cylon. Warn him, and maybe he can stop Raiden.

Yoshi even remembered the time circled at the top of the map: 7:45 p.m.

His heart pounded as reasoning opened up an unarguable way forward, like a prophet might part the sea.

Except for one detail.

Yoshi strained to recall the grid's sector numbers the flags had been stuck into—his passing observation didn't seem to have captured them.

The prophet lost power, the sea flooded over the blueprint, and Joe Joe's image splashed away.

I should just call the police.

But there was something else twinkling like broken glass underneath the watery remains of Joe Joe's plan—another plan, bigger and bolder. The shimmering lattice of its undefined form filled Yoshi with as much dread as tremulous excitement.

Coming, coming, coming.

The return of the sensation surprised him, but its energy had altered into something no longer ominous, but promising.

The station intercom echoed through the bar, calling for all passengers for the train on Platform 5 to board immediately.

"Well, that's me, Dizzy," Leon said, slapping Yoshi on the back.

As Leon leaned over to pick up his bag, his musky scent reminded Yoshi of the day they met. He stood and hugged Leon again.

"Thank you for being a good guy. I'm going to miss you."

"Things work out how they're meant to work out. Now, whatever you do, do it with smarts. Gray wants to control the city's view of reality. He's probably not gonna like anyone messing with that."

Yoshi blinked as if he'd been slapped. "You throw that in now?"

"What I'm sayin' is, there's a time to be bold and a time to be smart."

Leon winked and bowed, then threw his bag over his shoulder and headed toward the escalator. His words left Yoshi paralyzed in the floating space between the mountain and the trees, frozen like the moment on the cliff when he could only watch the tsunami wash everything away.

But maybe this time I can do something. I do know how Kai will be dressed, where he'll be, and when.

Joe Joe reappeared in the midst of his thoughts and poked the blueprint again. Yoshi could see—he could imagine—arriving at the District's control area, getting through the gate using Haru's job, and spotting a gold helmet in the crowd.

His heart pounded, and the other plan returned, its lattice forming shapes and symbols under Joe Joe's.

Daunted by what it hinted at, Yoshi told himself he was just going to warn Kai. That was trouble enough.

Sight

Haru answered after two rings, his shiny, round head appearing on the screen in front of digital portraits of his stable of actors. He wore thick spectacles that enlarged his eyes and a blindingly confident smile. But restrained desperation still laced his tone.

"Yoshi, how are you?"

"Hi, Haru. Sorry for not getting back to you straight away. Been laying low since Maya."

"Of course, of course. Now, you mentioned your contract finished before the event, so I figured you're free to take on new work?"

"I am."

"Perfect. Well, as it would happen, I'm providing actors to pilot virtual rovers at the Maya event tonight—a last minute detail due to the unexpected masses. They don't have enough of those actoids prepped, so they're going for virtual crowd control. All you'll need to do is—"

"I can do it."

"Great," Haru replied with a startled glee, and his headlight smile went high beam. "That's great."

"What time do I have to be there?"

"Right, let me see." Haru's chunky fingers, sporting rings of turquoise and tiger-eye, scratched his polished head. "Call-time's in two hours, is that a problem? I've been trying to reach you—"

"It's fine." Yoshi was already exiting the hotel foyer onto the main road. To the right, people lined up for arriving buses, and, behind them, a line for share-pods snaked back from the road.

"Actually Yoshi, you need to be suited up thirty minutes prior. So, can you be there in, say, an hour?"

"Done."

"Excellent. Okay. Sending the brief and access pass now. This is going to be the start of a new you, Yoshi, I'm sure of it. Knock 'em dead. Just, ah…"

"I'll be careful, Haru. Thanks."

"Great. Talk to you after the event."

As the screen swallowed Haru's face, Yoshi tapped his watch to summon Driver. But instead of the usual ETA message, Driver called him back.

"Hello, sir. Where is it you were wanting to go?"

His skin prickled at the intelligence—no, the *surveillance*—of Driver's response, and his destination snagged in his throat.

"Are you far away?" he stalled.

"I'm here at the hotel, sir. Where is it you were wanting to go?"

Looking west up the road, Yoshi spotted the auto-pod parked at the end of the hotel's charging bay. The wind picked up.

"Never mind. I was thinking of heading up to the look-out, but it's breezier outside than I thought. I've changed my mind. Thanks."

He tapped off the call and headed in the opposite direction to join the line for the share-pods. While he waited, he set his watch to incognito mode. Within ten minutes, he climbed into a pod and sped off down the road, ducking as he passed Maya's spying machine still parked in the bay.

As the pod drove through a salute of towering pine trees on either side, he listened to the brief.

"Welcome Rover. The Maya District premier will showcase the ultimate in immersive entertainment, and you'll be a part of bringing this game-changing experience to Shibido. Following a welcome from Maya CEO Tyler Gray, attendees will be treated to a screening of *Dreams For All*, the exciting sequel to the cult classic *One Man Dreaming*. The film will be projected onto the sea-wall in an ode to the traditional cinema experience. As the film ends, Maya District will activate in the VIP area. Actoids will enter, seamlessly immersing the guests into a continuation of the film with the storyline focusing on the VIPs as the heroes. The immersion will last approximately twenty minutes, and a giant screen projection will share the VIPs' experience with the wider audience.

"Due to the growing excitement, attendance has risen higher than expected, and crowds are filling neighboring areas. As a friendly presence of order, you'll be piloting a virtual panda-man rover that will be seen and heard by all Lenz's and MR goggles tuned into the event channel."

Yoshi tapped his consent to the terms and conditions, skipped the Rover etiquette, and spent the thirty-minute ride down the serpentine road searching through streamed video of the event in case he could catch sight of a gold Cylon.

Emerging at the mountain's base, the pod zipped out along the elevated highway toward the city outskirts. The dying rays of the sun infused the sky with coppery pinks. A twinkling array of Christmas illuminations lit up High Scape's edge, but far less than the year before, replaced by their virtual clones in the channels. By the time the pod drove out from under the Scape's eastern edge, the sunset had burned off and twilight had slipped into something violet and studded with early stars.

A semi-circle of towering floodlights extended out from the sea-wall, with swarms of media drones flitting around their fierce electrical glow like moths. Projections of giant red theater curtains draped the wall, but pedestrians flooding the streets blocked everything else below it.

Yoshi's stomach clenched at the thought of what chaos two hacked scramblers might cause with such a crowd.

Temporary barricades detoured the pod north. As he passed the sky-bridge, Yoshi could finally see into Maya District. Awash in the over-exposure of the floodlights, the bones of Gray's dream revealed itself—a stark shell of a suburb, filled with half-blind people believing in things that weren't really there. In the center stood the VIP's raised platform, the size of a city block and populated by several small buildings and ramps.

As the pod eased to a stop outside the fenced control area, six caped *Short-Term Security* guards herded a group of protesters away. Yoshi scanned the troublemakers, hoping again he might spot a Cylon, but the group dispersed and disappeared among the revelers.

He checked the time—7:03 p.m.—and headed toward the gated entrance. A guard stepped out of a small booth, and it took Yoshi a few seconds to realize it was Jin.

"You come back to offer me that security job, Mr. Goto?"

"Jin, what are you doing here? I thought you got let go?"

"As you can see, they're a little understaffed, and I had nothing else to do." Jin's eyes narrowed. "Actually, I thought you and the rest of the cast were let go, too?"

"My contract with Maya finished, but an agency recruited me for this." He loaded the access pass on his watch, hoping to pass through without any further questioning.

"Can't escape Maya, either, then, huh?"

Yoshi shrugged. "A job's a job."

"Ain't that the truth, then?"

Yoshi almost said it, almost told Jin the truth and handed over the responsibility to a man in uniform like he'd been taught to do. But he had to give Kai a chance with the truth first. If that failed, he promised himself he would tell Jin and the police.

But he was running out of time.

"Hey, you," a voice called from inside the compound. A short man, round as a boulder, stood halfway between the gate and the main building. He pointed a fat finger at Yoshi. "Are you from Star Production?"

"Yes. Are you the Rover Manager?"

"You're late, get in here."

Yoshi waved in acknowledgement and turned back to Jin. Yoshi found himself enjoying a brief moment looking at someone with only one Lenz and no strabismus—the normality seemed to ground Yoshi in the midst of all the craziness.

"Great to see you, Jin. And don't forget to send me your number. Crazy crap *does* happen."

As Yoshi headed across the yard, Jin called out.

"Just don't go makin' me late again, Mr. Goto. Or my wife gonna kill us *both* this time."

Yoshi kept his head down, hoping his name didn't spark any unwanted interest.

As he followed the Rover Manager toward the building's wide entrance, he glimpsed the concrete structure among the old buildings behind the control area. The stick-torch symbol on its side caught residual floodlight and appeared to float off the wall in 3D. The other radical plan that stirred in him at the station pulsed in his subconscious like sonar in the dark.

Inside the main control building, people headed in and out of three tunnel-like corridors. To the right, a long, narrow window opened onto the event's main control room. A small army worked at giant monitors in front of one mammoth screen displaying a drone view of the brightly lit district. The event's Sight glowed in the corner—1.2 billion and rising.

As the manager neared the far corridor, a technician trolleyed a large generator in front of them.

"Coming through."

"That's meant to be set up already," the manger huffed and pulled Yoshi out of way. "That's for your orb. He still needs to connect it. Let me talk you through some regulations while he sets up."

The manager's eyes darted around their sockets as they read from some virtual document. Half-listening, Yoshi returned his gaze to the control room, where three smaller screens showed the spot-lit VIP area. A crowd of fifty or so—senators, project partners, select journalists, and the selected fans from Nebulae—laughed and smiled in poses for the drones filming their every move. Bipedal waiter bots tiptoed around them with flutes of bubbling champagne on their backs. Behind them, plain, open-walled buildings and ramps covered the back two thirds of the dais. Artificial smoke masked its perimeter and, no doubt, hid the actoids waiting backstage.

Yoshi recognized the Mayor's thin, pale figure, ghastly elegant in a white gown, as she chatted to the enigmatic Ken Morita. To the side, on her own, stood Nina, the punk girl fan who'd won the Nebulae competition—panic quickened his heartbeat at the memory of her being zapped by the scrambler.

A sharp-toned voice called from behind him, and Yoshi froze, every muscle tensed with dread as Lavinda's words whip-lashed the Rover Manager.

"Rover Manager, what is going on? We go live in fifteen minutes. I wanted all the rovers embedded in the crowd by now so they're arrival doesn't distract from Gray. What have you been doing?"

"My apologies, Communications Manager. Just a small delay with the last orb. Ready in five minutes!"

Yoshi remained facing the control room window and prayed Lavinda didn't recognize him from behind. As she demanded a better explanation, trapping Yoshi to the spot, a familiar figure in the control room walked by the window, like a shark swimming past in an aquarium. Exquisite panic squeezed Yoshi—Tyler Gray turned and looked straight over him.

After an excruciatingly taut moment, Gray walked away and Lavinda finished her interrogation and left.

"Follow me," the Rover Manager snapped, sweat beading his forehead.

Trembling with relief, Yoshi followed him into a long, narrow room where a row of immersion orbs lined the left wall. Pilots were already strapped in and walking on the motion pads. Rows of monitors covered the opposite wall, each screen showing a different viewpoint of the event. A blue glow identified the virtual panda-men among the crowd as they re-directed wayward pedestrians toward the VIP area.

The manager stopped by the last orb, labelled *Alpha,* where the technician still worked on connecting the generator.

"Strap in as soon as the tech is done," he said, before walking back to a control lectern by the entrance.

As the manager turned his back, Yoshi scanned the monitors. There were at least twenty, each one overlaid with a sector number. Recalling Raiden's map, he searched his memory again for the gold flag's sector number, but he couldn't remember. Doubt seeped into his plan.

"She's ready," said the technician.

"Okay," Yoshi replied, still scanning for any sign of Kai.

"She's ready now," the technician repeated firmly.

Swearing silently, Yoshi turned away. But just as he did so, a flash of gold caught his eye. He stepped back to the monitors, but whatever it was seemed to have already disappeared.

Damn it.

"Hey, you," barked the manager, "you need to strap in now."

Without taking his eyes from the screens, Yoshi climbed into the *Alpha* orb and pulled on the harness. Stretching the goggles over his head, he spotted another golden flash. A shiny, gold Cylon helmet moved through the crowd in a monitor marked Sector 7A.

"Ah, Rover Manager," he called out, "just a quick question—do you know where Sector 7A is? My friend's there and I'm just wondering if I'll see him."

Angry disbelief contorted the manager's face. "This isn't a social event, buddy. Get your goggles on *now*."

Yoshi glanced back at the monitor, but he'd lost Kai again. The sighting, however, had filled him with daring optimism.

He pulled the goggles on, and the green grid replaced the orb around him, the view transforming into a muted blue version of the room. Maya's rising Sight sat in the top left corner. He raised his hand and a virtual panda paw-hand appeared. Looking down, black and white fur covered his panda-man body.

"Okay, *Alpha*," said the manager through the orb's speakers, "your appearance coordinates are being generated—that's the sector your rover will cover. I'll be in your car but keep an eye on the VIP feed in your vision to remain aware of the main proceedings. Remember, anyone logged into the Lenz channels, via Lenz or MR goggles, will see and hear you, so remain in character at all times. And do not allow your virtual rover to pass through the attendees, it is very impolite to ruin the illusion!"

A small screen displayed in the top left of Yoshi's view showing the VIP area. A counter appeared next to it, set at ten seconds. Like a magic wish being granted, a semi-transparent map of all the sectors overlaid his view, highlighting his own—5C. He spotted 7A on the same side of the event, just closer to the VIP area.

"Start walking," said the manager. "Make sure you cover all of your sector, and keep the crowd engaged. On my cue, turn and point toward the stage for the start of Gray's presentation. Stay around the edges until the VIPs have finished their District experience, and then you'll be extracted. Let's go. Augmentation in ten seconds."

The counter in Yoshi's vision started. He began walking and the motion pad kicked in. A blue glow throbbed in his sector, alerting those around it that a virtual rover was teleporting into that location. They politely made way for his arrival and the countdown hit zero.

The room disappeared in a burst of excited voices, elaborate costumes, and vivid colors. His focus adjusted instinctively back to the closeness of the augmented view, and he found it impossible to tell the real costumes from the virtual. Although not physically present, the electric atmosphere made its way through time and space into his being, filling him with the joyful December spirit of something wonderful coming.

The crowd in 5C wasn't as dense as sectors closer to the center, so he could move around freely without passing through anyone. As he guided attendees, he peered through the crowd toward 7A, but it was two sectors away diagonally and difficult to see.

After ten minutes, the Rover Manager cued him to give the crowd a final direction to move closer to the dais. The floodlights dimmed. The small screen in Yoshi's view showed the VIPs stepping aside as Gray walked out from the structures behind them. Wearing a sharp, navy suit, and back-dropped by the red curtained sea-wall, his spot lit image appeared across the District's buildings, and a deafening applause erupted.

The Maya CEO stopped at the front edge of the dais, and the red curtains behind him slipped back to reveal five giant screens projected on the sea-wall, showing the five districts around the world. Gray lifted his arms.

"Hello Japan. Hello, Germany, U.S., Great Britain, and Australia."

The crowd erupted in every city, their applause spiking before settling. When Gray continued, his tone was as smooth as velvet.

"Tonight, I'm going to share with you an *experience* that will *revolutionize* your every day. Because that's what Maya does, we *revolutionize*. Our most important products aren't hardware and games, they're possibility and believability. Because you expect your entertainment to surround you, to immerse you, District Maya will *transport* you."

He paused to take in another burst of cheering. Enchanted by the contagious excitement, Yoshi momentarily forgot his mission.

"With the Lenz, Maya turned the entire wearables industry inside-out by placing an interface in your eye, immersing you in the most seamless mixed-reality experience. In 2038, we introduced you to the *yujin*, the most human-like and intelligent android assistant. And yes, there have been some glitches."

In all five cities, the crowds roared with laughter, but Gray remained gracious and humble as he raised his voice.

"But as anyone who was at Nebulae witnessed, the *yujin* are now fully functional and completely indistinguishable from ourselves."

The laughter turned into applause and whistling, forcing Gray to pace for a minute until the worldwide audience calmed down.

"In 2039, we brought you the *enhanced* Lenz—an easy-to-administer eye drop that colonized a safe yet complex technology in your eye, allowing you to immerse yourself in your favorite filters, uninterrupted. And with the updated Lenz, we brought you the Mirage, a ground-breaking AI-based filter that analyzes your viewing behavior and social media profiles to show you the world you most want to see. Your Mirage knows you better than you do. It's your higher self, your guru. It knows when you're sleeping, it knows when you're awake, and it works like magic."

Another theatrical pause for a devoted applause.

"We've given you the ability to see what you most want to see. We've given you companions that can be whatever you want them to be. And now, we're giving you a real-world space where these technologies come together to make each of you the *star* of *the world* you most want to be *in*. And to make this the most immersive experience ever, we've again stripped away any interface, so that your fantasy begins and ends without you even noticing it. No gates, no check-in, no login, just seamlessly enter and leave the Maya world as you please. But I promise you, you won't want to leave.

"The Lenz, the actoids, and now Maya District—each of these technologies form part of one larger mythology. Because that's what Maya builds—myths and legends that come alive with you as the hero."

Gray had to raise his voice again over the cheering.

"Tonight, the world will share our VIPs' experience of the first ever fully augmented real-world district, a preview of what you can experience when Maya District opens on 5th January."

"But, first, let me tell you a story, a prelude to thousands more all about you. Get ready to enter your dreams. Let's do this!"

The thunderous roar of cheers, whistles and stomping hit Yoshi like the crash of a giant wave. The spotlight dimmed and Gray slipped out of view. As the five screens faded off, the district fell into darkness, and a hush fell over the crowd. Yoshi gazed at the sea-wall like a kid on his first visit to the cinema.

Shapes and symbols coalesced across the buildings all around them, and then merged into giant letters that swooped together on the sea-wall to form *One Man Dreaming*. Then, just as they did at Nebulae, the words dissolved and reformed into *Dreams For All*. A silent, almost tangible excitement gripped the crowds across the world as the title vanished, immediately replaced by a silhouette of someone very familiar.

Yoshi's chest heaved with excitement.

The shot closed in and panned around the silhouette to reveal an intimate close-up of Joe Joe's face. Another spontaneous cheer shook the ground, but Yoshi stood silent, transfixed. Giant projections of Joe Joe bled out onto the buildings all through the district, surrounding Yoshi with his likeness. It was like standing inside a memory he never knew he had, a déjà vu of a déjà vu.

Keep moving, he reminded himself.

He tore away from the sorcery to focus on weaving through the captivated attendees without passing through them. He edged along the sector's perimeter for five minutes, and then headed through 6B toward 7A.

"Alpha," Rover Manager warned, "watch your zone."

Ignoring him, Yoshi made his way through 7A toward the outer edge, guessing Kai would position himself there so he could escape as soon as he activated the scrambler. But after another five minutes of searching, he still couldn't see any sign of the gold Cylon.

Loud, fast-paced action exploded across the seawall and surrounding buildings, as the Algorlines trapped Joe Joe and the Liveys at the edge of a towering skyscraper. Knowing what followed, Yoshi was once again spellbound by the exquisite replication of his alter ego come to life all around him.

Joe Joe leapt off the skyscraper. Leon and the other Liveys jumped after him, the Algorlines munching the roof where the heroes had stood only seconds before. The Liveys whooped as they plummeted, just as they had done during the scanning. As they landed among a clearing of ruins, a bright light flashed out of the screens and swamped the district, blinding the audience, and forcing Yoshi to shield his eyes.

In his momentary blindness, Yoshi again saw Joe Joe in his mind's eye pointing at Raiden's map of the district. Although Yoshi couldn't articulate even to himself how he knew, he understood the lattice was expanding his awareness and allowing him to anticipate an emerging pattern. What it suggested was more complex and absurd than just warning Kai, and what it asked of him terrified him—he'd never wanted anything like real heroism on his shoulders, it was just something to be in a movie.

The light faded, and he blinked to find the road under his feet had turned to rubble. Crumbled ruins had replaced the district's blank buildings, and High Scape, the sea-wall, and Low Ground, had all disappeared. Only the VIP dais remained, and the five giant screens had reappeared and floated behind the dais. The Stratodel twinkled in the sky far above each dais, like a common star uniting the five countries. The VIPs stood motionless in a hanging silence, as all the attendees around the world realized they'd been transported into the film's final scene.

"Alpha," snapped Rover Manager in Yoshi's ear, "you're wide of your sector. Pull back to 5C."

"Just trying to get around a big group without disturbing them," Yoshi lied, and he pressed on.

But the audiences' eyes flickered as they stared at their shared illusion in silent awe, their hearts and minds fully immersed in the commercialized magic, and the delicate moment made it difficult to navigate without disturbing the audience.

He reached the edge of the sector, but after scanning the crowd, a rising dread loosened the screws on his nerves and panic rattled in its cage.

Kai, where are you?

As smoke cleared on the five screens, a lone character appeared on the dais in each city—Joe Joe in

Shibido, Suzy Lee Bingo in Germany, Leon in the U.S., Bamboo Run in Great Britain, and Dhven in Australia. The crowd erupted again as the actoid stars unstrapped their parachutes and crossed the dais. They prompted the VIPs to help them find a portal to reach the Stratodel and escape the Algorlines. Embracing the narrative, the VIPs from each country raced into the buildings on their dais. Although the crowd could see the VIPs running through plain buildings, the giant screen showed them racing with the actoids through a stylized city of ruined streets. Both the trick and its realism enthralled the audience.

Another message appeared in Yoshi's view:

Rover extraction in six minutes.

He checked the time—7:39 p.m.—and then he searched the sector's edge again. But still nothing. A hysterical urge to run surged through him, to hand over the responsibility 'to a uniform before it was too late. He reached up to yank off the goggles—

A flash of gold sparked among the crowd a few yards away, and Yoshi's heart leapt like a startled bird. A gold Cylon emerged to stop and glance around.

Yoshi hurried over. Forgetting he was virtual, he reached for Kai's arm, but his panda hand waved straight through Kai's gold costume. Startled by the apparition, Kai jerked back and looked directly at Yoshi.

"Kai," Yoshi whispered, hoping Kai could hear him, too. "It's me, Yoshi."

Behind the tinted MR visor, Kai's eyes widened with shock.

"Yoshi? Is that you? What are you doing here? And why are you a panda-man?"

"I came to warn you. There's five hundred thousand people here. You need to stop."

Kai's brow knotted. "There's not that many—"

"Trains of people have been coming through all afternoon. The crowd stretches back almost to High Scape."

A rotund woman to their left shushed them.

"You're overreacting," Kai whispered, "this is just—"

"Look at their faces, Kai." Yoshi waved at the crowd, their eyes quivering as their focus struggled between the closeness of the Lenz's augmentation and the distance of the dais. "You said yourself, they're in trauma. They don't need any more of it. You don't need to go this far."

"I've got to do something," Kai insisted.

"Doing something doesn't mean you're doing the right something. This is too brutal. There's a better way."

As Yoshi said the last words, the radical idea forming in his unconscious rose up and unfolded itself like reverse origami, revealing a concept unrestrained by any algorithm—the boy from the underground was calling out to the people of Shibido from the limbo of their trauma with a truth they needed to feel. And if he could see the boy, then he was Taka, like his Grandpapa. And if he was Taka, he had to pick up the torch.

Shards of color from the film flashed across Kai's doubt-twisted face. "You better start making sense, Yoshi, 'cause I'm ready to do this now."

"You don't look ready."

Kai looked away. "I know exactly what I'm doing. Maya shut down the Minaki's ceremony, so we're shutting down theirs."

The ceremony.

And that unfolded more of Joe Joe's plan in Yoshi's mind—the Minaki had built a Taka hut in the underground garage, and he had to lead the citizens to the ceremony to expose them to the hut's magic. How he was meant to do that, he had no idea. But as soon as he doubted himself, Naomi's words came to him:

…our brains are willing to make great leaps of faith, especially when we're desperate.

Unsure if he was having delusions of grandeur or some spiritual awakening (or even if there was a difference), he couldn't resist a sudden, giddy excitement to share the crazy notion with Kai.

"Let's take them to the ceremony."

"Who? What are you talking about?"

"It doesn't matter who or how many. We just need a few people to see. Then they'll share it with others. That's how it works."

Kai's eyes flickered with hope before doubt clouded over again.

"How what works? What are you talking about?"

But Raiden's voice cut Kai off from a communicator on his shoulder.

"You ready?"

The woman shushed them again, and Kai scrambled to turn his communicator down. On the seawall behind him, the VIPs neared the edge of the ruined city. A shimmering portal floated above the road only a block away from them, revealing a glimpse into the gardens of the Stratodel.

Yoshi held Kai's gaze, willing him to stop. The audience stared in breathless anticipation. Kai shook his head and pulled the communicator toward his mouth.

"Raiden, wait. I'm not sure—"

"Don't lose it now, Kai," Raiden warned. "Maya's Sight has hit 1.5 billion. It's time to scramble."

"This could get really crazy."

"It needs to get crazy. We're all passive terrorists."

Kai looked up at Yoshi, then closed his eyes as if realizing something stupid. "You lied about the crowd size, didn't you, Raiden?"

"You're freaking out, Kai. Take a deep breath. On three. One."

"Raiden, no—"

"Two."

"Wait—"

"Hit it."

"Don't!"

As the VIPs across the world jumped toward the portals on all five floating screens, the video streams broke apart. The sea-wall's stained landscape jutted into the fanciful city illusion, and the district flickered between the two states, like the broken emergency light in the underground. The crowd gasped and stepped back in one sudden shift, and the large woman to their left fainted to the ground with a thump.

Yoshi's world solidified into pitch black.

Portal

Flailing wildly, he called out Kai's name, but swearing voices from behind startled him into silence. Confused and shaken by Raiden's scrambler zapping him back into the orb room, he unstrapped and jumped out.

The other pilots stumbled blind around the room like drunks, their eyes struggling to focus. A burly man pressed fearfully against an orb, his eyes wide with desperation and his voice shaking with panic.

"It's all a blur."

"Same for me," called another, still tangled in her harness. "What is going *on*?"

The Rover Manager fumbled along the wall toward the exit.

"Something's happened to the Lenz. Everyone get out of the orbs and follow the corridor lights to the emergency zone."

"We can't see!" yelled the pilot as she finally freed herself from her harness.

"Follow the blue glow," the manager said, controlling the shake in his voice. "The blue lights on the floor. Follow them to the exit."

But Yoshi's vision was fine. He turned to the wall of monitors to see the entire district sitting in darkness, silhouetted in the dim glow of the city. Five-hundred-thousand people stood frozen, like statues in a dream.

Breaking the faux serenity, a mid-air explosion tore through the dark above the VIP dais, its bloom of flames illuminating those below. Security guards floundered around the base, confused by their malfunctioning optics, while the crowd in front stampeded away and collided in panic. Three more mid-air explosions popped above the district edge as media drones collided and spiraled like out-of-control torpedoes toward the ground. The district erupted into chaos.

Whatever Raiden's scrambler had done, it had affected more than the Lenz's frequency.

Yoshi scanned sector 7A and spotted a gold figure leading a small group away from the mayhem. After a few seconds of relief, his every muscle tensed and his head screamed *run*, to flee the commotion before he was caught, or before he did something *really* stupid.

But his reflection floating over the disaster confronted him and demanded to know what he really believed. Could he *really* imagine a change happening through that many people? Was that his *real* Outlook for the future, or was it just fanciful thinking?

As the other pilots disappeared from the room, his head flooded with what had been *coming, coming,*

coming, but what could only now flow through his unblocked memory in its full clarity—not another disaster, but the truth of his Grandpapa's incoherent storytelling. It didn't matter if his stories made sense or not, it was his actions that brought them to life and allowed their *luma* to flow. His Grandpapa had been trying to teach him from within the prison of his dementia. But instead of using performance as a method of connecting to others, Yoshi had used it as a means of dissociating from his fears.

He suddenly understood why the lattice showed him the pattern. It was a map to a place and time where three strands came together—an invisible tribe waiting with a ceremony, a group of blind people waiting for some magic, and an angry man with a device that just tore a hole in the wall between them.

Infused with raw, invigorating instinct, he ran down the hall to the main entry room. But as he headed toward the exit, a door swung open on his left. He darted sideways, too slow, and collided with someone storming out.

Clutching his smarting head, he looked up and froze. Gray stared back at him, mouth dropped open and eyes flaring with disbelief. He wore spectacles that appeared to allow him to see fine without the Lenz.

"*You? You* did this?"

"No, Mr. Gray," Yoshi hurried to explain. "No, I tried to stop it."

Gray's eyes burned luminous with fury and his hands clenched into white-knuckled fists.

"*You did this?*"

"No, I—"

Gray lunged, but a muscled arm wrapped around his chest and pulled him back. Gray wrestled against Jin's hold like a wild dog on a leash.

"Please, sir," Jin whispered as he dragged Gray back, "there's cameras all around."

Gray settled, but his chest heaved with anger, and his eyes didn't leave Yoshi.

Before any of them could speak again, another man wearing glasses popped out from the doorway.

"Mr. Gray, the VIPs are on their own. Security are running blind without their Lenzes. I've got no one to send to get them."

Gray shook off Jin's arm and wiped back a loose wick of his slicked hair. He pointed at Yoshi as he commanded Jin.

"Lock him in a cupboard if you have to, but *do not* let him leave."

"Okay, then, sir," Jin said in a calming voice. He grabbed Yoshi by the arm and steered him fast toward the entry.

"Don't let him leave!" Gray yelled before heading back into the control room.

"Jin," Yoshi whispered, "I can help the VIPs."

"Best you keep quiet, Mr. Goto."

"I can get them out of there."

Jin yanked Yoshi to a stop and held him close to his face. Jin's Lenz eye looked a little drooped, by his other was clear as daylight.

"Did you have anything to do with this?"

"I was trying to stop it."

"You *knew* this was going to happen? Why didn't you call the police? Why didn't you tell *me*?"

Yoshi hung his head. He still struggled against the responsibility being demanded of him, but the inner idol of island calm had grown as big his him and now wore his body like a second skin. He looked Jin in the eye.

"I stopped someone I cared about doing something stupid. But I couldn't stop the others. Now, I *can* help the VIPs."

Without another word, Jin dragged him outside and into the compound dimly lit with emergency lights. A group of guards wearing emergency MR goggles struggled with a mass exodus of staff knotting with a swarm of confused and panicked attendees.

Jin kept going, pulling Yoshi around the control building and toward a side gate. He unlocked it and swung it open onto the esplanade, on the VIP side of the barrier. He gestured to Yoshi to lead.

"You're gonna help me get the VIPs to safety."

After a quick glance in the direction of the concrete ramp entrance, with the stick-torch shimmering ghost-like from its side, Yoshi took off toward the VIP platform with Jin following.

Only a low barrier separated them both from the complete chaos exploding inside Maya District. It was like a zombie apocalypse, the sort of scene Yoshi had watched so many times, only now he was running right by its volatile reality.

Hundreds of terrified people, half-blind and hands held forward, staggered between tangles of confused and fallen strangers. Some stood paralyzed, mouths open and eyes wide, as they struggled to make sense of their distorted vision. Others ran in all directions, disorientated, and smacking into each other or tripping over others. Drones sporadically collided in the air, their sparking bodies spinning off into the buildings. Spot-fires flared in the dark all around, silhouetting the thousands as they scattered deeper into the district or down streets leading back to High Scape. The siren of a fire truck blipped as its tires hit the gutter and launched itself into the district's main street, scattering the crowd.

Yoshi and Jin reached the base of the dais to find the security guards busy trying to help those calling for help. Yoshi ran up the side stairs, and Jin followed.

As they reached the top, an ear-busting bang exploded in the night sky to the right—two drones spiraled mid-air in a flaming embrace. They smashed into a tall, blank building in the middle of the district, and its top burst into flames, lighting up like a giant tribal torch.

A yelp called Yoshi's attention back to the platform—Ken Morita lay sprawled over a prone body lying in an awkward heap.

"What is going on here?" Ken demanded.

By the way the still body's lower legs bent underneath it, Yoshi knew it was an actoid. But the blinded Ken Morita didn't, and he was freaking out as he backed away on his hands and ass. Another journalist helped Ken to his feet, and the rest of the media group huddled around them, their damaged vision straining to make sense of the blur. Yoshi spotted the Mayor, crouched down and hugging a shaken elderly man. Jin helped a red-haired woman to her feet, but by the bewildered look on his face, the situation overwhelmed him, too.

None of them seemed able to formulate any visual construct in their minds of what was happening—leaving them extremely susceptible to suggestion.

Except Nina, standing at the front edge, turning her shiny, bald head side-to-side, gazing with pure, blind joy as if she thought the blurred chaos was all part of the event.

That's the mind-set I need to get the others into.

Yoshi filled with a super-lucid energy, like his brain had become some sort of cosmic antennae, tuned to more directly receive the subliminal signals he'd been receiving. He breathed deep, inducing a kind of meditative state, as he lowered himself into Joe Joe's character and prepared to hijack the desperate VIPs' predisposition to illusion.

"Everyone, stay calm, alright?" he called out with Joe Joe's recognizable drawl.

All heads snapped toward his voice. Relief lightened their frightened faces, but the wild fullness of their eyes betrayed their uncertainty. Jin shot him a questioning look.

"Is that you, Joe Joe?" asked Nina, glancing around with her crossed eyes.

"Looks a little too big, to me," replied a man standing close and squinting at Yoshi.

"And you all look a little a blind to me. So, I need you all to listen. The Algorlines are attacking and we got separated from the others. The portal shut before we could get through. It's just us now, alright? Leon will open another portal, but we have to get to it."

He glanced at Jin who nodded to show he was prepared to go along with the charade.

"Why are things so blurry?" the Mayor demanded.

"It's just a bit of portal blindness from its closing flash. It'll pass. But right now, we have to rely on each other. And we have to hurry."

"This is so real," exclaimed Nina.

The others' faces brimmed with a daring curiosity, their eagerness to immerse in the drama chasing away their doubts.

"So, what do we do, then?" Jin called from the back of the group, pretending to be one of them.

"We have to use our senses. Form a line, hold hands, and follow me."

As the group fumbled for each other, the Mayor assisted the older man to stand, and Jin helped them both join the group. Yoshi went to Nina and led her from the edge to join the others.

"I need your help," he whispered.

Her eyes widened, thrilled to be included in the story. "Of course, yes!"

"We can't have anyone doubting the mission, alright?"

"Of course."

"I need you to back me up and help keep anyone who drops their Outlook to stay on track. Can you do that?"

Her smile beamed almost brighter than the flaming tower in the distance.

"You got it, Joe Joe."

"Alright," he called out. "Let's do this."

Returning to the line, he took the hand of the red-haired woman at the head of the group. "Follow my voice."

One by one, they followed Yoshi down the stairs, and he coaxed them along the esplanade toward the control area. Nina immersed herself in her part, ad-libbing like a pro, and Jin hurried along the stragglers.

As they reached the control area's gate, Yoshi led them past it and toward the torch building in the old area. Jin raced up to him from the rear, but by the time he reached the front of the line, Yoshi had already started ushering the group around the corner to the stairs.

"What are you doing? Where are you taking them?"

"This will lead them out the other side of the underground garage, where it's safer."

"I'm not a fool, Yoshi."

Yoshi put a hand on Jin's shoulder. "I need you to trust me, Jin. There's something down there they need to see. Something that may make some good out of all this."

"You need to start making sense right now."

"The islanders. They have a ceremony on tonight. It's a very special healing ceremony."

Uncertainty froze Jin as he watched the group holding the wall to guide themselves down the stairs. "That's where the islanders live?"

Yoshi nodded. "I need you to make sure there's someone to meet us at the other end, at the south access ramp. Can you do that for me, please?"

Jin chewed his lip.

"This is that crazy crap you were talkin' about, right? My wife is going to be so mad." He took off back toward the control area.

Yoshi took a deep breath to contain a fragile awe of his own daring, and then ran down the stairs to the VIPs.

He found them huddled by the entrance, peering in. The wariness on their faces had transformed into a delightful, child-like disorientation, but they hesitated to go in any further.

"Okay," Yoshi called out, "everyone, catch your breath."

He took a few steps in and peered into the parking area for any sign of the Minaki or their ceremony. The dim light had rendered the graffiti on the ceiling and sloped wall as subtle, primitive markings. Oblong puddles dotted the ground, mirroring pieces of the illustrated ceiling like holes in space and time. But any further ahead, the parking area seemed to dissolve into darkness. The stillness worried him.

"What is this place?" Morita asked, his nose twitching like a snow hare.

Nina outstretched a hand to feel the damp wall. Sweat patches bloomed under her arms and exertion glistened on her thick neck.

"It's so real."

"Yes," agreed the Mayor, her hand covering her nose. "And the stench. *So* real." But she said it with a faint smile, as if secretly delighted by her revulsion.

Their enthusiasm spread throughout the group, moving them all forward, hands held out in front like a troupe of amateur mime artists. Yoshi stepped out into the center of the path, so his silhouette was strong for their blurred vision to follow.

"We're under the city now. This is the only area safe from the Algorlines where Leon can open another portal for us. We've got to keep moving so we're at the right spot at the right time."

The underground was darker than Yoshi remembered, the safety lights just timid glows along the wall. The acrid aroma of rusty, damp cement pressed against him. After almost fifteen minutes, hc found no sign of the Minaki—no mats, no D-lamps, nothing. He began to fear he'd imagined them, and everything.

Ken Morita ambled up beside him, the edges of his smile holding it back in a grimace. He held a hand to the side of his face and spoke softly.

"This is still part of the event, isn't it?"

Yoshi thought of the young girl back at the mall, her finger twirling the Santa beard, her little mind not sure if she wanted the truth.

"I don't know what you're talking about," Joe Joe replied. "We've got to find the portal. We'll be in the

Stratodel very soon, alright? You should let the others know."

A childish grin transformed Morita's doubt.

"Yes, yes, of course." He felt his way back to the other reporters, and excited whispers fluttered the information throughout the group.

But, as Yoshi led them deeper into the underground, the others began questioning everything.

"When do we see properly again?" the Mayor asked. "This is getting tedious."

"When do we get to the Stratodel?" asked another.

"Will you stop narrating your thoughts," Ken shout-whispered. "You're ruining it for the rest of us."

"Not long now," Yoshi replied with a confidence he didn't really have. "We're nearly there."

He pressed on toward the T-junction, where the flickering light would come into view, and the *Taka* hut would be just on the other side—he was sure of it.

But on reaching the junction, he found only solid darkness stretching ahead, the flickering light finally blown. The small alcove of light in the distance teased him forward, but it seemed far away. Fearing he'd lose the group's focus, he spun and waved them on, infusing his movements with turbulence.

"Quickly, I can see the portal ahead, but it looks like it's closing. We've got to hurry."

The group drew in close and hastened forward. Sweat trickled down their temples, and their brows and mouths twisted with concentration. Their whispering fell silent, submerging them in an abstract melody of shuffled footsteps and echoing drips. But in the absence of any decent light, the darkness became heavy and overwhelming. Shoes scuffed the ground as some struggled to maintain their balance. Yoshi's own depth perception faltered.

Desperate for a break from the darkness, he remembered Kai's lighter. He snatched it out of his pocket and flicked the spark wheel. But the brave flame barely reached more than a few feet around them.

Someone yelped from the side, and Yoshi spun to see the Mayor stumbling into the sloped wall. Sharp exclamations rippled through the group, freezing them. Yoshi raced over to help the Mayor right herself.

"Is everything okay?" called out someone from behind.

"Everything's fine," said Nina, her breaking voice betraying her own doubt. "It's so immersive, isn't it?"

"No," said the Mayor, looking up at Yoshi, her eyes struggling to pull focus on him. "Something's not right about all this."

"I don't like this, either," replied the red-haired woman, her words quivering with leashed panic. Her palpable anxiety bled into the others, and a group fear compressed the space around them. "My vision is clearing. This place doesn't look part of the district."

"Where are we?" another voice called out.

"Stay with me," Yoshi said. "We're nearly through."

The Mayor recomposed her stance and dared to declare aloud the group's collective thought. "We should leave."

She started walking back, and several others peeled off from the group to follow.

No no no.

Then he saw it, like a ghost in his peripheral—the torch symbol on the slope where the Mayor had stumbled. Alerted into action, he bolted up to the boy's shrine and held up the lighter. Stepping through swirls of dust, he plucked the stick-torch from its resting place against the back wall. The wood light in his hand, he ran back down to the group and light the torch's tip.

A strong flame flickered and enlarged, its warm glow engulfing the VIPs and illuminating their faces. The Mayor halted, and the others stopped with her. Yoshi walked around them all with the torch held high to draw them back together.

"We're just getting to the best part, alright?"

Glancing back at the long stretch of dark behind her, the Mayor nodded. Yoshi kept the torch high and led them forward. A vibrant warmth flared from his heart to his forehead, as if a bright light shone out of *him*.

Shine your light.

A familiar ecstatic sensation welled up through his legs and torso and spilled out into his arms and head. The floor began to disappear beneath him, and he felt himself drifting away from his body, reminding him of his out of body experience in the school play.

Don't get lost in there.

He reached through the ether to his hand on the torch and gripped it tight. The hard, smoothed grain grounded him, and he willed himself back into his body.

"Look," shouted Nina, stepping forward. "There's the portal!"

Ahead, the giant abstract structures came into view, forming a glowing tunnel out of the darkness. Yoshi's heart leapt with relief. Unseen D-Lamps highlighted segments of the structures and cast Escher-like shadows on the walls, floors, and ceiling. A clicking fluttered through the air, signaling to Yoshi that the Minaki were close. He sensed himself shifting back to the dual reality experience, but this time maintaining a balance. His body moved through the underground while his awareness watched from another realm, floating in some fourth dimension between the world he knew and something that came after.

His excited pulse throbbed in his ears, grounding him, as he led the group out of the dark and into the light of the *Taka* hut.

Tsunami

The structures arched high over them, framing the graffiti on the walls and ceiling behind in broken pieces. A breeze blew through, rustling plastic sheets stretched taut across the branches, and their quiver dappled the floor. The compressed humidity drew a forest mustiness from the cement, and the clicking echoed through the canopy of the make-shift hut.

Moving further in, the torch light revealed a crescent of various-sized oblong shapes drawn on the cement floor. The others drew in close, and the transpersonal radar in Yoshi's head pinged. He lowered the torch to illuminate the markings—they formed a crescent of reef-ringed islands, smaller at one end, just like the map of the Agu-shi archipelago he had seen on the Minaki article.

The clicking and rustling grew louder. Another breeze blew through, and the flickering light on the floor made the map shimmer and seem to enlarge, as if they all fell in slow motion toward it.

Following his instinct, he raised the torch again, revealing a vivid scene stretching all around them. The play of light and shadow expanded the walls backward with illusionary depth, giving life to the graffiti's colors and shapes, transforming them into abstract branches, flowers and birds. He moved the light from side to side, making the structures appear to gently sway, animating the scene to light up the shapes and symbols hiding in the VIPs' consciousness. Their faces twitched with a conflicting amazement as their minds struggled to process what was happening. Even Yoshi felt his senses tricked. He could *smell* the pungent mulch of a forest floor, *feel* the breeze on the back of his neck, and he could almost believe they had all been transported to a forested island.

By the look of wonder in the others' eyes, they were experiencing the same visionary mode he'd experienced on Meti. He let them drift in their imagination, to wander among the vision, to let it create for them an altered state of consciousness, as it had done for him, so that they would not only see what they needed to but *feel* it.

As he led them onwards, the structures pulled back, moved by unseen hands. The group drew together. Fatigue glazed their eyes, reminding Yoshi of how disorientated and intensely vulnerable he was just before his own vision.

Then the clicking fell silent, and a short figure stepped out from the shadows ahead. Yoshi halted, shocked by the sight of the boy. Hushed exclamations confirmed the others saw him, too.

Terror gripped the boy's strewn face, and his chest began to rise and fall deeply. The air bristled, the moment delicate as an eggshell. The fear in the boy's face reached out to the group as he lifted one arm and pointed behind them. They spun to see the structures lined up in a wall and slowly edging toward them, their shadows stretching across the floor like supernatural fingers reaching out to the VIPs' feet. The VIPs' shuffled backward, huddling together, their faces lustrous with fear as the ceremony's magic took up residence in their exhausted minds.

But a desolate dread filled Yoshi that he'd lead them to something more traumatic than what Raiden had planned for them, that perhaps Raiden was right— the city needed to revisit their grief, to finish feeling it, to pass through their fear of something *coming, coming, coming* to release their minds from being set on one terrible future that would repeat the past.

He gripped the torch tight again and hoped that whatever happened next, the controlled exposure of ceremony would guide them through it.

As the wall of structures kept coming, a ragged group of Minaki emerged from the shadows and walked in front. The flickering torch light rippled across their clothes and skin, making them appear translucent. Behind them, the structures' illuminated edges sharpened into the towering, hostile shapes of top-heavy waves about to break.

Distressed murmurs arose from the VIPs, and a knowing welled in their faces, as if an overwhelming memory breached the surface of their consciousness. The rustling grew into a loud white noise, like water rushing toward them.

Exhausted, delirious, and hypnotized by their fear, they quivered like terrified children and huddled behind Yoshi.

"No," whispered the Mayor.

"No, it's not there!" called Ken. "There's nothing there."

"Don't make me look!"

"I don't want to see!"

A powerful sensation rushed through Yoshi, like he was channeling the VIP's emotions. But there were so many he was overwhelmed; he couldn't tell if they belonged to the VIPs, the Minaki, or to the others who had come.

From behind them, the boy called out one word.

"Tsunami."

A shrill cry pierced the air, and the Minaki burst forth from the wave in a mad run toward the group. The structures closed in from all sides. The VIP's cried aloud and huddled together. Yoshi no longer had any idea what was happening or what he was doing. He held up the torch defensively as the Minaki bared down on them.

But the islanders veered off at the last second and ran a circle around the terrified group. Their rush spun Yoshi into the huddle, and he dropped the torch. A hand pulled him in close, and he turned to see the Mayor's strained face. Clutching each other, they peered out at the arms and legs rushing about them. The pounding of the tribe's feet sounded like the mindless, unstoppable force of a devastating surge. The light in the underground shifted, exposing the structures in the background for what they were— debris from people's lives, flashing in glimpses through the islanders' limbs, as if they were all caught together in a swirling surge plowing through the streets and houses of a flooded town.

Yoshi couldn't watch anymore, and he pulled back into the group. Their faces were wrecked by nightmares flooding back, of loved ones lost, of the destruction witnessed, and all the memories they'd hid from in their Mirage.

The group collapsed onto their knees, their hands splayed before them. The Minaki's footsteps slowed, and the rushing noise faded away. Yoshi looked up to see the islanders stop and face the group. The jungle illusion behind them had completely gone, replaced by the silent, lamp-lit cement of the abandoned parking area. The VIPs remained prone, sweat and tears forming damp patches on the ground around them, like they'd just struggled out of the ocean onto the mercy of a foreign shore.

A warm, callused hand wrapped over Yoshi's, and he turned to see Singlet's dark eyes and sun-aged face. Yoshi was struck by a strong sense of presence, and he realized his consciousness no longer operated in two places at once. Singlets patted his hand and smiled.

Slowly, the Minaki moved in among the group, one tribe member kneeling beside a citizen and easing them up into a sitting position. The Mayor blinked and looked into the eyes of the girl holding her hand. For a second, Yoshi feared she might recoil in shock, but her tear-streaked face remained serene, as if seeing someone she had not seen for a long time. Her lips trembled, and she clasped both hands over the girl's.

Gradually, each citizen lifted their head, their drying eyes filled with exhaustion and relief. They faced the islander by their side, their sight seeming to have settled. In the calm, collective euphoria, the hut's heaviness ebbed away. The more they surrendered to the stillness, the more profound it became, exposing a primal connection to each other, of a sadness and loss shared, citizen and islander alike.

Singlets helped Yoshi to his feet, and the Minaki led them all toward another row of tree-like structures, brightly lit by many D-lamps, but blocking the way ahead. As they approached, Yoshi noticed objects littering the ground around them, a menagerie of salvaged personal items neatly spaced out across the cement—a faux jade hairbrush with a handle shaped like a mermaid's tail; a buckled lunch box; a rusted bunch of keys with a worn KFC key ring; a ripped, yellow raincoat; a flattened football; a twisted pair of lens-less spectacles; a faded, red sneaker; a baby's sock.

The Minaki released their wards' hands and walked gently among the objects, their heads down. Yoshi and the others watched in respectful, silent anticipation. In turn, each Minaki stooped to pick up an item, and then they held it to their chests, imagining, or remembering, who it may have belonged to. There was murmuring, like prayer, reminding Yoshi of the one he'd said to his parents in the hospital.

The Minaki walked forward again and hung their items on the starkly lit structures, like ornaments on a Christmas tree, before they disappeared through the lamp glow.

Realizing there was one person he needed to say a proper goodbye to, Yoshi searched the items for something he could connect to his Grandpapa. The soft footsteps of the others followed.

After a moment, he found what he was looking for—a toy boat. Although it didn't look anything like the upturned boat of the hut on Meti, it reminded him of it all the same. He picked it up and held it with both hands, and a secret fear unlocked itself in his heart—had his Grandpapa forgiven him for not being there when he died?

His secret shame welled in his chest, and a tear escaped his eye to splash onto the boat's bough. But a warmth suffused through his body, absorbing the fear, and a familiar presence passed through him. Then it was gone, leaving an unexpected and powerful enlightenment blooming in his chest. It felt like pride.

Saying a silent goodbye to Grandpapa Goto, he walked up to the nearest structure and placed the boat in between two lower branches. He glanced behind to see several others holding an item to their chests, their eyes closed, and lips pressed together. He left them to finish, and he walked through the cleansing brightness of the warm lamp light.

He emerged from the glow into a bare stretch of the underground. The Minaki were nowhere to be seen. Gradually, all the others came through, blinking as if waking up. Their knowing faces suggested a common, unspoken awareness of the ineffable force that had, for a profound few moments, opened their eyes to the truth—that they themselves were the real refugees, displaced from any deeper connection to the present, past or future.

Yoshi led them toward the south exit, and they moved in silence as one through the underground. With every step, the air grew cooler, and his body felt lighter but stronger. An expansive feeling spritzed the air, elevating his mind and lightening his heart. He saw a clarity now sparkling in the eyes of those around him, and he became aware of a deep and true positivity emerging from the sadness they'd experienced.

Brimming with an eagerness to respond, they picked up their pace and left the debris behind.

***

The group emerged from the ramp into an unusual coolness, like a great pressure had been released from the city's atmosphere. Ash floated down with confetti grace, and the air smelled of burnt rubber and fritzed electronics. The full moon had risen to its zenith, suspended directly above the Christmas light glow of High Scape. Although sirens rang in the distance, an unusual quiet hung over the city.

Reaching the road's edge, Yoshi looked right toward Maya District, its empty suburb brushed with moonscape tones and a surreal after-cinema feeling. Smoke curled out from the burned areas, like the district were a charred patch from a giant's campfire where stories had been told late into the night. Auto-dozers scooped fallen drones scattered like fried mosquitos.

Gasps popped through the group at the return of their Lenzes, their eyes glowing like cats in the night. But the eyes of some remained dark. The Mayor touched her lower eyelid, and her Lenz remained off. She looked a mess, her silver wave of hair collapsed and hanging in strands over her face. She glanced at Yoshi, her dark eyes focusing on him properly for the first time.

There was a new emotion in her face, an alert readiness. It shined on the faces of them all.

A siren blipped from down the street, and headlights flashed, spotlighting the group. As an ambulance raced to a stop in front of them, another ambulance came around the corner and pulled up by the first. Yoshi had to cover his eyes against the light as elongated silhouettes ran toward them with torches.

"You all done with your sight-seeing, then?" called a familiar voice.

Jin strode out of the light with a flock of paramedics. He winked at Yoshi before helping the rescue team guide the group to the bus stop. They sat everyone down and wrapped them in silver emergency blankets, lining them up like giant burritos. Three paramedics flustered around the Mayor, but she brushed the extra attention away.

A female paramedic squatted down in front of Yoshi; he recognized her golden curls and dark mustache from his ride on the rescue helicopter. She blinked and tilted her head.

"You again?"

She shone a small torch into each of his eyes and asked about his condition before sitting back and looking him up and down.

"So, what happened to you this time?"

Yoshi opened his mouth to say something, but the ceremony seemed too abstract to articulate and too profound to speak about so soon. Or perhaps what he felt was that he might be dropping a spoiler for something the paramedic, and every other citizen, had yet to experience.

Ken Morita saved him from the awkward silence.

"We had one of the most immersive experiences I've ever had. Maya have outdone themselves, a grand mix of alternate reality and cultural therapy. A fitting commentary on our time, with the unexpected turn of events forcing us into the underworld of our misdirected ideals and forming from them a path through the wall of our denial to the possibility of alternate futures."

The Mayor blinked at Morita's over-articulated outburst—completely unlike the usual saccharin, hype-focused commentary he'd always given. Yoshi recognized the same surge of raw energy he'd felt after coming back from Meti. The paramedic nodded in resignation to not getting any sense from anyone.

"Thank you, Mr. Morita. You just sit tight and relax there, okay?"

She smiled and moved to the next burrito.

As the rescue teams bombarded the others with questions, a steadfast serenity remained on all their faces. Yoshi shared a candid smile with some of them, recognizing a sense of solidarity and an unspoken agreement to not discuss the ceremony—at least, not yet.

The paramedic finished with the Mayor, and she looked around to take in the world with her naked vision. Yoshi faced the night sky and realized why it seemed so quiet—there were no drones.

Two buses arrived and the paramedics assisted the group aboard. Nina and the reporter chatted as they headed to the first bus, and Yoshi and the Mayor were directed onto the second. As he climbed on, Yoshi felt like he was making his way backstage after a show, the excitement over, but the energy still lingering. He glanced back at the access ramp, wondering when he'd see Singlets again.

As the bus pulled away from the stop, its motion rocking him calm, his concern for Kai returned. He scrolled through the news on his watch.

The cause of the blackout is not clear; however, initial reports suspect the use of Maya's own scramblers. It's believed police are questioning two persons of interest in Shibido, but no other details have been provided. We still await comment from Maya CEO Tyler Gray, but there's no doubt the future of Maya District is in question.

Shibido's emergency response teams, however, have received nothing but praise for their prompt and efficient evacuation of the event. The total number injured has reached seventy-six, but all with only minor injuries— wait... I'm just getting word... I'm just getting word the missing VIPs have been found, alive and safe.

A hand tapped Yoshi on his shoulder, and he turned to see the Mayor. She'd tied her wild, silver strands back into a tight bun, like someone's grandmother.

"Thank you," she said.

He shifted in his seat, uncomfortable with the recognition for what the Minaki had done through him. The Mayor nodded slow and deep and looked out the window.

Behind her, all the other passengers faced out to the district. Although many had kept their Lenzes deactivated, their eyes twinkled with the memory of where their minds had taken them. Wrapped in their silver blankets, they no longer looked like burritos;

they looked like brave scouts returning from the future with a sacred technology.

By the time the buses arrived at the hospital, a weighty lightness had engulfed Yoshi. Was it possible to feel light and heavy at once? Everything around him seemed more solid and static than he'd ever experienced, his body as present as stone, yet inside he floated like a balloon.

As nurses ushered him and the others through the emergency area for a thorough examination, he surrendered to the residual prosaic-like profundity of the ceremony. By the time he laid back on a dorm bed, his last thought burnt out like a falling star.

Gift

Morning light streamed through a wide window overlooking High Scape. In a muted media screen floating in the sunlit glass, Ken Morita reported from the edge of Maya District, its featureless buildings behind him draped in the sea-wall's morning shadow. From outside the room, soft voices mingled with faint metallic noises.

"Good morning, Mr. Goto," said a cheery voice from the doorway. A short man in a crisp white coat walked in. "I'm Doctor Kim. How are you feeling?"

A sleepy haze fuzzed Yoshi's mind as he propped himself up on his elbows. "I'm fine, I think. What time is it?"

"Just after ten. You slept well—unlike the others—so we kept you overnight for observation. Let me have a look here."

As the doctor checked a medical screen at the end of the bed, Yoshi looked at the news again. The story's Sight ticked over in the left-hand corner of the screen, picking up new viewers by the second.

"Is that Ken Morita?"

"Indeed. He refused to wait for my all-clear, said he had work to do. He's been reporting all night, going on about an invisible tribe and magical ceremonies. I'm worried he's had a bump on the head."

Yoshi wondered how Morita was coping with the ceremony experience. He gestured to raise the volume.

"Regardless of the cause, I believe Maya's intent was to deliver an experience that would change the city. It was brave and heroic of Tyler Gray, as the creator of the Lenz, to expose its flaw so that we might see our own flaws."

"*Heroic*?" Yoshi almost shouted.

"…where only twelve hours ago fifty of us VIPs emerged from a first-hand tour of the Shibido we have forgotten. There are over three hundred people living under the esplanade—islanders known as the Minaki, displaced by rising sea-levels from a distant archipelago called Agu-shi. They have been living here for over eight months, ignored by the council, and forgotten by ourselves."

Yoshi recognized Morita's post-vision excitement—he was trying to resolve a highly stimulated imagination demanding to be used in more powerful and meaningful ways.

"I have spoken with the Minaki," Morita continued, "and although they have declined to speak on camera, they have expressed their desire to maintain their dignity and sense of identity. Therefore, I call upon the council to demand Maya offer the undamaged areas of Maya District as temporary housing for all of Shibido's homeless, citizen and migrant alike. And further, I propose a skill registry, to capture the skills of all those residing in the district so they may be engaged by you, dear viewers, to allow them to assist you, in return for food, shelter, supplies and simple conversation."

Doctor Kim stepped to Yoshi's side and asked to shine a light into his eyes. Yoshi turned the news' volume back down.

"Are you feeling any aches or pains or drowsiness?" the doctor asked.

"No, I feel fine."

"Then you're okay to leave as soon as you feel ready. The police have been asking after you, so expect a call from them. And the Mayor asked me to tell you she'd like to see you before you leave. She's just next door, first one on the right. You can discharge at the front desk on Level One. Take care, Mr. Goto."

As soon as Doctor Kim left the room, all the unresolved issues from the last twenty-four hours clamored for Yoshi's attention.

His contract would be nulled for sure, but was he still Yoshi Goto or Jack Kobayashi? Had Gray told the police about him being at the premier? Would they buy his story about leading the VIPs to safety? What had the VIPs said? What happens next?

The future stared back at him with a blank face.

He took a few deep breaths, and all the questions settled. Regardless of what anyone else believed, or what was on any documentation, he knew who he was. Whatever happened next, he would deal with it, one step at a time.

He rolled over and placed his feet on the floor. The cold set off a memory of being in the hospital after Meti. He glanced at the doorway, half-expecting Gray to appear with some wild new offer. He had to see him as soon as possible, otherwise he didn't know whether to go home or back to Mountain Station.

First things first.

He straightened his clothes—his shirt still smelled of the underground's spiced, earthy incense—and splashed his face at the sink, then he headed to the Mayor's room. He paused at the door, wondering if she was still under the influence of the ceremony, or if the demands of her job had pulled her back into the alternate reality of politics. He took a deep breath and knocked.

"Come in."

He eased the door open to see her smiling from her bed by the window. Propped up on plush pillows, she wore a knitted, aubergine scarf draped over her hospital gown, and her hair had been sprayed back up into her trademark silver wave. Her pale face and dark circles betrayed her sleeplessness, but her eyes glimmered with vigilance. She waved the volume down on the media screen where Morita continued to report from the district.

"Mr. Goto, come in. How are you?"

"I'm fine, Mayor Wada. How are you?"

"I'm fine, too. They won't let me leave, though; they're worried about an ongoing heart condition of mine. To be honest, I've been awake all night, but I'm eager to get moving."

She patted an empty spot on the bed, but Yoshi remained where he was.

"What happened with Gray? Why is Morita calling him a hero? He had nothing to do with what happened in the underground—"

"I know. I know Gray's goals; I've been pandering to them for the last year. But I spoke to him last night, after speaking to that fool Morita. Morita and I agreed something happened in the underground garage that we don't fully understand." The Mayor paused, chewing her lip as she fought back a moment of emotion. "But we are certain the public are not going to buy into some foreign quasi-religious ceremony. We need to find a way so that the message—or whatever it was the ceremony shared with us—will land more softly with the city, and so Gray won't lose everything."

"Why are you protecting him?"

"The world doesn't need another villain to blame. Gray gave us something we needed at the time. We all bought into the Lenz, and we're not going to stop using it."

"You're protecting your donators."

"No." The Mayor huffed. "It's complex. I've got my party's policies to consider. Look, there's no point reacting hysterically, banning this, crucifying that. The Lenz isn't a bad thing. The Mirage isn't a bad thing, in moderation."

"But, Morita—"

"Ah, yes, Morita, the entertainer reporter become the entertainment. I asked him not to say anything publicly just yet, because nothing's been confirmed with Gray, and there are other factions to consider. He's just trying to up his Sight, and he's dropping me in hot water at the same time."

"He's seen something he can't explain, but it touched him, and he feels it's his duty to report it."

"Oh, he's been 'touched' alright. But if he thinks I've had some epiphany to throw my party's policies under the bus, he can think again. These things take time."

"With all respect, Mayor, you politicians take too long. He's keeping you to your word."

By the way the Mayor twisted the edges of her scarf, Yoshi could see the loyalty to her work already winding its constricting tentacles around her. He wondered if the shift in her perspective would lose its curious spark and become too inconvenient to maintain. He wondered the same of himself.

The Mayor let her scarf go and patted the bed again. Sitting down, Yoshi noticed the Lenz's luminous ring had returned to her eyes. She caught him looking, and she tapped her temple.

"I can't do my job without it, but I've toned down my Mirage." She paused, a serene calm on her face. "That ceremony, it showed us what we *needed* to see, didn't it?"

Yoshi hesitated, having never before discussed his *Taka* experience with anyone other than the Minaki. He nodded.

"I think that's what it's about."

"Your parents would be proud," she said and smiled at his confused look. "When I learned we'd been led out of the event into the Minaki's ceremony, I just had to know *who* had led us there. It took some deconstructing—controversial actor, survivor of the Shift tsunamis, and recent survivor of a cargo drone crash on Meti. You're more like a character from one your movies. And your Great Grandpapa was Minaki."

"My Great Grandpapa was?"

The Mayor's face conflicted with emotions Yoshi couldn't read. "Yes, it's in the records. I thought you must have known."

"I only knew my Grandpapa, and he was ill by the time I was old enough to ask those sorts of questions. I never looked far back into my family history. I didn't know them so I just… I think it was just too hard for me."

"It's not easy looking back when you know it means letting go. Sometimes ignoring things that have changed is a way of keeping them as they were." The Mayor blinked away the conflict lingering on her face. "You know, I didn't retain much knowledge of the Minaki from when they first arrived—I admit, we politicians have let them down. *I* let them down. But, after a little reading, I now know what a *Taka* hut is, and, I think, perhaps, the Minaki would consider me *Taka* now, too?"

"They believe everyone has to be *Taka* some time."

"What does it mean to be *Taka*? What do they expect us to do or be?"

"I think the *Taka's* role is to maintain the well-being of their community by helping those who become stuck. They believe in this energy—"

"*Luma.*"

"Yes, *luma*. They believe it's like a collective soul energy of everything, and it flows through us. We're all trading in this energy every day, but when trauma hits, we feel like we lose part of our soul, so we turn inwards and horde our remaining *luma*. Their ceremonies help unblock this, to heal." He recalled the sensation of being in two places at once, and how he had to hold the torch tight but let it go at the same time. "But you can't share it with others if you don't allow it to flow freely through yourself. You have to feel it, listen to it, act on it. It's instinctual, and that's what makes it special, you have to let it shine out of *you*. So, I think that's why the Minaki believe everyone should take turns leading the ceremonies, in their own way, because… I think being *Taka* is as much about healing yourself as healing others."

The Mayor raised her eyebrows. "Sounds like you understand them a lot better than you think you do."

Yoshi surprised himself, too, but he shook his head. "I'm just interpreting what I've learnt recently. You should talk directly to them. Like Morita."

Yoshi gestured to the media screen where Morita reported from outside the underground garage's south exit. The scene cut to an aerial view of Maya District, its structures almost invisible in the morning shadow of the sea-wall. But Yoshi's attention was consumed by what stood in the middle of a charred, empty block—a seven-tiered tree, illuminated from underneath by a circle of D-lamps.

"What is that?"

The Mayor clasped a hand over his, and her eyes glistened. "You haven't seen it?"

"No."

She squeezed his hand. "Watch."

The scene cut to CCTV footage of the Minaki hauling parts of the *Taka* hut structures along a street through pre-dawn dimness. Yoshi realized the report had cut back in time to show where the tree had come from.

Another cut, and the Minaki reached the burnt-out block that had been cleared by the auto-dozers. The islanders arranged the arched structures into seven circles and roped their stems together to create seven different sized tiers of branches. They then stacked the tiers on top of each other to form the giant tree.

The video's Sight floated in the top right of the screen—1.9 billion, nearly everyone with access to the channels.

"It's a gift," the Mayor said, her voice soft with awe. "When the city woke up, there it was. The Minaki must have been exhausted. After they built the tree, they just laid down under it and went to sleep."

Colored objects dotted the branches, and Yoshi recognized the items as the ones the VIPs had hung on them in the underground. The screen cut back to the original drone shot of the tree, revealing the Minaki sleeping around its base. People tip-toed past them to place items under the tree—blankets, pillows, baskets of fruit and wrapped food.

Yoshi leaned forward, spotting a familiar bald-headed girl among the gift-givers.

"Is that...?"

"Nina Fuji. She was up all night, too, calling me about getting resources to the homeless. She's been leading people there with donations since sunrise. She's got more energy than any of us."

Yoshi wondered how the other VIPs were, if the idol awoken inside of them had stayed awake, if they all sensed the small shifts inside them were the clicks of the ceremony safe cracking the flow of *luma* back through the city.

"Everyone reacts differently to *Taka* magic."

"'Magic,' Mr. Goto?"

"That's what the Minaki call it. All the VIPs have been initiated, they're all feeling what you and Morita are feeling, but they'll all react in different ways. Nina's started the collection with the others. Morita is encouraging a different perspective."

The Mayor smiled with embarrassment. "And I have to start doing my damn job, right? But what of the ceremony now? I thought it might be something we'd share with others."

Kai's words came back to Yoshi.

Don't just wait… engage…

"We need to respond to the gift. It's a gesture, asking us to make what happens next something between all of us. Perhaps the ceremony has changed for a bigger audience."

"They're traders, essentially, aren't they?"

"From what I've read, yes, as a ritual of keeping *luma* flowing. What are you thinking?"

"I'm not sure, yet. They made those structures out of old and discarded things. Perhaps a market of some kind, around that tree, for all the homeless to trade their crafts. Give them a sense of purpose and perhaps income."

"They need more than a market."

"It would be a start, to give them back some dignity. It is as important as shelter." The Mayor looked back at Yoshi. "I'll need reliable people to help me think this through and ensure we act. Know anyone looking for a job?" She smiled knowingly, and Yoshi laughed.

"Looking for work has been my full-time job. I think it's time I tried something else. Actually," he said, thinking of Mico and Jin. "I know two other hard workers. One you might remember—the security guard who brought the ambulances. And another friend of mine, Mico. He works harder than anyone in Shibido, and... he's Minaki—you could ask him all your questions about *Taka*."

"I want to talk to both of your friends."

A knock sounded at the door, and a nurse poked his head into the room. "Mr. Goto? There's someone here to see you."

"Thank you, nurse."

Yoshi turned back to the Mayor who bowed and held out her hand.

"Thank you, Mr. Goto. I'll be in touch with you, I promise. We're friends now."

"Thank you, Mayor Wada," he said, surprised by how many friends he had gained. "I hope they let you out soon."

"Well, they better, or I'll climb out the window and hail an auto-pod myself. By the way, you're a hero now, you know? I hope you've got a good agent."

Yoshi laughed at the irony. He bowed a farewell and headed to the doorway, but the Mayor called him back.

"Mr. Goto." She paused, her face again conflicted with the same emotion as when Yoshi admitted he didn't know his heritage. "How did you know about the Minaki's ceremony?"

The question spidered up Yoshi's back.

"Mayor Wada, I—"

"Did you know the scramblers were going to be used?"

Yoshi locked up, unable to move or speak. He panicked for an explanation, but the Mayor spoke before he could.

"Villainy and heroism are not as black and white as the movies, are they, Mr. Goto?"

She bowed her head again and looked at the news in the window where the Minaki's tree floated over the view of High Scape.

Reeling from the confrontation, Yoshi left the room and stopped to take a breath in the hallway twinkling with tinsel and baubles.

Halfway down the left side, a stranger sat on a bench. He wore a white bandage wrapped around his head and had one arm in a cast and sling. As Yoshi approached, the stranger looked up, and Yoshi's heart wagged its tail.

"Kai?

"Yoshi," Kai said, scrambling to his feet. He wore the same shirt he had on the day he protested outside new Gate and carried a red gift box under his cast arm. A small rose of blood stained the bandage around his head.

Mixed emotions filled Yoshi—he didn't know if he wanted to punch Kai or hug him. He nodded at Kai's wounds instead.

"What happened to you?"

Kai flushed with embarrassment and glanced around before lowering his voice.

"When Raiden's scrambler went off, I helped some people out of the district. The least I could do, right? Some of them were as blind as bats. Anyway, when I went back to help others, I got knocked over in the chaos and got trampled on."

"You were an ass. You know that, right?"

"I'm so sorry, Yoshi. I was all caught up trying to be a hero. And I was wrong about you, about everything. You came back for me, even after I pushed you away. You risked a lot to warn me."

Yoshi stroked the bandage around the blood stain.

"I had to. But are you okay?"

"I'm sorer than I've ever been, but I deserve it. The police got Raiden and Akio. But, anyway, what about you? What happened?"

Yoshi looked down, thinking of how to explain everything. Kai didn't know anything about Meti, his vision, or the boy—he only knew Yoshi as the troubled actor who knocked a kid out of a sleigh, crashed a Christmas tree, stole a robot, and sold his identity.

"I took the VIPs to the ceremony."

Kai's face lit up. "You did? How? What happened?"

"They met the Minaki."

"And?"

Unable to hold back a second longer, Yoshi drew Kai close. "I'll tell you about it later." And he quietened him with a kiss.

The hallway noises merged into a faint white-noise, like leaves rustling in a breeze. After a timeless float around the soft anchor of their lips, Kai pulled back, his eyes filled with a subtle sadness.

"What's wrong?" Yoshi asked.

"I just wish I'd helped and been part of the ceremony. Not to be a hero or anything, but just, you know, to have made some actual difference."

Yoshi dove a hand into his pocket and pulled out the lighter. "You *were* there. And I was there because you made a difference to me."

Kai's face lightened, chased away by an abashed look in his eyes. "Can you forgive me for being such an ass?"

"I'll do my best," Yoshi laughed. "I know where your heart is at. And you've taken a risk, yourself, coming here. The police must be looking for you."

Kai shook his head.

"They're not after me. They think it was just Raiden and Akio. They didn't snitch on me. I got off lucky." He raised his cast arm. "So, what do I call you now since you sold your identity?"

"I don't know what's happening with that. I left the train station last night to warn you before my new ID was confirmed, and Gray saw me at the event."

Kai scoffed at the mention of the Maya CEO. The silky luster of his amber-flecked eyes seemed to flare.

"The media is making him out to be some kind of hero, like the event was meant to 'open our minds', if the black-out hadn't happened. Can you believe it?"

"I know, I know," Yoshi said, squeezing Kai's hand. "But the Mayor's onto it, don't worry."

The flare settled and Kai shook his head.

"Sorry, you don't need me firing up right now. Look, if you need a place to crash until you sort things out, you can stay with me. I've only got one futon, but I've got a couch I can sleep on."

Yoshi pulled Kai in close and kissed him again, silently suggesting an alternative solution. After a moment that could have been ten, they pulled themselves apart and headed down the tinseled hallway, hand in hand.

Reaching the front desk, Yoshi signed the discharge form with his own name without thinking.

"I need to go see Gray," he said to Kai, as they walked outside to the drop-off area.

"Is that a good idea?"

"I want to." He *did* want to. In fact, he felt driven to see Gray, like the Maya CEO was another new friend he needed to check on.

As if summoned by their discussion, a shiny, black auto-pod pulled up in front of them and opened its door.

"Hello, Mr. Goto," said Driver. "Mr. Tyler Gray asks to speak with you. Please, would you allow me to take you to him?"

Kai gripped Yoshi's arm, but Yoshi smiled reassuringly in return.

"I've got to face this."

"I'm coming with you," Kai said, and he climbed in first.

They rode in silence through the Christmas Eve quiet of High Scape's streets, Kai giving Yoshi time to gather his thoughts. But instead of mapping out what he'd say to Gray, all Yoshi could think about was that the sooner he spoke to him, the sooner their futures could begin.

As they pulled up to the studios, Kai kissed Yoshi on the cheek. "I'll wait here. Be careful."

"Thank you."

Yoshi climbed out and headed to the gate where a self-scanning device had replaced Jin. He crossed the cul-de-sac and entered the tower, the video walls of the long corridor now dormant. As he approached the foyer, the *yujin* stepped out and bowed.

"Welcome back, Mr. Goto. Mr. Gray is expecting you."

The *yujin's* natural mannerisms rendered it completely indiscernible from a human. Noticing Yoshi staring, the host looked up at him and scratched his nose.

"Can I help you with anything else, Mr. Goto?"

Yoshi blinked and looked away, as embarrassed as if he'd been caught staring at a real person.

"No, I'm fine, thank you."

"You're welcome, sir. Wonderful Day."

As the elevator rose, Yoshi shook off the uncanny feeling from the perfected *yujin* and cleared his mind until the elevator doors opened.

Gray stood at the mirrored foyer's window, his back rigid. He remained facing out to sea as he spoke.

"I don't have much time for pleasantries. The police and Council are demanding all my attention before I leave. Suffice to say your actions have negated our contract. You can keep your identity, and your payment is being rescinded."

As Yoshi crossed the buffed floor, his reflections on either side spread out like wings.

"Mr. Gray, I had to—"

"There's been a change of direction with Maya District, as I'm sure you've heard. Although the black-out affected only those at the event, 'glitch' memes have scared off over 460 million active users, and Sight time is down more than I care to admit. Maya is no longer the media's darling, but a humiliated manufacturer of malfunction. I'm bleeding cash, and Maya City is on hold, perhaps forever. But the only thing I can think about is what happened in that abandoned parking garage. None of the VIPs speak any sense about it. What did you *do* to them?"

"I just tried to get them to safety."

Grinnnd. "You did *something*. You bribed them, scared them. You *changed* them."

Yoshi hesitated, contemplating whether he should mention the vision.

"The Minaki's ceremony changed them."

"The what?"

"The islander refugees that you had moved on, and their ceremony you shut down. I took the VIPs to their ceremony." He took in a breath of courage. "Why don't you go down there, to the tree, go see them for yourself?"

Gray held his gaze on the sea, clouds rolling through his reflection. His next words fell heavy in the still of the foyer.

"The tsunami took my son."

"I'm sorry," Yoshi said, sensing a residual power of the ceremony flowing between them. "I didn't know."

Gray's stance softened.

"He was just six-years-old. He loved to play along the original sea-wall, swinging his lightsaber at some invisible foe. He said he was fighting the wall, to stop it getting any higher. He said the land and the sea needed to be together. Quite an imagination, wouldn't you say?"

Dizziness swamped Yoshi, and his sense of self seemed to detach from his body and orbit the room. He saw, in his mind's eye, the boy from the underground lunging across the top of the sea-wall, swinging his stick in the rain. Gray's voice played like a voice-over.

"I'd taken Eli to the food hall for dinner that night, overlooking the esplanade. He'd gotten bored because I was on my laptop for the whole meal. I should have taken him to Mixed World, like he wanted, but if he played along the wall I could keep an eye on him while I kept working. I was obsessed with an idea, you see, an augmented technology like no other. I worked on it like a demon, my laptop always in front of me, so I never saw it coming.

"I remember pausing for a moment to check on Eli. It was a beautiful, peaceful evening, the ocean twinkling in the night. When I first saw the wave out at sea, I froze with incomprehension, this sparkling line stretched across the bay. And it was growing. When Eli stopped his playing to face it, I realized the sparkling wasn't getting bigger, it was rushing closer. By then, the wall of water surged over the beach. I banged the window, screaming at Eli to run, but he had no time and nowhere to go.

"All I could do was stand at the window and watch the wave surge over and swipe him off the wall, tossing him like a broken *yujin* toward me, until he disappeared under the wash right below the food hall, right under my feet." Gray tilted his head down. His tone softened, almost pleaded. "Can this ceremony free me from the burden of that memory, Mr. Goto?"

Yoshi pulled himself back into the present, his body shaking with disbelief. Outside, the rain faltered, as if it might turn off, followed by the walls dropping away to reveal themselves as propped-up stage sets hiding a studio audience just waiting to shout, "You've been punked!", the last few weeks all just some elaborate experiment, some extension of Maya District with him as the unaware hero of his own movie.

But the clouds rained on. He opened his mouth to tell Gray the ghost of his son had led them both to this point in time and space, but he couldn't find the words to explain such a thing. He wasn't even sure if he truly believed it. How could anyone know if something like that could be real or not?

He put a slow hand on Gray's shoulder.

"I lost my parents and my home in the Shift. I think I stopped feeling anything so I couldn't lose someone else I might care about. The ceremony helped me feel my grief, to let it flow through me, so it could change. There's no algorithm for how to do that. But isn't it good to know that it *can* change, or be changed, that no matter the past, that there's never really one future? Imagine that."

Yoshi removed his hand. Gray's chest rose and fell slowly and deeply, like the sea rolled through him.

"When you experience the Earth's power striking at you so personally, yet so indifferently… It's my fault Eli died."

Instinct screamed at Yoshi to say something about the boy, to compel Gray to seek out what he couldn't see. But the words still failed him, and Gray talked on.

"All I had left was my idea, a lens to help us see things differently, to forget the inescapable horrors of the past, or, at least, to not see the end we all know is coming."

"But we don't know that," Yoshi said, his mind still searching for a way to reach Gray. "What did you say in your office when you offered to buy my identity? 'We seek distraction because we know to be too aware is a curse.' We needed distraction after the Shift from the saturation of terrible news. We needed a break from it while our hearts and minds processed it." He didn't know where his words were coming from, some mash up of snippets his new friends had said that were coming together as he spoke. "Maybe, now, though, the Lenz could help us remember both the trauma and the beauty of the past, while, at the same time,"—*like some dual reality experience*—"help us imagine our own dream for the future, not some algorithm's."

It was the best he could do. He hung his head, wishing his time as *Taka* had lasted just a little longer, so he'd know what to say and how to say it. But both he and Gray seemed to have run out of words, and the room filled with an awkward silence. Gray gazed out to sea where sun rays bronzed the ocean, as if nothing else existed.

"I should go," Yoshi said, bowing to Gray's back before returning to the elevator.

As he stepped inside, Gray turned his head to the side.

"The ocean is still coming. Some fashionably new 'spiritual' perspective won't stop it."

And then it came to Yoshi, *through* him, from the lungs of a drowned child given voice again, if only momentarily, by a ceremony of soul.

"Maybe…maybe it's trying to push us all back together."

The elevator door shut, snap-shotting an image in Yoshi's mind of Gray standing at the floor-to-ceiling window, the cloud armada outside breaking up inside his reflection.

The elevator's six sides hummed around Yoshi as it transported him through time and space, his own mind still struggling with what he believed. Could something as devastating as the Earth Shift have a purpose, to deliver *Taka* magic to where it was most needed? Yoshi wondered if there'd somehow been ceremonies in the other cities, if there were now seeds of 'magic' also planted in Australia, Germany, the U.S., and Great Britain—other *Taka* recruited as the core pillars of a sacred technology now scaffolding itself through some theta layer of the world, with *luma* its Wi-Fi, and the heart and mind its devices.

Or was that just the imagination of a child?

And was it magic, really? Wasn't the ceremony just some interactive performance using optical illusion to take advantage of a traumatized audience desperate for meaning?

Except for one thing:

They all saw Eli.

Like the symbols on the hut's ceiling, the mystery spoke to him on a level where reason couldn't function. The best he could do was accept that the uncertainty itself was some kind of magic. The *coming, coming, coming* would always be there, but it could be anything, the uncertainty a gift, a constant whisper of hope—but it couldn't be articulated any more than that, for if it were, it would stop being what it was: undefined and full of possibility.

And then he understood what *luma* really was—hope *and* grief, always changing, the extremes connecting everyone, but not just as a passive force, but as a living energy that needed to be maintained, shared and used.

The elevator doors dinged open.

***

By the time he returned to the pod, the sky had cleared to disparate flocks of altocumulus. Kai sat slumped in the seat, watching news on a screen floating in the front window. He sat up as Yoshi climbed in.

"You okay?"

"I'm good. I'm still Yoshi Goto."

"It's good to have you back."

Kai squeezed his hand and gave Driver his address. As the pod pulled away, Yoshi looked up at Maya's shining tower and imagined Gray still standing at the window.

"I think he's going to be okay, too."

"Forget him, what about your contract?"

"He said my actions negated it. But I still have the payment from the first contract, so I'm okay for a while."

"And you can act again?"

"I guess I can. But the Mayor offered me a job."

"That's great. I just hope she keeps her promises better than her policies. Keeping you by her side will no doubt get her more votes, though. Considering how fast popularity shifts, it could just be all talk."

"All the VIPs met the Minaki in the underground. We might see some changes in other ways."

"People have been immersed in their Mirages a long time. They'll need to decompress; it'll take a while."

"I guess that's the difference between evolution and revolution, Mr. Feisty." He play-punched Kai's shoulder, realizing he might have to be Kai's 'Tora', and that was okay.

"Alright, alright. We just don't know if we have much time, do we? Maybe you can do something with your new fame. Have you checked your Sight?"

Yoshi cringed. "I think I was getting use to not being Yoshi Goto."

"Acting wasn't the escape you thought it was, huh? Maybe you can find a different way to use what you got."

A new lattice of nascent ideas flickered through Yoshi's mind, and his skin goose-bumped in response.

"Hey, why don't we go see the tree tomorrow?"

Kai's cheeks flushed. "I was thinking of going to see Raiden."

The pod hit a bump.

"You don't owe him anything, you know?"

"He kept my name out of everything. His head may not be in the right place, but his heart is, and I'm worried that's because people have given up on him in the past."

As much as Yoshi disliked Kai's sense of loyalty to Raiden, he found himself admiring it for what it was—Kai wanted to heal the same pain in another. Did that make Kai *Taka*, too? Maybe, like the ice melt and ocean rise, the ceremony's effects would compound and make their changes sooner.

"Well," Yoshi said, thinking of Mico and Jin, "I've got to go see a couple of friends, too, so I'll do that while you check on Raiden. If you can do it without being overheard, let him know the VIPs met the Minaki."

Kai squeezed Yoshi's hand.

"Oh," Kai exclaimed, reaching to take something from the seat next to him. "I meant to give you this."

He handed Yoshi the red gift box he'd had under his arm in the hospital. Nodding a thank you, Yoshi unclasped the folded seal and smiled at the delicately crafted strawberry shortcake inside.

"It's not Christmas Eve without traditional Japanese Christmas cake," Kai said.

Yoshi blushed, warmed by the gesture but also embarrassed he didn't have a gift to give in return. But he knew it was okay.

"Thank you very much. We can share it tonight."

They curled into each other and watched the news in the front window overlaid on the city view. Morita still reported from Maya District, his mustache bouncing up and down as he spoke.

"And, now, to some brighter news. A trainee fisherman on a Canadian fishing boat has captured authenticated photographic evidence that show polar bears are still with us."

Kai sprang upright. "No way."

The screen cut to a shaky video of seven furry, white bears—two adults and four cubs—trotting through a field of pink flowers by a choppy bay.

Morita's voice-over continued.

"Last seen in the wild before the Earth Shift, polar bears were thought to have been starved into extinction by the loss of ice—until now. These bears appear much smaller than average, with thinner fur, but scientists are quite certain they are, indeed, polar bears who have survived in the northern coastal areas of Canada. Experts believe the bear's survival may be due to a fast adaption to a vegetarian diet, defying earlier predictions that they would not survive without more protein. Our reporter caught up with the trainee who spotted the bears on his first day on the job."

The footage cut to the excited fisherman, and Yoshi's jaw dropped. Shrouded in a furry-lined Eskimo hood, Leon beamed a smile as bright as a glacier in sunlight.

"Oh, man," he gushed. "They looked just-off-the-ice-pure-white and mag-nif-fee-cent. What I'm saying is, they were glowing. Did you know a group of polar bears is called a celebration? Ain't that somethin'?"

"That guy looks familiar," Kai said. "Is he familiar to you?"

Yoshi didn't answer, transfixed and humbled by the sight of things he thought he would never see again. The video replayed the bears trotting through the flowers as Morita delivered his final words.

"Strict access to the area has been enforced while wildlife protection organizations monitor the bears, their primary goal now to ensure this celebration can continue to adapt and thrive again."

If you enjoyed The Lenz, please help this independent author by leaving a review on Amazon and/or Goodreads.

Also by Damien Lutz on Amazon:
Amanojaku

ABOUT THE AUTHOR

Damien Lutz is a writer and UX Designer living in Sydney, Australia. He also creates artwork and interactive experiences based on his stories, which can be seen at www.damienlutz.com.au/author

Praise for Lutz's *Amanojaku*:
"A multilayered protagonist and stellar setting help guide this sci-fi narrative to an unforgettable coda."
- *Kirkus Reviews*
"I would recommend this book to anyone who enjoys gritty sci-fi and has fond memories of Blade Runner."
- *San Francisco Book Review*

Follow Lutz on Facebook:
www.facebook.com/damienlutzauthor

Follow Lutz's Amazon Author Page:
www.amazon.com/-/e/B00V29EKCM

Follow Lutz on Goodreads:
www.goodreads.com/author/show/13707607.Damien_
Lutz